ROADSIDE ASSISTANCE

MARIE HARTE

sourcebooks
casablanca

Published by Sourcebooks Casablanca, an imprint of Sourcebooks, Inc.
P.O. Box 4410, Naperville, Illinois 60567-4410
(630) 961-3900
Fax: (630) 961-2168
www.sourcebooks.com

Printed and bound in Canada.
MBP 10 9 8 7 6 5 4 3 2 1

For D&R. I love you.
And to all the women out there who never
feel good enough, this one's for you.

Chapter 1

Foley Sanders stared at the door, where minutes ago one sexy, pissed off woman had stalked out of the garage. She'd worked the hell out of those black heels. They'd rapped against the concrete floor, the angry staccato an unsubtle reminder to get out of her way. Talk about a fine pair of legs. To his chagrin, he wasn't the only one who'd noticed. The guys had stared after her as if they'd never seen a woman before. He wanted to be better than that, but...

God love him—*a redhead*. The woman had wine-red hair so dark it looked almost brown. And that body... She had curves, a lot of them. And height.

Man, talk about Santa coming to town early. Just breathing, the woman qualified as a statuesque knockout. But angry? A serious threat to his sanity. Now how to calm her down... Oh, right. Find and kill Dale, then get their cars out of her lot.

He glanced around for their young service writer and saw nothing but steady business. With three lifts and space to spare, there was never an excuse for downtime in Webster's Garage. Lining the back of the shop and the rear wall, multidrawer mechanic toolboxes separated several workstations. A few calendars, sadly of *clothed* women, cars, and motorcycles, adorned the red and brown brick walls.

But no Dale to be found.

Foley wondered if strangling the guy would annoy his bosses. Not Liam so much. The hard-ass was old-school when it came to screwups. Del, though. She might be a problem. Ever since getting engaged to McCauley, she'd been going hot and cold on discipline around the place. One minute jumping down his throat for something, the next babying their twenty-one-year-old service writer like he was four.

"Dale," he yelled, then remembered the kid had taken off early today.

"He's not here, genius. Probably wants to beat the snow." Johnny Devlin, one of the mouthier mechanics in the garage, lovingly stated the obvious. With Seattle's winter nearly officially here, the weather seemed to be getting worse. "Boy had plans to help his sister move, I think. He'll be in first thing Monday morning."

"Hell." Foley rubbed his eyes, irritated. He needed to get a bunch of cars moved out of the fiery siren's lot before she had them towed. Had Dale left the keys where Del normally kept them? Or had he taken to reorganizing again, so no one could find anything without the kid's help?

Johnny went back to cheerfully whistling a Christmas tune while Credence Clearwater Revival came on the radio to replace some seriously awful folk music. Thank God. Now if Foley could just get Johnny to shut up.

"*Must* you whistle?" he growled, a headache brewing as the temperature started to get to him. They kept the garage bay doors closed, but the cold didn't seem to care, and the T-shirt and jeans he wore under his coveralls weren't doing him any favors.

The bastard grinned back at him. "I must." Johnny

had recently fallen in love and now considered himself a dating guru. Well, technically the little bastard *was* pretty good with the ladies. He had a pretty face, a big brain, and had grown up around a bevy of strippers, so he had the female perspective down pat. Still, Foley would rather pull out his own teeth than admit Johnny knew more than he did about chicks.

Women, not chicks, you Neanderthal, he imagined his mother saying before slapping him on the back of the head. He rubbed the imagined smack and sighed.

"Ha! I found it." His best friend, Sam, victoriously raised his previously misplaced air ratchet and narrowed his gaze on Foley. "Quit fucking with my gear."

Foley frowned, still off-kilter from the angry beauty in heels. "I told you I didn't touch your tools. You need to clean up that mess." He nodded at Sam's tool bench, a clutter of disorganization that hurt to look at.

After nearly two decades spent around Sam and Sam's chaos in regards to living, Foley should have known better than to try. But he figured one of these days Sam might actually heed his advice.

"I'm not seeing the problem." Sam shrugged and tapped the ratchet into his huge palm. "You seeing a problem, big man? Want me to fix it? How about I fix *you*?"

He glanced at Sam's thick, tattooed biceps, then at his own, and raised a brow. "I know you don't seriously think you can take me down."

Sam's scowl lightened into what—for Sam—could be considered a grin. "You want to go, *boss man*?"

"Must chafe your ass that Del and Liam left me in charge." Foley crossed his arms over his chest, amused at the thought of Sam taking the lead. His buddy didn't want the responsibility. He just liked needling Foley for being a—quote—*kiss ass*. Foley continued his rant. "But then, what choice did they have?" He looked at Johnny, monkeying under the hood of a Honda. "The happy whistler who can't think beyond his new girlfriend?" A glance at Lou, who leaned against his workbench, smirking at them. "The resident Romeo who's better with a paint gun than a wrench?"

"Watch it, hombre, or I'll paint your face a new color." Lou didn't put any heat behind his words, but his mammoth frame would be a challenge if it came to a fight. He was as big as Foley, though not as badass. Then again, Foley had never actually battled the garage's resident know-it-all. He wondered, between them, who might actually win, and could see Lou thinking the same, his lips curling into a grin.

Thoughts of fighting brought Foley's attention back to Sam. "Or you." Foley scrutinized his buddy, teasing to conceal the worry he'd been feeling. "You're practically all skin and bones. Eat a sandwich, jackass. It won't kill you. Unless you're starving yourself to impress Shaya?"

Sam snorted. "Shaya likes me just fine."

"You mean she likes the wad of bills you shove down her G-string at Strutts," Lou said under his breath.

Sam turned a cold eye on him. "Anytime you want to throw down, Cortez. I'm game."

Johnny took a break from his work, straightened, and faced them. "Guys, it's almost Christmas."

"So what? Santa ain't bringin' Sam a personality. What can I do but help him adjust to good cheer?" Lou offered.

"Fuck off, Lou," Sam snapped.

Johnny pleaded, "Tone down the testosterone, would you?"

Lou took a threatening step toward Sam, then stopped, grinned, and held out a hand. "Pay up, Hamilton. I told you he'd make sure none of us shake the peace around here. Getting laid has made our Johnny a lover, not a fighter."

Foley laughed. They placed bets on everything in the garage, and Johnny's maddening good mood was fair game. Good to know Foley wasn't the only one who could use less whistling, more classic rock.

Sam gave Johnny a sad look as he put a five in Lou's hand. "Johnny, Johnny. All that happiness is turning you into a pussy. Does Lara know what she's getting with you, man?"

"Turning into?" Foley repeated. "I thought he was born that way." He laughed at the finger Johnny shot him.

Then in a sly tone, Johnny said, "Calling me names and betting on me isn't getting you guys any closer to an invite to dinner next weekend."

Foley and Sam exchanged a glance. Free food changed things.

Sam coughed. "I don't suppose Lara would make anything special for us. Like say, chocolate chip cookies?"

"I don't know." Johnny rubbed his greasy nails on his coveralls. "How sorry are you for being a dick?"

"*I'm* sorry Sam's a dick," Lou apologized, ignoring Sam's suggestion of where to stick his head. "And that you have to constantly deal with lowbrow humor from the badass bros."

Foley rolled his eyes. They'd been calling him and

Sam that for years, and he hated to admit it, but he liked the title.

"Lowbrow, my ass," Sam muttered.

Lou shrugged. "Just my opinion." He turned to Foley. "But then, I'm just a lowly peon working for the big man."

"Please." The guys always ribbed Foley whenever the Websters left him in charge. "Like you work for anyone but yourself." All of them contracted their work for a percentage. With the raw talent and experience Webster's had pooled the past few years with their current team of mechanics, it was no wonder the garage had overflowing lots and no time to spare anymore.

"That's true." Lou grinned. "But right now, I'm more than glad Del and Liam left you in charge. I wouldn't want to be you when you're standing in front of them, explaining why all our cars got towed away."

Foley had been trying to avoid the pressing need to fix the situation. "Shit."

"Good thing Del's not here to collect on all the swearing," Johnny just *had* to remind them.

As one, they glanced at the change-filled glass jar on a nearby counter. The ROP—Rattle of Oppression, as they'd taken to calling it—had been getting filled on a weekly basis. The boss had decided that to keep from swearing at her upcoming wedding, she'd practice clean speech at work. Unfortunately, if she had to talk nice, she expected them all to do the same.

Foley grinned. "You have to admit it's a challenge. Even Liam has cut back on his 'fucks' and 'goddamns.'"

The guys chuckled.

Foley finished putting his tools away, then realized

he'd only given himself a ten-minute reprieve. "Oh hell. I'll be at the coffee shop dealing with our angry neighbor. If you guys leave before I get back, have a good weekend. And, Johnny? I'm marking down in my calendar about dinner next weekend."

"With cookies, right?" Sam asked.

"Maybe." Johnny shrugged. "Lara seems to like you, though I have no idea why."

Foley removed his coveralls and hung them in his locker in the break room, leaving him in jeans, steel-toed boots, and a thin T-shirt. When working, he tended to run hot. But as soon as he stopped, the cold hit him. He washed his hands thoroughly and tried to finger-comb his hair, wanting to make a better impression on his would-be lover. He grabbed his jacket and headed toward the exit.

Johnny hummed the funeral march, which earned a rare chuckle from Sam.

Lou called out, "Good luck, *jefe*."

"Quit calling me boss," he barked.

"Okay, walking dead man." Lou laughed. "Wonder if she'll puncture a lung with those heels. Might be worth it to see." Lou made as if to follow him, and Foley ordered him to stay the hell away.

He didn't need an audience when he worked his charms on that delectable redhead. And he especially didn't need any unasked for competition when it came to getting that first date. That was, if he could convince her not to stomp his head in with those four-inch heels.

He grinned. He loved them mean.

His grin faded, and he turned around and headed for the service desk. First, he had to find those damn keys.

—∿∿—

Cynthia Nichols had done some stupid things in her time, but not wearing a jacket in this weather ranked among her top five. Her earlier phone conversation had made her so blasted angry she'd torn out of the shop without thinking. She shivered and glanced at the mass of vehicles taking up her customers' spots and swore at all things car related. Spotting a familiar face outside, she waved.

Hurrying through the door, she inhaled the scent of coffee and freshly baked goods and let out a sigh. Nichols Caffè Bar—her most recent acquisition and newest workplace.

Warmth unfurled. She finally felt at home. For years she'd been investing in businesses, getting them going, then leaving once they turned a profit. But this was the first one she'd decided to work and keep as her own. A family-run company, since she owned half of it, and her brother and sister-in-law owned the other half.

"Where have you been?" Nina, said sister-in-law, asked before calling out a name for the cup on the counter.

The customer collected it with a thanks and headed to a back table. For a Friday late afternoon, they had a decent enough crowd. Icy roads and snow had been forecasted for later in the day, so she hadn't thought too many Seattleites would stick around. But for coffee, her fellow caffeine addicts would apparently brave the weather.

"Hold that thought." Cyn grabbed a hot cocoa and a bag of muffins and took them outside to Francine. The older woman typically passed by on her way to her nephew's workplace. He'd drive her home after her daily walk. Francine had to be in her seventies, but rain, shine, or snow, the woman refused to miss her exercise.

"Before you say anything," Cyn said to forestall the prickly woman, "it's the holidays. Take the cocoa and the muffins and indulge my Christmas spirit. Please?"

Francine lived on a budget, and it showed. Yet the woman had her pride. Hell, so did Cyn. But she hated the thought of Francine going without, especially during the holidays.

"You're a real pain in my ass, you know that?" Francine frowned, then gave a grudging nod and accepted the treats. "Thanks, Cyn. Stay warm. See you next year." She gave a smile. "Micky's taking me to Vegas for a few days. He won a free trip."

"Enjoy yourself. And watch those slots."

Francine cackled and shuffled away.

Cyn watched her go, shook her head, and joined Nina again.

"You're a soft touch. That woman is going to live to be two hundred, she's that mean."

"She's just misunderstood."

Nina raised a brow. "The last time I asked if she wanted a free coffee or pastry, she shot me the finger."

"She's got her pride." Cyn chuckled. "That or she just doesn't like you."

"Whatever. So where were you?" Nina asked again.

Cyn joined her behind the counter. "I went over to Webster's Garage to talk to the idiot in charge."

Nina frowned. "I like Liam, and I wouldn't exactly call Del an idiot. Not to her face."

Cyn understood. The gang at Webster's was decidedly… rough. Liam Webster had to be in his late fifties, yet the man looked like he could bench-press *her*—and she hadn't been a lightweight since the fourth grade.

Del, his daughter, had ash-blond hair, a few piercings, tattoos, and the meanest glare on a woman Cyn had ever seen. She had been nice and polite the few times Cyn had run into her, but Cyn had sensed a predator behind those cold gray eyes from the first.

Eyes a lot like those of the testosterone-laden idiot she'd just lambasted with a bit of redheaded temper. Dear God, where did the Websters find their mechanics? San Quentin? Rikers? Baddies-R-Us?

Aware her sister-in-law waited for an answer, Cyn said, "The Websters are out of town, so they left Foley Sanders in charge."

Nina sighed. "Foley."

"Hey. You're married to my brother, remember?" Cyn frowned. "Do the names Vinnie and Alex ring a bell? You know, your *children*?"

Nina laughed. "Hard to forget a house full of boys and your manly brother. Hubba hubba."

"Ew. Forget I asked."

"But Foley Sanders." Nina wiggled her brows. "He's so big and strong and just…yum."

Nina wasn't lying. Which made Cyn dislike him all the more. She knew all about guys like Foley. Men who had looks and muscle, the envy of other men, and the fantasies of heterosexual women. Men who acted like they didn't mind what a girl looked like, then dumped her for a skinnier, younger model.

"Yum or not, it's his job to be responsible for the garage, and you'll notice that over half our lot is full of cars that don't belong to us." She knew for a fact that they had come from Webster's because she'd seen their blue-haired clerk parking them randomly in the lot earlier today.

"So who else was there?" Nina prodded.

"Three other brutes." Sexy, big, and handsome men with tattoos and attitude. The kind of men her mother had long ago taught her to be wary of.

"God, kill me now. It's a good thing I'm happily married to my own stud. I can't believe how close we are to all that man candy." Nina practically glowed. "Sam is so hunky but scary. He's got those tattoos all over. I wonder how far down they go?"

"*Nina*."

"Then there's Lou. The brooding Latin lover. I swear, he gives me goose bumps when I see him."

"What?"

"Johnny Devlin's a real charmer. He's the one that looks like a cover model. He flirts a good game, but he's never been serious. Probably because I'm married." Nina fingered her ring.

"So glad you remembered," Cyn muttered, now trying not to laugh. Nina was a petite beauty with blond hair, green eyes, and a sunny personality. It had been a no-brainer as to what her brother saw in Nina. After twelve years, they still had a happy, healthy marriage and two handsome sons to prove it. "I don't think I've ever heard you go on about the Webster guys before."

"My dear husband has." Nina grinned. "But hey, I let Matt have that girlie calendar in his office at home, so we're even."

"You mean his Grannies for Nannies, calendar? The one my mom was in to promote her side babysitting business?"

"Hey, they're women. They count."

Cyn laughed. "That's just mean."

"And funny. But it's all good. Matt's friends with Liam and his guys. Del too. They're actually a nice bunch of people. And they buy a lot from us. Don't make enemies," Nina warned.

Too late. In the month she'd been working in the shop, Cyn had only encountered Del and Liam. A good thing, because she had man issues she was still trying to get over. But a lifetime of disappointments made it a long process.

She now felt a little bad about her behavior in the garage. It was Sanders's misfortune that she'd talked with one of her chauvinistic ex-business partners prior to dealing with the car situation. Dan Fawkes was such a dick. The word *scruples* had never entered his pretty little head.

"Sweetheart, let me handle things. We can renegotiate your portion of the distributions, can't we? I know it's hard to understand, but—"

"I understand perfectly." She'd wanted to "sweetheart" him right in the balls, considering they'd already haggled over her fair compensation, per her signed contract. *"I did all the work, and you're taking all the credit."*

"Now you know that's not true. I'm just better at math. You're the creative side to our arrangement. And the pretty one. Why, without you on board, I doubt Oglevy would have agreed to talk to me in the first place." So patronizing. *"Don't worry about it, Cyn. Leave the boring stuff to me. I'll do the calculations for you, and you can—"*

She'd disconnected before he could say any more, texting only to let him know her lawyer would be in touch. She'd ignored his subsequent texts and emails. The oily bastard.

If he thought he could cheat her out of her entitled shareholder distributions, he could think again. She never let anyone screw her over when it came to business.

Now her personal life, on the other hand… That had taken a beating one too many times. But she'd learned. Or so she told herself.

She and Nina worked together to help a few more customers. Funny how the rushes came and went with no discernible pattern, not counting the morning craziness.

"Have I mentioned I'm thinking about becoming the neighborhood cat lady?" she said to Nina just as the bell over the front door chimed again. She finished cleaning up after the last order, not looking at Nina. But her friend's silence made her curious.

A glance at Nina's smirk had her groaning inside, because trouble was sure to follow.

"Hey, *Foley*," Nina said with way too much pleasure. "How are you?"

"Lookin' good, Nina. How's Matt?"

"He's great. And if he's smart, he's done all his Christmas shopping by now. Not like last year's fiasco."

The deep chuckle went straight through Cyn…and had her bristling at her reaction.

"I, ah, I'm here to apologize to your friend, actually."

Cyn took that as her cue to turn around. Hell. Foley Sanders looked even better under the bright lights of the shop. She tried to pretend she wasn't studying him as intently as he studied her.

But damn, where the hell had he come from? He topped her own grand six feet by a few inches, and even despite his jacket, she couldn't detect any body fat on the man. He had broad shoulders and—as she vividly recalled from eyeballing him at the garage—huge, tattooed arms.

Short black hair framed a handsome face. Rough and manly. He had a five-o'clock shadow, and that rumpled hair look that on her would have appeared messy but on him shouted "sexy." Bright gray eyes watched her with caution, showing he had a measure of intelligence under all that muscle and ink.

She steeled herself not to get taken in by so much manliness. *Neighborhood cat lady, remember? Besides, his cars are littering the parking lot! Men suck. He's probably only into skinny chicks anyway.*

That made her feel better, imagining his intolerance for real women.

But real women can be any size. Plump or stick thin, fat or slender, tall or… Shut up, Cyn! This isn't time for a life lesson. Deal with Conan and love your gender later.

"Yes?" she said with an icy politeness that had Nina trying to bite back a grin.

"I'm sorry. I think we got off on the wrong foot." He smiled, but she wasn't buying the charm. "I'm Foley Sanders." He held out a hand.

Nina stepped on her foot, and she jerked toward Foley before realizing it. She glared at Nina before reminding herself to be a professional. She'd dealt with overwhelming men before and would no doubt again. So she pasted a smile on her face. "Cyn Nichols."

He blinked. "You're related to Matt?"

"Yes, is there a problem with that?" She didn't even have to pretend to be tired of that question. Matt was so handsome and in shape and popular. What tree had they shaken her out of?

"Not at all." His grin broadened. "I just hadn't realized Matt had such a hot sister."

She blinked. "What?"

"Before I somehow piss you off again, I'm here to get the cars," he said in a hurry. "Dale, our new guy, must have parked them in the wrong spot. Apparently our agreement was with the sewing place next door, not your parking lot. And I'm sorry I never answered your calls. I misplaced my phone again." He gave her a disarming smile that—damn it—worked.

She felt herself blushing. "Oh. Sorry if I came on a little strong." A little? Even she knew she'd been over-the-top bitchy. "It's just that we had some complaints with customers, and I couldn't understand why no one had gotten back to me." She still didn't understand that. What professional these days ever parted with his or her cell phone? But he'd made amends, so she could forgive him the lapse. "So you'll move the cars?"

He held up a ring of tagged keys. "Right away, Ms. Nichols."

"How do you know I'm not a Mrs.?" she asked, annoyed with the assumption. Was she so unattractive and ungainly she couldn't land a man?

He had the gall to wink and nodded to her hand. "No ring. Trust me. First thing I checked…after that dress. That's a really, really nice dress you're wearing." He let out a small sigh and left before she could think of something to say.

Like *I'm sorry for being so damn defensive about my size. It's not you, it's me. But then, it's guys like you who made me this way. Well, you and my mother.*

Thoughts of her mother scared her straight. She'd told herself time and time again to stop letting Ella Nichols dictate her feelings about herself. She just needed to follow her own advice.

"Ahem."

Knowing she had to face the inevitable, she looked at the smug woman standing next to her and groaned at Nina's wide smile.

"You and Foley Sanders. Oh my God, will you guys have the best-looking, tallest babies or what?"

Chapter 2

"WOULD YOU SHUSH." CYN LOOKED AROUND TO MAKE sure no one stood close enough to hear them. "First of all, I'm off men."

Nina's eyes grew to the size of quarters. "So you're into girls now?"

"No, Ms. Nosy. It's called celibacy. Well, that and cats." Though she'd never owned a cat before, they had a reputation for being independent. She could do with companions who didn't ask too much of her but gave her company nonetheless.

"Um, okay." Nina let out a whistle. "Even after I just witnessed a fine, *fine* man flirt with you, you're still turning to celibacy? Honey, he had that 'I'm gonna eat you up' look that every woman wants. I say take a chance."

"I say no. I'm done with men." *Or at least I'm trying to be done with men.* "Five minutes into a date, and I'm watching what I'm eating and gauging everything I say instead of just being me. I don't need that." *And I'm tired of hoping I'll one day find Mr. Right.*

"Jon was a moron," Nina said plainly. "Why let him color your idea of men?"

"Because he was just one in a long line of them. I've dated my share of judgmental jerks over the years, and frankly, I'm tired."

"You're a serial dater, for sure," Nina said.

"Tall, short, thick, skinny. I used to date with an

open mind. My only qualification was that my dates had to be intelligent."

"I get that. But muscles never hurt." Nina leered at the doorway through which Foley had exited.

"But even after all those guys, I never found one who actually liked me for me."

"That's bullshit."

Cyn stared. "What?"

"I said that's bullshit. You've had plenty of guys like you. You're smart and gorgeous, but you use any excuse to stay single."

"I do not." Offended, Cyn gave Nina the evil eye.

No doubt used to such a look from Cyn's brother, Nina ignored it. "Oh? What about Michael?"

"He ate twenty-four hours a day—at my expense," she exaggerated, though his eating habits had been both costly and bordering on a binge disorder. She would be the last person to discriminate based on size, but Michael had put health far behind him in his goal to eat as much as he could. "His grocery bills rivaled my mortgage."

"He was training for a marathon."

"And he could barely run around the block."

"But he thought you could do no wrong," Nina continued. "What about Frank?"

"Which one?"

"Both."

"Frank Sheffield was a mama's boy. Frank Barkin hated gays."

"Well, there's that I guess." Nina rubbed her chin. "How about—"

"Let me stop you right there. Todd was too religious. Deke not religious enough. Fred—"

"What does 'not religious enough' mean?"

"He was a nihilist. All doom and gloom. I'm not saying he had to believe in God, but believing in something besides the end of the world would have been nice."

"Oh." Nina tried again. "How about—"

"Just stop. Look. I've seen plenty of my friends get divorced, and then I see my parents together after forty years, and you and Mattie totally happy."

"He hates when you call him Mattie."

Cyn gave an evil, younger-sister smile. "I know. But I also know that marriage is hard work. If I can't enter into that kind of a relationship with a man I like and respect, and who respects me, it's all downhill from there."

"I suppose so. But I still say you're too fixated on the negative. Because even when a nice guy likes you, you look for flaws, because you don't think you're pretty enough, which is just weird. You're one of the most beautiful women I know."

Uncomfortable with Nina's effusive praise, which so contradicted what Cyn had grown up hearing, she changed the subject to a new line of pastries they'd considered showcasing in the store. They continued to work, Cyn helping out behind the counter because the newness of the business excited her. Plus, she had an addiction to coffee. Just being in the shop was enough to make her happy.

They joked with each other and young Nell, who was in the back washing dishes. But Nina kept glancing at the door.

"Stop it." It had been over half an hour since Sanders

had left. Cyn knew. She'd discreetly checked her watch a few times.

"What?"

"I don't buy that innocent tone. So help me, if you try—"

The door bell jingled, and he walked in, looking too damn fine. The flush on his cheeks and sparkle in his eyes only enhanced his rugged good looks.

Before Cyn could think of what to say to him other than *Thanks* and *Get the hell out before I forget myself*, Nina handed him a hot cocoa.

"On the house." Nina smiled.

Sanders accepted it with thanks. "This is just what I needed. It's getting really cold out there."

"But no snow yet?"

"No." He took a sip, his gaze resting on Cyn. "But if it does and ices over, tomorrow won't be pleasant."

"That's for sure. But we'll be open. Someone's got to feed and caffeinate the masses." Nina said something else while Cyn rang up a waiting customer.

Sanders continued to stand off to the side by the counter, making small talk with Nina about his fellow mechanics.

Without anyone else to wait on, Cyn decided to be the bigger person—no pun intended—and nodded to the man. "Thanks for moving the cars."

"No problem. I'm sorry they were there to begin with."

He sounded sincere, and she'd been taught to forgive those who truly wished for forgiveness. But she refused to apologize again for her justly given tirade. Maybe if he thought she was mean, he'd leave her alone. She had only so much willpower, and her heart hadn't mended from her last live-in disappointment, even eight months after the fact. She'd wasted two years on the man, only to have her relationship collapse on itself because Jon hadn't accepted that she was always going to be a bigger girl, and she was okay with her size. Well, mostly okay with it.

"Have a nice weekend." She turned and headed to bus a few tables.

A large shadow followed her.

She swallowed a testy retort and instead used her polite voice. "Um, can I help you with something?" When he said nothing, she turned to see him staring at her.

Okay, rudeness justified a like response.

"Well?" she snapped, her heart racing at the slow start of his panty-melting grin.

"Would you like to have dinner with me sometime?"

She buried her biological *hell yes* with a realistic *no*. Guys this hot wanted only one thing, then went on their merry way. "Thanks, but no." Most men would leave it at that.

"Why not?" He took another sip of cocoa, his gaze unwavering.

She swallowed a smirk at his persistence, because he'd proven her instincts right. Foley Sanders did not like to lose.

"I'm not into men anymore."

"You're into women?"

She sighed. Loudly. "Did Nina put you up to this?"

"Huh?"

"No, it means I'm off dating. Period. Men are trouble." She looked him up and down. "And I'll bet you're a lot more trouble than you're worth."

"Ouch."

"Yet you don't deny it."

"But, Cyn." He moved closer, and she froze. His voice seemed impossibly deep, and the way he said her name made her want to roll over and beg. "Some trouble is good for the soul."

"Not the kind you'd be bringing." She knew that instinctively. "But you seem like a nice guy." No, he didn't. "It's not personal. Just a lifestyle change." She paused for effect. "I'm celibate. No sex. So even if we did go out, you'd be getting nothing."

"Not even a kiss?" He smiled at her.

Unbelieving bastard. "Nope. Not even. Now I'm sorry, but I have to get back to work. Not all of us can laze around on a Friday afternoon." She pointedly looked at him, gave him her "I'm judging you as not worthy" stare, then turned her back on him.

She felt him step away after a moment. But his low laughter reached her before he left. As did his promise that sounded more like a threat. "See you later, Cyn."

Moments later, she felt another body behind her and knew exactly who it was. "Not now, Nina. I swear, if you blab any nonsense about me and Sanders to Matt, I will fill your boys with candy and hook them on ultra-violent video games."

Nina snorted. "Nice try. They're already playing those games, and they've systematically found the candy stashes their father has hidden around the house."

Cyn had to laugh at that. "Matt's always sucked at hiding things."

"So try to come up with something better while I design your wedding invitations. Hmm. Mrs. Cynthia Sanders has a ring to it, don't you think?"

"You're fired."

"Ha. I own half of this baby. And don't you forget it."
Nina left with a snicker.

And this is why you never do business with family.

Saturday morning, Foley watched his mother make
breakfast for him and Sam. He felt bad. It had been a
few weeks since he'd shared a meal with her. Foley
loved Eileen Sanders more than anything else in the
world. The woman had buried a husband she loved
when Foley was just four years old. Then she'd raised
his troublemaking ass on her own ever since. To have
taken in Sam as well? He liked to tease that she'd get
into heaven one day for sheer guts alone.

A glance at Sam's shy smile when Eileen scolded
him to eat made him love her all the more. Especially
because Foley knew if he couldn't get Sam to do right,
he could always count on his mom to step in and kick
Sam in the tail.

"Sam, you eat these damn pancakes or I'll shove 'em
down your throat. You hear me, boy?"

Though Sam could break her in half without trying,
he nodded dutifully and started shoveling down the
food, though not with the gusto he normally reserved
for filling his big body.

Fucking Louise Hamilton. Even after all the years
apart, Sam's mother continued to drag Sam back into
misery. Foley had mentioned Louise in the car, since
he'd overheard Sam talking to her, but Sam refused to
talk about her, a glare his only response.

Ever since Sam had been just a sickly, skinny little

prick mouthing off to anyone and everyone back in the sixth grade, Foley and his mom had been caring for him in one way or another. Sure, they'd all gone through rough patches. Some juvie crap, that awful mess in prison they both hated to dwell on. And Sam's continued refusal to get help for the messes his mother created. But through it all, they'd become a family. With Sam, Foley and his mom could both work on the guy, and he needed the affection so damn badly that all of them came out for the better when he let them help.

"When do Liam and Del come back?" Eileen asked.

Sam started answering with his mouth full, until she gave him "the look," and he shut it.

Foley smirked at him, accepting the hidden finger Sam shot him as his due. "After Christmas. They're doing it up this year because Del's engaged to that smothering McCauley clan."

"Now, Foley, that's not nice." Eileen glared at him. She loved Liam Webster for taking Foley in. Like he'd been some wayward waif. Far from it. He and Sam had been doing just fine on their own, taking classes while working at various garages. But he'd admit he'd found a home at Webster's.

Still, nothing he could say would change her mind about Liam and his "heart of gold." Of course, she'd never heard the old man go off on him or swear like a sailor.

For a while, Foley had wondered if maybe his mom and Liam might make a go of it. But Liam's propensity for dating topless dancers, and his struggle to get over his dead wife—who'd passed *thirty friggin' years ago*—had cautioned Foley to keep his mom away.

"Yeah, well, Mike McCauley is okay, I guess," he

admitted. "He makes Del happy. But I think she just hooked up with him to get to his kid." Colin was a seven-year-old ball of energy always good for a laugh and feel-good moment. To Foley's surprise, he liked showing the kid power tools and the treasures to be found under the hood of a muscle car. He'd never thought too hard about having kids, but around Colin and all the freaking happiness in the garage lately, he'd wondered...

"Colin's a good kid," Sam agreed, his mouth now free of food.

"Exactly. Because his father is raising him right." She pointedly looked at Foley and Sam as she settled pancakes on Foley's plate. She added a bunch of sausage to the table too.

God. Foley *loved* his mom. He started wolfing down his breakfast.

She continued, "Everyone makes mistakes, but it's how you deal with the aftermath that makes you a man."

They groaned, and Sam begged, "Not today, Eileen."

"Sam Hamilton, you eat my pancakes, you take my advice."

"Well, I'm not all that hungry, so I—"

"Eat!" She shoved another stack on his plate.

"Better do what she says," Foley advised, trying not to laugh. "You know she gets mean when she thinks we aren't listening."

"She's mean all the time," Sam grumbled and forked another mouthful of carbs.

She rubbed Sam's head, as only his mother could do and get away with unscathed, and returned to the stove. After fiddling a bit, she returned to the table and sat with them to eat.

"So, boys. Anyone you're dating lately?"

They shrugged, as usual, making her work to get answers. Foley had been grudgingly sharing with his mom forever, but it had taken Sam a lot longer to trust she'd accept him no matter his faults. Eileen never judged. She listened, offered unasked-for advice, then smiled and waved them on their way.

And maybe that was part of his problem with women. Foley tuned out as Sam talked about a passing romance with a woman heading out of town. Maybe if Eileen Sanders hadn't been such a terrific role model of what a woman should be, Foley wouldn't have stuck to casual dating for so long. His mom didn't put herself above others and had a generous heart. Even better, she'd never taken shit from him or Sam. She wasn't afraid to say it like she saw it.

The realization stunned him, but it made sense. How could Foley settle for anything less when it came to finding a woman he'd want to keep around?

An image of sexy Cyn Nichols came to mind. A fiery redhead who'd looked interested even as she'd told him to screw off—in nicer words than he'd thought she might use. Hell. He liked her. Obviously she was hot. He wanted to do her in the worst way. She had a rounded, voluptuous quality that put him in mind of Marilyn Monroe—one of his mom's favorite actresses he'd been forced to watch when younger. But that pinup build was definitely his type.

Even better, she worked close by with people he liked. Matt and Nina Nichols had always been personable when he'd visited their shop. Not treating him like he'd steal half their inventory, just because he looked like a prison escapee—as Del liked to describe him.

He grinned. Del could be mean. Probably why they got on so well. She didn't take his shit. Just like Cyn hadn't taken his crap either.

He didn't go for cruelty in a woman, but he liked sass. And he fucking *loved* red hair.

Shit. He was getting a hard-on at the breakfast table— near his mother. He focused on wiping his plate clean, on Lou's last paint job, on his last disaster of a hookup… and finally lost his erection. Just as he rose and poured them all more coffee, Eileen dropped a bombshell.

"There's a man I'd like you to meet. He and I have been dating for a few months, and I—"

He dropped into his seat like a stone. "*What?* How have you been dating and I didn't know?"

"Yeah," Sam growled. "We need to look this guy over, make sure he's—"

"*This* is why I didn't say anything." Eileen shook her head. "I wanted to get to know Jacob before you two scared him away. I like him."

Foley and Sam exchanged a look.

Foley's mother had turned fifty-three a month ago and looked like a knockout. She kept in terrific shape, a fan of yoga and strength training, so he could see guys wanting to shack up with her. Long dark hair, gray eyes, a thin, oval face. Then there was her even prettier personality. So yeah, he and Sam kept an eye on her. For all that Eileen could act like a mother bear around her kids, she had an inability to weed out the morons from the good guys.

Over the years she'd dated a few losers, but she'd

always put him and Sam first. He knew for a fact that her typical MO was to settle for some action on the side, though he tried to ignore the fact that his mother had *needs*.

But she'd never dated anyone she'd kept a secret before. *That I know of.* "Okay, who is this guy? Tell us all about him."

"No."

Sam blinked. "What do you mean, no? Why won't you tell us about your new boyfriend? Does he scare you? Did he threaten you?" Sam looked murderous.

Talk about making a leap. "Easy, man. Jesus, I doubt she'd be with someone who threatened her." At least, Foley hoped not.

"Simmer down, you two." Eileen sipped her coffee. "Jacob is a very nice man. He's a dentist, as a matter of fact. I helped his daughter and son-in-law with a rental a few months ago. We clicked and started dating."

Eileen worked as a building manager for several rental properties on the south side. She'd continued to grow her business through sound decisions and sheer grit. And now she even owned a few buildings she managed. She was the best landlord Foley had ever had.

"Wait. A few *months*?" Foley didn't like his mom having secrets. Granted, he didn't figure she told him everything about her life, but a guy she'd been seeing for this long meant business.

"Seriously, Eileen. What's up with that?" Sam sounded gruff.

Hurt.

Before Foley could reassure him, Eileen stepped in. "Oh, relax. I fully intended to introduce him if we got more involved. At first it was a few dates. He's handsome, and I wanted to make sure he wasn't out just to get a piece of ass."

Foley wiped a hand down his face. "Mom."

"Oh. Uh, good." Sam flushed.

"But I soon realized Jacob is the real deal. He divorced his wife over ten years ago and has been happily single since. He makes his own money, a very nice living, as a matter of fact. He has a daughter and son-in-law and a grandson on the way." She gave Foley and Sam a piercing look. "He's obviously much more successful than I am."

Foley frowned. "You make a decent living, and you're just as smart as some stupid dentist."

She glared. "I *meant* he found a way to raise his daughter to be a fine woman who married well and is giving him grandchildren." Then she gave her trademark pained sigh. "Where did I go wrong?"

He and Sam shared a commiserating groan. They'd been hearing the grandkid speech for years.

"You saved me from a life of crime," Sam offered— the Hail Mary of defenses. "I'd definitely still be in jail if it wasn't for you and Foley. I don't think you went wrong at all."

"Oh, sweetie. You're my boy." Eileen leaned close to kiss Sam on the cheek. "Of course I didn't go wrong with you."

And he calls me a kiss ass.

Then Eileen turned that militant gleam on him.

Foley hurried to keep her off grandbabies. "Exactly. You owe me, Hamilton. So stop whining about cleaning the bathroom at home and settle your debts."

His mother tried to hide a smile, but Foley saw it. Sam did too, because he had to work to mask his own. As usual, bringing up his sorry excuse for a past turned Eileen's attention from her favorite complaint about grandkids to pity for Sam.

"Fine. I'll clean it this week. But my room is off limits."

Foley cringed. "I'm thinking of calling *Hoarders* and getting you on the show."

"Up yours." Sam shot him an obscene gesture.

"Sam," Eileen warned.

"But he started it."

"Oh, for fuck's sake," Foley swore.

His mother scowled.

"It's okay, Eileen." Sam sighed. "It's not his fault." The sparkle in Sam's eyes warned Foley to be wary. "He's been having a tough time dealing since this hot chick blew him off yesterday in front of everyone."

"Oh?"

Foley mentally consigned Sam to the depths of dating hell.

"*Totally* blew you off," Sam said to him with a smirk. "Maybe I'll take my turn and—"

Foley gritted his teeth, knowing he was being played but unable to stop himself. "Try it and lose some teeth."

"Well, well. I'm not the only one with secrets." Eileen leaned forward and sipped her coffee. "Tell me more, Sam."

"Well, she—"

"Nothing to tell." Foley jerked to his feet, grabbed his and Sam's plates, and dumped them in the sink. "Some chick got PO'd because Dale parked our cars in her lot by accident. I fixed it. End of story." Sam, the bastard, refused to follow Foley's lead.

He kicked back in his chair and raised a brow. "End of story?" He turned to Eileen. "She's just Foley's type. A gorgeous, stacked redhead. Seemed pretty smart and sure the hell rocked a dress and heels."

"Is that right?" Eileen practically purred.

"I'll be in the car." Foley leaned down to kiss his mother's cheek. "Love ya, Mom, but I have shit to do today. And before Sam goes filling your head with nonsense, the woman is fine, yeah. But I think she's married." A total lie, but he didn't want his mother on his case.

Eileen let out a sigh. "Oh. Well, but maybe—"

Foley left before his mother could say any more.

When Sam joined him five minutes later, Foley had built up a head of steam.

"Hey, easy." Sam held up his hands in surrender. "I was playing her."

"What?"

"I got her so hooked on your lack of a love life she slipped up and gave me her boyfriend's number."

"She did?" His mother was usually slicker than that.

"Actually, I distracted her then looked him up on her phone."

Foley grunted.

"Dr. Jacob Wynn. I'm thinking I need my teeth cleaned."

"Sounds like a plan." Foley nodded. "But you still owe me for telling her about Cyn. What the fuck, man?"

"Lay off about Louise, I lay off about Cyn."

Foley sighed. Sam's mother had always been a touchy subject. "Agreed."

"Good. Now let's stop somewhere to eat first. Aggravating you made me hungry again."

The perfect excuse to swing by a certain coffee shop. "You up for some coffee and pastries?"

Sam immediately clued in. "As a matter of fact, I am. Especially if they come with a hot redhead on the side. You called dibs, fine. But I get the impression she's not interested."

"She is. She just doesn't know it yet."

Sam snorted.

"Coffee first. Dentist after. But no scaring the redhead away."

"Dude, I don't think you *can* scare a woman like that. Ten bucks says she shoots you down hard."

"I can't take that bet. But give me 'til next week, and we'll bet again. I just need to work my magic, and she'll be putty in my hands."

"You do know roofies are illegal."

Foley told him where to go, and Sam shot back something even more obnoxious. A good way to start the weekend. Especially with Cyn on his mind.

Chapter 3

CYN HAD DRESSED FOR THE WEATHER TODAY. BOOTS, jeans, and a thick sweater would combat the cold this Saturday. Though it hadn't snowed, the icy roads last night had made travel more than a little hazardous. Closing up early would ease her fears about getting stuck out in the dark with a flaky battery.

The weather hadn't scared the customers. Today Nichols had a decent crowd. People continued to shop and prepare for the holidays, and the peppermint cocoa sold like crazy. A little girl at the counter oohed and aahed over their Santa-shaped cookies and chattered about Christmas. If only Cyn could enjoy the holidays so well.

Another Christmas spent at her parents'. Another joyous day watching her perfect brother and his perfect family live up to her mother's expectations while Ella Nichols subtly complained—in excruciating detail—about everything Cyn was doing wrong with her life.

If only "Silent Night" could be taken literally.

Nell and Gino continued to serve behind the counter while Cyn brought out another tray of Kim's orange cranberry muffins and toasted pumpkin scones. She would have indulged, but she'd made the mistake of stepping on the scale earlier. Two more pounds had jumped out of that bottle of wine she'd shared with Nina last night. Or it might have been the thuggish gang of Christmas cookies forcing her to take "just one bite."

"I hate Christmas," she muttered to herself then grabbed a bottle of eco-friendly cleanser and a clean rag to wipe down tables.

She'd just finished clearing the last of them when a familiar sense of anticipation and annoyance broke out over her. She wasn't surprised to turn around and see Foley Sanders staring at her. She swallowed hard and forced a polite, "Hello."

His wide smile did nothing but stir her ovaries into happy leaps of joy. She glanced at his equally large and scary mechanic friend standing next to him. Talk about presence. The pair had a combination of sexy danger and charisma that attracted and repelled Cyn in the same breath. Tatted, muscular, and wary—as if they would attack anyone who came too near—the men seemed more lethal than anyone she'd ever met. At the same time, Sanders had a softness in his eyes that invited her to look closer and peel back the layers of the man.

"Hi, Cyn." He held a coffee and bag of goodies in one hand and motioned to his companion. "This is Sam. You met him yesterday at the shop."

"We didn't actually meet," Sam said in a low, gravelly voice. "She was bitching you out about the cars."

Not nice of him to bring that up, was it?

Good Lord, but Sam might as well have had the word "menacing" tattooed on his forehead—in addition to the wealth of ink she'd seen over his forearms and biceps the other day.

"That's right," she replied, all sweetness and cream. "I came in to correct a fucked-up situation."

Sanders sighed. Sam blinked then grunted at her and sat at the table she'd cleared.

"Yeah, well, it's all good now, right?" Sanders gave her a subtle once-over and sipped from his cup, joining his friend at the table.

"It is." She decided to be pleasant. Not his fault his friend had the manners of a goat. "Enjoy your coffee."

"Cocoa." Sam lifted it in toast to her. "And it's damn good. You might have attitude, but you've earned it. The drink and food is fuckin' amazing."

She tried not to but couldn't help it. She found Sam's honesty charming. "Thanks. Appreciate the *fuckin'* compliment."

That earned a laugh from them both. Before Sanders could draw her into conversation, she left them to return to the back, where she planned to try to get some work done away from temptation. And she didn't mean the food.

After half an hour dithering online, looking at memes on Facebook, she gave her spreadsheets a disinterested glance and yawned. It had just passed noon, and by the sounds in the shop, the crowd continued to remain steady.

She'd finally delved into progress on a small candy store in Issaquah she'd invested in when someone knocked at the door.

"Yes?" She didn't glance up, finishing her calculations. Awesome. They'd finally turned a profit.

"So you busy?"

Having expected Gino or Nell, she jerked her head up to see Foley Sanders occupying her doorway. "Um, what?"

He tucked his hands into his front pockets, filling out

a pair of jeans and a sweatshirt like the clothes had been
made just for him. "I really am sorry about yesterday."
He grimaced. "And about Sam."

She grinned. "Yesterday's over. And Sam is fine. I
appreciate honesty."

"You do?"

"Actually, yes. Why? Does that surprise you?"

"Not really." The look on his face unnerved her, because
she couldn't read him. "You seem like a smart woman.
I already know you're not afraid of confrontation."

"True enough." Her palms felt sweaty. Waiting for
him to get to the point while trying to seem blasé took
energy. Man, he was good-looking. And way out of
her league.

"So you want honesty. Okay. You're beautiful. I
want to go out with you. How does dinner sound?"

She blinked. Talk about direct. On the one hand,
she liked him the more for it. On the other, now she
had to respond in kind. "I thought I told you yesterday
I don't date."

"I didn't ask for a date. I asked you out to dinner.
I don't see why we can't be friends who happen to
eat together."

He looked awkward, standing in an odd way. "Are
you hunching your shoulders for some reason?"

"Do I look smaller? Less threatening? Sam said
you're probably scared of me, so I'm trying to look easy-
going." He sighed and straightened to his full height.

She snorted. "Yeah, right. And for the record, I'm
not scared of you. I just don't know what you want. I
told you before. I'm not into one-night stands. Or sex
of any kind."

"Now that's just a shame, but okay. I get it. Look, I'm not into forcing women into anything." He shrugged. "Frankly, I don't have to."

"Nice ego you have there."

"Hey, you want honesty. There it is. I'm sorry we got off on the wrong foot yesterday."

Shoot. He sounded sincere. Nothing cut through her defenses faster than a real apology. It took a person of worth to recognize his or her fault and atone. Especially when she'd been the one with the "attitude," as Sam had said.

Her cheeks heated. "I am too. But I don't want to lead you on in any way. No sex. You want to be friends. That's what you're saying."

"I'd like a lot more than friendship. But if friendship is all you're offering right now, sure, why not? Never hurts to have a friend who makes killer cocoa and muffins."

She had to hand it to him. Despite not looking the least bit smaller or less threatening, he'd disarmed her. "How about lunch next week instead of dinner?"

"Lunch works. And I understand. Seriously. No sex, no hint of sex, not even a glimmer of it on the horizon."

She wished he'd stop saying "sex," because she kept envisioning him without his clothes on. In bed. Right next to her. So much for her bid for celibacy.

Cyn cleared her throat. "Right. Okay. Lunch. And we'll go dutch."

"My treat. I'll probably end up annoying you, so at least if I'm buying, you'll feel like you have to be nicer than normal to me." His sly grin made the temperature in the room rise. "I know it's tough. But I'll grow on you."

"Like mold?"

"I prefer to think of myself as a creeping vine. And

hey, if after lunch you haven't changed your mind about jumping my bones, at least you'll like me by then. I'm a charming guy."

She had to a laugh. "Persistent and honest. Okay. Lunch it is."

He winked. "Talk to you next week, Cyn." Sanders turned on his heel and left.

Cyn stared blankly at her monitor until Gino interrupted with a question about their new scones' ingredients. Pulled back into reality, she dealt with allergy issues and a few finicky customers, all the while wondering if she was woman enough to withstand Foley Sanders's lethal charm.

⁓

The following Tuesday afternoon, Cyn sat across from Foley—she couldn't very well keep thinking of him as Sanders now that he'd insisted on paying for her lunch—at a small café in Fremont. Foley had asked her to pick the place, and considering he planned to pay for it, she'd chosen a decent, normally priced café she usually visited when she wanted a tasty yet healthy meal.

"I've been here before." Foley smiled at her across the small table, which felt smaller by the moment.

If he shifted his knee, they'd touch.

"Me too. I come here when I can. I like the food."

"Yeah." He stared at her. "You always look pretty."

She flushed. "Uh, thanks." She sipped her water, hoping he didn't realize she'd taken extra care with her appearance today. Jeans and a sweater. Nothing fancy, though she'd often been told the deep burgundy weave complemented her coloring. "So…"

"So…" He grinned. "Funny seeing you without something to say."

"Hey. You're the one who wanted lunch. Talk."

He seemed pleased. "You first. Tell me about yourself."

"What's there to tell?"

"How come you're not already married with kids?"

She paused, but he didn't seem to realize his rudeness. "Men are assholes. Why aren't you married with kids?"

"I scare people." He shrugged. "What can I say? I'm a big guy, and I'm not as smooth as some guys out there. So, back to your 'men are assholes' comment. Explain that."

"Seriously? You don't think that's a little personal?"

"Sure it is. But I want to know about you. Hey, you're the one who wanted honesty."

She did. Kind of. "You're a very literal guy, aren't you?"

He laughed. "Pretty much. I don't like games." His grin faded. "Last woman I dated seriously confused me. We agreed to be casual, then, because I followed *her* rules, *I* was the bad guy."

"Oh?"

"Yeah. I mean, you say up front what's what, then you're damned because of it. What's the deal with women who do that?"

"Not knowing the specifics, I can't say. But maybe she thought you wanted something else."

"I was pretty clear on what I wanted."

"I'll bet."

He raised a brow. "I'm detecting a judgmental tone. Hmm."

She hated that she now felt like her mother. "Sorry. It's just… Sometimes guys think they're saying one thing, but they're actually saying another." She frowned. "My ex kept trying to change me. Hey, I am what I am. You don't like it, don't let the door hit you on the ass on the way out."

Foley nodded. "Yeah, that. Same here. So this chick I'm talking about. I just wanted to be friends with her. Well, friends with benefits. I told her that—in those exact words. She wanted the same thing, or so she said. Next thing I know, she's wanting to hang out all the time and going on and on about babies." He paused. "Far as I know, FWB stands for Friends With Benefits, not Friends With Babies."

She felt for him and tried not to laugh. Friends With Babies. Yikes.

"I'm thirty-three. Old enough to start thinking about kids, I guess. But I'd kind of like to have them with someone I'm serious about, you know?" he said.

"I get it."

"As if the baby lady wasn't bad enough, my mother is constantly on my ass about grandkids. Jesus, it's not like I have an expiration date. Or do I?"

She laughed with him. Their food came, and they ate while agreeing about the complexities of dating.

"But since we're just gonna be friends and all," Foley interjected, "I want to know about *you*."

"What about me?"

"Just pick a topic and run with it. Don't be difficult, Red."

"Red? Really? I've been called so many nicknames over the years. *Red* is the most unoriginal I can think of."

Foley frowned. "So Firecrotch would be better?"

She'd been taking a drink and had to swallow, so as not to choke, and still ended up coughing.

After shoving her water at her, he watched with concern as she cleared her throat. "Ah, so that's a no on Firecrotch."

She coughed and shook her head. "That's not only offensive, it's sexist."

"How so? A dude can be a firecrotch. I mean, technically, he's got hair—"

"*No*. Okay? Just, no." She finally caught her breath and glared. "Hell, Foley. Warn a girl next time."

He smirked. "Sorry."

"No you're not."

"If you'd just tell me a little bit about yourself, I'd probably be on my best behavior."

The twinkle in his eyes drew her. Handsome, funny, and naughty. She was liking him more and more—against her better judgment. Slowly but surely, her desire to remain free of male entanglements was shifting in favor of giving Foley a chance. She liked the guy, and she hadn't genuinely *liked* anyone of the male species—not a relative—since her ex.

"Fine," she gave in. "I'm thirty-four and come from an overbearing Italian family. I co-own the bakery with my brother and Nina. Recently bought into it since I decided to move back to town. I also invest in other smaller companies, which I do smartly thanks to a business degree I earned from the University of Washington."

"An intelligent woman. Nice. What else?"

"What else?" His approval warmed her. A lot of guys seemed to be put off by her admission of college and financial success. "Um, well. I've dated my share of men, but nothing ever clicked."

"Men are assholes. I heard you before."

"About time."

He grinned. "No wild stories about your exes?"

"That would take us way past lunch."

"I feel you." He took a drink and pushed his empty plate away. "What about your family?"

"We're close, and we all live in town." Not so close to her mother, but she refused to go into that with him. "You've met Matt and Nina, and they have two boys I'm crazy about. My nephews are a handful. Then there's my mom and dad. I have a bunch of relatives in the Portland area too, but we only gather for reunions or major life events. Graduations, stuff like that. And that's all there is to know about me."

"Where do you live?"

"Why?"

"Suspicious much?" He sighed. "I'm curious. I'm not asking for an address. Just a general location."

"North Beacon Hill."

He nodded, looking pleased. "Me too. My mom manages properties, and she got me and Sam a great town house."

Time to learn about him. "You and Sam live together?"

"Yep. He's as tight as a brother can be, even if we're not biologically related."

"And? Keep going." She pushed aside her empty plate. "You wanted to learn about me, now it's your turn."

"I *knew* you'd be interested." He grinned.

She rolled her eyes. "Well?"

He shrugged. "My mom and I are tight. My dad died when I was a kid. Now it's just me and her and Sam." He frowned. "And some guy she's apparently interested in."

"Oh?"

"Yeah, some dentist. She says he's a decent guy. But we'll see."

Protective of his mother. She liked that. "No ex-wives? Clingy girlfriends?"

"Nope." He stared into her eyes. "I'm all yours."

"Friends, remember?"

"Sure. I'm all yours…as a friend."

He continued to just stare at her, making the temperature rise. Somehow he made her feel indecent in a sweater that covered her from chin to waist. She cleared her throat. "What about work? You're a mechanic, right?"

"Yeah. I've had my share of schooling, for tech though. Not business. Emissions, A/C, trade stuff. I love my job. Fixing things, especially cars, that's my wheelhouse."

"Nice to do what you love."

"I know." He nodded. "Hmm. What else?"

"How long have you worked for Del?"

"I've worked for *Liam* for four years." He leaned back from his chair and linked his hands behind his head. "Del joined him as a partner a couple years ago. She's great, even if she is a hard-ass. I like her."

"I don't know her well, but Nina and Matt speak highly of her."

"She's good people. All the guys are, really. We went through some bumpy roads with the crew until Del and Liam weeded the losers out. Now it's Johnny, me, Sam, and Lou. Us and the Websters. We're a good crew."

"Sounds like it."

They sat in silence for a moment, but she didn't find it uncomfortable. Foley was so much more than she'd expected.

He glanced at her plate. "You sure put it away."

She followed his gaze, confused. "Excuse me?"

"Your food. I like that."

She went from liking him to being unsure. It was like Jon, Mitch, Mike, all of them all over again.

"You like that I eat my food?" Was this some weird way of mentioning her weight? Men hoping for a chance with her typically waited until they'd at least slept with her before trying to slim her down.

"Yeah." He dropped his hands to the table. "Some women pick at their food like rabbits—ordering salads and skimping on eating. Like faking it's going to impress me." He huffed. "I like a real woman. You eat meat and bread and don't skimp on an appetite. I like your size." His gaze wandered over her. "You're friggin' hot."

Cyn blinked. *Her size?* He was really going there on the first date? "So you're saying I'm big, and you like that I'm fat?"

He finally looked up from her breasts, apparently realizing she didn't sound thrilled with him. "Huh? You're not fat."

"Thanks for that." Now she felt embarrassed, because she'd drawn attention to her size—which didn't need to be pointed out to anyone with a pair of eyes.

"I mean, you're tall. Stacked. A big girl. You have meat on your bones. Something to hold on to."

Oh hell. She'd found a guy who seemed somewhat decent, one she wouldn't mind dating even. But instead of just liking her for her personality, he wanted her because of her assumed fat rolls. A chubby-chaser. Joy. Could she just once find a guy who'd look into her eyes, think her pretty enough to want to get to know better, then fall for what was *inside* the outer package?

"Foley, thanks for the meal, but I'm done."

"No dessert?"

"I think this 'big girl' ate enough, don't you?"

He groaned and closed his eyes. "I knew I'd say something stupid. Come on. You're supposed to forgive me for being an idiot, right? I think you're hot as hell. You have to know you're sexy, pretty, built—"

"Like a tank of Jell-O. Thanks so much."

"Cyn—"

"I think it's great you're into big girls," she told him, not wanting to be a complete bitch again. She liked the fact that there were men in the world who saw a different standard of beauty in women than what the magazines advertised. All her previous boyfriends had wanted to change her. Foley didn't seem to want that, yet instead of feeling flattered, she felt…disappointed.

Damn it, she was more than numbers on a scale.

He looked embarrassed, and she felt worse, because he shouldn't be shamed for being attracted to a type. "I'm not into—"

"Big girls need love too." She meant that. But just once she wanted to be desired for her sparkling wit, her laugh, her opinions. "But I'm more than a big girl. Thanks for lunch."

Cyn left before she succumbed to the burning in her eyes.

She'd had her share of boyfriends throughout the years. She'd dieted, exercised, and starved herself until she'd lost weight to please them. But she'd never been and would never be thin or small. A six-foot-tall woman, she'd last fit into a size fourteen in high school.

Men liked her face and her breasts. They loved her

hair. But they seemed to differ when it came to her body. They either wanted her thinner or more athletic, but never as she was. Foley, at least, had been honest.

Hell, she'd told him she hadn't wanted a relationship. So why did his attitude make her feel bad? They could be friends. No problem.

She left in her car, pleased she'd insisted on them driving separately.

Yeah, she and Foley could be friends—*distant* friends.

Time to get back to work and focus on what really mattered. Making a living so she could retire in peace in another thirty-plus years—alone and lonely, with no one but her imaginary cats to keep her company.

Foley didn't know how he'd shoved both feet in his mouth so fast, but yeah, he'd done it. He stared at her empty chair, sincerely confused about how their lunch date had gone from awesome to shitty in the span of seconds.

They'd been doing so well. She'd shared details about herself. He'd told her how close he was to Sam and his mom. She seemed to have no problem with him—until he'd mentioned what she ate. He still had no idea why that should be a big deal. The woman was gorgeous, and she obviously knew she'd never be a stick. But who the hell wanted that?

The whole package had to attract him, at this age at least. Years ago he'd been a dog. He'd readily admit that. But now he wanted a woman with looks, brains, attitude, and strength.

Cyn seemed to possess all that. Talking to her had

been easy and engaging. She didn't let him steamroll the conversation. The superficial part of him acknowledged he'd never seen a more beautiful woman. Her face could have launched a dozen or more magazine covers. And what guy didn't want more than a handful in the breast department?

Well, fuck, he was hard again.

He calmed himself, remembering her confusion, her anger, and her poorly concealed hurt. Man, he'd stepped in it big-time. Now he had to make things better. Somehow.

Except he had no idea how to go about apologizing. Any way he thought about it, he'd end up reminding her that he'd called her a *big girl*. And while he'd meant it as a compliment—he was a big guy, after all—she'd apparently been insulted.

"Women."

He paid the bill and left in a huff. By the time he'd gotten back to work and involved in a Wrangler's suspension problems, he hadn't gotten any further with a solution to his dilemma.

"So what happened on your date?" Lou asked.

Sam and his big mouth. "It was okay." It was a disaster.

"You don't look happy." Lou didn't move from his position by the Jeep.

Foley stepped out from under the lift. "I'm thrilled to be at work. Life is just grand."

"Oh man. She shot you down?" Lou didn't laugh at him, so Foley decided to take a chance.

He glanced around and saw Johnny buried in a Chevy, so he leaned closer and whispered, "She left me sitting with my thumb up my ass. We were getting along great, then somehow she thought I called her fat or some shit, and she took off."

"What exactly did you say to her before she got upset?" Foley ran down their conversation.

Lou groaned. "Foley, you never comment on what a woman eats or doesn't eat. Are you *loco* or just stupid?"

"We were being honest with each other." Foley was confused. "I never called her fat. You've seen her. She's fucking built, man."

"Woman hears 'big,' she's hearing 'fat.' I'll bet she's dealt with a lot of bullshit over her size for a long time. She's tall for a woman, then you add her curves. Between guys wanting a piece of her and other women being jealous of her, adds up to issues, my friend." Lou sighed then smiled. "Issues I'd be happy to help her get over. She really is one sexy woman."

"Yeah, yeah, Lou. Keep it in your pants."

Lou chuckled. "Dealing with dickheads has probably made her sensitive. Then you said something that added to that. You're screwed."

Just what he didn't need to hear.

"But look at the bright side."

"Yeah?"

Lou gave him a big old smile. "*I* didn't call her anything. And I have a sudden thirst for coffee."

Foley would have slugged him if Sam hadn't entered the garage.

"How'd the date go?"

"Big mouth." He slugged Sam instead.

Chapter 4

"YES, MOM. I'LL BE THERE SATURDAY NIGHT, LIKE I TOLD you." Cyn sat in her running car, her hands in front of the heaters, and swore to herself as her mother continued to talk. The parking lot had emptied an hour ago, but Cyn had stayed behind at the coffee shop to do more paperwork.

Nina would have stuck around to badger her about the lunch she refused to talk about, but fortunately one of her boys needed a ride Matt had been unable to provide.

"So are you bringing anyone?" Ella Nichols nagged. She'd been asking that same question every time they talked. "Our Christmas party is growing. I can't wait!"

"I'm coming by myself. Should be more fun that way. You know, not having to entertain a guy and instead focusing on friends and family."

"Oh, honey. You and Jon have been broken up for eight long months. Time to start fresh, don't you think? You don't want to be alone forever."

Maybe I do. After two years of time and effort, I thought I'd found a prince. Instead, he turned out to be a warty little frog. "It's not about Jon. It's about me. I like being by myself, and I'm too busy for a man right now anyway."

"Too busy for a relationship? Please." Her mother lived and breathed the word *marriage*. Cyn had grown up being taught that a woman's future should be all

about finding the right man—which meant always looking one's best, no matter what it took.

"Don't worry about me. I'll be basking in the love
you and Dad and Mattie and Nina share. Like a Hallmark
special, don't you think?"

"Cynthia, please don't be sarcastic. I hate when you
do that."

Maybe she'd overdone that saccharine sweetness a
bit. "Fine. Sorry. Look, I said I'll be there. I just want to
enjoy the holidays, okay? And I really am busy. Taking
on Nichols has added to my workload, what with keeping everything afloat. Moving back here put a strain on
my other businesses, Mom." A gentle reminder. A lie,
but a good one.

Cyn had been a silent partner in a number of businesses for years. And she'd never had to live in one
location to manage them. That meant travel, but at the
time, she'd liked not being tied down to any one place or
person. And that need to be mobile gave her the perfect
excuse to stay away from home.

"I know, sweetie." Her mother softened her voice.
"I'm so glad you're finally back for good. We'll see you
Saturday night, then."

"Right. And remember, I'm coming to see family
and friends. No playing matchmaker. We talked about
this." Family gatherings were not an excuse to meddle
in Cyn's nonexistent love life.

"Fine, fine. I have to go. Your father's calling me."

Though Cyn hadn't heard him, Ella disconnected
before Cyn could say good-bye.

Annoyed, because she had a feeling her mother would
do what she wanted regardless of Cyn's wishes, Cyn put

her car in gear and drove to the game store where she'd ordered her oldest nephew Vinnie's Christmas present. She ended up finding something for Alex too and left with a lighter heart.

She loved watching her nephews at Christmas. Though being held to her mother's standard and being found lacking had always hurt, her brother had never made her feel less than wonderful. Matt loved his little sister. He'd always looked out for her. As had her father, who thought his little girl could do no wrong. Hell, even Nina's addition to the Nichols clan had produced laughter and smiles, not tears. Nina was a best friend and sister-in-law all wrapped up in a pretty package.

Only Ella Nichols continued to be a malignant shadow on family togetherness. Cyn was never good enough for her mother. Why she thought that might change because she'd finally come home, she didn't know. Cyn was smarter than that.

As she drove home from Queen Anne, she wondered what she'd hoped to achieve by living in the city, too close to ignore a summons from her mom. The family deferred to Ella, and since Ella only wanted what was best for her children and husband, had never done any wrong as far as they could see, they all thought Cyn overreacted to the constant barrage of subtle teardowns and insults.

If only Cyn tried harder. If only Cyn could hold up to the true beauty within. Work harder. Exercise more. Eat less. *Be* less around men so they could seem *more —more needy, more annoying, more arrogant*. Cyn had watched her mother concede to her father throughout their marriage, because a good woman put her husband

and family first. Her mother hadn't gone to college. Instead, she'd raised her children, put all her hopes and dreams into supporting them—at a cost to herself.

"Not my fault she made that decision." Cyn frowned and turned off the radio, which was too full of cheer for her dour mood.

Ella had given birth to a baby girl who hated dance and the color pink, and refused to kowtow to a man for anything. Cyn didn't hate men. Far from it. She just wanted to find someone she didn't have to stand behind. She wanted to stand abreast of a partner, to be equal. To find a man who wouldn't mind her financial success, her smarts, or her bigger than socially acceptable body.

"Someone who couldn't care less that I'm a *big girl*." She scowled, thinking about Foley. He hadn't come into the shop or called in two days, since their disaster of a lunch. She appreciated that he'd finally gotten the message that she wasn't interested, even as some perverse part of her wished he'd tried to convince her to give him another chance. After so long being single, part of her had actually been tempted to go out with him again.

Yes, eight months was a long time to go without a date. Enough time to heal from Jon's betrayal, but not enough time to forget. She didn't want to go back to her empty house yet, so she drove past the coffee shop, reminding herself that *it*, and not a man, shaped her passions and dreams.

She turned south, thinking to head toward the park to take in some quiet time and watch the snowflakes melt into the water. On her way, she skidded on some black ice and shrieked. Thank God the roads were mostly clear. The snow had started to really come down, and after righting the car, she did her best to calm her racing heart.

A few minutes later, her car just…died.

"Crap." She managed to use momentum to park at the side of the dark, mostly empty road.

To her dismay, the bright headlights of a large vehicle sidled up behind her. She reached for her phone on the dash shelf and found it gone. Must have slipped to the floor when she'd skidded on the ice. She locked her doors and prayed whoever had found her was a decent person, and not the serial killer her imagination conjured.

Whoever it was, even in the dark, she could tell he was big. Suddenly the clouds overhead moved and the moon lit the snowy ground over which he walked, revealing familiar boots. Her gaze darted up to see the man was wearing a jacket she'd seen before.

Her breathing had elevated to panting, despite realizing the identity of her Good Samaritan. Great, now her windows had fogged.

When he arrived at her window, he knocked. "Cyn?"

"Foley? What are you doing out here?" She didn't believe in coincidence.

"Not stalking you, since I have a bad feeling that's what you're thinking."

She flushed. "I wasn't thinking that. Exactly."

"Yeah, right." He shook his head, still talking to her through the car window. "You planning to roll down the window, or are you afraid I'll drag you through it and have my wicked way with you? You know, since I'm so into *big girls*."

He just had to bring that up. By now, her face felt so hot it threatened to burn up her car. "I can't roll down the window. My battery died."

"What?" he said louder.

She unlocked her car door and opened it, immediately regretting the cold wind that swept her. "My battery died. The car's been giving me issues, but then the issues disappeared, so I thought I was okay."

"Dumb." Foley looked big, handsome, and tired. "Get out so I can get in."

She did, and he gently nudged her aside, then entered the car. When he turned the key, nothing happened.

"I told you. My battery died."

"Yeah, but why? How old is it?"

She frowned. "I don't know. I've had the car for two years." She shivered when some snow drifted down the back of her neck.

Foley must have noticed, because he frowned. "Come on. Lock up, and I'll give you a ride home. We can fix this tomorrow."

"We?"

He looked up at her, brows raised. "Unless you'd rather change out the battery right now? Got a spare in your car? Some tools?"

"Well, no, but—"

"Then there's the fact that there might be more wrong than just the battery. Next time I might not be in the neighborhood to save your pretty ass."

She glared. "Speaking of which, what *are* you doing here?"

"I can tell you here, now, in the cold and the dark. Where muggers are probably waiting to take advantage...

Or we can go back to your place, where you can make me some nice hot chocolate, and I can explain."

"Maybe I don't have any hot chocolate."

He just looked at her.

"Fine. I do." Her weakness, chocolate in any form. Well, that and sexy assholes, apparently, as evidenced by her body's reaction to seeing Foley again.

After grabbing her purse and keys, she locked her car and followed him to his SUV. He opened the door but didn't help her step up and in, for which she was grateful. She really didn't need to be any closer to him than she had to be. For some reason, he smelled good. Even after what must have been a full day's work, the man didn't stink.

And his car... "This is neat."

"Glad you think so." He entered and started them toward North Beacon Hill. "Address?"

She gave it to him. "I meant your car is tidy. Neat. For some reason, when I see you, I think hot mess."

He clenched his jaw. "You're welcome for the rescue."

"I could have called my brother." But she wouldn't have. The roads were getting worse, and she'd rather he stayed with Nina and the boys. Her father, maybe?

"Are you going to be this bitchy all the time?"

She blinked at him, then smiled against her will. "Probably."

He shook his head and muttered something under his breath she couldn't understand.

"What's that?"

"Never mind."

They pulled in front of her cute cottage in no time, their drive unbroken by talk or music. She knew she should thank him. What was it about the guy that brought out the worst in her? She'd never tolerate the attitude she'd been giving him from anyone else. Around him, even she didn't much like herself.

"Foley, I'm sorry. Thank you for the rescue."

He seemed mollified. "You're welcome."

"But I was about to call my dad to come and—" His narrowed eyes had her swallowing the rest of what she'd planned to say. "Thank you."

"How about that hot chocolate?"

She nodded, and they left his car and entered her house. She hung up her jacket and his and removed her shoes. "You too. No shoes if you want cocoa."

He removed his boots while she set the kettle on the stove. He joined her in the kitchen, the small island separating them, and glanced around. "Nice place."

The cottage had room. Three bedrooms, two baths, and a nice-sized open kitchen/living room floor plan. Cyn kept it clean and clutter-free. A buttery-gold painted the walls, adorned with artwork from places she'd visited. Fresh flowers sat on the dining room table that shared space with her open living area. Her television she kept in a spare bedroom, making the fireplace the focal point.

She smiled, proud of her home. "I like it."

"Who'd you get the flowers from?"

Foley sounded jealous, and she loved it. *Man, I really am a bitch.* "A lovely florist named Joey."

He frowned. "Yeah?"

"Joey prefers roses, but *she* also likes a nice Christmas bouquet. *She* happens to be my go-to when I'm buying flowers."

He relaxed. "Oh." He stuck his hands in his pockets. A sign of nerves, she realized, intrigued.

"Now tell me how you just happened to be in the neighborhood when my car died."

"Yeah, well, this is tricky."

"How so?"

"You already think badly of me. I don't want to add to it."

"Might as well."

"Thanks." He huffed. "Okay, I've been trying to find the right way to apologize for Tuesday."

Watching him squirm pleased the vindictive "big girl" in her, but him bringing up their disaster of a date also reminded her why it had been a disaster. Now she felt uncomfortable as well.

"Never mind. It's over with. We're friends."

"Bullshit. I gave it a few days, then figured, you're stubborn. Thorny. Might as well let you rip into me so I can get my two cents in."

"I'm sorry. Thorny?"

He gave a surprising grin. "My mom's description of a woman with issues. Thorny. It applies to you, honey."

"Honey? Forgotten my name so soon?"

Instead of taking issue with her tone, he laughed. "Oh yeah, thorny. For the record, *Cynthia*, I am not into 'big girls.' I like women of all shapes and sizes. And yeah, I like them pretty, I'll admit." He walked around the island and closed the space between them, forcing her to back into the counter so he wouldn't be on top of her.

"Um, space?"

"No." He cupped her cheeks, startling her. "I love

redheads. I love a woman with curves, and more, a woman with a brain who's not afraid to use it."

She swallowed, loudly.

His grin grew. "I also love a woman who's a little bit mean."

"A little bit?"

"Or a lot," he added, his gaze settling on her mouth. "I know you said you don't want a relationship. You don't want sex."

"Um, yes. I said that." *But I didn't mean it,* her reproductive organs shouted.

"How about a kiss, then, to apologize for hurting your feelings?"

She felt small, having made so many assumptions about Foley when she'd once again been reacting wrongly due to her own screwed-up issues. "It's okay. I'm the one who's—"

He leaned closer, his lips almost brushing hers. She looked directly into bright gray eyes so clear they looked like diamonds. "Just a little kiss," he whispered.

She nodded without thinking and closed her eyes when he pressed firm lips against her mouth.

The kiss, like Foley, made a statement. It packed a punch she hadn't been prepared for because that spark of contact lit her up like a firecracker.

He moaned. Or she moaned, but it was definitely her pulling him closer and deepening the kiss. She pushed her tongue into his mouth and grabbed his shoulders tightly.

For a second, he held still, and she feared she'd misread everything.

Then he breathed a "yes" into her mouth and took control.

Good. God.

Foley kissed as if starved for her. He deepened the contact, angling his head and his body so that one thigh rode between her legs. Then he moved his hands from her cheeks, guiding hers from his shoulders to wrap around his neck.

He put his large palms on either side of her hips, then dragged her closer, so that her chest brushed against the hard plane of his.

She inhaled on a moan, her nipples like tiny spikes of need against his broad chest. The kiss of apology had turned into tumultuous desire in the span of a heartbeat. Cyn knew she should pull back, should slow them down, but the sheer arousal he'd spiked demanded she end it another way.

She hooked her leg around his and felt him huge and hard against her.

He ripped his mouth from hers to kiss up and down her neck, sucking hard at her pulse. His hold on her waist shifted, one hand still on her hip while the other had slid under her sweater and now grazed her bare flesh, gliding up her sensitive ribs.

"Oh," she breathed as he drew closer to her breasts.

"Fuck, Cyn. You're so soft," Foley whispered into her ear before he nipped the lobe.

At that moment, he found her breast and palmed the large globe through her silk bra, rubbing her taut nipple.

"Man, you feel good." Foley kissed her again, squeezing and teasing her breast, then moving to do the same to the other.

She could feel her body respond, could sense the intensity of it all while experiencing an almost out-of-body pleasure. No one had ever, in her entire life, turned her on like this with a kiss and some petting.

And her hungry body wanted more.

She pulled back to stare into his face, seeing the need emblazoned there, the beauty of hunger in his eyes. She let go of his neck to stop him from playing with her breast, her hand over his through her sweater.

He stopped the moment she touched him, watching with a predatory stillness. But when she guided that hand lower, he relaxed, groaned, and kissed her again. He didn't need further encouragement as his hand slid down her belly.

In seconds he'd unfastened her jeans, then glided beneath her panties, seeking the heat of her.

The second his fingers slid through her folds, she ate at his mouth like a woman desperate for affection. She knew it, could feel it, and didn't care. She'd never been so quick or close to orgasm, and from just a little bit of touch. Damn it, she wanted this. Wanted *him*, right now.

Foley didn't stop. Not that she wanted him to. He shoved a thick finger inside her while rubbing her clit with his thumb. The ravenous kiss was a contest in wills, until she succumbed to his demands and let him take charge once more.

Her reward—an intense orgasm that swept through her and caused mini earthquakes inside her. She heard a shriek, Foley's encouragement, and felt him rocking against her with an erection that threatened to rival Mount Rainier in size.

Then he stilled and removed his hand. A moment later, the shrieking stopped.

"Good timing, eh?"

She opened her eyes to stare into the bright gleam of male satisfaction. "Timing?"

"You went off when the kettle did."

"Oh." The shrieking hadn't just been inside her. More than one way to let off steam. She would have laughed if she'd been able to think past the lethargy settling in her bones.

"I knew you'd be hot, but you fucking burned me." He brought his finger to his mouth and sucked. And that action had her readying for another go with him.

With Foley Sanders. A man she'd just remembered she wasn't sure she liked.

He must have seen her hesitation, because he pulled back from her, though the grin hadn't left his face.

She glanced down, surprised to see him still thick against the fly of his jeans. "You didn't... I mean, you, ah..."

"Not yet. I'm saving that for when I'm inside you."

Confused, relieved, and suddenly shy, she didn't know what to say, how to explain why she'd jumped him. "I'm not sure what happened."

"Chemistry, Cyn, that's what happened." He leaned close to kiss her again, but this time the contact was fleeting, over before it truly began. "Can I take a rain check on the hot chocolate?"

"Um, sure." God, when he kissed her, she found it difficult to think. Her gaze went to his erection again. "I just... I can't..." She blew out a breath. "I don't know what to say."

"Say thanks for the ride." His lips quirked. "The car ride. And say you'll call me later, so we can have a real date where you don't get mad at me. Yeah, Cyn, you're a big girl." His gaze on her breasts left her in no question as to what he meant this time. "And I'm a big guy." He cupped his arousal, and she fought the urge to fan herself. "I think we'll fit just right."

"I told you I didn't want sex." Yeah, sounded weak to her own ears.

He just looked at her.

She covered her face with her hands. "I couldn't help myself."

"Me neither. I'm still hard, and I know about a dozen women who'd help me get rid of this."

That had her staring at him in shock—and anger.

"But I don't want anyone else. I want *you*." He brought her hand between his legs and made her squeeze. He sucked in a breath. "Fuck, I want you. But I'm willing to wait. Call me when you're ready." Then he groaned and eased her hand from him. "But don't wait too long. I'd hate to die from blue balls." He found a piece of paper and a pen and wrote down his number. Then he left the kitchen, putting space between them. He put his boots on and grabbed his jacket. "Hell, who am I kidding? I'm going to go home and jack off, thinking about how you taste, how you feel. But it won't be the same. Call me," he repeated in a low growl and left.

Cyn weakly leaned against the counter, wondering how her life had spiraled way, *way* out of control. As she thought about all he'd said, she felt a giddy urge to laugh.

He'd liked her. *All of her*. Not a guy out to get with a big girl, but a man attracted to her face and her mind. And her body, of course. Jesus, had they fit together. And they hadn't even had sex, not fully.

If he's that good just touching you, imagine what he'll be like when you finally do *hook up all the way.*

Her panties were damp, her orgasm a full-body relief that made life brighter, sweeter. She fixed herself a cup of hot chocolate and wondered what to do about Foley.

Then she realized something that still bothered her—just how was it he'd been right where she needed him, exactly *when* she needed him? Needed, kissed, touched...

She sighed. If only she could forget about the way he'd played her body enough to figure him out.

Chapter 5

THE MOMENT FOLEY RETURNED HOME, HE LOCKED HIMSELF in his bedroom and masturbated to memories of Cyn. Which took about five seconds, then he cleaned up and slid between his sheets.

God, it had been all he could do not to shove deep inside her and come. Instead, he'd been the gentleman, giving her a good time while remembering her pledge of no sex. He didn't want her to regret being with him, and the idea of seducing her into something she didn't really want bothered him.

Fuck, but that woman could burn him just by looking at him. Cyn was the most beautiful woman he'd ever seen. And now he knew what she looked like when she came. Talk about good dreams.

The next morning after he woke, he lay in bed, staring at the ceiling, unable to get her out of his mind. He'd thought he might be able to persuade her into another date with a steamy kiss. In no scenario had he imagined she might take over the kiss, or that she'd let him get her off.

He groaned and took a firm grip on his morning wood. Just thinking about the woman turned him on, but now knowing how hot and wet she would feel around him, how sweet and passionate she'd get when aroused… He had to stop thinking about her or he'd be the laughingstock of the garage. Waving an erection around at work—not a good thing. Especially not around his unforgiving friends.

But he couldn't stop thinking about her. How she'd looked, felt, smelled. Tasted.

He started stroking himself, lost in memories of their kiss. Once again, he lasted all of two seconds before he gave himself up to the bliss overtaking his body, Cyn and her taste at the forefront of his mind.

After a quick shower, he dressed for work and headed for the kitchen, where he made himself a quick breakfast. Should he wake Sam or let the goon fend for himself? Foley hadn't heard Sam get in last night. Probably spending his time with Shaya before she left the city. Though Shaya didn't seem Sam's type—too aggressive and world-weary for his buddy—she'd been kind to him, and she'd taken the edge off a man who needed some release. A satisfied Sam wouldn't work so hard to fight his way out of everything. When Sam got some, the guy was easier to handle.

Kind of like Foley, come to think of it. He grinned, in one hell of a good mood, and was sipping his coffee when Sam entered the kitchen, clean and in what looked like a decent frame of mind.

Foley grinned. "Oh yeah, you got lucky."

Sam shot him the finger, poured some coffee, then hunted down a bagel. After slathering the thing in cream cheese, he joined Foley at the table. "Well?"

"Well what?"

"Tell me what went down with you last night." Sam shoved half the bagel in his mouth and kept talking. "You look like a well-fed dog. You fucked Cyn, didn't you?"

"Not exactly. But man, she is just…" He blew out a

breath. "I hate to keep saying hot, but it applies. Woman burned me to a crisp. She's amazing."

Sam studied him, finally swallowing his food before talking again. "So you guys are an item now?"

"Not exactly. I went by to talk to her—"

"Because you're a pussy who couldn't give it a few days." Sam shook his head. "Pathetic."

"—and ended up following her in her car. I was going to signal her to stop when she broke down. Bad battery. So I gave her a ride home."

"A ride, huh?"

"Grow up." But Foley laughed. "At her place, I was just going for a kiss. But somehow we got a little heavier." *Did we. Hell. There goes my dick again.*

"So what?"

"So now I'm not sure. She knows I'm not just into big chicks."

Sam laughed. "I can't believe she thought that. Damn. We all know you're a dog with a hard-on for anything with breasts. With you it's about pussy, not size."

"You should talk."

Sam snorted. "True. I like to fuck."

"I didn't want to take advantage, so I left it in her court. Told her to call me."

"Yeah?" Sam studied him.

"What?"

"You like this one."

"Um, yeah. Haven't you heard anything I've said?"

"No. You really like her. As in, this isn't just about dipping your dick."

"So what?" Foley fidgeted. "Cyn's different. She's gorgeous, yeah. But she's tough. Smart. Mean, and a little scared underneath. I don't know. She's cool, and I want to know more. It's no big deal. Just a while since I've dated a girl."

Sam finished his bagel and said with a grin, "What about Sue? You guys were tight."

"Asshole." Foley's disastrous relationship with Sue, a waitress at his favorite bar, Ray's, had almost ended his time there. As he'd told Cyn, Sue had agreed to some casual sex, and yeah, she'd been decent in bed. But then she'd changed the rules, wanting to be with him all the time, wanting to be exclusive. Then all that talk about kids had freaked him the hell out.

At least now they got along like they used to. A good thing, because Sue was a tough woman. Not just because of all the tats and piercings. The woman could handle herself with a knife. And man, he did not want to go there. Crazy and needy he could do without, even if they did give good head.

Now Cyn... He couldn't see her handling a blade like Sue. She'd cut deep with words, her brain her most effective weapon. And well, maybe her body too. Shee-it. How could the woman not realize how fucking beautiful she was? It was that vulnerability, that lack of awareness, that made her so amazing. Foley had never been attracted to perfection.

That small susceptibility, that need for acceptance, pulled at him. *I sure the hell hope she calls. And soon. Because no way am I over that woman. Not at all.*

—✥—

Sam watched his best friend and knew a moment of unease. Cyn Nichols was different. She fascinated Foley, and Sam could see why. On the surface, the woman had everything Foley liked in a girl—breasts, red hair, a body that wouldn't break from some rough handling, and attitude. Hell. Sam would do her in a heartbeat, no problem. He couldn't fault the guy's taste.

But Foley had been out with women he truly liked before. A few he'd even been serious about. Like his girlfriend Michelle, from high school, and then that uppity chick, Desiree. Sam hadn't liked her much, but he'd said little, not wanting Foley to dump a woman for his sake.

Because he knew Foley, and the guy had heart. He always put others ahead of himself, because that's the kind of guy he was. Not a selfish shit like Sam—who'd secretly been relieved and thrilled when Foley had dumped Desiree. Foley protected his mom and looked out for his family, to which Sam belonged, whether he wanted to or not. Eileen and Foley had decided to keep him a long time ago, and having a few brain cells that still worked, he'd accepted the claiming, no protest.

But Foley could be known to be *too* giving. To the detriment of his own happiness, sometimes. Michelle, Desiree, that last job in Fremont, the one before Webster's. They'd left because the manager hadn't liked Sam. Not Foley, *Sam*.

And now this Cyn Nichols. She mattered, because there was a light in Foley's eyes that had been missing for far too long.

What to do about her, though. Would she be good for Foley, or just another distraction his buddy didn't need? Hearing why she'd turned Foley away, Sam couldn't blame her. It also brought an aspect to her character he hadn't considered. She'd been hurt before, so she took that hurt and turned it into a shield, bitching at others, keeping them at a distance so they couldn't hurt her.

He knew all about that. And he respected her for her strength. But he didn't want her keeping Foley at a distance. Or did he?

A glance at Foley's glimmer of a smile worried him. Maybe he'd better keep a closer eye on Cyn, the way he'd continue to keep an eye on Eileen's Jacob.

He smiled at something Foley said, but his heart wasn't in it. He owed Foley, Eileen, even Louise. His miserable existence might not mean much to him, but he could help others, and he did. Even if they weren't aware of it.

Foley had a guardian angel, one covered in tats and with a prison record, but one who could kick serious ass when needed. He'd make sure to shield Foley from Cyn Nichols, if necessary. Women like that fucked a man up better than meth ever could. Addicting and deadly, despite looking innocent on the surface. He'd do some damage control with the woman, just as soon as his buddy stopped mooning over the chick.

"Shit, Foley. Quit drooling over your redhead, because if you walk around with a boner at work near Lou, he might just take you up on it."

Foley flushed. How cute. "Shut up, dickhead. Lou's straight, and you know it."

"Maybe, but I notice you're not denying the wood."

Foley jumped up from his seat and darted down the hall. "I have to go to the bathroom. And not to jerk off, Sam. Jesus."

Sam chuckled, his mood restored. Foley swearing,

razzing him. Not dreaming over some stupid woman.
Just him and Sam against the world. As it should be.

By Saturday afternoon, Cyn still hadn't called Foley. She
sat in her kitchen, staring at the scrap of paper he'd left
behind. She'd plugged his number into her phone under
"Big Man," knowing Nina would never look Foley up
under that name if she happened to nose through Cyn's
contacts. Cyn didn't nickname her associates. All business, even in her social life, she organized with flawless
attention to detail. Foley should have been filed under
S for Sanders.

She stared at his number again, wondering why she
kept dithering over what to do about him. The orgasm
had softened her toward him. The man clearly had skills.
He hadn't asked for more than sex, and God knew it had
been a while for her.

Why not enjoy him? She'd never been one for casual
sex, but Foley was nice. He'd helped her with her
car, which yes, had needed nothing more than a new
battery—or so Matt had said. She'd refused to go down
to Webster's, surrounded by so much testosterone and
Foley. Not when she had trouble keeping her thoughts—
and lips—to herself.

She blushed, still amazed she'd turned his nice kiss
into a friggin' orgasm. Yet for all the pleasure Foley had
given her, he hadn't taken his own. What kind of guy did
that? Especially with a woman as willing as she'd been.
Hell, he could have mounted her outside on her front
lawn and she wouldn't have said no.

"I'm so easy. And desperate." She groaned.

Fortunately, she had no one to hear her but herself. Nina and Matt had decided to put in time at the shop, while Cyn's nephews helped out their grandparents, getting ready for the annual holiday party.

Cyn had wondered if she should bring Foley—for about three seconds. Any scent of a man with her, and her mother would no doubt pester and degrade her into a bitter, self-doubting mess by the end of the evening.

As hard as Cyn had worked to overcome Ella's badgering, the little girl who lived on inside her constantly wondered if maybe Ella wasn't right. Cyn probably wasn't smart, funny, or independent enough to live on her own. And with her chubbiness, she couldn't hope to land a decent man, not without her mother's help.

Part of Ella was correct. Cyn didn't feel fully satisfied with life, despite her successes. Even her sexual encounter with Foley had been lacking something. A closeness? A reciprocal lust? Then again, the man had *not* been faking that monster in his pants.

Hell. She fanned herself, dying to know what he looked like naked. She wanted to see all those tattoos. She pushed the call button on her phone then hung up before it could ring.

Should I? Shouldn't I? Should I? Shouldn't I?

With one more week until the holidays, maybe she should wait until after Christmas for a date. He likely had plans with family. That dimension of his character further softened her. Foley loved his mother. And Sam, a man he considered a brother.

How could she not like a guy who cared for his family? She loved hers unconditionally, despite her mother's unintentional cruelty. Cyn knew that at heart,

Ella wanted only the best for her daughter, despite how much she hurt Cyn with her criticisms.

Love could be strange. Just because Foley loved his mother, Cyn shouldn't make him out to be a saint.

She dialed him anyway.

The phone started ringing. She brought it to her ear, her nerves on high alert as she waited on the call she'd been dying to make for two days.

"Hello?" he answered on the third ring.

Had he been making her wait for taking so long to call? Did he normally take so long to answer?

Could you stop being an idiot and just talk to the guy? "Hi, Foley."

She could almost see his lips curl as he smiled into the phone. "Well, well, Lady Gorgeous finally calls."

He thinks I'm pretty. She had to hold back a sigh. *Oh God, get a grip, Cyn.* "You told me to call," came out much more belligerently than she'd intended.

He chuckled. "So I did. How are you?"

"I'm good." Great. Now what? "Are you busy? Is this a bad time to talk?"

"Nah." She heard the sound of clanging in the background. "I'm trying to help Sam with his pathetic excuse for a car." A definite "Up yours" from Sam. "So you want to get together?"

"I think so," she said slowly, still not sure. "I have a family get-together I can't get out of tonight. But I was thinking—"

"That we could get together after? Sure, I'm game."

Not what she'd been planning to say, but thinking about dealing with her mother, she could do with someone who thought her beautiful. "It might be late."

"It's Saturday. I'll be up. Want to meet at your place or mine?" He paused and must have muffled the phone, because she heard Sam in the background. "Make that your place. Sam's a pain."

"Fuck you" came clearly through the phone, followed by Foley's "Back at ya, jackass."

She grinned. Sam's coarse language and blatant honesty made him more, not less, likable. At least, to her. "Okay. Can I text you when I'm leaving my parents'?"

"Sure. Talk to you soon, baby."

She hated pet names. "My name is Cyn. Remember it."

He laughed. "Okay, *honey*." He disconnected. The ass. So why was she smiling?

The party was in full swing when Cyn arrived. She'd meant to come fashionably late, so she wouldn't have to spend one-on-one time with her mother. Ella would be way too busy hostessing the party to corner Cyn.

She saw her father and brother, Nina and the boys. Several neighbors, family friends, and a few work associates of her father's. Vincent Nichols continued to manage his growing PR firm, though he had planned to retire years ago. He said he couldn't leave the business he loved, not yet. Personally, she thought he couldn't face life, 24–7, with Ella.

Biting back a grin, she greeted her family and brought the wine and flowers to her mother.

Ella Nichols bustled in the kitchen with several of her friends, nattering in Italian while the scent of rich marinara, lasagna, and baked chicken filled the air.

"Cynthia, there you are." Her mother chastised by

waving her finger. "You're late. Ah, but you brought me flowers. Thank you."

Ella Nichols, the ideal maternal figure. Loving, accepting, gracious. Until she got Cyn in private and lamented her daughter's myriad disappointments. To combat her mother's tactics, Cyn had learned to be with her mother only while in the presence of others.

"Sorry. Had to finish up some paperwork." Cyn lived by her spreadsheets.

"Yes, you're so successful now." Isa Noroni smiled. "Your mother's been telling us all about you."

"And still so pretty." Anna and her husband, Tom, had been friends with Cyn's parents forever. "Sweetie, it's been too long."

"Good to see you, Anna. Isa." To Anna, she said, "Is Tom here?"

"Probably eating something sweet he's not supposed to," Anna said drily. Tom, a well-known diabetic, had a propensity for sneaking cupcakes when no one was watching.

"I made a low-sugar carrot cake for him," Mary, another of Ella's friends, said. "Hi, sweetie. Good to see you."

"You too, Mary." Cyn smiled. She'd always enjoyed her mother's friends, Ella's bimonthly bridge group that continued to play together, even after fifteen years.

"You get more striking each time I see you. Why aren't you a model yet?" Mary asked.

Ella rolled her eyes. "Mary, really. My Cyn is no model."

Ah yes. The double-edged sword. Too thick to be a model and too…her mother would come up with something.

"She's too smart to spend her time on pictures and clothes."

Because all models were dim?

"Nothing wrong with fancy clothes and being pretty. How else do you find a man?" Isa added. "Not by looking like a cavewoman."

Behind her, Anna shook her head. "Men. Blah. Let's talk about something fun. Like this Nichols coffee shop that's getting so popular." Anna winked. "I love it, keeping it in the family. Matt told me he's already opening up two more. One in Green Lake and another in Tacoma. How exciting!"

Cyn needed to talk to her brother about that, because they hadn't exactly agreed on the Tacoma location. But she made small talk before escaping to find her father.

She encountered him talking to a tall, handsome guy around her age—one not wearing a wedding ring, damn it. With any luck, he hadn't been invited to become her plus one. Her parents might have neighbors or business acquaintances who happened to be young single men. Unfortunately, history had proved that the only unattached males who frequented Ella's parties were invited with a specific purpose.

"Cyn, honey, there you are." Her father pulled her into a hug. "Your mother monopolizes you too much." Over his shoulder, she spied Nina laughing at her and glancing at the man next to her father. Nina wiggled her brows.

Shoot. Definitely sensing a matchup.

Before she could flee, her father latched onto her arm.

"*Et tu, Brute?*" she said under her breath.

"Your mother worries," he answered in a whisper.

In a louder voice, he said, "Cyn, I'd like you to meet Cristo's son, Tony. You know Cristo, one of my business colleagues. Tony, this is my daughter, Cynthia."

She did her daughterly duty and shook his hand. "Call me Cyn."

Tony seemed nice. He hadn't ogled her breasts yet, though she'd taken care to dress conservatively in a knee-length skirt and button-down green shirt, draping a Christmas scarf around her neck. For added internal strength, she'd worn her favorite kick-ass leather boots, scored on a lucrative shopping trip in Venice, Italy.

"Pleasure to meet you." He wasn't as tall as Foley or as dangerous-looking, but his short brown hair framed an intelligent, attractive face. He wore glasses, which shielded his blue eyes and made him seem even more harmless.

He held her hand a second longer than he should have before letting go. She immediately went on alert.

"So how's your dad doing?" she asked, having met Cristo once, a year ago. Her father had also talked about him. A pleasant man devoted to his family, that she recalled.

Tony smiled, and it was a nice smile. Just not as nice as Foley's.

Right then and there, she ordered herself to stop thinking about Foley so much. She'd meet him later this evening. No sense in getting in over her head. It would be a long time before she put her absolute faith in a man not family.

"Dad is good. He would have come tonight but he had some business to finish up."

"On a Saturday night?"

"He's in Italy right now. He and Mom booked a business vacation. Plus, they're visiting family."

Her father excused himself to talk with more guests.

Cyn had always wanted to visit her relatives. "Where in Italy?"

"Catanzaro. The City Between Two Seas."

"I think Mom and Dad went there once."

"Have you ever been to Italy?"

"Rome and Florence twice, and I worked in a stop-over at Venice." She held out a leg. "I bought my favorite boots there."

"Nice. I'm partial to Sicily, myself. But don't tell your father. Sicilians and Italians don't mix."

"He won't mind. He's a weird blend of Sicilian and Scot, though I think my mom ignores the Sicilian part."

It turned out she and Tony knew a lot of the same people through their parents, and she enjoyed talking to him. But not once did she view him in any kind of romantic way. From the way he acted toward her, she thought he felt the same. Relief and enthusiasm for the night replaced the building dread inside her.

Twenty minutes later she left him to search out Nina. She found the troublemaker lip-locked with her brother in the hallway. She loved seeing her brother and sister-in-law still so enamored with each other. Theirs had been a true love match. How nice to know there were a few of them left in the world.

"Mat-tie," she sang, drawing out his name. "Just what are you up to in this dark hallway, away from the festivities, hmm?"

She heard him groan and mutter something uncomplimentary under his breath.

"That is no way to talk to your younger sister." Then she dropped the hammer. "So what's this nonsense about announcing our Tacoma expansion?"

Nina glanced from her to Mattie and moved away. "I think I'll go check on the boys."

"Afraid?"

"Very." Nina left.

Matt stared after his wife, then sighed and turned back to Cyn. "Where'd you hear that? Don't tell me. Mom."

"Mom's friends."

"Hell. She was supposed to keep quiet about that. I told her we're thinking about it. *Thinking*. Not doing."

"Not yet." Not until their numbers panned out.

Matt yanked her into his arms for a hug. "So how are you, Cyn?"

She moved back so she could breathe again. "Jeez. Are your arms bigger than they were a week ago?"

"Hey, I can either lift weights to stem my aggression or use my boys as dumbbells. And I hear Social Services frowns on knocking around kids." Matt sighed. "Vinnie is driving me nuts. He knows everything about everything lately, and he's getting a smart mouth. Then add in Alex, and I'm surprised I'm not bald from ripping my hair out."

"Wonder where they get that from. I mean, with you and Nina, it could go either way."

His eyes narrowed. "You know, it's winter break next week, and I'm thinking the boys need some quality aunt time."

"No. Uh-uh. The last time I invited them to sleep over, Alex conned me out of twenty bucks, and Vinnie somehow changed my ringtone to 'Baby Got Back.' Not amusing."

Matt laughed. "He's just having some fun with you. All his friends want to know when his pretty aunt is going to pick him up from school again. He was the most popular kid in sixth grade when you chaperoned their Halloween trip."

She shuddered. Pubescent nearly teenage boys. "Never again."

"At least you're the cool aunt he likes. He's going through an anti-mom-and-dad phase that's been tough on Nina. Me, I know he'll ride it out. But she dotes on those kids."

"A little too much, maybe. She's too much good cop. I keep telling her to be a little more bad cop."

"Like you, you mean?"

"Well, yeah."

"Good point. So tell me about you and Foley Sanders."

He slipped that in so subtly she nearly spilled the beans about her date later on. "Wh-what?" Nina, that traitor. *I'm gonna go bad cop all over her ass.*

"Well now." Matt rubbed his hands together. "I hear the giant has a crush on my baby sister. Want me to talk to him for you?"

"Shut up." Crap on a cracker, her cheeks felt hot.

"Blushing! Ha." Matt laughed.

"There is nothing going on."

"So you have no problem with me telling Mom—"

"*Okay,* fine. What will it take for you not to blab?" How was it her older brother could still push all her buttons so easily?

"We talk about the Tacoma plans this week."

"But the numbers—"

"Are there, you're just being supercautious. I like that about you, but no risk, no gain."

She sighed. "Fine."

"*And* you take the boys for one day next week. Just one is all I'm asking."

"You mean blackmailing."

"Foley Sanders," he said in a louder voice. "Does Mom know about him?"

She clapped a hand over his mouth and glanced around, relieved to see only her father nearby talking to friends in the living room. "I will *so* get you back."

He wriggled free. "Right."

"Besides, Mom's doing her best to set me up with Cristo's son. But luckily for me, he's not interested."

"You mean Tony? The guy staring at your ass right now?"

She closed her eyes and groaned.

"Or would that be his business partner, Al? Dad made sure to invite them both, doubling his odds of marrying you off. I'm sorry to say, but the guys are in on it, because I overheard Dad auctioning you off earlier. Something about four camels to the man who can take you off his hands."

"You're not funny, Matt. This is so embarrassing." She had no doubt her father had been following Ella's orders.

"Gee, Al seems to find your skirt as fascinating as Tony does."

"I think I hate you." She opened her eyes, wanting to slap the smirk off her brother's face.

"Well, you start telling everyone you're going to be the neighborhood cat lady, and we get concerned."

"I was joking," she snapped. Well, kind of.

"Next time make sure you're not joking when Mom can overhear you." Matt shook his head and propelled her out of the hallway to greet her would-be admirers. "I'll leave you with Tony, he of the many camels. Need to find my wife and tell her the good news about our sitter for next week."

"Jerk." She watched him go, then turned to see Tony and Al looking amused.

"Camels?" Tony asked.

"Long story." She cleared her throat, wishing the floor would swallow her whole. "Ah, how to say this… I'm not sure if my father bamboozled you into attending or not, but I'm actually really happy with my life right now." At their continued silence, she blurted, "Not looking for a boyfriend at the moment."

"I volunteered to come, if it makes you feel any better." Tony held a hand over his heart. "Honest. It was either this party or going out with my sister and her on-again, off-again boyfriend."

She knew all about problematic family. "Then I'm happy to have saved you."

"I saw your picture and begged to come," Al, a cute blond with dimples, who stood even with her own height, confessed. He had no problem staring directly at her chest before making eye contact again. "So what are you doing after the party?"

Tony frowned. "Now hold on. I wanted to come to avoid my sister, but I'd be more than happy to take in a club. Get a few drinks out in town. You up for it, Cyn?"

"Um, well…"

"Why not have both of us take her out?" Al asked.

"She could pick." He paused, and the odd look he and Tony shared disturbed her. "Or not."

"So what'll it take to get you to prefer men to cats?" Tony asked.

The guys snickered, and Cyn did her best to remember that fratricide was frowned upon in the state of Washington.

Chapter 6

BEFORE SHE LEFT THE PARTY, CYN MADE HER ROUNDS. Tony and Al had some weird kind of double entendre thing going on that left her feeling as if she missed out on many of their jokes. Their closeness was nice but a little…off. She had the distinct feeling both men wanted to take her out after the party, then take her to bed. Together.

She admitted to having a few fantasies about herself in a sexy guy sandwich, but she left them at the fantasy level. She'd had enough trouble dealing with one man. Two would probably lobotomize her.

After a subtle escape from the pair, she'd mingled, eaten her share of lasagna—her favorite—and had some decadent chocolate cake. Nina and Matt made her laugh. Vinnie and Alex had been overjoyed to hear they would be spending some time with their "cool aunt," which meant she'd need to pony up some money to show them a good time. Then the schemers had slunk away to a back bedroom to play more video games.

She should have joined them, but the beauty outside had drawn her. The snow fell in soft flakes, coating the ground and trees and making it look like a winter wonderland. A full moon bathed the grounds in a blue-white cover, and the stars twinkled against the black night sky.

Even the cold couldn't detract from the majesty of the quiet moment.

"Oh, there you are."

Crap. Ella had found her. With no one around to provide a buffer on the back deck, Cyn was doomed.

"Hi, Mom. Great party."

"Isn't it, though?" Ella laughed and came to stand next to Cyn. She wrapped a slender arm around Cyn's waist and squeezed. "I'm so glad you've come home, honey. I missed you."

Cyn started to relax. Maybe her mother had changed. It had been some time since she'd been alone with her.

Yet five seconds in her mother's presence and Cyn felt like the overgrown teenager she'd once been, uncomfortable in her big body. Taller than all the boys, filling out before most of her friends, and never as thin or graceful as her mother, no matter what she did.

"Work is going well?"

Cyn nodded. "It's great. Along with the other investments I've made, the coffee shop is keeping me happy and financially comfortable, for sure. I like working there."

"It's good for you. Helps you to be around people, I'd imagine. I don't know how you work so alone all the time. All done through computers and with those businesspeople and meetings in tall buildings." Ella laughed. "But you've made it work. I always knew you were smart."

"Thanks."

Cyn stepped away from her mom and turned so she could face her. "You look good, Mom. Happy." She did. Ella stood several inches shorter than Cyn. Her face had begun to wrinkle, but with laugh lines from a life well lived. Her black hair now peppered with silver, it still suited Ella's pixie-thin face and sparkling brown eyes. She had the build of a dancer, all lean lines and tone. Even at sixty, she exercised and kept herself in shape.

"I am happy. Your father and I are going on a cruise in February to celebrate our anniversary."

"That's great."

"Yep. Our fortieth anniversary."

"I know. Matt and I are still trying to figure out what to get you."

Ella grinned. "I hinted to Nina I wanted a party."

"We can do that." It would be fun.

"You can bring Tony with you, if you like. I know it's about family, but you—"

"Tony's nice, but I'm not looking for a boyfriend right now." Best to nip her mother's machinations right in the bud.

"What about Al? He's smart. You like them smart, don't you?"

"Mom, I—"

Her mother took her by the hand and squeezed. "Oh, Cynthia. You heard all my friends inside earlier. You're such a pretty girl. You just need to lose a few pounds, and the men will come rolling in. You'll see."

Don't swear at your mother. Not cool at Christmas, Cyn. In a firm voice, she said, "Mom, I'm happy the way I am."

"I noticed you eating a lot of cake and cookies." Ella frowned. "Are you doing yoga yet? Did you get that video I left for you?"

"It's the holidays. I had maybe two cookies and a slice of cake. I also had a fabulous piece of your famous lasagna." Still trying to keep the peace. Complimenting her mother's cooking should do the trick.

"Yes, you should have taken a smaller piece though." Ella chewed her lower lip. "Didn't you see the big bowl of salad Ida brought? I asked her to bring something you could eat."

Cyn saw red but kept her mouth shut through sheer force of will.

"I'm worried, sweetie." Ella rubbed her hand, then let Cyn go. She sighed. "You were so happy with Jon, and then he left you."

"I left him," Cyn corrected, but as usual, Ella seemed not to hear her.

"It was your weight, you know. Jon and I used to talk about you."

"*What?*"

"I was concerned. I didn't want you two to end, but I could tell he was losing interest. The phone calls and visits were more sporadic. And the way he stopped looking at you like you mattered…"

So Ella had interfered. Cyn had wondered. When she and Jon had parted, he'd said things that sounded as if they'd come straight from Ella's mouth. Cyn deliberately pushed her mother's words aside. It was either that or choke the woman.

"Looks matter, honey," Ella continued. "You're smart, but there are smarter women out there. And you're far from rich. Then add in the fact that you aren't getting any younger." Ella sighed. "Your brother has two children—almost teenagers. You're still not even married."

"I could just get pregnant. Why bother with a

husband?" Cyn said with false cheer. "Would that make you happy?"

Ella scowled then said something in Italian Cyn didn't understand. "What's wrong with me caring about your future?"

"Why can't you be proud of me for what I've already done?" Cyn asked her mother as she had so many times over the years. "I'm independent. On my way to being wealthy. I'm happy." *Or at least, I* was *happy before you cornered me out here*. "I've got great friends. So what if I'm still single? I don't understand why my not having a husband is a fate worse than death."

"Your aunt—"

Cyn groaned. "Not Aunt Sharon again. Mom, Aunt Sharon is gone. I know you loved her. But I really don't think her not having a husband contributed to her death."

Her mother wasn't rational about her deceased sister.

"Sharon was just like you. She was lonely." Her mother sighed. "I tried everything I knew to help her. All she wanted was a man, but no man would take her. Then she got sick and had no one to care for her."

"Um, it's a new era, Mom. Women don't need men to care for them. I—"

"She had baby fat she never grew out of. So pretty, but so ungainly. Mama tried her best, but so many of the men made fun of her."

The perils of growing up in a small provincial town in Italy, even in the twentieth century, apparently. Knowing she was beating her head against a brick wall, Cyn tried again. "All Sharon had to do was move out on her own. Grandma Isabelle was a dictator. You told me that."

"I loved her. She was my mother."

"Yes. And I love you too." A hint that her mother and her grandmother had more in common than blood. That overbearing personality had definitely passed through the generations.

Cyn gave up and leaned down to kiss her mother's cheek. "I'd better get in and talk to Nina again before I go." She still had her ace in the hole, and if her mother pushed her too far, Cyn would use it.

"You really shouldn't have had that lasagna, Cyn." Her mother glanced critically at her belly. "But Tony seemed to like you well enough. You should run back to him. What about—"

"I actually have a date I need to get to." Her mother's shock made the revelation worth it. "See you later." She darted off before her mother could start the inquisition. It had been so satisfying to mention her date with Foley. Telling her Mom made him seem more real. Even if she had no idea what to do about him when they got together. Sex? A relationship? Would he show up tonight, or would he make some excuse not to see her? She could too easily envision him cozying up to some pretty, skinny girl with breasts.

Only time would tell.

She heard her mother calling her, dashed through the house for her coat, and ran into Nina. "Nina, I have to go."

"Cyn! Honey, hold on a minute." Her mother was in hot pursuit.

Cyn chanced a glance back and saw Ella sidelined by her friends.

"Nina, hold her off for me, would you? I have to go

before I do something drastic. Like hang myself from the top of that tree."

Nina commiserated. "Go. I'll take care of her. Ah, the grandson should do it."

Cyn neared the front door after saying good-bye to her dad. She turned to see Nina whispering to Alex, who nodded. He looked over at Cyn, waved, then headed off to hug his grandmother.

"I love you, Grandma!" he yelled.

Overdone, but at least he'd taken the attention from Cyn. Nina rolled her eyes and shooed Cyn away.

She didn't have to be told twice. Once in the car, Cyn pulled out her phone and texted Foley. Oh, he of the magic hands. Shivering, she typed.

It was do-or-die time.

When Foley received Cyn's text, his entire body came to life yet again. He'd been on a roller coaster of highs and lows all night, his time at Ray's an oblivion as he ignored the guys making fun of him in favor of fantasies about his evening to come.

"It's just pathetic." Lou sighed and downed his beer. "We knew what to expect with Johnny. Lara had his nuts in a vise forever."

"I'm going to let that slide." Johnny tossed a dart and hit the board dead center.

"Only because it's true." Sam grabbed his darts and shoved Johnny aside. Predictably, he didn't hit anything. "Shit."

"But Foley is made of stronger stuff," Lou continued. "At least, I thought he was. Hey, lovesick, you're up."

Foley shook off a vision of Cyn wearing nothing but an apron as she posed in her kitchen. He forced himself to calm down before standing to take his turn with the darts, noticed the score sheet on the table, and groaned. "Hell, Sam. You're killing us, you know that?"

"Whatever. At least I'm here in the game." Sam frowned. "Not dreaming about my date with the witch."

Lou raised his glass. "To Foley and his *bruja*. May you make sweet magic together."

"That was lame." Sam drained his glass.

Foley let fly and hit a double twelve. "That's twenty-four, losers."

"Losers?" Johnny raised a brow. "Math is not his strong suit. Um, Foley? Lou and I are already winning by like sixty points."

"So? Twenty-four points is still pretty damn good." And he couldn't care less. He had a date with a sexy redhead in a half hour.

"I hate him in a good mood." Sam glared.

"You're just pissy because Shaya's gone." Johnny, brave guy, slapped Sam on the shoulder. "I feel you, man. Let me get the next round." He left, and they watched him flirt with the bartender—who was *not* his girlfriend.

Sam shook his head. "Lara must really love him."

"Please." Foley snorted. "He's only flirting with Rena because he can get away with it." Rena, the bartender, was Lara's best friend. She was also Del's cousin, and though all the guys had wanted to get with her at one time or another, reason prevailed. Screwing with the boss's family, literally or figuratively, was a damn stupid way to mess up a good thing.

And anyway, everyone loved Rena. No one wanted to break her heart. She was pretty, bubbly, and an all-around lovely woman. Way too nice for Foley.

Unlike Cyn.

Johnny returned, all smiles, with a full pitcher.

Sam just grunted while Johnny poured.

"Thanks." Lou sat back and stared at Foley.

"What?" Foley said. "Sorry, Lou. I'm taken."

Sam snickered.

Lou turned to him. "You know, Sam, one of these days you and I are going to go head-to-head. I wouldn't bet on you standing at the end."

"Bring it, Lou. For fuck's sake, make a move already. You have a bad habit of talking everything to death."

Foley glanced at Sam, unsure about his mood.

Lou, fortunately, took Sam in stride. "Don't worry. I won't take your shitty attitude personally. Shaya was good for you. Too good for you." The guys laughed, and Sam relaxed. "But my pity only goes so far. Doesn't mean you and Foley aren't going to have to pay for tonight's rounds. Face it. You guys lost."

They looked at the score pad Johnny had tallied.

"Hell." Sam blew out a breath. "We never win."

"Next time we split the teams," Foley said. "I get Johnny. Sam, you get Lou. Johnny and I'll spot you for the handicap."

Sam agreed while Lou swore at him.

Johnny laughed. "You guys are coming tomorrow, right?"

Lou nodded. "Yeah. Want us to bring something?"

"Beer or whatever you want to drink. Oh, and I hope you're not allergic to dogs." Johnny made a face. "Lara's fostering one ugly-ass puppy. I think she's trying to break me into getting a pet."

Sam lit up. "Dogs are cool. I knew I liked Lara."

Johnny frowned. "Yeah, well, don't like her too much. She's mine."

"Why not stamp her forehead so everyone knows?" Foley offered, just to needle the guy. "Or piss around her, like dogs do. Mark your territory, Fido."

Lou chuckled. "I would pay money to see that. Johnny pissing around the house to keep the competition away. Woman would kick your ass if you tried that."

Foley remembered that not too long ago Lara had put a hurt on her gropey ex-brother-in-law. He had to admire a woman who could open up some whoopass. He could easily imagine Cyn doing the same to some guy not worthy of her time. She'd gut him with those killer heels.

"Just go." Sam shoved at him. "You're killing the mood with that dopey grin. It's embarrassing. Johnny's about all I can handle at one time."

"Hey." Johnny scowled.

Foley stood, threw down some bills, then wished everyone a good night. He had some time to kill, but hell, even he realized he was not good company. He couldn't stop thinking about Cyn. Weird, because he'd dated his share of the ladies over the years. He'd often anticipated a night of good hard fucking. No biggie. It excited him, sure, but not to this degree.

Lately, because of Cyn, he found it hard to focus on anything but her. His appetite wasn't what it should be, and he wanted to smile all the time. Definitely unlike him and his cool-as-a-cucumber approach to dating.

On the drive to her place, he told himself to relax. To try not to act like he was so into her. A woman like Cyn would use anything to her advantage. While he respected that, the very strength that made her so attractive urged caution.

He pulled up in front of her house and saw the lights on. With nothing but his wits to lose, he locked up his car and stood on her front doorstep. Before he could ring the bell, the door opened.

"Come on in." Cyn stepped back, obviously waiting for him.

Pleased, he entered and felt his nerves return. *Get a handle, Sanders.* He handed her his jacket and removed his boots, all the while studying her.

She wore her beautiful hair down, and it lay in straight waves, curling around the tops of her breasts. The button-down green shirt she wore practically begged him to unbutton it, but he told himself to wait, to let her make the moves tonight. She wore a pair of flannel pajama pants with the shirt, as well as fuzzy red-and-green socks. Cute, and not at all the attire of a woman out to seduce a man.

Maybe tonight wasn't going to be about sex. Though he should have been more bummed out about that, he was happy just to be with her. A glance into her eyes showed her own wariness. Good to know he wasn't the only one unsure about things.

"So do I get to turn in that rain check for the cocoa tonight?"

Her slow smile warmed him. "Sure."

He followed her into the kitchen, unable to help remembering the last time they'd been there together.

Shoving his hands in his pockets so he wouldn't be tempted to jump her, he leaned back against the counter and asked, "So how was the party?"

She groaned. "We might need something stronger to talk about that."

"That bad?"

"You could say that." She took out some cookies and placed them on the counter. "Nina made them. Enjoy."

"Gingerbread men. Awesome."

"Hope you like the decorations. My nephews did them." Her smile showed she clearly cared for the boys.

"How old are they?"

"Alex is ten. Vinnie's eleven going on twenty."

"Coming up on the teenage years. Yikes."

"Yeah, and my sneaky brother blackmailed me into watching them one day next week. God help me."

He laughed. "Tell me about the party. What was bad about it? I thought you said you were close to your family."

"I am. It's a mother thing. I love her, but she drives me to drink." She sighed. "My mom's always been supercritical of me, but she only says or does stuff when no one's around to hear it."

He frowned. "That's not cool."

"She means well, but she doesn't understand the stuff she says is hurtful. My family thinks I make too big a deal about it." She shrugged. "Maybe they're right. She and I have been butting heads since I was little."

"My mom and I are tight, but I'm her little boy."

"Little?" Her once-over made him laugh.

"To her, always. Mothers and sons share a special bond. Like fathers and daughters, or so I'm told."

"That's true. My dad is awesome and supersweet to me, while my mom definitely has a soft spot for Matt. She's also big on marriage and babies." Cyn made a face. "And pleasing men. I'm a disappointment because I didn't marry at eighteen and have fourteen kids by now."

"Ouch."

"I know she loves me, but the woman drives me *nuts*." Then she changed the subject so fast she about gave him whiplash. "Look, Foley, I'm always going to be big. Six feet tall, and never mind about my weight."

He'd learned his lesson on that score. "Yes, ma'am."

She huffed. "I've starved myself. Exercised to death. Gone on a bazillion diets. Nothing works. This is me." She waved at her body, her tone aggressive. "I'm not going to change."

"I get it."

"Do you?" She ran a hand through her hair, and he wanted to comfort her, to tell her he didn't give a rat's ass what anyone said. She was beautiful. But she'd obviously been dealing with the issue for a long time. "I'm telling you this because my last boyfriend heard the same lecture, then proceeded to try to change me. And before you ask, I was the same at the beginning as I was at the end of our relationship.

"I know I'm a basket case about my size. It's just... I can't help it. This is me. You say you want sex."

And back to his favorite subject. His libido quickened. "No question. Do you?"

"After the last time we were in this kitchen, you have to know I'm attracted to you."

He smiled. Wide. "Yeah."

"But I've never done casual sex. It's not in me to do that. So if you want to have sex, then we're kind of going to be dating." She paused. "As in, we're monogamous."

He thought about what she'd said, and why her laying out rules he normally avoided didn't scare him in the slightest. "You know how red your face is right now?"

"Shut up." She fumed, but he could see her starting to relax. "I didn't think I wanted commitment. I'm not asking to marry you, or God forbid, get pregnant."

He nodded.

"But I can't just sleep with you, then have you go sleep with three other women next week. If you're with me, you're with *me*." Her cheeks had passed pink and rounded into sunburned red. "And not just for sex. We get to talk and go out together too. That's the deal. If you can't handle that, we don't have anything more to say."

Chapter 7

"SO YOU WANT A BOYFRIEND OUT OF THE DEAL?" FOLEY had struck gold without realizing how he'd done it.

She shrugged. "Boyfriend sounds kind of serious. I'd say I wanted a few dates, but that implies a casualness I can't handle if we're sleeping together. I can't randomly bed-hop and feel good about myself. I wish I could," she mumbled. "So boyfriend fits better than anything, I guess."

"Well now, if you're done?" At her nod, he said, "I like you, Cyn. Even when you flat out told me you didn't want sex, I had hopes."

"I got that."

"But I'd never force you to do anything you don't want."

"You were pushy to get me to go out with you."

"That's called persistence." He smiled, then grew serious. "I'm not kidding about us together. I don't want any confusion between us. I like you. A lot. You're pretty and smart, and I'm really, really attracted to you." Understatement of the year. "I don't want you smaller or blonder or nicer. I like you the way you are."

"Wait. Nicer?"

"So we can take this as slow or as fast as you want." He shrugged, hoping his hands in his pockets hid the fact that he had a massive hard-on. "I'm happy to sit around tonight drinking that hot chocolate I was promised. Hint hint."

Steam from the kettle soon turned into a whistle, and she fixed them both hot drinks. "Okay."

He tried to read her expression and couldn't. "Okay?"

"I think dating will work. We're only seeing each other, right?"

He nodded and let out a breath he hadn't realized he'd been holding. "Yeah. Sounds good to me."

He tugged her with him into the living room and sat them on the couch, but he didn't make a move. Not yet. "So tell me more about the party."

"You sure you want to know?"

"I asked, didn't I? One thing you'll learn about me, Cyn. I don't play games. I say what I mean."

She nodded. "The party was good, until my mother once again tried to set me up. It's like she doesn't think I can get a man on my own. And then she gave me a pep talk that made me want to shoot myself. Well, more like shoot her, but it's Christmas, and I'm pretty sure murder's a crime."

"Want me to talk to her?" he asked, only half joking.

She paused. "Um, no. Frankly, you'd scare her."

"With my good looks?" He gave an insincere grin, and she laughed.

"That or your tattoos. You have that bad-boy vibe all mothers try to steer their daughters away from." She narrowed her eyes. "Or sons. How do you feel about gay people?"

Another shift in subject. He needed to think fast to keep up with her. "Ah, do I need to feel one way or the other about them?"

"Answer the question."

He sighed. "This is a test, right? Okay, here goes. I

don't care much about sexual preference, color, religion, or politics. Just don't talk to me about them. And when I tell a guy no, I mean no." He smirked at her.

"Funny." She seemed relieved. "Sorry. I just don't want to waste time on you if you're biased or disagree with my lifestyle choices."

He raised a brow. "You're gay?"

"Why do you sound intrigued by the thought?"

He tried to look innocent and took a tentative sip of hot cocoa. It was so much better than the instant crap he had at home. "Well, one fine woman is one thing. But two fine women, together? That's gold."

"Really? Because I don't imagine you and Sam going at it to be sexy."

He nearly choked and saw her smirk. "You're evil. No wonder I can't stop thinking about you." *Shit*. He hadn't meant to admit that, but the shy smile that came after had him working hard to control the burst of feeling for her growing inside.

"Well, if it makes you feel better, the entire time Al and Tony were talking to me, I kept comparing them to you."

He sat straight. "Al and Tony, huh?"

"Tony's the son of one of my dad's friends. Al is his business partner. Though the way they worded a few things, I got the impression they might be a little closer than associates."

"Yeah?" Good. Gay guys weren't a threat. Sophisticated business types were.

"I could have been wrong, but..." She leaned closer and whispered, "I think I was invited into a threesome tonight."

"No shit?"

"The body language and a few things they said, it was weird." She blinked.

"Just weird? Not a little turn-on?"

"Foley." But that look on her face…

He chuckled. "Nice. So, my mean girlfriend is kinky. I like."

"Would you stop?"

"Hey, I've fantasized about doing two chicks at once. Never done it. Not sober, at least, not that I can remember."

"Funny."

"I'm kidding." He put the mug down and scooted closer to her on the couch. The hunted look in her deep brown eyes gratified him. Good to know she took him seriously. "I can't promise you a threesome. Just one of me. Sorry, I don't share."

"Neither do I," she said plainly. "So if you think you can sleep with me, then sleep around with anyone else, just don't." She leaned closer and poked him in the chest. "I'm taking a chance on you, going against my dream to be the neighborhood cat lady. Giving up celibacy for—"

He couldn't help it. He cut her off with a kiss and pulled her into his lap, cradling her into his body. The damn woman fit like she belonged there.

The passionate kiss increased his need for more of her, but he forced himself to go slow. No sense in showing her how little control he had when with her. He'd have to keep his pants on so as not to come in three seconds. He wanted to impress her with his staying power…if he could find any in his overcharged body.

Fuck, but she felt amazing against him. Tasting like chocolate, with full lips that parted and eased under his. He swept his tongue through her mouth, taking, insisting, and groaning when she squirmed over his lap.

He eased back and threaded his fingers in her soft hair. "No bullshit between us, okay?"

She was panting as loudly as he was and nodded.

"No games. I want you. You have to know that." He nudged her with his erection, and her eyes grew rounder. "You okay wanting me back?"

She stared at him, and he had a feeling he'd moved too fast.

"Yes."

Thank you, Jesus. "We'll go slow, baby. And yeah, I know your name is Cyn."

She grinned, her expression so sweet yet naughty. He felt something stretching, deep inside, something that had nothing to do with sex and everything to do with affection.

"Baby, huh? What should I call you?"

"Call me 'big boy.' It's honest, and it's something every guy likes to hear. I promise not to get pissy about it either."

"You're an ass, you know that?" She smiled, her fingers playing with the hair at his nape and turning him hotter and harder than he could handle with her right on top of him.

"*Your* ass, you mean." He moved her to straddle his waist, putting her chest flat against his. "I belong to you now." He groaned when she palmed his chest. "Feel my heart? It ain't the only thing pounding for you."

"I want to see your tattoos," she confessed. "I want to trace them with my fingers."

"So much for wanting to go slow. Shit. Take off my shirt."

She pulled the long-sleeved T-shirt off him and blinked. "You're huge."

"Touch me," he ordered, his voice hoarse.

She ran her hands over his pecs and abs, up to his shoulders and around his thick neck. "Wow. Your tattoos cover your upper body all over."

Cyn had such an animated face. She obviously liked the look of him, and he'd never been so thankful for good genetics and his gym membership than right now. He settled his hands on her waist while she dragged her nails over his tats, finding sensitive spots he hadn't realized were erogenous zones. But hell, everywhere she touched him, he went up in flames.

"Some kind of hot rod, skulls and dragons, tribal designs, but no naked women, hmm?" she teased as she watched the path of her nails. "You must work out a lot."

"Yeah." He wanted to be inside her. To touch that most intimate part of her.

"So strong." She glanced up and stared into his eyes.

Like a moment out of time, they connected. He stared into her eyes, saw the need she had, for more than sex, but to be cared for, protected. Foley had been born to take care of others, and in Cyn, he saw a woman of incredible beauty and strength, but possessing a vulnerability that could crush her were she not cared for.

"I'd never do anything to hurt you, Cyn," he promised. "Nothing but pleasure for you, my red-haired *bruja*." He smiled. "Lou called you a witch."

"Not nice." She frowned.

"Nah, it fits. You put a spell on me. Now let's find the bedroom so I can give you what you need."

She kissed him, a slow, deep caress that shook him to the quick. He felt more for this woman than for anyone he'd ever been with.

She slowly rose from his lap and tugged him with her down the hallway. "Follow me."

Anywhere, he pledged, half in love with her already.

This felt different. Cyn couldn't explain it, but looking into Foley's eyes, she saw the promise of so much more than fulfilled desire.

The man had depths she was only coming to understand. He followed with silent obedience, his footsteps soft on the hardwood floor. She heard only her own heartbeat pounding like a drum.

Despite planning to delve into a celibate lifestyle, to finally be free from the drama that came with relationships, she couldn't deny how much she wanted Foley. Even after hearing her rules, he hadn't balked, hadn't denied that tonight would be more than a quick roll in the hay. Granted, he could be agreeing to anything just to get between her legs, but she didn't think so.

Once in her bedroom, he stopped her. He pulled her to him and caged her in his strong arms. Shirtless, covered in tattoos and muscle-bound, he could have been the poster boy for the male form. So beautiful, so strong. His power was a huge turn-on.

"If I'm a witch, what are you?" she asked, breathless.

"Probably a troll." He quirked a grin, then lost it

when his gaze focused on her mouth. "I want you so bad. But we're gonna go slow. Even if it kills me."

"Safe sex, right? Condoms?" she had to say.

"Until you get to know me, I'll raincoat it. But I'll be dreaming about coming deep inside you at some point."

She'd never thought that a sexy thing, but having a naked Foley inside her thrilled her on another level. "Maybe."

"No maybe about it. I want you—just the way you are…flannel pants and all."

She laughed and flushed. "Okay, not my sexiest clothes."

"Doesn't matter what you're wearing." He put her hand between them, right over the huge bulge between his legs. "Proof. You can't ever doubt this."

"No," she agreed.

He took her hand away. "You let me be in charge this first time, okay? I want to last with you, but I'm afraid I'll come too soon if you play around." He sounded gruff, lusty, dominant.

Cyn knew she'd never forget tonight. Not as long as she lived.

"Okay. You're in charge." She bit her lower lip.

"Take off your shirt."

The moment of truth. Would he see her body and turn away? It was all well and good to touch her and—

"*Now*. Stop thinking so much." He gripped her ass and squeezed. Hard.

She tried to move back, but he wouldn't give her space. So she unbuttoned her shirt, her hands brushing against his bare chest as she moved. He felt like a furnace, so hot to the touch.

Once she'd unbuttoned her shirt, the sides fell apart, revealing her bra and belly.

Foley glanced down and stared. "Take off the bra but leave on the shirt."

"I can't—"

"Do it."

She frowned but did as he asked. She had to take off the blouse to get rid of her bra, but he helped her put the shirt back on, framing her torso while leaving her obviously naked breasts bare.

"Oh Christ. I'm not gonna last long at all." Foley bent his head and took one nipple in his mouth.

She moaned his name and clutched his head to her, amazed at how he could get to her with a simple kiss.

He caressed her, his hands all over her belly and breasts while he teased first one nipple, then the other with his mouth. The smooth glide of fabric over her back and arms increased sensation, and she loved how he continued to fondle her with both his hands and his mouth.

She squirmed, wanting more of him.

Then he pushed the shirt off, so that it fell over her forearms. He leaned back to stare at her. "I love your tits. They're so big. Look at how red your nipples are." He groaned and kissed her breasts again, aggressive then gentle.

"Faster," she urged when he continued to play.

It was as if he'd deliberately slowed to a crawl, laving her with slow licks and kisses. He was driving her insane.

Foley tugged the shirt down, her wrists pulled behind her. He kept her hands bound by the material.

When he jerked her arms together, the action thrust her breasts forward.

"Oh yeah. That's what I like." He lifted his gaze to hers and stepped closer, so his chest pressed hers once more. Then he moved, a slow glide that raked her taut nipples over his flesh.

"Foley," she moaned, astounded at how he made her feel. Hot and melty and needy.

"Yeah, baby. That's it. So good." He closed in for a kiss, continuing to slide his body against hers.

The kiss came slowly, deepening as she writhed against him. Being powerless to do more than follow his movements aroused her to such an extent that she couldn't think. She obeyed on instinct, doing whatever he wanted.

He finally tugged the shirt free of her wrists. She immediately circled his neck, tugging him closer while she toyed with his hair.

He moaned into her mouth, and she realized the firm pressure against her belly was the ridge of his erection as he ground against her.

"Come on, big boy," she teased and ran her lips down his throat. "Get naked."

"You first," he growled and walked her back, then gave a quick shove.

She landed on her bed with a startled *oomph*. Before she could move, Foley followed her and kissed his way down her belly. He knelt on the floor, his hands on her waist as he journeyed toward the waistline of her pants. He tugged them down, and she hoped he wouldn't think badly that she wore—

"*No underwear?* Shit, Cyn. You're killing me." Foley

didn't waste any time. He yanked her pants away, then her socks, and spread her thighs with those large, callused hands. Without missing a beat, he dove between her legs.

He sucked, kissed, and licked her into a frenzy. She gripped his head and rocked into his mouth, unable to stop. "Please," she kept moaning. She wanted him with her this time.

Sadly, she couldn't wait. "Foley, I'm coming."

"Yeah. Give it to me," he rumbled and sucked harder, shoving a finger inside her.

She cried out as ecstasy overwhelmed her. Her lover continued to kiss her while he thrust that finger in and out, until she had to stop him.

Breathing hard, she tugged him away by the hair. "Oh my God. Foley…" She wanted him closer. "Come here."

The bright gray of his eyes burned as he slid up her body, his rock hard, and gave her the kiss she wanted. She tasted herself on his mouth, and she liked knowing he'd wanted to please her. That he belonged to her, at least for tonight.

"Don't you want to come?" she asked and nibbled at his throat.

She felt him swallow. "Fuck, yeah. Almost did licking you up. You taste good."

He sounded like a wolf, all growly and fierce. The raw strength of muscle over her did nothing but make her want him even more.

"So take off those pants. Let me see you."

"You sure you're ready?"

"I think I can handle it," she teased.

"Handle *him*." He cupped himself. "I'm big. And I'm getting bigger just looking at you."

"Quit bragging already. Let me see."

He gave a mean grin, then left the bed to slowly peel off the rest of his clothes. He hadn't been lying. Foley was *huge*. He kept his gaze on hers while he stripped.

"Just…wow."

He grinned and held himself for her. *Definitely more than six inches* was all she could think as he dug into his jeans pocket and withdrew a line of condoms.

"One won't be enough," he said as way of explanation. He ripped open a packet and moved to put it on, when she stopped him.

"No, let me."

He swore and said, "Fine. But don't play, or I might go off."

She chuckled. "Off like a rocket, huh?"

"Yeah." He walked to the edge of the bed, and she sat up to meet him.

On her knees, naked and aroused, she knew she had to touch him. She took the condom from him but didn't put it on him right away. Instead, she ran a finger over his length.

He clenched his jaw, looking almost angry as he stared down at her.

She wanted to tease just a little more, so she cupped his balls, feeling the heavy heat of him. "You really are big, aren't you?"

"I'll come all over you if you don't put that fucking condom on and lie back. Now."

She trembled at his harsh tone, seduced by his dominance, and rolled the condom over him, hoping it would fit.

It did, but the latex only confirmed how wide and long he was.

"Now lay back and spread your legs."

She scooted back on the bed and did as ordered.

Foley blanketed her in seconds and kissed her, shoving a leg between hers to widen her thighs even farther.

The kiss was raw, passionate, and desperate. And she *loved* it.

She grabbed his thick biceps and held on while he positioned himself at her core.

"I'm gonna go slow. So slow you'll hate me."

"I already hate you." She arched up into him, trying to scat him inside her. But the bastard wouldn't move. Cyn was no small woman, and she had her own strength. But she couldn't get Foley to shift at all.

"Damn it. Wait," he snarled and started to enter her. He watched her face, unblinking, and gave her every solid inch of himself. "*Yes*."

He filled her up, almost uncomfortably so.

"So fuckin' good." Foley closed his eyes and pushed deeper, and she moaned at the pleasure.

Then he stopped talking. He opened his eyes and watched her watching him while he started to slide in and out of her. The gentle, slow taking turned rough, a claiming she welcomed from a man who seemed like he could handle all of her. Her breasts shook. Her flesh clamped around him with each thrust, trying to hold him deep.

The bed rocked as he moved faster, his face a mask of agonized pleasure.

Her climax rose again, because with every pass he grazed her clit. Filling her with his thick cock and rubbing against the bundle of nerves screaming with pleasure.

"I'm coming," he warned seconds before he ground hard and stilled.

His movements pushed her into her own orgasm, and she moaned his name as she clamped around him.

He swore and rotated his hips, still pumping until he had no more left to give.

After a few moments, they lay joined, breathing heavily and exhausted.

Foley leaned down to kiss her. She enjoyed letting him lead and softened under his firm lips. "Cyn, sweetheart." He withdrew slowly and shuddered. "Be right back." He left the bedroom and returned, joining her on the bed.

He drew her into his arms, so they lay on their sides, facing each other. He brushed her hair back from her face and kissed her, a gentle caress that soothed. "A weaker man would have had a heart attack."

"Good thing you're not weak."

"No shit." He kissed her cheeks and forehead, then hugged her tight. "That was fucking amazing. Gimme some time, and we'll go again."

"Really?" She felt worn out. Then again, she'd already come twice. In one night. A miracle.

"Yeah, really. I told you nabbing a younger man was the way to go." He chuckled when she tugged his chest hair.

She loved everything about his body. Foley had body hair, but not too much. His muscles were massive. Being with a man with his frame, she felt small and feminine for the first time in forever.

He cupped her breast and squeezed gently. "Oh yeah. A definite handful."

She blushed. "For you and your big hands."

"And *only* my hands," he said with an authority that pleased her. "I have to ask you something."

She rose on an elbow and watched him. "Go ahead."

"Why the hell would you think you could go without sex for the rest of your life? Cat lady? Please." His contented grin took the sting out of his words. "I have never in my life come so hard, baby. And I'm ready to do it again." He stared at her mouth. "Maybe something a little different this time."

"No blow jobs until I know you better." She read him like a book.

His sly grin made her insides tingle. "Good thing I got nothing but time."

"Sure of ourselves, are we?" She touched him, because she could. Man, what a body.

"Honey, I had you begging me to fuck you." He leaned back and tucked his hands behind his head. "You were hot for it."

"I wasn't the only one begging."

"Yeah?"

"Well, not in so many words, but that last kiss before you put yourself in me. That was pretty desperate." She sat over him, aligning their parts.

To her surprise, she felt him stir against her. So much for needing a little time to recover.

He gripped her hips, his lids heavy as he stared at her naked torso. "I admit. I was dying to come inside you. Hell, I nearly did that first time in your kitchen. You have no idea how hard it was to not fuck you that night, right on the counter."

She rocked over him, getting him wet from her arousal. "I didn't expect an orgasm that night. You're pretty good with your hands."

"And my tongue?" he taunted and stuck it out for her.

She rubbed her sex against his thickening erection. "I love your tongue. Bet you can't wait to feel mine." She chuckled, feeling his response. "Oh yeah. Just wait. You liked me touching your cock, holding your balls." She peppered in the dirty talk to see how he responded.

His eyes darkened. His nipples were hard, and watching his corded abs contract was a beauty all its own.

He started to remove his hands from behind his head.

"No. Keep your hands there, mister. I'm in charge this time."

He smirked at her. "Think you can make me beg... the way I made you?"

"I know I can." She dragged herself over the hard length of him and watched him swallow. Then she cupped her breasts and flicked her nipples, giving a breathy little moan that was in no way fake.

In a hoarse voice, he said, "Condoms are on the floor. Maybe you'd better get them. Fast."

She smiled. "Maybe I'd better."

Chapter 8

FOLEY HAD NO PROBLEM ADMITTING IT. HE'D BEEN pussy whipped. After spending the better part of the night with Cyn, she could have asked him to shave his head bald and tattoo *Lou Is Great* on his forehead, and he would have done it to make her happy.

Fuck. He'd never, *ever*, been so done in after sex.

He sat at his kitchen table, staring at nothing, at ten on Sunday morning. He would have slept through the night with Cyn, but he hadn't wanted to freak her out. So he'd left after she'd fallen asleep, making sure to prop a note where she'd find it, along with an invitation to Johnny's for dinner.

He couldn't help it. He wanted her with him. Wanted to see her with the guys and make some decisions regarding their "relationship" before his body made them for him. Because right now, thinking again about last night, he wanted to go ring shopping. Marriage, kids, everything and anything with the red-haired witch who'd set his whole fucking world on end.

"Must have been a good night," Sam said, joining him. Sam looked no worse for wear. His eyes were clear, his hair mussed but no extra bruises on his bare torso or fists that Foley could see.

Foley chose not to comment. Some things he did keep to himself after all. "How was Ray's?"

"Not bad." Sam shrugged and made some coffee.

"Hey, jackass, don't use so many scoops."

Sam shot him the finger. "Next time you make the brew. Maybe if you quit daydreaming about last night, I'd be drinking some weak Foley coffee by now. And where's my breakfast, bitch?"

Foley sighed. "No way are you ever going to find some woman with that mouth of yours."

Sam smirked. "Found plenty of women. None I want to keep."

Or who'd keep you went unsaid, because Sam never took those comments from Foley as jest. He had a sore spot about rejection. No surprise, considering the way Sam's mom treated him. The other guys could razz Sam about women, but if Foley did it, Sam took it to heart. The big marshmallow.

"So you're okay about Shaya being gone?" Foley stood, grabbed the coffee bag out of Sam's hands, and shoved him aside.

"Jerk. Yeah, I'm good."

"So were the guys betting on me?"

"Yep." Sam looked smug. "Two to one odds you fall for this one. Lou seems to think she's just your type. Physically, sure. She's got that Marilyn Monroe body going for her."

Foley chuckled. "I sometimes forget I wasn't the only one forced to watch those movies."

Sam shrugged. "They were okay. No nudity or swearing, though. And not near enough violence, but hey, what can you do with the older generation?"

"I dare you to say that around Eileen."

"I may look stupid, but I ain't that dumb."

"So you say." Foley looked in the refrigerator and

found the can of sweet rolls he'd hidden behind the mustard. He set the rolls on a cookie sheet, then heated the oven.

"Hey. I didn't know we still had some of those left."

"No shit. I hid them." Foley shoved the pan into the oven and set the timer.

Sam narrowed his eyes. "Hmm."

"Yeah, hmm. And it's your turn to go shopping."

Sam groaned. "Come on. Have pity. You've got a new piece of ass to tap, and I got nothing. Least you can do is—"

"Okay, time for a few ground rules." He straddled his seat backward. "First, Cyn is not 'a piece of ass.' Second, I invited her to dinner tonight. We're picking her up if she says yes, so be on your best behavior."

"I'm not a fuckin' dog."

"Easy on the swearing."

Sam growled. "Shit. Seriously?"

"Look, I like this one. Can we not scare her off until I see if she's as cool as I think she is?"

"I guess."

"Don't look so miserable. I don't put up with ass-holes, do I? Did I stay with Michelle?"

"Technically she dumped you."

Foley frowned. "I got rid of Desiree."

"She was okay."

"Bullshit. You hated her. And she was a little too selfish for me. I mean, I'm all for sharing my life, but not having it taken over."

Sam tapped his fingers on the table, a sure sign of his discomfort with the conversation. "You don't really think that pushy, mouthy redhead with the smokin' rack is going to let you set the pace? Man, she's tough. No way she'll let you lead her around."

Foley rolled his eyes. "I see we need another class on Relationships 101."

"What? *Relationships?* I thought you were just banging her."

"I said I invited her to dinner tonight." Hopefully Johnny wouldn't have a problem with that. Might be a good idea to text him in case Cyn said yes and Foley showed up with an extra body.

Sam tapped faster. "Yeah, but that's just to show her she's not a one-nighter, right? You just met the chick. How can this be a relationship?"

Foley waited for the coffee, still thinking about Cyn and how different she'd made him feel from his past girlfriends. Then again, maybe Sam had a point. Great sex could warp a guy's thinking.

"Look. Let's not get ahead of things. She and I hit it off." Big time. Probably best not to tell Sam that he and Cyn were officially dating, though. "I want to see more of her. So we'll have dinner tonight, and I can figure out if she's an actual bitch or just has bitchy tendencies. Okay?"

That seemed to mollify Sam, because he stopped tapping. "Makes sense." He glanced at the oven. "But I'm still not going shopping."

Foley frowned. "Yeah? 'Cause I'm thinking you are." He stared at Sam and picked up his cell phone.

"What are you doing?"

"I'm telling Mom."

"Are you serious?" Sam gaped. "What are you? Six?"

Foley held the phone to his ear. "It's ringing."

Sam's expression darkened like a thundercloud.

"You really don't want my mother to think you're a dickhead, do you? No more than she already thinks it, I mean. Calling Cyn, her future daughter, a one-night stand? Insulting the mother of her grandkids?"

"*What?*" Sam wore panic well.

Foley disconnected and shoved the phone into his back pocket. "That's what my mother will think. If I'm dating some chick, the same one *you* convinced her I'm into, she'll be all wedding bells and shit. And then you come around and mess that up with some tough talk about how Cyn is a bitch? A piece of ass? Eileen will skin you alive."

"You are seriously messed up, you know that?" Sam paused. "So you're not going to marry her or anything, right?"

"Hell no. I just met the woman." Foley snorted. "Even I'm not so hard up I'll put a ring on a woman just because she slept with me. Even if she did ring my bell every time," he added, still not sure how that had happened. An orgasm was an orgasm—unless a guy was inside Cyn Nichols apparently. Then it became a religious experience.

"Hey, I'm not kidding when it comes to food," Foley continued. "Your turn to get the stuff. Or do you want to go back to us shopping separately? I'm good with that."

"No, no." Sam paused. "I fucking *hate* shopping." He swore, creatively, for a solid minute.

"You done?"

"Shit for brains. Yeah, now I'm done." The timer went off. "But I get extra cream cheese on my sweet rolls. You owe me."

"Still not sure how that shakes down, but whatever."

Foley ate, all the while tasting Cyn on his lips and remembering the radiance of her joy when she'd come apart in his arms.

———⁂———

Cyn couldn't believe she'd been invited to dinner with Foley's *friends*. From sex to a real date around real people. He was taking this boyfriend/girlfriend relationship seriously.

To a guy, bringing a girl into his inner circle was like a girl bringing a man home to her mother. She didn't know how she felt about it. On the one hand, Foley wasn't treating her like some girl he'd banged for a night and had finished with. On the other, meeting his friends brought them to a deeper level than she felt comfortable with.

She thought she'd have more time to get used to the idea of Foley as her new boyfriend. *Put up or shut up*, she told herself. She'd wanted Foley to treat her like she mattered, and he was. She waited anxiously by her front door, wearing jeans and a pretty blouse that brought out the gold flecks in her eyes. Her jacket was the thin, sporty kind. Because if she'd worn a puffy version, with her size, she'd look like the Stay Puft Marshmallow Man.

Foley pulled up in a black muscle car, one that looked a lot like the tattoo on his chest. Talk about some amazing ink. She wondered who had done his artwork. Or if it had hurt to have so much drawn on his body.

She saw Sam get out of the car next to him and move to the backseat. *Oh boy*.

Cyn hustled outside and locked up behind her, then met Foley at the passenger side. As usual, he looked ridiculously sexy. His dark hair was tousled, his five-o'clock shadow present, instilling all kinds of thoughts about what his raspy cheeks would feel like against the insides of her thighs.

"You're letting all the heat out," Sam complained from the cramped backseat.

"Oh, sorry. I should sit back there."

Sam nodded. "Yeah, you should. I—"

"Ignore him. I think he's on his period." Foley nodded for Cyn to get in the car.

"His period? Really?" She got in and buckled up as they tore down the road. "That's a little harsh."

"Especially since I'm like, a guy." Sam snorted. Then he said, "That's a little sexist too, isn't it, Cyn?"

She turned so she could see him, and the dark expression on his face warned her Foley might like her, but Sam hadn't yet made up his mind. "True. Actually, more than a little sexist."

"Sorry," Foley mumbled.

She glared at Foley. "You don't sound sorry."

Sam agreed. "You don't."

"Hey. No ganging up on the *big boy*." Foley winked at her.

Not going there with Sam in the car. "So where's the SUV?"

"At home. I thought my car would impress you better. It purrs, and it's *big*. You know you like them *big*."

Sam snickered.

She ignored her blush. "Are all your friends like you?"

"Strong and sexy?"

"Obnoxious and pigheaded," she countered.

Sam chimed in, "She's got you there."

"Really?" Foley turned the corner, and Cyn held onto the dash for dear life. "'Cause I'm thinking you're a friend, Sam, and you're even more obnoxious and pigheaded than I am." He grinned at Cyn. "And that's saying something."

"Whatever." Sam sneered. "Dick."

"What did I say about the swearing? Jackass."

Cyn looked from Foley to Sam, awash in their camaraderie and wanting to wade deeper. "So, Sam, you're a mechanic too?"

He just looked at her.

"Tap once for yes, twice for no."

"Smart-ass." He sighed. "Yeah, I'm a mechanic. So?"

"He's not one for small talk, is he?" she asked Foley, who chuckled and shook his head. She turned back to Sam. "What do you do for fun?"

His suddenly lecherous expression told her she didn't want to know.

"Never mind. So this dinner invite. It's okay with your friends?" she said to Foley.

"Sure. Johnny's all about impressing us with his incredible girlfriend. None of us can understand why Lara puts up with him. So tonight is more a curiosity about them than about us."

"Don't forget the free meal," Sam added.

"That too." Foley made a sad face at her, then focused once more on the road. "None of us can cook."

"By none of you, you mean…"

"Sam, me, Johnny, and Lou. Though I think Lou's been lying about that. Once I went by his house and smelled something amazing."

"He said it was his mom. I asked." Sam shrugged. "But knowing Lou, probably lying. Dude is supergood at everything. It's annoying."

"Yeah. Try not to make eye contact with him," Foley teased. Or at least, she thought he teased.

"Is he the one who called me a witch? Or was that one of you guys?"

"That was Lou," Sam said quickly.

"Hmm."

They listened to classic rock as Foley capably drove them through the cleared roads. The temperature had heated enough to melt the stubborn ice from the pavement.

"How's your car?" Foley asked.

"Okay. Matt changed the battery, and he said that's all it was."

"Your brother's a mechanic?" Sam asked.

"He likes to think he is."

Foley frowned at the road. "Why didn't you bring it to me?"

"That's like a gazelle walking into the lion's den. No thanks."

He shook his head. "I am so maligned."

"Big word, Foley," Sam taunted. "No need to impress her, dude. You already bang—"

"Shut up," Foley interrupted before Cyn could.

She turned to glare at Sam. "You always this big an asshole? Or should I feel special?"

He blinked at her, then turned to glance out the window. But she swore she saw his lips curl.

Facing front again, she saw Foley giving her a look. "Something you wanted to say?"

He smiled. Then he laughed. "I like your style, baby."

"Oh, he knows my name." She huffed. "Big boy, please."

He cracked up as they pulled in front of an older house in a nice neighborhood. The place could use some paint, but the outside looked tidy enough. An SUV and a glossy black truck sat in the driveway.

As they left the car, the front door opened, and she recognized one of the guys from Webster's waving them in.

"Hurry. Lara just took cookies out of the oven."

Sam darted around her and Foley and tore into the house.

"Lara's known for her cookies," Foley explained. "And like I said, we really can't cook."

Good to know. "So I could make you microwave popcorn, and I'd be a goddess?"

He tugged her closer and planted a kiss that made her weak at the knees. "Nah. We know all about microwave-able crap. Now if you swallowed me whole while I came down your throat, then I'd worship on my knees."

"Foley. Shush."

He laughed and put an arm around her shoulder, then drew her inside with him.

Enveloped immediately by good smells, she let Foley take her coat. He tossed it and his over the couch and dragged her into the kitchen, where three large men stood around a slender brunette fussing over the stove.

"Get out. I mean it! The cookies are for dessert. Jeez. It's like being attacked by piranhas."

Cyn laughed, and everyone turned around to stare at her.

Foley introduced her. "Guys, this is Cyn. You

remember, the hard-ass that bitched me out about Dale and those cars?"

She elbowed him and was rewarded with a grunt. "Nice, Foley. I'm Cyn Nichols. I run Nichols Caffé with my brother and sister-in-law. It's the shop a few doors down from Webster's."

Foley frowned but had yet to take his arm from around her shoulders. "This is the gang. Lou, Johnny, Sam you know, and Lara."

Everyone said hello, and Cyn couldn't help comparing the rough-looking men, seeing similarities despite their obvious differences. "What do they feed you guys at that garage? Or is weightlifting a requirement?"

Johnny, the leanest of the guys—which wasn't saying much—preened and flexed. "Yeah, she said it. And she meant it. She thinks I'm huge. See, Lara? Women still love me."

Lara shook her head. "One of these days that fat head won't fit through the door."

Everyone laughed.

"Hi, Cyn. I'm Lara, Johnny's fiancée. Well, as soon as he gets the stones to ask me."

The guys made fun of him while Johnny turned red. "That's a damn lie! I already asked you. She's making me wait."

"That's right." Lara beamed. "I'm currently going through nursing school and working at Ray's on the side. No time for a man."

"I hear you." Cyn accepted the beer Lara offered.

"Really? So what am I?" Foley looked wounded. Then ruined it by grinning.

"A pity date. Meh. It's Christmas."

Johnny grinned. "Oh, I like her."

Lou whistled. "Damn, son. That's harsh." He held out his hand to Cyn. "We met briefly before. I'm Lou Cortez. Single and eager to please." He wiggled his brows.

"I'll bet you are."

Handsome, like the others, rough, and a definite ladies' man. He was Latino with a slight accent that made him that much sexier.

Lou grinned and kissed the back of her hand, and then Foley was there, shoving Lou back. "Okay, Casanova. Give it a rest."

Johnny and Lara shared an amused glance before Johnny said, "I'm Johnny, but you know that. I'm the pretty one at the garage." She could well believe that. Strikingly handsome, tall, and with a killer grin, he'd all too easily charm the panties off a girl. "I'm the one who gets things done while the badass bros and Romeo play around."

"Badass bros?"

To her delight, Foley flushed. "Stupid nickname."

Sam opened the fridge and buried his head in it. "Yeah, stupid."

"I like it." She gave Foley a wide grin. "Badass bros." She laughed. "*Big* badass bros sounds even better."

"Be nice," Foley growled. "Ignore her. She's hot for me, but she's fighting it."

"Yeah, we can tell," Sam deadpanned. He gave her a look she couldn't read, but then Lara distracted her by calling her over.

"Guys, get lost. Go compare whose is bigger or something. I want to talk to Cyn."

"No need to compare," Johnny said. "We all know I'm—"

"Pitiful, yeah, you are. Pitifully small," Sam cut in. "No, wait. That's what Sue said about Foley, right?"

Everyone grew silent.

Cyn turned around with a smirk. "Really? Then Sue didn't know what she was doing. I don't call him my *big boy* for nothing."

The guys slapped Foley on the back, teasing the "big boy." Foley smiled at her and mouthed, "I'm going to get you for that." Then he shoved Sam out of the kitchen into the living room, and the others followed.

Sectioned off as it was, Cyn and Lara had the kitchen and dining area to themselves.

"Nice save," Lara said with a sincere smile. She had long, dark brown hair, deep brown eyes, and an athletic figure Cyn envied. Boobs and tone, slender all over but where it counted.

Cyn sighed. "Thanks." She paused. "So Sue?"

"A mistake. She works with me at the bar."

"Oh, wait. Ray's." Relief filled her "I know about her." Lara blinked. "You do?"

"Foley mentioned it on our first disaster of a date."

"Oh, this I have to hear."

"To make a long story short, he complimented me for cleaning my plate and led me to believe he had a fetish for big girls."

Lara laughed, long and hard. "Awesome. That's about right. Foley sticking his foot in his mouth for sure."

"You've known him long?"

"Ever since I've been working at Ray's. A good four, almost five years now. The guys come in a lot. It's a rough place, but most of the people are decent and hardworking, even if they look like prison escapees," she said drily.

"So a lot like the guys, just not as big or sexy."

Lara grinned. "Exactly." She eyeballed Cyn. "So you're the one who jumped Foley's case. I heard about you."

Cyn flushed. "I was having an off day."

"Hey, don't apologize for it. I'm sure if you were annoyed, the guys deserved it."

"According to Foley, someone named Dale was to blame. But it wasn't Foley's fault I was in a bad mood. I'd just come from dealing with one of my ex–business partners, who thinks women aren't capable of thought. Or math. Or business, apparently." But at least her lawyer had taken care of that shareholder nonsense for her.

"Ah."

"Yeah. So he'd aggravated me, then I had to go deal with the sexy *male* mechanics I hear so much about. My sister-in-law has vowed never to move from our current location, because she lives for when Webster's guys come in for coffee."

"Oh, I've met her. Nina, right?"

"Yes, and before you ask, she's happily married to my brother. She just likes to look."

"Hell, we all do." Lara crooked her finger, and when Cyn leaned closer, she said, "So that crack about 'big boy.' Interesting."

Cyn smiled.

"My Johnny's a keeper, but I have to watch myself with compliments, or he really will find it hard to fit through the door. Has an ego the size of Texas."

"Don't they all?" Cyn laughed, and Lara joined her. In Lara, Cyn thought she'd found a new friend she could really grow to like. "Now tell me, are the rumors about your cookies true?"

"Taste one and see." Lara offered her one.

Cyn accepted the warm treat and had a fleeting thought of her mother cautioning her to forego anything that might add to her waistline. She took a big bite instead.

Chapter 9

FOLEY DIDN'T KNOW WHAT HAD COME OVER HIS friend. "What the hell, Sam?"

"Yeah, dude. Dick move mentioning Sue." Lou crossed his arms over his chest. "Never bring up an ex-flame, and not around a new woman."

"No wonder you're single." Johnny shook his head.

"Sorry, okay?" Sam kept his voice down. "I was joking, not thinking."

Foley sighed. Sam did look miserable. "No biggie. Just don't bring up anybody else."

"Laundry list of them, is there, Foley?" Lou chuckled. "A lot of unhappy women missing their *big boy*?"

Foley flushed.

Johnny's wide grin boded trouble. "Maybe we could make shirts for the garage. Webster's Big Boys. Swing a big dick, save a mighty dollar. Something like that."

Lou rubbed his chin. "Hmm. Clever. I'll mention it to Del."

"You guys are assholes, you know that?" Foley blew out a breath, pleased to see Sam relaxing again.

Cyn had held her own. Not intimidated by his friends or mention of an ex. He hoped to hell she remembered he'd mentioned Sue before. Then she'd know for sure he wanted nothing to do with the woman.

"So you and Cyn. It's serious?" Johnny asked. "I mean, you never bring your sex friends to dinner."

"Not that we've been invited to that many," Sam argued. "You get a woman who can cook, and this is what? The third time we've been invited? That's so lame, dickbag."

Johnny shared a glance with Lou. "Is he somehow missing the fact that I actually invited him tonight? Because I'm thinking he is."

"Seems like," Lou agreed.

Foley thought they'd forgotten Johnny's question until Sam poked him in the shoulder. "Well?"

"Well what?"

Sam ignored Foley's glare. "Are you guys serious?"

They'd had this same discussion earlier. Not cool of Sam to bring up something personal in front of the guys. Foley gave him a warning look, but Sam ignored it. "She and I are new, okay? I thought I'd bring her around, spend some time with her. It's no big deal."

Johnny and Lou glanced at each other again.

"What?" Foley snapped.

Sam had to add, "I get the attraction. I mean, she's got really nice tits."

"*Sam.*"

The guys grinned.

"Sorry. Breasts."

Foley pinched the bridge of his nose. "Can we please talk about something else?"

"You guys got plans for Christmas?" Johnny asked. "Lara and I are spending it with her family. Dad's got a new girlfriend, so we'll split time with him and his lady on Christmas Eve." He paused to look at Sam. "And no cracks about poles or—"

"Cracks?" Sam said.

Foley tried not to laugh. Johnny's father ran a

successful strip club, and most of his girlfriends had been strippers, hence references to poles and ass cracks.

Lou coughed to hide laughter. "Right. Well, I'm spending the holiday with my mom, aunts, cousins, and sisters."

"All girls, right? You have how many of them?"

Lou sighed. "Too many to count. Maybe fifteen?"

Foley cringed. "Damn. I can barely handle my mom. She and Sam and me are hanging at her place, I guess." Sam nodded to confirm. "And her new boyfriend's too."

Lou raised a brow. "Yeah? How you liking him?"

"We'll see. I'm meeting him for the first time on Christmas." Which made him wonder if dentist guy would be bringing his daughter and her family with him. Hell, he hoped not. Bad enough he'd have to watch his mom flirt with some guy Foley hadn't okayed yet. Too bad he and Sam hadn't had the time to swing by his office. Now he'd have to make up his mind over the guy during the holidays.

"What about Cyn?" Johnny asked. "Going to spend time with her?"

Sam crossed his arms. "Yeah, are you?"

Even for Foley, that seemed to be rushing things. Holidays were for family, not new girlfriends. So why did the thought of giving the relationship some space worry him?

He forced himself to look unconcerned. "We might go out, but I'm sure she'll spend the holiday with her family. I mean, we just started—"

"Hooking up?" Sam interrupted.

"—dating recently." What the hell had crawled up Sam's ass? "You don't like her?"

Everyone watched Sam. Though his buddy gave no signs of anxiety, Foley could tell Sam was bothered.

"Nah. She's okay. Just wondered where you were going with this one."

"This one? It's not like I have a fucking scorecard with names and stats," Foley snapped.

"Touchy." Sam shook his head.

Realizing he was getting bent out of shape over some harmless teasing, Foley relented. "Maybe I am. Woman freaking rocked my world. I don't want things to end yet." He slapped Sam in the back of the head.

"Hey."

"So watch your damn mouth."

"Good advice," Lou said. "Words to live by."

Johnny nodded. "The Bible according to Foley."

Sam, getting into the spirit of *fuck with Foley* night, added, "Wisdom indeed, young grasshopper."

"You know what? Fuck all of you."

They looked over his shoulder, and he just knew Cyn was standing there.

"So, ah, it's time for dinner," she said. "Lara suggests you wash up first. And, Foley, you might want to eat some of that soap. Someone's got a dirty mouth." She snickered. "Lara, guess what Foley said?"

—~~~—

The meal went off without a hitch. Sam watched as Cyn charmed the friggin' guys and Lara. Lara, who had a head on her shoulders, a kind heart, and could see past bullshit, liked Cyn.

Hell, Sam did too. She'd been funny but not a glory hound, sitting back to listen until asked a question. She gave her opinion and didn't back down, even when Lou started putting the verbal screws to her about the idea of a flat tax, which had bored the piss out of him.

Even better—or worse, depending upon his viewpoint, which continued to shift during dinner—she kept looking at Foley like she wanted to know more about him. She smiled and studied him when she didn't think anyone was looking. That told Sam more about her than he wanted to know.

He didn't want to like her. Now he didn't know what to do about her. Especially since she'd been so damn pleasant and funny throughout the meal. He kept waiting for her to act like she was better than everyone, which she clearly was. She had an education and money, came from a nice family—according to what he knew about the coffee shop people—and had an air of competence anyone could see.

And she liked Foley. *Fuck*. She even had good taste.

"Sam?"

He glanced up, only to see Cyn staring at him. "What?"

"I asked what you thought about dogs. Lara went into her bedroom to find the puppy that's supposed to be hiding under the bed." Cyn grinned, and Sam hated that suddenly he could totally relate to what Foley saw in her. "Except he's been hugging my foot all through dinner." She leaned down and picked up a pit bull mix no bigger than a breadbox. "Oh my gosh, he's adorable."

Johnny held his head in his hands. "No. We're not getting a dog."

Lara returned and smirked at Johnny. "Of course not." She winked at Cyn.

"We're too busy. You have school. I have work."

"Work?" Foley looked confused. "Is that what you call what you do at the garage?"

Cyn chuckled.

"What's that?" Johnny glared.

"Oh please," Foley huffed. "We all know you're a genius with a wrench. Easy, little guy."

Johnny flipped him off.

"Hey, don't be so loud or aggressive. You'll scare the puppy." Sam tried not to look so taken with the furry thing as he stared at it. "It's so small." And fucking adorable.

Sam wanted to hold the tiny fella. He had a soft spot for animals. Always had. People could be cruel. He absolutely hated mistreatment of innocence of any kind. But especially to animals that couldn't help trying to love on a guy.

Cyn stood, and the puppy yelped. She soothed it, stroking its head and ears while mothering him against her bountiful chest.

"Lucky dog," Lou teased.

Foley glared. "What's that?"

"Not a thing, man. Not a thing."

Cyn ignored them and circled the table to give Sam the puppy. "Wow. He looks even smaller in your giant arms."

He swallowed around a ball in his throat. "Yeah." The puppy licked him, and he looked down at it so no one would see him acting like a pussy, holding a stupid dog. A glance at the furball made him smile. "I think he's a she." Trying to get a handle on his emotions, he turned himself cold and uncaring again—while being gentle with the puppy.

"Oh, a girl." Lara batted her eyelashes at Johnny. "Please?"

"Lara." Johnny groaned. "You know we're too busy for him—her."

"But my sister isn't. The girls would love her! And just think, we can dog-sit."

"Not a bad idea." Johnny glommed onto it like glue. "I'm sold."

Sam saw Lara look at Cyn and smirk before she noticed him noticing.

Sly. He appreciated that. He shook his head at Johnny. "Sucker."

"What? I'm trying to save a dog's life while saving mine too. The pup's cute, but you wouldn't think a dog that small could shit as much as she does. My back hurts from scooping up so much poop."

"Johnny!" Lara frowned. "We're eating."

"Oh, sorry. What can I say? I'm not a fan of early morning walks and dog duty."

"Then you should not have a dog." Sam petted the girl, letting her snuggle closer.

"You should," Cyn said to him. "You're good with her."

"Sam's a pet person. Animals love him." Foley sounded like a proud older brother. Until he ruined it with, "Which is weird, because usually animals can sense evil."

Everyone around him laughed, and Sam felt himself smiling too. A great night with his friends…and Cyn. While holding a puppy in his arms, drinking beer and eating burgers with the promise of Lara's cookies for dessert, Sam thought that Cyn kind of looked like a good thing for his friend.

He rubbed the puppy's belly.

But where would that leave him?

Three days after the family Christmas party, where Cyn had confessed to having a date, Nina continued to nag. They worked side by side in the shop while Matt did paperwork in the back.

"So you're really dating Foley. *My* Foley."

Cyn turned to Nina. "Whose Foley?"

"Oh, you know what I mean. When your mom mentioned you had a date at Sunday night dinner, I thought you'd lied to get out of the party early. But I saw him in here yesterday, and he was definitely making eyes at you. Come on, Cyn. It's me. Your best friend."

"Who keeps writing 'Mrs. Cynthia Sanders' on all my notepads?" Cyn growled, trying not to find Nina's efforts so amusing.

"It's a catchy name, though." Nina sighed. "Fine. I'll stop. Just tell me what I want to hear."

Cyn hadn't been keeping it a major secret...exactly. Foley's friends all knew. Foley made no bones about watching her like he owned her when they saw each other, which simultaneously thrilled and annoyed her. As a woman wanting a sexy, bossy-in-bed boyfriend, Cyn had hit the jackpot with Foley. But as a successful, independent businesswoman, she didn't appreciate feeling like any man's subordinate.

Then again, Foley never actually made me feel beneath him. Protected, not demeaned in any way. Odd. He's the first man to—

"Cyn!" Nina snapped her fingers in front of

Cyn's nose. "Stay with me. Foley. You. Dating? Not dating?"

Cyn blew out a breath. "Fine. We're dating. But we're new, so don't—"

"Be right back." Nina raced into the back, leaving Cyn to deal with the influx of customers who'd entered.

She finished serving the last one and checked the time. Five o'clock. Nearly quitting time for her. She'd come in early, and Nina would stay later with Matt. The rest of their help had alternated days off through Christmas. She and Nina had argued about keeping the place open, but now Cyn was glad she'd lost. She wanted her time off, now that she had someone special to spend it with. Family was great, but family didn't kiss her the way Foley did.

Matt and Nina walked out of the back together, evil grins on their faces.

Cyn contained a groan. "Shoot me now."

"So. You and Foley Sanders, huh?" Matt leaned against the back counter and studied her. Big, protective, all-knowing brother. "I don't know if I'm okay with that."

Feeling confrontational, she glared at her brother and Nina, as if daring them to have a problem with who she was dating.

Matt continued, "He seems nice enough, but he's got a shady past."

"Seriously?"

"But since you've been in such a dry spell lately, I'll let it slide." Matt gave her a superior smile. "Finally a guy I can't smash under my shoe. You always pick the douchiest boyfriends."

"Hey. Not fair. What about Jon?" A pregnant pause. "Never mind."

Nina and Matt chuckled. "Exactly," Matt said.

Cyn groaned. "You two aren't going to give me a hard time about this, are you? I mean, Foley and I aren't serious. Just hanging out and—"

Nina tsked. "Make sure to use protection."

Matt gagged. "Nina, please. Don't say stuff like that when I'm around."

"Oh, grow up. You're going to make me have the sex talk with Alex when it's his time, aren't you?" She turned to Cyn. "When I told Vinnie a year ago, Matt closeted himself in his study and refused to come out for an entire day."

"That's a lie." He straightened. "I talked with Vinnie about stuff later. In private. Just us guys."

Cyn shook her head. "He always has been a prude. I can't believe you married him."

"I'm right here." Matt frowned.

Nina nodded. "I know. He's cute, so he's got that going for him. And I like his body. But it's been a work in progress to get him to experiment in bed."

Matt turned around without another word and headed back to the office.

Nina and Cyn watched him go.

"Is it wrong I love tormenting my brother?"

"Yes, it is. And I'm a terrible wife because it amuses me." Nina glanced away from her departing husband to the front of the store and bit her lip, then choked on a laugh. "Oh man. Your day is now complete. Look who's coming to see you."

Cyn turned to see Foley courteously holding the door open—for her mother.

"Don't say anything until I get Matt. He won't want

to miss this." Nina darted away and returned seconds later, the pair of them breathless and standing behind the counter, watching it all unfold.

Cyn looked around for somewhere to hide.

"Cyn, sweetie." Her mother walked to the counter and placed her hands down flat. "You haven't returned my calls." She turned to the others. "Matt, Nina."

Behind her, Foley glanced from her petite mother to her and back again.

"Believe it." Cyn sighed.

"What?" her mother asked.

"Mom. Nice to see you. Can I get you an Americana?" Her mother's usual.

"That works. And a muffin too." Ella refused the offer of free food and paid Nina while Cyn made her the coffee and Matt grabbed her a muffin. Behind her, Foley said nothing.

"Isn't this nice. Full service." Her mother winked at Cyn. "Now come talk to me. I'm sure Nina and Matt can manage without you."

"Sure can, Mom," Matt said in a chipper tone. "You take your time."

Cyn shot him a death glare before following her mother to a nearby table. It was all she could do not to reach out to Foley. But she could only process one thing at a time when it came to family.

She'd artfully dodged her mother's calls by sending texts and leaving phone messages when she'd known her mother would be unavailable to talk. The reprieve would only have lasted until she saw her mother again for Christmas, but Cyn would take anything she could get.

She heard Foley place his order in a low voice. He said something that made Matt laugh. She could only imagine. Lord.

She sat with her mother and waited for it.

Ella didn't disappoint and dove right in. "Now, about this man you're dating. Who is he? How do you know him?"

"Ah, well…" Behind her, Foley stood waiting, a shit-eating grin on his face. "Would you like to meet him?"

"I would, yes."

Cyn nodded to the empty chair next to her.

"Now?" Her mother blinked.

Foley sat. Today he wore a T-shirt under his jacket. When he hung it on his chair, he treated Cyn to a mouthwatering view of his powerful, colorful forearms.

Her mother's eyes threatened to bug out of their sockets. For that alone, Cyn wanted to kiss him. So she did.

She leaned close and gave him a peck on the lips. A big move for her, considering it had taken her months of dating Jon before she'd been openly affectionate with him in front of her family.

"Hi, Mrs. Nichols. I'm Foley, Cyn's boyfriend," Foley said before she could. He seemed to have no problem throwing the b-word around.

"Is that so?" Ella sounded cautious.

Foley was everything Cyn had never brought home. Bigger than life, dangerous, and not one to back down. Not some academic or genius in the business world, with a portfolio longer than her arm. Foley was blue-collar badass all the way.

Ella cleared her throat. "So, Foley. How long have you lived in Seattle?"

"Born and raised here."

"Your parents?"

"Just my mom and me. My dad died when I was a kid."

"Ah." Ella studied him.

Foley didn't flinch.

"Have you ever been married before?" The inquisition was well under way.

"Mom."

"No, let him answer the question. He should have nothing to hide." Ella remained firm.

Cyn wanted to crawl under the table. Thirty-four years old, and still having to deal with an overbearing parent. When it came to business, she took no prisoners. Yet when with her mother, all her old insecurities returned, and her confidence took a nosedive. How screwed up to want to please her mother while at the same time wanting to leave the woman and her judgments far behind. Cyn loved her mom, but she didn't always like her.

"So, have you been married?" Ella asked Foley again.

"Legally, in the States?"

Cyn heard a thread of humor in his tone and started to relax.

"As opposed to what?" Ella asked, her fingers tight around her coffee cup.

Foley kicked back in his seat. "Well, I mean, a wedding in Mexico to a piñata shaped like a banana. That probably wouldn't count, right?"

Her mother pursed her lips.

Cyn fought a laugh. "He's teasing, Mom."

"I should hope so."

Foley chuckled. "Just kidding, Mrs. Nichols. Nope. Never married. No kids, no troubles. Just me floating in a world of nuts and bolts and the guys I work with."

"What do you do for a living?"

Next thing, Ella would be asking for bank statements and credit approval ratings. "Mom, enough, okay?"

Foley grabbed her hand under the table and squeezed.

"Your funeral," she muttered. A glance behind her, at the counter, showed Nina and Matt focused on their table. They had yet to blink.

"I'm only doing what a concerned parent would do." Ella sniffed. "He looks like a criminal."

"Oh Lord." Cyn dropped her head into her hands.

"Nah. I'm done with prison. That was years ago."

Her mother just stared. Cyn couldn't tell if he was serious or not. Intrigued, she wanted to know more.

"Now I'm just a hard-working meth dealer. I own this corner and the heroin lab down the street. But I don't employ underage children. Only ex-cons and guys with at least a GED."

Cyn's jaw dropped.

Her mother choked on the sip of coffee she'd taken while Foley chuckled. "Hey, I'm just kid—"

"*This* is your boyfriend?" Ella was not pleased. "How long has this been going on?"

Not pleased herself, Cyn answered, "Since I found out I was pregnant."

She wanted to slap a hand over her own mouth. Now her mother *and* Foley looked horrified. But their shared alarm caused her to burst into uncontrollable—and a touch hysterical—laughter.

Her mother said something in Italian Cyn didn't need

translated. "I've obviously come at a bad time. I'll talk to you later." Ella stood.

"Hey now. I was just kidding, Mrs. Nichols." Foley didn't sound put off by her mother at all. "I work two doors down at Webster's Garage. I'm one of the mechanics there. All legal. I swear."

"How nice for you." Ella looked angry, bewildered, and…old. "I'll come back another time to talk to you, Cynthia. Good-bye, Foley." She turned and left.

"Hmm." Foley stared after her. "I'm sensing a touch of awkwardness." Understatement of the year. "Do you think she liked me?"

Cyn laughed again, unable to contain it. "Oh yeah. She was totally into you. I could tell."

Matt joined them and took a seat next to Foley. "What was all that about?"

"The part about your sister being pregnant or me being a meth dealer?"

Matt just stared.

Chapter 10

FOLEY DIDN'T KNOW WHAT HAD COME OVER HIM, BUT he hadn't liked the way Cyn's mother had tried to interrogate her—over him. Having discussed the woman with Cyn, he now understood a little more about their dynamic.

Had Foley not known of their relation, he wouldn't have guessed them to be mother and daughter. Ella Nichols was petite and pretty, but constrained. Not a knockout like her daughter. Cyn simmered like a pot about to boil over. All sexiness and aggression and life, just waiting to be let loose.

Having experienced her passion and laughter, he knew what she had to offer. Yet seated with her mother, it had felt as if a lid had been placed over her, keeping her down. Just watching her nervous expression and her shoulders slump had pissed him off. Ella's judgmental tone hadn't helped matters.

"I'm sorry," Matt said, cupping his ear. "Meth dealer? Pregnant sister? I think I've had too many cups of coffee today. I'm obviously hearing things."

"Of course you are." Cyn frowned. "Foley was joking. As usual, Mom got pushy and nosy. Instead of being nice, she questioned him as if ready to book him on charges."

Foley decided to keep mention of his actual prison time for another day.

"So you're not pregnant." Matt waited.

"Oh my God. *No*." She turned a becoming shade of pink.

"Well, not that we know of," Foley had to add.

She punched him in the arm. "No, Matt. I am not." Then she shot Foley an evil smile. "At least, not by Foley."

"Ack. Stop talking. I think I'm hemorrhaging internally." Matt groaned and put his head down. "My little sister cannot be in the family way. That would mean she's doing things I can't think about."

Foley laughed, and even Cyn cracked a smile.

"Oh, go back to your wicked wife and have your fun. I can't believe you sicced Mom on me."

"Yeah right." Matt snorted. "She had her own agenda from the minute she walked in." Matt glanced at Foley. "So you guys are dating." He narrowed his eyes and wore his serious face, the one that meant business. "You screw her over, I'll make your life hell." Then he gave Foley a pleasant smile. "Enjoy your coffee."

"Ah, thanks." Foley watched him go, reassessing Cyn's brother. Matt was a big guy. Not as big as Foley, but the man looked as if he'd be a tough one to put down.

"Why are you looking at him like that? He was kidding."

"Yeah, sure." No, Matt had been serious. Foley liked him the more for it.

"Well, you met my mom. I'm sorry she was being so nasty."

"Hey, don't sweat it. Wait 'til you meet my mom."

Cyn gave him a cautious look. "Oh?"

Foley realized he might be moving too fast. Considering he wanted a lot more from Cyn than she probably felt okay about giving him, he knew to back off. Bide his time. Be strategic.

And Johnny thought he didn't have the smarts to be in charge.

"My mom has this thing about a big dinner after the holiday. I was hoping to bribe you into coming over. You can show her you're not a stripper or hooker, and she'll get off my ass about dating."

When Cyn just gaped at him, he laughed. "Kidding. Man, you're just like your mom."

"Not winning you any points, Sanders."

"Ouch. Sorry." He flinched at the glare she shot him. "My mom is a sweetheart. Seriously. I wanted to invite you over for dinner sometime, but I can't cook. My mom is big on cooking for me and all my friends, so it's no biggie to swing by. She's not going to think we're getting ready to head down the aisle or anything. She's pretty chill about my social life."

"Oh." Cyn reached for his hand on the table. "Okay then."

He liked her touching him. A lot.

He cleared his throat. "So when are we hanging out again? I have some time tomorrow." They'd discussed Christmas plans and had family to consider. Their relationship being so new, they'd decided to take things slowly.

Yet here Foley sat, unable to stay away, just two days after the best sex of his life with a woman who wouldn't leave his thoughts.

"I have my nephews tomorrow." She made a face. "They'll be fun, but they're balls of energy."

"Want to show them the garage? I can let them check out some tools and stuff. Do they like cars?"

"Oh." She brightened. "That would be nice. We're going to take in a movie and walk around a park, maybe. And we'll eat many, many times tomorrow. They have bottomless stomachs."

"Ha. Sounds familiar. You guys will have a good time."

She smiled at him, and his heart raced. "Would you like to join us?"

Not wanting to appear too desperate for her with an immediate *hell yes*, he opted for subtlety. "Well… what's in it for me?"

"You can spend time with boys. I doubt you get a lot of that, unless you have some nephews or kids you've forgotten about."

"Like I told your mom, I'm kidless."

"You'll get fed when you're with us."

"Hmm. Keep going."

She huffed. "You'll get to be with me. There. That should do it."

"Yeah, but you're bossy. And you have lousy taste in men. Just ask your mom."

She laughed. "You have me there."

Do I have you? "Just one more thing."

"And that would be?"

"After the boys go home tomorrow night. What do I get then?"

She leaned close and whispered, "Spend the day with us and find out."

⚬⚬⚬

And so Foley found himself driving to Cyn's house in the late afternoon on Wednesday to pick up her and her nephews. They'd had an influx of work, so he hadn't been able to spend the entire day with her and the boys, but he'd managed to get out a little early. He parked and rang the doorbell, wondering what to expect.

A tall youth answered the door. He only stood a head and a half shorter than Foley but had yet to grow into his frame. All skin and bones.

He looked like Matt, with dark hair and dark eyes. "My dad's a cop. And he's in the back." A good-looking kid…with a smart mouth.

Foley sighed. "Is your aunt here?"

His younger brother slid beside him. He looked up at Foley, and his eyes grew wide. "Stranger danger! Stranger danger!" he yelled.

"*What* is going on?" Cyn roared from behind them. "Is that Foley?"

"You mean prisoner 652408?" the older boy asked.

"Damn it, Vinnie. Let him in. Bad enough your grandma gave him a hassle yesterday. Don't you do it too, or no popcorn and no movie."

Cyn hopped into view behind them, struggling into a sock. "Hey, Foley. Just push past the obnoxious twins."

The younger boy frowned. "We aren't twins. I get the looks, he gets… Well, he's tall."

Vinnie scowled. "Shut up, Alex."

Foley walked toward them, which had the boys automatically backing away. He heard the door close behind him, but he was intent on only one thing. He grabbed Cyn before she toppled over, struggling with that stubborn sock.

"Oh, thanks."

He nodded, then pulled her in and kissed the breath

out of her. When he finished, he had a hard time easing himself down. "There. Now, where are we headed?" He turned to see her nephews gaping at them. "What?"

"N-nothing." Alex grinned. He looked like the spitting image of his older brother but had green eyes. "You're Aunt Cyn's boyfriend."

"Yep."

"The meth dealer," Vinnie muttered.

"*Vincent Nichols*." Cyn straightened. "Where did you hear that?"

Vinnie gave Foley a challenging look. "Oh, it's going around."

"Probably Matt," Foley offered.

"My brother is an imbecile. Feel free to tell him that," she told the boys. "Foley, to answer your question, how about we visit the garage first? The movie isn't until five thirty."

Foley nodded. "Sounds good. Get your coats, and let's go."

Following the boys, he walked next to Cyn. "Well, this should be fun."

She chuckled. "They're only giving you a hard time because my brother put them up to it. Alex will be the easy one. Vinnie's a tougher nut to crack—just like his father."

"And aunt."

"Thanks a lot."

He grinned and waited for the boys to get into the backseat. He shut the door, then turned to smile at her. "Hey. Think about how hard I had to work to get you to go out with me. If I hadn't come along that night when your car died, I—"

"You know, you never did tell me how you just happened to be there when I broke down."

He'd expected her suspicion and was pleased to see it, because that meant he was getting to really know her. "So untrusting. And you wonder where the boys get it."

She flushed. "Not fair. I asked a legitimate question."

"Truth was I'd swung around to your shop to apologize and saw you pull away, so I followed you. And no, that's not stalkerish at all."

"Really."

Okay, it had been. "Really. I figured to pull past you and deal with you another time. And then you slowed down and stalled on the side of the road. I had a civic duty, as a mechanic, to help."

"Uh-huh."

"Oh, for fuck's sake."

She slapped a hand over his mouth. "Foley. Language."

He licked her palm, and her eyes narrowed, but she didn't remove her hand.

"You want a treat later, after the boys are gone? Behave."

He growled, wanting his treat now. A glance at the car showed the boys glued to the byplay between him and their aunt, their faces pressed to the window. In a low voice, he said, "You're lucky they're in the backseat. Otherwise I'd have you bare-ass naked on the hood of my car while I pounded into that sweet pussy."

Her jaw dropped. Let her stew on that while he ignored his need to bury himself inside her again.

He drove them to Webster's, fielding questions from the Nichols' kids the entire way. He had to hand it to Vinnie. The kid had smarts, for sure.

"So you've been a meth dealer—I'm sorry—a mechanic, for how long?"

Cyn grinned.

Foley sighed. "It's like your grandmother is here with us, as we speak." In the rearview, he saw Vinnie smirk. "Since I got out of high school. My buddy Sam and I are like brothers. We went to school together, then became mechanics together."

"How?" Alex asked. "Did you have to go to school to be a mechanic? I hate school."

"Alex." Cyn frowned.

"Sam and I kind of drove around the West Coast after high school for a while. We always liked cars, so we went to trade school down in Sacramento for a year. We worked at different shops after that, learning and taking other classes. Emissions and A/C work is big, so we tried to focus on those. It didn't take long before we came back to Washington. My mom lives here. So we settled back in Seattle."

Silence filled the SUV until Cyn asked, "Are you glad you came back? It must have been exciting to travel."

"It was. But I missed home." He'd missed his mother—what he considered home.

"Aunt Cyn traveled a lot too," Alex said. "She's been all over the place. She even lived in Boston."

"Yeah?"

Cyn nodded. "I spent a year in Boston, some time in Philadelphia, then I traveled down to Baltimore. The East Coast is very different from the West Coast."

"Yep. We've gone to Disney World," Vinnie said. "Florida drivers are for shit."

"Vinnie!"

"He's not wrong." Foley bit his lip to keep from laughing at Cyn's outrage. "Sam and I hit Orlando once years ago. Man, it was so hot the mosquitoes were crying."

"Did you go to Disney World?" Alex asked.

"Nah. Too expensive. And I think we scared security."

Cyn laughed. "I'll bet."

"How come you have so many tattoos?" Vinnie asked. "Don't they hurt to get?"

"Sure do." Foley pulled into the parking lot at Webster's. "But girls seem to like them."

The boys looked to their aunt.

She shrugged. "I think they're pretty."

"*Pretty?*" Foley frowned. "Seriously? Not scary, tough, manly? Hell, Cyn. I've got snakes and skulls and cars on me. Pretty?"

"You could get a unicorn," Cyn said. "That would be pretty."

Foley and the boys stared at her. "Girls, am I right?" he said.

The boys nodded.

"Aunt Cyn." Alex shook his head. "No unicorns. When I get a tattoo, I'll get a cool car. Or a monster with three heads."

"Or a naked lady," Vinnie added with a sly glance at his aunt.

She pinched the bridge of her nose. "God save me."

Foley chuckled. "Come on, guys. I'll show you where real men work. And none of us have unicorn tattoos."

"How about butterflies?" Cyn asked.

"Now you're just being ridiculous." Foley ushered them inside, where he found Sam and Johnny working. "Hey, guys."

Johnny and Sam stopped what they were doing and joined the group. "Hey there." Johnny smiled. "Who's this?"

"Johnny, Sam, you know Cyn. These are her nephews, Vinnie and Alex."

Johnny wiped off his hands and held one out to the boys, who shook it while staring at his colorful forearms visible beneath his rolled-up sleeves. "Hey, guys."

"Hi." Vinnie kept a wary eye on Sam.

"Sam, smile. You're scaring the kids." Foley nudged him.

Sam grunted, but he stopped looking so menacing. The big guy was a sucker for animals and kids. A soft heart surrounded by a hard shell of attitude. He wore a short-sleeved shirt, and his many tats were visible on his arms and around his neck. Taking a subjective step back, Foley admitted that had he not known Sam, he'd give the guy a wide berth.

"So, you guys want to see what we do here?" Sam asked.

The kids seemed interested. "I do," Alex said.

"Me too." Vinnie nodded. "Our dad has a lot of tools, and he's going to teach us to build an engine when we're older."

"Good idea," Sam said.

Cyn watched him like a hawk, but Sam did no more than show the boys different tools and cars they'd been working on. Johnny joined him and answered questions.

"That section is yours, isn't it?" Cyn asked Foley, pointing at his bench.

"Yep. How did you know?"

"I've seen Johnny over there before." She pointed to

Johnny's tools. "And that area next to yours is just so disorganized. It's not you."

"True." He crossed his arms, enjoying himself. He liked her seeing where he worked. Even more, he enjoyed her interest. Cyn seemed to want to know more about him. A good sign that she considered him more than just a boyfriend-labeled hookup.

"Yeah. You're Mr. Bossy. Mr. Organization. I bet you're methodical when it comes to your work."

"He is," Johnny agreed, having overheard them. "A complete logic monster. But there's nothing Foley can't fix."

"He's good, huh?" Vinnie asked, glancing over at Foley.

"My boy's got game…in the garage." Sam snorted. "Don't know about the rest of his life, though."

"Please. You should talk." Foley slung an arm around Cyn, and Sam frowned.

Now what to do about that? For some reason, Sam didn't approve of Cyn. And that bothered him. Foley respected Sam's opinion. Another reason he wanted Cyn and his mom to meet. He wanted Eileen's opinion of her. Foley really, *really* liked Cyn. A lot. Sam might be weird about him dating a woman for any number of reasons. But Eileen would tell him if she didn't think Cyn was good for him. And she'd tell him from a place of truth, not jealousy or fear. As much as his mom wanted grandkids, she wouldn't want them from a woman of little worth.

Vinnie didn't seem to like Foley's arm around his aunt either. He walked back to her, Alex in tow, and subtly inserted himself between them. He tugged her hand. "Come on, Aunt Cyn. You can touch the air tools," Sam said."

She joined the boys, oohing and aahing over the tools and engines. Foley answered questions and watched, enjoying her with the boys. She was naturally maternal, keeping an eye on them while letting them have fun. He showed the kids the lift, where they stored the oil, the computer where they could order parts and study diagnostics, and more.

Then Cyn warned him they needed to get to the movies.

The time had passed in a blur, and to his bemusement, he realized he'd enjoyed answering Vinnie and Alex's many questions.

Before the boys left, they thanked Johnny and Sam for their time. Vinnie especially seemed to like Sam, because he shook Sam's hand, staring at Sam's tattoo-covered forearms as if committing them to memory before leaving.

Sam nodded. "Have fun at the movies. What are you guys seeing?"

"The latest superhero movie, I think." Cyn sighed. "Something with no kissing or romance, I'm sure."

"There's usually a little romance in those movies," Johnny said.

"Oh good. My nephews hate the kissing parts, and I get a kick out of torturing them." She waved, ignoring the kids' groans. "Thanks, Johnny, Sam. The boys enjoyed it."

"What about me?" Foley frowned.

"You get a special thanks." She kissed him, a full smack on the lips.

"Oh." He swallowed hard. "Well, then."

"Hey, Cyn. Where's mine?" Johnny asked. "I feel neglected."

"Whatever." Sam snorted. "Any lips but Lara's touch you, and your girlfriend will rip your lips *off*."

"He has a point." Foley grinned, feeling on top of life all of a sudden. "Later, slackers. Make sure you lock up."

Sam flipped him off, and Johnny called him a name not meant for small ears—a good thing the kids had gone back into the SUV.

They arrived at the theater with time to spare. The movie had just the right amount of action and humor. Sitting with Cyn and her nephews gave Foley a funny feeling inside. He glanced over at them all enraptured in the film. It felt like he was sitting with his own family, taking in the flick.

His own family.

He had never before been ready for something so permanent, but now, things had changed. Sex with Cyn had been amazing. And meaningful. Not just a physical release, but an emotional one as well. He wished he could read her better, to know what she really thought about him. He also realized they'd only been seeing each other for a short time. Hell, doing the math, only a week and a half had passed since their first meeting. Yet he felt as if he'd known her for a lot longer.

With no other way to explain it, she fit. They were different in many ways. She had her degrees and businesses, thinking all the time. He had clever hands and a brain that solved puzzles. He liked to fix things. She organized.

Yet they both loved family. For all that her mother

had annoyed her, Cyn remained loyal. She'd moved back to Seattle to be with her people. As had Foley.

Vinnie slipped by them to head to the bathroom, and Foley decided to get a refill on his drink, to maybe stop thinking so hard about the future and just enjoy the now.

He whispered to Cyn, "Be right back. You need anything?"

She shook her head and shooed him away, fascinated with some muscled stud in tights on screen. She looked just like Alex, fixated on the action.

Chuckling to himself, Foley got his refill then went in search of Vinnie, just to make sure the kid was okay. The theater wasn't a bad place, but weirdos could be found anywhere.

He went down the hallway toward the men's room and saw a teenager having a heated conversation with Vinnie outside the restroom.

Not liking the look of things, Foley paused some distance away and sipped his soda, watching.

"So are you blowing the coach or what?" the larger boy asked.

Not a friendly talk, apparently. The boy with Vinnie stood a head taller, had more bulk, and wore the typical damaged jeans and a Seahawks sweatshirt. Not a bad-looking kid, except for the air of menace surrounding him.

"Jim, get lost." Vinnie tried to go around him, but Jim wouldn't let him. Instead, the boy crowded Vinnie's personal space. "I already told you. Coach played me because I'm better."

Considering Vinnie had mentioned basketball a few times in the car, Foley figured this altercation had to be about Vinnie's all-star basketball performance this season. Nice to see the kid had confidence though— *"Coach played me because I'm better." You go, Vinnie.*

Foley drank and watched, determined not to step in unless the fight got out of hand. He was a firm believer in letting people, kids included, fight their own battles.

"Oh, I'll bet you're better. Better at sucking dick."

Seriously? Jim had to be in middle school with Vinnie if they were on the same team. Nice mouth for a seventh or eighth grader.

Then again, Foley had been swearing since losing his first tooth. Who was he to judge?

Vinnie rolled his eyes. "You're so homophobic it's obvious."

Jim flushed. "What are you talking about?"

"It means you might as well come out and accept yourself. Honestly, no one on the team would care."

"What?" Jim shoved Vinnie back into the wall. "You calling *me* gay, you pole-smoker? Seriously?"

Foley took a step in their direction, still not noticed by the kids too intent on each other to spot him. Time to stop the violence before it turned too physical.

"See. I don't even know what that means," Vinnie said. "Whatever. I'm done." Vinnie tried to move around him again, but Jim shoved him back even harder.

Now Vinnie looked both scared and angry.

"You don't know anything," Jim spat. "I'm not gay. I'm dating Kyra Fields, asshole."

"You wish."

A tall man who looked like Jim exited the restroom. He appeared decent enough, but Foley could read trouble on the guy. The small beady eyes were a dead giveaway. He didn't seem to notice Foley, focused on his boy and Vinnie. "Problem, Jim?"

"Yeah. This jerk is calling me a fag." Jim snickered. "I think Vinnie's got a crush."

The man joined the boys, and Foley decided to give him a chance to make things right with his prick of a kid. "Is that right?" He stared at Vinnie, who appeared visibly nervous. "Is this the boy who took your place on the team? Vinnie Nichols, right?"

"Yeah," Jim sneered. "Our 'star center.'"

"The kid who couldn't find his ass if I handed it to him?" Jim's father asked, aggressive and way too involved in a kid's fight, especially one his own son had started.

Jim glanced from Vinnie to his father and took a surprising step back. He seemed suddenly nervous, and Foley didn't like any of it. "He's just a dickhead, Dad. I put him in his place. Let's go back to the movie."

Foley walked toward them, still unnoticed.

"Not yet." The man put a hand on Vinnie's shoulder, and Foley saw red.

He set his soda down on a nearby bench before reaching them. "Problem?"

Vinnie looked relieved to see him.

"Not your business. Take off," the dad said without looking at him.

"How about we try this again?" In a threatening growl, Foley warned, "Take your goddamn hand off Vinnie's shoulder before I break it off and shove it up your ass."

The man took a hard look at Foley and blinked. He released Vinnie, and Vinnie hurried over to Foley's side, his eyes wide.

Foley put a hand on his arm to reassure him. "Why don't you go join your aunt and brother while I talk to Jim's dad? Oh, and take my soda with you." He nodded behind him.

"Okay." Vinnie darted away.

Foley closed the slight distance between himself and Jim's father and saw Jim take another step back. One large bully and a smaller one in the making.

To the boy, he said, "Jim, is it?"

"Yeah," Jim answered, trying to sound belligerent but coming off as shaky.

"Instead of giving Vinnie shit because he took your spot on the team, maybe you can try to win back your position next season." Assuming their season this year had ended. "Vinnie was right. All your anti-gay talk just makes it look like you're trying to cover for some hidden tendencies. Lay off the hate, kid. Trust me, it won't help you in the long run."

As he spoke, he saw the kid's dad become angrier. Obviously Jim got his bias honestly—from his father.

"Who the fuck do you think you are?" Jim's dad stood toe-to-toe with Foley. A big mistake.

That extra step closer triggered Foley's need to attack. Ever since his stint in prison, he'd never let any guy get this close without taking him out. Lesson learned…the hard way.

Foley was more than ready to plant his fist in the guy's face. Jim at least had the sense to step far away. "Buddy, you really want to act the fool in front of your kid?" He pushed up his sleeves, doing his best to remember to be civilized. This wasn't Ray's or one of Sam's illegal fights. It was a family theater, for God's sake.

"Don't talk to my son, you piece of shit." The man put his hand on Foley's chest, as if to shove him away.

In seconds, Foley stepped aside and jerked the guy around. He twisted the asshole's arm behind his back, shoving him face-first against the wall. "You want to take this outside? Let's go. I got nothing better to do than teach a fuckhead like you some manners. No wonder your kid's a little jerk. He's watching you mouth off to eleven-year-old boys." Foley huffed. "What a man. But you know what? I'm not eleven. So what say you and I go outside, and I pound you into next week?" Foley jerked the guy's arm, making him cry out.

"I'm sorry. Okay?" Dickhead's voice had risen an octave.

"Yeah, you are. How about you tell Jim the right way to behave?"

"How about you go to h—"

Foley jerked his arm again, and Jim's father hiked up on his toes and screeched.

"Try again, dickhead." Any minute now someone would arrive to use the restroom. They needed to take this outside, but Foley wanted to make his point clear.

"Dad, come on." Jim sounded close to tears, and Foley would have felt bad about doing this in front of him, but young Jim needed to learn some manners. "I'm sorry, mister. I am."

"How about you, *Dad*?" Foley asked. "You sorry for picking on a sixth grader? For teaching your kid wrong? You sorry about that?" Then, just for fun, he leaned closer and whispered in the guy's ear, "You know what we do to pussies like you in prison? Got any idea of how much fun it is to make a tough guy like you scream?" He leaned into him with his chest.

"*I'm sorry*. I'm so sorry, I am." The guy started pleading, repeating himself and sounding so scared Foley worried he'd piss in his pants.

Satisfied he'd gotten his point across, he let go and stepped back, on alert in case the jerk found a hidden well of courage and tried to launch a punch. But Jim's father was all apologies as he hurried to protect his ass. He turned, kept his back to the wall, and cradled his arm, inching away from Foley.

"Jim won't come near Vinnie again. No way. I swear. Big mistake. No problem with you, guy. None at all." He stared at Foley's tats in horror, no doubt imagining the colorful artwork to be gang- or prison-related. What an idiot.

"Yeah? Is that right, Jim?" Foley put enough of a threat in his voice to convince both father and son to back off.

"I'm sorry. I won't talk to Vinnie ever again." The boy didn't bother wiping the tears from his eyes.

Father and son raced away, and Foley grunted with satisfaction. After he took a quick pee break, he came out and found Vinnie waiting for him with his soda, a wide grin on his face.

"Why aren't you inside?"

"I've been waiting for you. I was hiding around the corner."

Shit. "You saw all that?"

"You were *awesome*." Vinnie beamed. "Jim is the biggest jerk at school. He's mean all the time and picks on everyone. I usually avoid him. All my friends do. But then I took the spot he thought was his on the basketball team, and he got worse. Dad said to ignore him until I couldn't anymore. But you were so much better. I think he cried."

Foley tried to feel bad about that but couldn't. The kid had been a prejudiced little creep.

"Yeah, well, I was only interested in making his dick of a father cry. You have any more problems with him, let me know, would you?"

"I don't think Jim will mess with me anymore. And I *know* his dad won't." Vinnie clenched his fist in triumph. "That rocked!"

Foley had a feeling knocking assholes around was not the way the Nichols family handled conflict. "Um, okay. But don't tell your aunt. I don't want her to think I started any trouble."

Vinnie turned an invisible key over his lips and pretended to toss it away. Then he handed Foley his drink. Pleased the kid wasn't suffering from the altercation, Foley ruffled Vinnie's hair. He and Vinnie returned to their seats.

"You okay?" Cyn whispered. "You guys took a while."

"We're fine," Vinnie whispered back. "Foley's awesome."

"Ah, okay." Cyn gave Foley a questioning look.

"Just a guy thing."

She looked like she wanted to ask him more questions, but then something on the screen blew up and took her attention. They enjoyed the rest of the film.

All the while, Vinnie kept glancing over at Foley and smiling.

Chapter 11

Cyn had no idea what to make of Vinnie's sudden turnaround in regard to Foley, but she didn't want to change his mind. Alex, too, seemed to view Foley as his own personal hero, with both boys wanting to sit by Foley in the pizzeria. They chattered nonstop about boy stuff while she watched with amusement.

Who would have thought Foley would be so good with children?

He was patient, amused, and tolerant of their endless fart jokes and questions about cars, his tattoos, and what he was like in school at their age.

She shook her head at the fascinating man. "Why am I not surprised you got into fights in high school?"

"And after high school. And a few years after that. Oh, and Monday with Sam…" He chuckled. "Hey, I never claimed to be a saint."

Her nephews hung onto his every word, eating their pizza as he talked.

"Where I grew up, you had to be tough. Nobody gave us the 'Don't Be a Bully' talk in school. You had to learn to stand up for yourself. I did."

"I see."

He shrugged and took a huge bite of pizza. But at least he didn't talk with his mouth full. She hated that. His mother had obviously drilled manners into the guy.

"Are the tattoos a way of looking tough?" *Or are they to make you supersexy?*

"I got them over the years because I think they're cool."

"They're so cool," Vinnie agreed.

"They really are," Alex added.

Foley rolled up his sleeves, showing off his art while she took more notice of his muscle. "Sam's got a matching skull and snake. Something we did when we were younger." She noticed some dates beneath the skull and reminded herself to ask him about them later.

"Do you have a tattoo?" he asked.

She glanced up to see all three of them staring at her. "Who, me?" She started to tell him he should know, then saw the boys' interest, as well as the gleam in his eyes. "Wouldn't you like to know?"

He grinned. "I sure would."

Alex screwed up his face. "Ew. You're not going to kiss or anything, are you? Because seeing that in the movie almost made me throw up."

Vinnie sighed. "He's young. It will pass."

"Oh?" Cyn raised a brow. "This sounds interesting. So this aversion to kissing has passed you, has it? Who's the girl *you're* crushing on, Vin?"

He flushed.

Foley chuckled. "Come on, Cyn. You can't ask a guy that."

"Why not?"

"Because it's private. Hell, even now, when my mom tries to get in my business, I make her work hard for the answer."

"But you still tell her."

"Well, she's my mom."

Cyn stuck out her tongue at him, having fun. "Momma's boy."

"You don't want to go there, do you? Because my mother wasn't grilling you the other day. Aren't you thirty-four years old, or something?"

"Oh. That hurt." Vinnie grinned. "He's talking about Grandma, Aunt Cyn."

"I know that, you monster." Score one for Foley. "Hey, you want dessert? Hush up. That goes for all of you," she warned, looking each one of them in the eye.

Foley smirked. And *wham*, she wanted him something fierce right then and there.

He must have seen something in her eyes, because his gaze dropped to her mouth. "Hey guys, want a few quarters for the video games?"

The boys went gratefully.

"And stay together," Foley warned.

Vinnie nodded, no longer smiling, and made sure to keep in sight.

"What's that about?" she asked.

"Nothing. I just worry about jerks around. We live in a city, you know. You have to be careful with kids."

She reached across the table and clutched his hand tightly. "Okay, you big worrywart." She gave him a tender smile. "You're good with them. Thanks."

He looked uncomfortable. "It's no big deal. They're nice kids."

She gripped him tighter then let go. "They are. And they're on their best behavior with you here. What did you do to make them like you? Something when I wasn't looking."

"Yeah, I gave them each a twenty," he said wryly.

"Really?"

"No. It's my winsome personality. The same one that won you over." He waited while she laughed at that, then said, seriously, "You're really good with them yourself. You're going to make one hell of a mother someday."

What a sweet thing to say. "Thanks, Foley."

"Even if it's not my baby currently in that sexy belly."

"Shut up." She blushed. "I'll pay for that later with my mom, but it was so worth it to see the look on her face…and on yours." She laughed again.

"Smart-ass."

They left with the boys sometime later, dropping them off at Matt and Nina's. Cyn and Foley had a short talk with Matt, who didn't seem surprised to see him there.

"Glad you guys had a nice night." Matt nodded. "The last time they went out with one of Cyn's boyfriends, I think they spiked his drink with hot sauce."

Foley glared at her. "Thanks for the warning." That she *hadn't* given him.

"I didn't want to prejudice you against them." Her wide smile didn't seem to be fooling him. "You had a good time, and they loved you. It's all good in the end, isn't it?"

Matt grinned. "Oh yeah. That's female logic, all right."

"No shit."

She frowned at Foley. "No swearing."

Vinnie and Alex appeared and pushed past their dad. "Bye, Foley." Alex shook his hand.

"Bye, little man." Foley gave Alex a firm shake and grinned.

Vinnie surprised the hell out of everyone, Foley

especially, it seemed, by giving him a hug before darting away.

Matt blinked. "I think that's the first time Vinnie's hugged anyone not family." He narrowed his eyes. "What the hell happened tonight?"

"Nothing exciting." Foley put his arm around Cyn's shoulders. "But I did give him some quarters for video games."

"Hmm." Matt watched him with suspicion.

"You're welcome, big brother." Cyn poked Matt in the chest. What an ingrate. "I hope you and Nina enjoyed my babysitting."

"You have bony fingers." Matt winced.

Foley shifted and pulled her closer. "Be nice to your sister, Matt. She's my girl now. No picking on her, or you have to deal with me."

His deep voice gave her shivers.

"Trust me, Foley. She doesn't need anyone fighting her battles. Girl has a mean streak a mile wide."

Cyn's wicked smile spoke volumes.

"But hey, you want her? She's all yours."

Cyn didn't like her brother's warped sense of humor. "I am not a handoff in some kind of relay race, *Mattie*."

Her brother grimaced. "*Matt*. I hate when you call me Mattie."

On a rant, Cyn continued, "You can't just turn me over to Foley, because you don't own me, moron. I'm a person, and I have—*Hey*."

"You can yell at him later." Foley dragged her by the hand back to the SUV.

"Thank you, God. And thank you, Foley," Matt called out before shutting the door.

Foley reminded her, "He doesn't own you, because I do. We have a debt to settle, woman."

"A debt? I—Oh." She remembered all too well what he wanted, and she was eager to give it to him. Now what to do with a testosterone-fueled bad boy all her own?

They made it back to her house in no time and entered in silence. Nerves and excitement tangled inside her, and she wondered if she should make a move. She decided to take it slow, to be smooth about it. Before she could turn to thank him for such a fun evening, he had his lips on hers and shoved her against the back of the door.

He reached next to her to lock it, then took off her jacket and shrugged out of his while he kept kissing her. He finally let her break for air and kissed his way up and down her neck.

"Foley." She ran her fingers through his hair. "In a rush, sexy?" She wasn't complaining. Far from it.

"I haven't had you since Saturday night. I'm dying to get inside you again."

They'd made the most of that Saturday, though. "What are you waiting for?"

He growled something low in his throat, then yanked off her top and bra. He palmed her breasts, teasing and pinching, until she'd drenched her panties.

"You wet for me, baby?"

"Yes," she hissed and yanked him close for another kiss.

His hand snaked under her jeans and underwear, yet he didn't move where she needed him most. She tried to grind into him, but the bastard kept playing with her. She tore her mouth from his and nipped his throat.

"In me," she demanded.

But Foley wouldn't be rushed. He kissed his way

down to her breasts and took her nipple in his mouth. She pulled at his thick shoulders, wanting him naked too.

Instead, he toyed with the closure of her jeans. She toed off her shoes while he shoved down her pants and panties. He let go of her breast only to remove the rest of her clothes, then straightened.

She loved that she had to look up to meet his gaze.

"Turn around." He didn't give her much choice as he turned her to face the door. She heard his zipper go down.

"Wh-what are you going to do?"

"Hmm, what do you think?" He pressed against her, and she felt his erection along her backside. "I bet this would feel so good somewhere else, hmm?"

She instinctively thrust back against him, wanting him inside her.

He held her hips and ground against her, sliding that cock between her legs, through her cream, but not penetrating. "How about if I slip inside, just for a tease, before I put the condom on? How would that feel?"

Before she could answer, he plucked her clit with thick fingers, and she jerked back against him.

"Cheater," she breathed.

His low laugh accompanied another push, but this time he bent his knees and positioned himself at the entrance to her sex.

"Fuck, that's good." He pushed in and out without penetrating more than an inch, not giving her nearly enough.

She rocked back to increase the sensation, then angled so he'd slide fully inside her.

He swore and continued to push, filling her up.

He stopped after an interminably long time and settled deep. Skin to skin. No condom.

Oh my God.

"Damn, Cyn. You feel so fucking hot."

"So do you," she moaned.

He slowly withdrew, only to slam inside her again.

She cried out, wanting more. She knew it was dangerous, having Foley in her without protection. Not fearing for disease as much as that she'd lose control and let him ride her into a potential pregnancy.

Yet she couldn't stop herself from grinding against him, fucking *him* as much as letting him fuck her.

"Stop." He grabbed her hips to still her and withdrew in a hurry. She heard him rip a packet and waited while he donned a condom. Then he spread her ankles for better access. "You want me? Want this?" He shoved back inside her so fast and deep he took her breath away.

The sensation was indescribable, and she teetered on the verge of orgasm.

He continued to take her, nothing slow or gentle about their connection. The fierceness of his claiming touched her, and when he grazed her clit with his fingers and shoved deep, he surprised a climax out of her, overwhelming her with sensation.

Foley muttered her name as he followed her into orgasm. He gripped her hips and emptied into her. As he brushed the backs of her legs, his jeans hit her skin.

The fact that he'd remained clothed while she'd been totally naked excited her anew. She clamped down on him, hard, and earned another groan from her skilled lover.

He stroked her back, petting her as he withdrew.

She turned to see him remove the condom and tuck himself back into his jeans. "Well, that was fun."

He didn't smile, didn't joke. His intense gaze roamed her face and body, then rested on her mouth. "We're just getting started. Get into bed and wait for me."

He left, presumably to dispose of the condom, and returned without his shirt. She hadn't moved, unable to do more than process her pleasure. He frowned at her while he stripped off his clothes. A large, muscular man covered in defining ink from his arms to his chest. She had *never* seen a man better put together than Foley.

"I said get in bed."

"No." She put her hands on her hips, trying to remain in control when her entire body wanted to curl into a ball and lay at his feet. "Make me."

His eyes lit up. "Okay."

In a heartbeat, he scooped her into his arms.

"*Foley.*"

The novelty of being carried shocked her into stillness, so that they reached her bedroom without a fight.

Before she could protest, he dumped her on the bed and followed her into it.

"You're heavy," she protested, though she craved his heat.

"You're fine as shit."

She grinned. "So romantic."

"Yet so true. Look at those tits. That belly, those thighs. And let's not forget that ass." He licked his lips. "Time for fun with numbers."

"Huh?"

"What's after sixty-eight?" he asked then kissed her.

When she could reason again, she answered, "Sixty-nine?"

"My favorite number."

When his meaning sank in, she blushed. She couldn't help it. "Foley."

His sexy smile faded. "I swear to you I'm clean. I'm planning to see the doctor right after Christmas to get a checkup and prove it, but until then, you have to take me on faith. Or not." He sighed. "Hell, I'm game for anything you want. You have no idea how amazing it is to make love to you. Condom or no condom. I just want to make you feel good, okay?"

She shouldn't trust him. He was a guy, and like all guys, sex came first, repercussions after. She knew she generalized, but her experience with men had sadly taught her this truth. Yet Foley was different. He looked at her and saw *her*, not just her breasts or her ass, though he seemed to like them well enough. He'd been so good with her nephews. A genuine caretaker, not a man out to make himself look good by pretending to like the boys.

Vinnie had *hugged him*. Alex had smiled at him.

Foley, a man she'd known not even two weeks, made her *want*. God, she'd claimed him as her boyfriend—a sexy, giving lover who treated her with respect while also letting her feel feminine. Desired.

She tugged him closer and kissed him, showing him how she felt. And he took it, kissing her back with a rawness, an honest passion, that held nothing back.

She broke from the kiss and whispered, "Turn around."

He froze. "You sure?"

"You want me to change my mind?"

He moved so fast she had to laugh. And then humor was the last thing on her mind when he delved between her legs to kiss her. He straddled her head, that thick cock swinging over her. Already he'd grown semihard again, his balls large, like the man. She moved her arm out from his knee and gripped his thick shaft, positioning him at her lips.

Tense, he stopped all movement, then started eating her in earnest when she tugged him down, so that his erection slid into her mouth.

He groaned as he drew her to another raging climax, all the while pumping into her mouth, growing more difficult to contain, so hard and thick.

They strained, thrusting and moaning together, a shared experience of lust and affection and conviction that pushed Cyn into another world of pleasure. Granted the ability to truly care for a man she found worthy, one she'd trust with the most intimate level of her health and well-being, was a turn-on like no other.

Foley petted and stroked her, giving as much pleasure as he received. Until Cyn couldn't bear any more. She sucked, drawing him into her mouth in deep pulls as she crested her orgasm, the rapture more than she could stand.

He followed, tensing and jetting down her throat while he continued to lick her into a shivery mess.

They lapped at each other until neither could move, done in by so much sensation.

Foley pulled away first and turned around, laying over her once more. Breathing hard, his lips slick, he stared down into her eyes and kissed her.

Then he rolled onto his back and took her with him. She felt his chest rise and fall, the beating of his heart beneath hers.

"Cyn. Baby." He hugged her, then kissed her cheek. "You broke me. I mean, down to nothing. I don't think I can move again. At all."

She smiled against his chest. "Me too."

He groaned. "I can feel those sexy breasts against me, and I can't chub up. I mean, I want to. But I am *done*."

"Again with all the love words."

He chuckled. "I'll give them to you. Just as soon as my brain starts working. Fuck me, but you have some serious skills."

She heard him yawn. Between one heartbeat and the next, he slipped into sleep. She trembled, caught between the heat of his body and the cold sweeping over her back. Without waking him, she found a blanket and returned to bed, covering them in it.

She watched him for a while, seeing the tender side of Foley while he slept. Still a formidable man, a generous lover and rough-and-tumble fighter, but he looked boyish in his peaceable dreams.

"What am I going to do with you?" she whispered and stroked his hair.

He mumbled in his sleep and turned toward her, hugging her close. And for the first time in eight months, she succumbed to temptation and slept in a man's arms. In her bed. Letting him inch piece by piece toward her heart.

When Cyn woke the next day, she found Foley staring down at her. "Morning."

He didn't speak.

She realized she no doubt had a bad case of bed head, in addition to dragon breath and a real need to pee. Darting out of bed and rushing to the bathroom in a hurry, she fixed her problems and returned to see him lying on his back, his hands linked behind his head as he stared at the ceiling.

"Good morning," she said again and slid into bed next to him, hoping he hadn't looked too hard at her in the light of day. She'd felt confident about herself last night, but this morning was a different story. Part of her, that ugly part she hated, wondered if he'd seen her true self and was disgusted that he'd succumbed to his libido. The realization that he'd once again slept with a fat chick couldn't be pleasant. He'd had to push past her thick, fleshy thighs last night to get to her sweet spot. Inside, she cringed.

"I wish I knew what you were thinking," he admitted.

To her consternation, the blanket over him grew tented.

She swallowed around a dry throat. "I guess I'm thinking my bed head and dragon breath hasn't put you off."

His slow grin worked its way past her insecurities. "Nah. I keep remembering you coming and sucking the life out of me. That's got me seriously excited to see you again."

He lunged for her and rolled her under him while she could do little more than shriek.

"God. You're fast."

He nuzzled her neck. "Maybe you should be more worried about *me* having dragon breath."

Before she could reply, he kissed her.

"You taste like toothpaste. Cheater."

"Damn right. No way I want you backing away from me after last night." He kissed her again. "I got up before you and cleaned up a little. Hope you don't mind I borrowed your toothpaste. Used my finger though. I swear I didn't get cooties on your toothbrush."

She made a face at him. "I didn't think that."

His expression softened. "Thank you, Cyn."

"For believing you didn't use my toothbrush?"

"For trusting me last night. It meant a lot to me." He had to be referring to their unprotected sixty-nine.

She blushed, which was stupid because she lay naked under him—also naked. "It meant a lot to me too."

He didn't smile, didn't make light of her confession or his. "I wish we didn't have family crap to deal with. I want to spend more time with you."

"Me too." She swallowed. "But maybe this is good. We're moving really fast." *At least, I am*.

He nodded. "I know. I don't usually go all out with a chick I just met. And you and I have only really been friendly for a week or so." He sighed and leaned his forehead against hers. "But I know you in so many ways. It's weird."

She was giddy to realize he felt it too. That it wasn't just her. "*You're* weird," she teased, trying to lighten the mood.

He pulled back. "Is that right?" He nudged the blanket wrapped around them out of the way.

Before she knew it, he angled between her thighs and pushed—right up into her.

"*Oh*." She gripped his biceps, watching as his smile faded and he moved in and out of her. Even strokes that didn't grow faster, even when her body tensed up and his breathing quickened.

"Come around me," he said between pants. "I'll pull out. I swear. But I want to feel you squeeze me when you come."

Stupid, irresponsible, dangerous… Yet she trusted

him, and she wanted to feel him in her this time when she rocked into sexual oblivion. She curled her legs around him and linked her ankles behind his back.

His face grew tortured, but he continued to move steadily, in and out of her. Then he ground against her pelvis and shoved hard, and she came, moaning his name.

He withdrew and pumped against her belly, leaving a mess while she shuddered, still awash in pleasure.

"No question," he said, breathless. "You're my early Christmas present from Santa."

She stroked his back and unlocked her ankles. "Yeah, what you just said." She cracked her jaw on a yawn. "And you once again wore me out. Just give me a few minutes…"

When she woke again, she found a note next to her on a pillow.

"Sorry I had to run, but I promised Sam I'd meet him for some last-minute shopping. Your present is on the table. Foley."

Not a "Love, Foley." Just "Foley."

She could live with that for now.

Then what she'd thought hit her, and she wanted to smack herself. She had a boyfriend. One she cared for, she admitted. Why did she have to try to mess up a good thing with the l-word and thoughts of permanence?

She—

Wait. He left me a present?

She cringed at the stickiness on her belly and hurried into the shower. But the hot water lulled her into spending more time there. When she'd finished and dressed, the time read ten o'clock.

After making herself some eggs and coffee, she circled

the small, prettily wrapped present on her dining table, wondering when he'd gotten her something. And why.

She felt bad that she had nothing for him, but their whirlwind romance had come on so suddenly. Nothing with Foley was a simple *wham bam, I'm done*. Every time with him had been fraught with feelings, emotional as well as sexual. To know he felt similarly affected…

She sighed. "Oh, Foley. You big goof. How am I falling so fast for you? Have I learned nothing from Jon? I'm not a stupid woman. Or am I?"

Cyn stared at the present for a good hour, mulling over when or if she should open it before Christmas.

Which was tomorrow.

Realizing how much she had to do before the big day, she hurried into her spare room, where a bunch of unwrapped presents awaited her attention. She also had a Christmas Eve dinner to prepare for. What the heck would she bring to Matt and Nina's?

As she planned and wrapped, she kept thinking about that present on her table.

Foley, that big lug, had gotten to her.

And she had no idea what to do about him.

Chapter 12

FOLEY WATCHED HIS MOTHER UNWRAP ANOTHER GIFT. This one a perfume she liked. Sam had bought it for her, and she exclaimed how much she loved it. Sam grinned.

Foley felt so incredibly relaxed and happy. He sipped his eggnog, wondering how life had gotten so good.

But then, good sex had that effect on a guy. Though he hadn't talked to Cyn since yesterday, except to respond to her Merry Christmas text this morning, he couldn't stop thinking about her.

The woman had taken him into her body. Into her mouth. She'd swallowed him down. They'd been skin to skin. Man, that was some serious commitment on her part, he knew. And it meant the world to him.

He sighed and finished off the sweet drink, watching as Sam picked up the present Foley had bought for him.

Every Christmas, as was tradition, they slept over at his mother's house, then had a casual breakfast and opened presents under her tree. Foley and Sam wore the pajamas she'd given them last night. Another tradition of opening one early Christmas gift, started because Eileen didn't tolerate boxer shorts or holey underwear—not the religious kind, he thought with a grin—when taking pictures of opening gifts.

He'd already opened his stuff from Sam. A *Darts for Dummies* book, which secretly Foley planned to put to good use, and a brew kit to make his own beer. Just what he'd been dying to try. Trust Sam to be thoughtful in between being an ass. Man, he loved the guy.

"Hmm. Feels heavy." Sam grinned at Foley.

"It's a book for your big fat head."

"Foley." Eileen tried not to smile. "Be nice. It's Christmas."

"Mom, that was nice. I could have said for his fat fucking head. But I didn't."

"Good to know." She sighed.

Sam and Foley laughed, and Sam opened up a gift that had been on his wish list for a long time. He marveled at the metal die cast of his dream car, a 1967 L88 Corvette, which had cost a pretty penny. "Damn, Foley. You even got the colors right." Red with black interior.

"Not that hard to figure out. You've had the poster for the car since we were kids. And that picture on your chest is telling, dumbass."

Sam smiled, and his joy gave Foley a full feeling, the good kind from eating fine food with people you love. Sam had never enjoyed the holiday season until Foley and Eileen had shown him what it meant to be a part of a real family. Even when Sam got bogged down with life, dealing with his bitch of a mother or issues of unworthiness and anger, Christmas normally brought out the happy kid in him, the one Foley and his mom had worked so hard to make shine.

"Yeah, well, I would have gotten you your favorite gift, but I thought the darts and beer would be better. And I figured you don't need a blowup doll now that you have your own girlfriend."

Foley chuckled. "You're an ass, you know that? Hey, Mom, did Santa put coal in Sam's stocking or what?"

"Hmm. I'm thinking he probably put it in both your stockings." She tugged at his ear, and Foley yelped. "Holding back on me, hmm? What's this about a girlfriend?"

"It's Christmas. No badgering on Christmas," Foley pleaded. "At least not until we've had your homemade cinnamon rolls."

Eileen stared at him, then sighed. "Fine. But I'm going to get you to talk, boy. See if I don't."

"Love you, Mom." Foley smiled at his mother while giving Sam the finger.

Sam laughed. "Yeah, Eileen. I love you, too."

She rose and smiled. "This is what the holidays are for. Spending time with the people you love." As she puttered in the kitchen, she said, "Oh, and tomorrow? Be here at two. We're going to brunch with Jacob and his family."

Foley and Sam looked at each other.

"What's that?" Foley asked and stood, in search of caffeine. She hadn't added that part about Jacob's family, had she? Dealing with Jacob would be bad enough.

"You heard me. Now, I didn't bring Jacob here for Christmas, even though I wanted to share our happiness with him. Because this is our time—for you, me, and Sam."

Sam grunted his approval.

"But Jacob means something to me. I want you two to get to know him. So tomorrow, both of you dress nice. Sam Hamilton, don't you even *think* of scrubbing down."

"Come on, Eileen." Sam paused, then sang in tune, "*Come on, Eileen.*"

Foley tried not to smile at the reference to a popular song his mother loathed.

"And, Foley," she continued on a tear, ignoring Sam, "I want you being nice to Jacob. No death glares or threatening looks."

"Hey, I'm the nice one. Blame Sam for that."

"I don't think so. He follows your lead. Always has."

Sam didn't argue. "That's true. I do."

"Ass."

"This is important to me." She turned to look both of them in the eye. "I want you to like him, and I know you will if you give him a chance."

Foley couldn't resist her hopeful expression. "I'll try, but no promises. If he's a jerk and he's not good enough for you, he's gone."

"That's fair. Just remember, your girlfriend has to jump through my hoops too."

"And mine," Sam added.

"And Sam's. So you might want to keep that in mind while you're running Jacob through the gauntlet."

She had him there. "No problem. Cyn can hold her own."

"So can Jacob."

Oh, it was on. "Merry Christmas," Foley said with forced cheer.

His mother gave him her best insincere smile. "Ho, ho, ho, my little elf. I can't *wait* to meet your lady friend."

Sam stared at the two of them and shook his head. "Love is for suckers."

Eileen stared at him for a moment in silence then chuckled. "Oh, honey. You know what you just did?" She turned to Foley. "When they say it and they mean it, that's when it happens."

Foley agreed. "Sam, you just signed your own relationship warrant. You are now officially doomed to find yourself committed." Just as he'd been blindsided by an angry redhead in heels after thinking no way in hell would he ever have what Liam, Del, or Johnny had.

"Huh?" Sam blinked, baffled.

"Don't worry, buddy. You have your looks. Brains aren't a requirement."

"What are you talking about?"

"Hell if I know." Foley was dying for a cinnamon roll. Something sweet to remind him of Cyn. "I'm just a sucker."

Cyn sat in a comfortable pair of jeans and her favorite sweatshirt, one of Matt's old castoffs that was worn, soft, and huge on her. So nice to not worry about clingy fabric or looking perfect as she sat with her family at her parents' house Christmas afternoon.

Having attended Mass earlier that morning, they'd returned home and eaten a big brunch, enough to tide them over until dinner.

She'd spent her time glued to Nina's side and eaten whatever the heck she wanted. She'd ignored her mother's frowns, and fortunately, Ella said nothing about Cyn's consumption of sweets and all things bad for her.

Alex and Vinnie bolstered her good cheer, asking a dozen questions about Foley, wanting to see him again.

"I swear, I'm still shocked that they liked him so much." Cyn shook her head while the boys played with their new electronic gadgets. "I mean, *I* like him. But Vinnie can be a tough one."

"That's because Matt coached him to be mean to your boyfriends," Nina explained. "Only the ones who can tolerate bratty nephews are worth keeping."

Jonathon, her ex, had taken to Alex more than Vinnie. But he'd been patient enough, and over time, Vinnie had warmed to him. But both boys had taken to Foley right away.

Matt joined them on the couch, having left his father in the kitchen with his mother. "What are we watching?"

"*Miracle on 34th Street,*" Cyn answered. "I love this movie."

"We were just talking about how much the boys like Foley," Nina told him.

Matt frowned, physically picked up his wife and moved her over, so he could sit between Cyn and Nina.

"Hey." Nina huffed. "All you had to do was ask."

"But then I'd have no cxcuse to put my hands on my delectable wife." He wiggled his brows like a lecher.

"Ew. There isn't going to be any kissing here, is there?" Cyn teased, sounding a lot like her nephews.

Matt kissed his wife then shoved Cyn back by her forehead. "Kiss that, twerp."

"Cut it out or I'll take all your presents back." She'd gotten him a baseball cap with his favorite basketball team's logo on it, a matching team jersey, and a real girlie calendar, one *without* grandmothers wearing Christmas sweaters.

"I'm sorry, I swear."

Nina gave a mock growl. "I can't believe you bought my husband a nudie calendar."

Vinnie looked up from his phone, and his eyes grew wide.

"It's a joke, Vinnie. No boobs for you."

He flushed. "Not funny, Aunt Cyn." Then he left the room.

Alex followed, still playing his game and tripping along the hallway.

"Speaking of boobs…" Matt paused. "I know what happened with Foley and Vinnie."

Cyn sat back and, not seeing her mother, put her feet on the coffee table. "Now what are you talking about?"

"It didn't make sense to me that nothing happened on your date with the boys. They never like anyone new, and especially not your boyfriends."

"You act like there have been so many." Cyn frowned.

"Yeah. We all know she's perpetually dateless," Nina offered with a grin.

"Don't help, Nina."

Matt sat with a weird look on his face.

Cyn sobered. "Well?"

He glanced around. Not spotting his parents or the boys, answered, "Apparently Vinnie had a run-in with Jim Nelson, that jerky kid on the basketball team who has disciplinary issues at school."

"Wait. When was this?"

"When you were at the movies."

Cyn had thought Vinnie had been an awful long time in the bathroom. "I *knew* it. He and Foley were gone a little too long." Foley, that liar. Wait until she had a word with him about keeping things from her.

"What happened?" Nina asked her husband. "Man, you take forever to tell a story."

"He does," Cyn agreed.

Matt scowled. "Shut up. Not you, honey. You, Cyn."

"Because he knows I'll make him pay later," Nina said.

Cyn rolled her eyes. "Still not hearing the story."

"Apparently Foley found Jim picking on Vinnie outside the bathroom. Then Jim's father joined him and got a little aggressive."

"*What?*" Nina's eyes grew round. "A grown man picking on my son? Let's go kick his ass. Christmas or no Christmas, no one messes with my boy but me."

"Simmer down, She-Hulk." To her brother, Cyn asked, "What did Foley do, exactly?"

"Your badass boyfriend jacked the elder Nelson up against the wall and nearly broke his arm. Then he made Jim and his dad apologize and swear to leave Vinnie alone. Vinnie didn't catch what Foley said to the kid's dad, but whatever it was had the dad nearly running from the theater. Vinnie said it was awesome. Foley looked like a prison escapee on a rampage. Vin's words, not mine."

Nina sighed. "I love Foley. If you won't marry him, I will."

"Ahem. Bigamy is illegal in Washington," Matt reminded his wife.

"Only if you get caught."

Cyn wasn't hearing them. She remembered Foley joking about illegal doings and prison with her mom. What if he'd been serious? What did she really know about him, anyway?

He kissed like he had all the time in the world. He was protective of those he cared for. He had no problem jacking up a guy threatening her nephew, and he hadn't bragged about it. He was honest—that she knew—and he seemed to be really into her.

He'd given her a present, and it sat on her dining table at home, burning a hole through her brain.

"So are you going to marry him?" Nina asked again.

Cyn blinked and saw her sister-in-law and brother staring at her. "Seriously? We just met."

"But we know and like him." Nina pinched Matt. "Don't we?"

"Ow. Stop abusing me, bigamist wannabe." Matt rubbed his side. "I like what I know of him. I have to admit, the way he dealt with Nelson has me wanting to give him a medal. Not sure if I like Vinnie thinking violence is the solution to his problems, though." Matt frowned.

"Want me to talk to Foley?" Cyn planned to talk to him regardless.

Matt shook his head. "No. I wasn't supposed to say anything. Besides, Jim pushed Vinnie around a few times. Then the dad laid a hand on him."

Nina tensed. "*What?*"

"That's when Foley about broke his arm," Matt explained. "So I guess violence was justified."

"You're damn right it was."

Cyn imagined she could see smoke steaming from Nina's nose. "Ah, you might want to relax, Nina. Foley handled it. Vinnie's fine. And it's Christmas."

"Peace on Earth, yeah yeah." Nina blew out a breath. "That Nelson is so lucky Foley dealt with him and not me. I'd have gone for his balls."

Matt winced. "My Nina does *not* play around."

Cyn laughed. "At work she scares teenagers and grown men and women alike."

"Why do you think I do most of my work at home?"

"Funny guy, aren't you? Say what you want, but Foley

is my new hero." Nina sighed, saw Matt's arched brows, and amended, "Aside from you, of course, my darling."

Matt shook his head. "Whatever. Can we please watch the movie?"

"You started it, but fine."

A dreaded voice interrupted. "Feet off the table, young lady."

Damn. Snagged by her mother.

Cyn spent the next two hours with family, laughing as they played board games and ate dinner. Fun continued as the day wore on. But she knew she wouldn't be able to avoid it forever. She found herself helping her mother with the dishes while everyone else played another game.

The day had gone surprisingly well. Once again Cyn felt conflicted about her mother. Ella had gone above and beyond with her gifts this year, buying Cyn a pricey painting she'd had her eye on since attending a gallery opening months ago with her parents.

Times like these made it difficult to remember why she hated being alone with her mom. Ella had been fun, sweet, and giving all day. Cyn's dad had beamed, proclaimed himself the luckiest man on the planet, and bragged about having the best wife in the world.

A full day of family happiness in a world where couples divorced every minute of every day. She knew she was fortunate to have parents who loved each other and their children and did their best to support one another.

Hell, her mother had even gone all in on the charity she and her friends supported, donating time and baking for a shelter downtown. She'd spent her Christmas Eve at the soup kitchen, alongside her husband, serving those less fortunate.

Cyn looked at her mom while drying the dishes. Her mother did look older, but when she smiled, she had a beauty all her own. "I love you, Mom."

Ella smiled back. "I love you too, sweetie. You're such a good girl. I'm lucky to have you."

Cyn felt warm inside.

Her mother continued to wash dishes in silence, then said, "I'm sorry about the other day. I didn't mean to offend you or your...boyfriend." That came out stilted, but Ella seemed sincere.

All of a sudden, Cyn felt guilty for having taken joy in irritating her mother. "Well, I'm sorry for teasing you. Foley was just being funny. He didn't mean to upset you either."

"It's just... I want you to be happy. Matt and Nina, the boys, they make a family."

"Nina's great." Matt had certainly gotten lucky with her.

"I want you to find someone just as special. You're such a pretty girl." Her mother lifted a soapy hand and wiped a bubble on Cyn's nose. "If I ride you about your size, it's only because I want everyone to see what I see underneath. You know that." Ella's eyes looked teary, and Cyn felt awful, both because her mom loved her and because her mom still couldn't see beyond her size.

"Mom, don't cry."

"I'm sorry." Ella sniffed. "I just love you so much, and you have so much untapped potential."

Cyn's eyes watered too, both from seeing her mother sad and from the fact that her mother still considered her inferior. "Mom—"

"That Foley. He's handsome enough. Too handsome for you. You can't trust the good-looking ones."

"Oh? What about Jonathan?"

"He was smart, dear. He liked you for your intellect. But Foley. What can he see in you?"

"Maybe that I'm special?" she dared say out loud.

Her mother talked over her. "That mean glint in his eye. And that talk about prison… I don't know. I don't trust him. And I sure don't trust him with my vulnerable girl. A little bit of attention, and he's in your bed. Oh, Cynthia. You always do give way too easily."

Great. Now I'm an ugly, stupid whore. Cyn bit her lip and tried to stay positive. "I'm sure he was teasing, Mom."

"A man like that gets looked at and flirted with by a lot of pretty girls. I hope you're being careful with sex. You could pick up all kinds of nasty diseases."

"*Mom.*" Cyn drew in a breath and let it out slowly. "Foley is a good man. Despite what you apparently think about me, I'm not a cheap date. A handsome man who pays attention to me does not automatically get invited to sleep with me." She focused on Foley. "I like Foley. A lot. He respects me."

"Is that so?" Her mother snorted. "Then maybe when I gently hint that you shouldn't have another cookie, you should listen. If you want to hold onto this Foley, you'll need to work at it. Think about it. You were with Jon for two years, and he still left in the end."

"Because I told him to go."

"Really? I remember your tears after the breakup. He tried to make it work, but you wouldn't listen."

Because he'd badgered her for weeks to lose more weight and "stop eating like a pig." Back when she'd been twenty pounds *lighter*. He'd also had the nerve to insist she put her career on hold while they supported *his* rise toward corporate stardom. The jackass needed a skinny trophy wife who stayed at home to take care of his needs. Not a businesswoman with sense and a larger-than-normal dress size. "God, Mom. Can we not talk about this today? It's Christmas."

"I'm trying to help you. Lose a few pounds. Give Tony a call. Lose Foley, sweetie. He's no good for you. He'll only break your heart when someone better comes along."

As though Cyn wasn't and would never be good enough.

Cyn just stared at her mother, wondering how the woman could say and mean the things she did and not realize her daughter would be hurt by them.

Ella sighed. "I always sound terrible. I know I do." She wiped a tear. "But I mean well. You're a good girl, sweetie. I want the best for you. You might not see it, because you've been dealing with weight issues your whole life. Just like Aunt Sharon. I loved her so much, but she was lonely. I get scared when I think of you like that, and I can't imagine losing you too."

Her mother cried and hugged Cyn.

Cyn didn't know what to do, so she hugged her mother back, trying to comfort her while half wishing she'd never moved back to Seattle. "Mom, it's okay. I'm not Aunt Sharon." *Who killed herself twenty years ago. I miss her, but can we please let this go?* "I'm fine and I'm happy. My life is good."

"I'm sorry for worrying. You're a smart girl. I only wish all men were as good as your father and brother.

Jon was, but, well, he's not here, is he?" Ella sighed, patted Cyn on the shoulder, and stepped back. "I'm sorry. Ignore me, Cynthia. You and Foley will be just fine. You trust him, and I'm sure he's attentive to you even when other women are around. Skinnier, prettier girls won't matter in the long run. Not if he's in love."

Cyn and Foley were new. She hadn't been out with him enough to know if he'd flirt with other women in her presence, or how he'd behave if some *skinnier, prettier girl* hit on him while she was there.

On her own, Cyn had looks and grace. But standing next to someone like Nina, she couldn't compare. Her belly to no belly. Thick thighs to toned thighs. Even her face looked fuller than it should, no doubt thanks to all those gingerbread men she'd devoured in the last few days.

Stupid Christmas season. And *whamo*. Ella had struck again. Holiday ruined.

"Let's stop all this foolish talk." Her mother shoved her hands back in the soapy water and finished the remaining dishes. "Today is a day for fun and celebration. How about if I promise that the next time I sit with you and Foley, I'll behave and apologize for being so mean to the poor young man?"

"Great." Cyn tried to put on a cheery face, but she couldn't help wondering. How long could the newness of sexual attraction last before Foley's eye wandered? Would he eventually turn into Jon, wanting her to be something she wasn't?

The rest of the evening passed in a blur until Cyn finally found herself at home with a glass of wine, staring into a blazing fire. She wondered what Foley was up to, and if he thought about her at all.

She stared at the gaily wrapped present in front of her, half afraid to open it.

"Screw it."

Refusing to let her mother get to her, she put down her glass and reached for the present, charmed at the uneven taping and wrinkles in the paper. Something to make her smile again after her hellish evening with Ella.

The package was too large to be jewelry—thank goodness—but too small to be anything she recognized. Not a piece of clothing, for sure. After unwrapping it and discarding the bow, she opened the box.

Inside, she found a small booklet of coupons, each of which had been handwritten by Foley. She had her option of bowling, a striptease, flowers and chocolates, a movie night, and several other activities that made her blush just reading them. A tiny framed picture of a smiling Foley had also been included, which made her laugh. The sticky note attached to the back of it read: "Now I'm always with you, lucky girl."

Last, she found a gift card to an expensive chocolate shop in Queen Anne she liked to drool over. A sticky note had been attached to it as well.

"Something sweet for my sweet. Yeah, clichéd." Which he'd spelled wrong. "But I like your vices. Yes to chocolate, no to other men." This time he'd signed it. *Yours, Foley.*

She felt shivery, excited, and laughed.

Her mother's words faded as if they'd never existed.

Foley liked Cyn for herself. He didn't want her to be someone different.

Not yet at least.

She'd treasure their time together, so that when it

ended, she'd have good memories. Unlike her relationship with Jon, she knew to hold a piece of herself back, so when they ended, she'd rebound faster and easier. She had to be cautious with this one, because Foley, unlike the others, had gotten close so quickly. Just by being himself.

A danger, a thrill, and a perverse way to torture herself all in one.

"My own Christmas present from hell. Foley Sanders." She sighed and drank more wine, holding her picture of Foley close. She fell asleep with it against her heart.

Chapter 13

FOLEY SAT WITH SAM, EILEEN, JACOB, AND THE REST OF Jacob's family in a big-ass house on Bainbridge Island. The guy had money coming out the ass, and he lived a ferry ride from Eileen.

A good thing—the guy wasn't so close he'd be underfoot all the time. A bad thing—Eileen would have an excuse to spend the night if she "lost track of time" while out with the guy.

"So, Foley, Eileen tells me you and Sam are mechanics." Jacob smiled.

Dr. Jacob Wynn, DDS, had straight white teeth, blue eyes behind designer frames, and an all-around terrific smile. He also had a spankin' house, a nice family, and damn it, the dude had manners—his mother's kryptonite. The guy could have three wives and a closet full of dead bodies, but as long as he said "please" before knifing her, she'd allow it.

Sam nudged him.

"Oh, er, yeah. I work with Sam at Webster's Garage on Rainier."

"How long have you been doing that?"

Foley glanced at his mother, who gave him a look that told him to behave. *Thirty-three friggin' years old, and still threatened by a woman less than half my size. Pathetic.* "Since I got out of—"

"High school," Eileen interrupted with a smile. "My boys have always been mechanically inclined."

He and Sam shared a glance. So. She'd changed her mind about full disclosure to the new guy. She didn't want any mention of their prison sentence. Interesting.

She hadn't told him or Sam to hide the fact that they'd done time. Not that they ever brought it up in casual conversation. But she sure hadn't let him mention it now.

Foley wasn't sure he liked this Jacob Wynn.

His mother seemed different about this one. She'd dated before, but she hadn't kept anyone a secret. And from what he recalled, she'd never dated a guy with money.

Ah well, what the hell? If she wanted to bang a rich dude, who was he to judge? He wanted Cyn for her body and her mind. Mostly her body. Nah, her mind turned him on just as much.

He smiled at the thought.

"You two are lucky," Jacob was saying. He had salt-and-pepper hair, a decent enough physique, though Foley thought he could break the guy's back without too much trouble, and a nice wardrobe. He wore slacks. At home. For brunch.

"I can change my oil and my own brake pads," Noel, his son-in-law, added with a self-deprecating smile. He was about Foley's age and had a techie vibe. "But that's about it."

Foley liked him and the daughter, Jan. "Yeah, well, I can fix a car, but I can't fix a computer."

Noel grinned. "Microsoft is my game. Coding is my name."

"Please. Not in public." Jan grimaced.

Her father and Eileen laughed. Foley couldn't help a grin, and even Sam gave a half smirk at Noel's red face.

Uh-oh. I'm going to get it tonight," Jan teased, looking every glowing inch of a pregnant woman. Her tiny baby bump did little to detract from her prettiness. It enhanced it.

"Yeah, no foot rub for you, brat." Noel squeezed her knee, and she jumped. "Ha. I know all your tickle spots. Behave."

The cuteness was a bit sickening, but the pair seemed to care for each other, and they'd been supernice to his mom. Not fake-nice either, but genuine.

Sam stood and asked for directions to the bathroom. Jacob showed him the way, disappearing down the hall with Sam behind him.

"Is Sam okay?" Jan asked after Sam had gone.

Eileen nodded. "Don't mind him. For Sam, that's his happy face."

"Oh." Jan looked at Foley. "No offense, but you guys look like you could rip my car doors off if you wanted to."

Foley grinned. "Depends on the make and model of your car."

Noel laughed. "Don't ask her. She's clueless."

"Hey. I know where to put my key and how to shift into drive."

"That's really all you need," Eileen agreed. "When you need a tire changed or something fixed, you take your car to the dealer."

"Mom." Foley groaned. "What have I said about the dealer?"

"I know. A rip-off. Sorry, honey. I mean to a garage."

"Thanks."

Jacob returned. "I don't mind saying I wouldn't want

to make Sam mad. I turned around and realized he's a good head and a half taller than I am."

"Yeah? Well he's not too big for me to pop in the tush if he gets mouthy." Eileen grinned.

Tush? The real Eileen would have said *ass*. Why was she cleaning up her language for slick dental guy?

Foley wanted to find fault in the man, but damned if he could. Since arriving for their brunch half an hour ago, Jacob had been polite, witty, and sweet to Eileen.

Foley liked the guy as a casual hookup for his mom. But as something more important in her life? That didn't sit well.

Which made him feel weird, because ever since Foley could remember, he'd been the man in Eileen Sanders's life. He didn't know how to deal with the presence of Jacob Wynn. Because Eileen seemed attached to Jacob since they'd arrived, treating Sam and Foley to maternal smiles and a slight distance Foley understood as a warning. To behave, and to allow some other guy to take over.

Take over what, numbnuts? He's just dating your mom. No biggie.

Man, he was dying to talk to Cyn again. What would she make of the situation? And more pressing, did she like her Christmas gift?

Sam returned, and Jacob ushered them all into his posh dining room, where the table had been set for royalty.

"Holy shit. Are we expecting the queen?" Sam muttered.

Jan must have heard him, because she snickered.

"What?" Noel asked.

"Nothing." She winked at Sam, who gave her an actual grin.

Everyone sat at the large round table, decked out

with a red tablecloth, a matching floral centerpiece done in Christmas colors in a cool-looking vase, cloth napkins, silver napkin *rings*, and friggin' porcelain dinner plates with crystal glassware. Eileen and Jan sat on either side of Jacob. Sam sat next to Eileen, with Foley next to him and a lot of space before he could reach Noel. Damn. The table could easily accommodate a good nine or ten guests.

Above them a crystal chandelier gave off a subtle glow. Jacob's house looked like it had been decorated by an interior decorator. Greenery and red ribbons wound around the wood staircase and grand mantel in the living room. He had antiquey furniture that Foley feared breaking if he sat too fast, so he'd been careful where he planted his ass.

Foley heard sounds from the kitchen and frowned. "Someone else is here?"

Jacob nodded. "I'm having the meal catered. Don't think I do this all the time, but I wanted to impress Eileen's boys—her word, not mine."

Sam nodded. "I'm impressed."

Foley was too. "So you have a lot of money."

"Foley." Eileen gasped.

"What? He's got a big house, has his private dock out back—I saw the boat. And he's having brunch catered." To Jacob, he said, "Am I wrong thinking you're loaded?"

Next to him, Sam tried not to laugh and coughed to cover up.

Foley glanced over at Jan and Noel, who stared at him in surprise.

"I'm sorry. Is this a big secret?" Now he felt stupid and gauche—the word a writer friend of Del's had flashed around the garage a time or two while researching some book of hers.

Jacob took a long sip of water from a fancy crystal glass that probably cost more than Foley's electric bill. "Not a secret any longer, apparently." Jacob laughed, and Eileen relaxed, though she shot Foley a hard look.

"What?" He shrugged. "I'm just saying it's a good thing. I don't want a guy after my mom for her money. She's not exactly poor."

"Foley Sanders. Behave," Eileen admonished.

Foley took a sip of his water, not surprised to find it crisp, cold, and delicious. It took a lot to refrain from drinking with his pinkie out, as if one of the Richie Riches.

"I'm not trying to be rude. I'm just saying—"

"He's saying you're okay, Jacob," Sam interrupted. "That's what he's saying."

"Yeah, that's all." Foley put down his glass. "See, my mom is too nice. The last few guys she dated hit her up for rent money. So we hit them up for a repayment of the 'loan' later."

His mom slapped a hand over her eyes and prayed for strength.

"I meant hit up as in talked to them. I didn't actually hit them," Foley explained.

Noel and Jan continued to stare at him, open-mouthed. Even Jacob watched him with caution.

"He's not lying," Sam said, backing him up. And Foley wasn't. He'd told her exes to pay up while *Sam* had pounded some sense into them.

"Right. I'm not." Foley took his napkin and placed it over his lap, the way his mom had. "So what's for brunch? I'm starved."

His mother groaned, and Noel and Jan laughed.

Jan raised a glass to him. "You know, Dad told us to be on our best behavior, but if you can ask about money, can we ask about all the tattoos? Are you guys gang-bangers or what?"

"*Jan.*" Jacob turned red.

"I like her," Sam said. At Noel's frown, Sam added, "But not that much. Sorry, dude, not into other guys' pregnant wives."

"Good."

Foley turned to Sam. "Man, that was tacky."

"And asking about money wasn't?" Sam snorted. "No wonder Cyn turned you down the first time you asked her out. You're a mess in social situations."

"*Me?*" Foley couldn't believe Sam had the nerve to say that. "I'm not the one hitting on a hot pregnant chick who's married."

Jan blushed.

"You are hot," Noel agreed.

"She is," Sam said. "But I wasn't hitting on her. I like her honesty. Too many rich assholes are just that, assholes. I'm not thinking Eileen's dentist is a dick either."

Jacob gave a weak, "Thanks."

"Where's that mimosa you promised?" Eileen asked Jacob, sounding desperate.

"Coming right up." Jacob escaped to the kitchen and returned moments later with a waiter bearing drinks. "Please. Make sure those two get plenty." He nodded at Sam and Foley.

"Told you I liked him." Sam nodded at Jacob. "Now about the tats, we got them after a few rough years after high school. But no naked ladies. Eileen frowned on that." He rolled up his sleeves and showed off his arms. Then he nodded to Foley to do the same.

When Jacob leaned closer to get a look, Eileen sighed. "You can clean 'em up, but you can't take 'em out."

Jacob glanced at his daughter and nodded. "I know."

———ww———

Forty-five minutes later, Jan giggled at something Noel said, though she'd been drinking straight-up orange juice, minus the champagne.

"So when are you due, sweetie?" Eileen asked her.

"End of March. We're so excited." She and Noel held hands on top of the table.

Foley sat back, stuffed on a scrambled-egg-and-lobster dish, shrimp cocktail, some weird pâté, and a hash mix that had been amazing. The truffles—mushrooms for the rich as opposed to the prepackaged veggies at the grocery store—had tasted surprisingly good, considering he didn't normally like mushrooms on his pizza or otherwise. And the booze with breakfast only added to the good times.

His mom had finally relaxed, smiling and joking, so she'd apparently forgiven him for being rude. Sue him. Best to get out the issues from the get-go. He didn't want the guy soaking up his mom's money or taking advantage of her. Did that make him a bad guy? Hell no. It made him a concerned son.

His phone buzzed, and his heart raced. "Ah, I'll be right back." He left the table for the bathroom. Jesus, could the guy make do with just a toilet and sink? But no. The bathroom was the size of Foley's kitchen. The toilet was one of those eco-friendly types that practically wiped your own ass when you finished. The sink was large and modern and had a faucet stuck out of the wall. The artsy mirror and funky lights highlighted the expensive-looking tile on the floors and the backsplash of the sink.

And, because you never knew when you might want to hang out by a toilet, a plush chair and side table occupied the sidewall, over which a painting stood watch.

Foley took out his phone to take a picture of the place to share with the guys. Then he sat in the chair and read his text. A note from Del: Be back on Monday. U better not have f'd up the garage. Merry Xmas.

Though disappointed the text hadn't been from Cyn, he nevertheless had to smile. He'd missed Del and Liam. The garage felt better with the Websters in it. And Jekyll, he thought, liking when she brought the growing puppy with her because it made Sam more manageable. Plus it was damn cute.

He sent Cyn a picture of the bathroom and a text, unable to wait for her to send one first. In rich guys hous w/ mom & sam, makng stupid talk & geting in truble. What up with u?

He took advantage of his location and used the bathroom, startled when the damn toilet flushed itself before he could, then washed his hands with some foofy-smelling soap. The towel he used to dry his hands felt like silk. *Of course it does, because everything in Jacob's house is expensive, tasteful, and cool.*

Knowing he couldn't wait forever for Cyn to text back, he moved to the door.

The phone vibrated.

To his pleased surprise, she texted back. Wow. Nice

toilet. LOL I remember how bad you are at being tactful. Be nice. Have your mom's back. Can't wait to see you again.

PS. LOVE the present. When can I use my coupons?

He grinned, his good mood restored, and tucked his phone away. Then he left the bathroom and found the gathering still in full swing.

"So I knew at a young age Foley would be a handful."

As he sat, he noted the amused looks on everyone's faces. Sam in particular wore a wicked smile.

"Oh boy. What's she been saying?"

Jacob swallowed a laugh. "Just that I should be careful or you might egg my house, toilet paper my trees, and misspell a bunch of curse words all over my car in neon purple soap."

"Mom." Foley flushed. "Spelling was never my strong suit."

"Seriously. He sucks."

"Sam."

Jan speared a strawberry off her husband's plate. "Don't worry about it. That's what your wife will be for. I married Noel so he'd fix my computers. I'm terrible with them. But he can't even boil an egg, so I cook. We're even."

Noel scratched his head. "I think I'm ahead. I work the computers, the car, the bills, the TV remote. Hmm. What else?"

"Well I grocery shop, buy your clothes, iron your pants, your shirts, I—"

"We get the picture," Jacob interrupted. "It's no big deal to be good at some things but not others."

"Yeah? So what are you not good at that my mom is?" Foley asked. "And keep it clean. There's a kid in the room." He nodded at Jan's stomach.

His mom blushed. "Foley, you are in so much trouble when we get home."

"Where have I heard that before?" He sighed, and the others laughed.

Jacob seemed to take the question seriously. His eyes sparkled behind his trendy glasses, which made him look smart and no doubt added to his appeal. "I'm not great at being spontaneous, but your mom is an expert at that." She blushed, and he continued, "I'm not the best when dealing with people outside of work. I can cook, but I don't like to. And it's been said I'm a little too uncomfortable with confrontation." Jacob paused and looked into Eileen's eyes.

He took her hand in his on the table.

"But your mother, Foley, has energy to spare. She can pull me out of a bad mood with a smile. She's amazing when it comes to handling people. A social expert, in my opinion."

"Oh, now you're flattering me." Eileen had her heart in her voice.

"Just speaking the truth," Jacob said. "She's an amazing cook, and she's terrific when it comes to diffusing tense situations."

"What does that mean?" Foley asked, confused.

"Just the other day she came to visit me at work when an alarmed patient had a tantrum about her insurance coverage. Now we have nothing to do with that, but my elderly patient wouldn't even let us try to help before she started yelling about being ripped off and taken advantage of. Before my assistants could step in, your mother calmed her down and had the older lady laughing at something, when moments ago she'd been screaming. Your mother is magic in more ways than one."

Then he leaned over and kissed Eileen on the lips. *Bam*.

Foley watched in shock as his mom kissed Jacob back.

Jan and Noel were grinning like fools, but Foley didn't know what to think. He knew his mother and Jacob were close. Obviously they would kiss and hold hands and cuddle. He knew this. But seeing it shook him, which made little sense.

Even worse, he could tell Jacob meant everything he'd said. The guy had the hots for Eileen big time. He sounded like a moron in love.

Sam turned and looked at Foley. He raised a brow but said nothing.

"Oh, Jacob. You're so sweet," she gushed. Then she turned back to Foley. "I wanted to let you know that I'll be staying here through New Year's. Jacob and I have a few parties to go to."

"Nice." Noel smiled. "Jan and I will be having a party too, in Fremont, if anyone would like to come."

Decent of him to extend the invite, but no way in hell Foley wanted to bring in the New Year with a tame crowd like the one in front of him.

He knew Sam felt the same, so he wasn't surprised when Sam declined. "Thanks, but we already have plans."

"Well then." Eileen turned to Foley. "Get out."

"Huh?"

"Eileen," Jacob sputtered.

She chuckled. "Relax, Jacob. The boy likes me to speak plainly." She turned back to Foley. "Brunch is over, and we all survived. Now you can go."

Thank God. He and Sam stood without being asked a third time.

"Thanks for the food. It was great." Sam nodded and shook hands with everyone. "Good luck on the kid," he said to Jan.

She gave him a peck on the cheek, and Sam turned red. "Thanks, Sam."

"Hey." Noel gave a mock frown, then ruined it by smiling. "You ever have computer problems, give me a call. Eileen has my number."

"Sure. You need your car fixed, call Webster's."

"Will do." Noel put a hand on his wife's shoulder, but he didn't seem possessive or upset. Just affectionate. He was confident in her love and care, so he didn't need to behave like an ass. Kind of the way Jacob was with Eileen. Smooth, loving. Not trying too hard to impress Foley by acting all big and bad.

Foley wished the guy would have been an asshole. But no, he had no reason to be upset with his mom's notion to shack up with the guy through the New Year. He walked over to Jacob and shook his hand, secretly reveling in how much bigger he was than the dentist. Oh yeah. This guy fucked over Eileen, Foley would tear him apart.

"Thanks, Jacob. For everything. Keep treating my mom right," he warned.

"Foley." Eileen grabbed him by the hand.

Jacob didn't seem to mind. He met Foley's stare, no hint of malice or fear in his gaze. "Your mom is lucky to have you. And you don't need to worry. I'll take good care of Eileen. If I don't, I'm pretty sure she'll kick my butt right into the Sound."

Foley laughed at that. He released Jacob's hand and patted the guy on the back. "You're okay, Jacob." He said good-bye to Noel and Jan, then let his mom lead him and Sam to his SUV.

"Sam was a stellar example of behavior today." Eileen kissed him on the cheek and, smart guy that he was, Sam hurried to get inside the vehicle and shut the door, leaving on a good note. "But you…" She smacked Foley on the back of the head.

"*Ow*. Damn it."

"What is *wrong* with you? Didn't I tell you to be nice?"

He glanced down at himself. "I wore my best clothes." Clean jeans and a nice sweater he broke out only on special occasions. "I didn't swear too much."

She just watched him, her gray eyes narrowed.

"Sorry, okay?" he blurted. "The guy is nice, and you like him a lot. I just wanted to make sure he'd be good to you. I love you, Mom."

She softened and kissed him on the cheek. "I love you too, you bonehead. Jacob is okay, sweetie. Really. If he wasn't, I would kick his ass." And she wondered where he got his mouth.

"Yeah. I get that. But he's rich." He didn't like that so much. Sure the guy wasn't using his mom for her money, but if he turned into a total jackoff, he could prove a real problem hiding behind his wallet. Foley knew the type. Like Lara's ex-brother-in-law. Johnny's girlfriend had been through hell because of that rich prick.

"He's comfortable, not exactly rich. And since when has it ever been okay to ask someone about their wealth?" She put her hands on her hips. "I raised you better than that."

"Yeah, well…" He shuffled his feet, feeling ten years old again. "He's okay, I guess."

"He's better than okay." She bit her lip, then confessed. "I love him, Foley. He's the man for me."

He had to swallow to speak, and he felt his future changing with every heartbeat. "Yeah?"

"He's mentioned marriage a few times, but I wanted us to get to know each other's families first. He's an amazing man."

Foley tried to lighten the mood. "You don't *have* to marry him, do you?"

"What?"

"He didn't knock you up or anything, did he?"

His mom turned beet-red. "Foley Sanders. Get in that car and go home." She laughed through her embarrassment. "A baby. Are you fucking nuts?"

"Does he know you swear like a sailor?"

"Like a Marine, boy. Your daddy was no crackerjack." He chuckled.

"And yes, he knows. Just like he knows about you and Sam and that mess after high school. I didn't want you saying anything in front of Jan or Noel because that's your business, not theirs."

"And his business, I guess," Foley said, not sure why he was angry when she'd only told her guy the truth. She wasn't hiding a damn thing from Jacob—*her guy*. *Fuck*.

"I wanted to be honest with him. The same way he was honest with me about his life." She paused. "Jan isn't his biological daughter," she said in a low voice. "Jacob found out years ago that his wife had been cheating on him throughout their marriage. They aren't sure who her father is, sad to say. But he's never told her, and he loves her anyway. He's a solid man."

"Damn." Sucked to be Jacob.

"He's not perfect. But I don't want perfection. I want someone I can love and who can love me." She looked so darn pretty with that smile. "He told me he loves me, Foley. I know he means it."

"Well, um, I'm happy for you. I guess."

"You guess?"

"It's weird, okay? You've never been like this about any other guy."

"I know, but when it's right, it's right."

He sighed. "I'm glad you're happy. I love you, Mom."

"I love you too, baby." Her slow smile turned wicked. "Oh, and I can't wait to meet Cyn. I wonder how much money *she* makes?"

"I gotta go."

Her laughter followed him into his truck.

Sam relaxed against the seat he'd kicked back, his eyes closed. "Long conversation. Did she ream you a new one?"

"Pretty much."

"Then can we go? Wake me up when we board the ferry. I love sitting up top, even in the cold."

"Will do."

A pause.

"You know, I liked him. For what it's worth." Sam liked the guy. Would wonders never cease?

"Fuck. I liked him too, okay? Now I need to deal with it."

"Yeah, you do."

Yeah, I know.

Chapter 14

CYN WAITED ANXIOUSLY FOR FOLEY TO ARRIVE. SHE hadn't seen him in three days. To her surprise, it felt like forever. All her self-warnings to keep him at arm's length, to not get too attached, disappeared any time she looked at that damn picture.

His sly grin in the photo was all Foley. Naughty, fun, sexy. When she thought about him, she smiled.

The doorbell rang, and she rubbed her sweaty hands on her jeans, took a deep breath, and let it out slowly. Then she walked to the door. She gave herself a quick study in the mirror over the side table by the entry.

Hair long and wavy. Check. Body-hugging cotton T-shirt under cashmere cardigan—check. Jeans to appear casual when feeling anything but—and check.

She spotted Foley's head through the window at the top of her door, so she opened it. "Hello?"

He gave her a thorough once-over, smiled, and kissed the breath out of her. Before she knew it, he'd stepped them both inside, locked up behind them, and continued to kiss her as he backed her against the door.

When she thought she might pass out from a lack of oxygen, he pulled back, panting. "Man, I missed you."

"I can see that."

He smiled. "Merry Christmas."

"You too." She pulled him in for a tender kiss. "I love my gift."

"Yeah?" He lit up like a kid at Christmas, and boy did the expression fit.

"In fact, I have a coupon I plan on using tonight."

"Hot damn." He lifted one hand to show he had a six-pack with him. How had she missed that? "Awesome. I brought the beer."

"Because beer goes so well with a foot rub?"

"Ah, hell. I knew you'd choose that one first." But he didn't sound upset. He sounded amused.

"So tell me about your holiday. What did you get?" she asked as she followed him into her kitchen.

"A new sweater and a Seahawks signed football from my mom, and a book and beer set from Sam. Oh man. You got a fully loaded pizza? You are the absolute best." He turned and took her in his arms again.

"Hey, watch the beer."

"Good point." He placed the booze on the table and kissed her breathless.

She didn't understand how he turned her on with simple kisses. Every time. She'd had plenty of boyfriends that were sexy, handsome, smart. None of them had gotten her hot and bothered with just a kiss.

"You don't know how bad I want to unzip, bend you over, and fuck the hell out of you."

Yes, yes, yes, her loins insisted. She blew out a breath, drawing on her patience, and he did the same.

"Sorry," he apologized. "I'm trying to be good. I wanted to talk to you, not just do you."

"Good to know I'm not just a piece of meat."

"No offense, but you're not meat. *That's* meat." He pointed to the pizza and drew in a deep breath. "I think I'm about to have a food orgasm."

"Really?" She stared at him. "Let's see that *O*-face, sexy. Or is it now an *F*-face?"

"Huh?"

"Food-face. Have you ever had an orgasm from eating?"

He seemed to consider the question. "Well, once, I guess. But I was hungry and horny and not quite myself. So I was eating this chick and jerking off and—"

"Gah. Stop talking. I don't want to hear it."

He laughed. "Such a lightweight. No, Cyn. I haven't gotten off while downing a burger and fries. I'm not Caligula, you know."

She raised a brow.

"Yeah, I know who he is. I watch the history channel. Roman emperor of torture and orgies. If anyone had sex with food, it was that guy."

"Um, right." She laughed with him, accepting his embrace once more.

"You know, just talking to you makes me feel good. Am I a pussy for saying that?"

"Admitting you like talking to me might *get you* pussy, but I don't think it makes you one."

"Excellent." He winked at her and dug into the pizza, putting slices on the plates she'd set out. "So where do you want to eat?"

"We can sit in the living room. You are over sixteen, aren't you?"

He paused in the act of grabbing them beers. "What?"

"That's what I tell my nephews when they try to drink in the living room. That you have to be over sixteen to take a drink from the kitchen."

"You have a lot of rules, don't you?"

"So what?" She accepted the beer and plate he

handed her and followed him to the couch. "Rules make life easier."

"And boring. Then again, breaking those rules can be a damn good time."

"Figures. You're the rule breaker, I'm the rule maker."

"So poetic." He polished off a slice while she watched, stunned. "What?"

"Did you even chew any of that? Or did you just swallow it whole? It's like watching a shark chomp down its dinner."

He flushed. "Sorry. I haven't had anything to eat today."

"Why not?"

"I promised my mom I'd help out with a few chores while she's bumping uglies with her rich boyfriend." He grimaced. "I can't believe I just said that. My mom isn't supposed to have an ugly."

She tried not to laugh, but he looked so miserable she couldn't help it. She took his plate and fetched him another slice, as well as a few napkins, and returned. "Tell me everything. I'm dying to hear this."

"Sam and I spent the day after Christmas with Mom, dentist guy, and dentist guy's daughter and son-in-law. Oh, and the daughter, Jan, is pregnant."

"This matters to the story, I take it?"

"Yeah, because my mom thinks Jacob—that's dentist guy—must be amazing, because not only is he some douche with money, but he has a daughter he married off to some computer wiz, plus he's got a bonus grandkid on the way. I'm just some lame-o mechanic going nowhere fast."

"She said that?" Poor Foley.

"Nah, but I know she was thinking it."

"I thought you and your mom were close." She took a bite of pizza, savoring the delicious grease and cheese and…calories. She heard her mother's voice in her head, the doubts that Foley would stick around a woman he found unattractive.

I'll just have one slice. That's all.

"We are." He sighed. "I might have acted like an ass a little bit. But I didn't mean to."

"You an ass? No." He pretended not to see the look she gave him. "Well? Details, man. How were you an ass? Be specific."

He put down his slice of pizza and blew out a breath. "We had to take the ferry to Jacob's place. He lives on Bainbridge Island."

"Oh, I love it over there."

"Yeah, it's great," he said, morose, and pushed his slice around on his plate. "So the guy has a killer house, all fancy and rich and shit. He's got chandeliers and had a catered brunch *Catered. Brunch.* Dude served freakin' mimosas in champagne glasses! We had lobster and shrimp. Frittatas, I think. The food was great, but I couldn't spell half of it."

"You can't spell, period."

"Smart-ass." He lost his annoyed expression. "Anyway, so we're all there, around his fancy table, eating fancy food, and—"

"I get it. He's fancy. You said that. Move on."

He glared at her, and she felt those butterflies in her belly fluttering. She loved when Foley turned a little mean. Was it wrong to egg him on? Maybe.

"So I flat-out asked if he had money. I mean, it's obvious."

"You asked about money? That's usually not done."

"I just wanted him to know I knew, and that I was glad about it. I don't want some guy taking advantage of my mom. She works hard for her money. And trust me, she's a soft touch. I've had to watch out for her with a few scummy exes."

She patted his muscular shoulder. Man, he was huge. "You're a good guy, Foley."

He flushed and turned back to his pizza, taking a big bite.

That flush turned her all gooey inside.

"I didn't mean to be rude," he said with his mouth full. He stopped to swallow and swig some beer, then continued. "But it was weird. I just…"

"What?"

"Seeing her happy was great, but it kind of… Shit. It's stupid."

"No, what?" She moved closer, her hand on his knee. "You can tell me," she said gently, sensing he needed to get something off his chest.

"I've always been there for my mom. My dad died when I was little. And Mom always put me first. I knew she dated, but I never met the guy unless she got serious, and that didn't happen that often. She worked hard to put food on the table and keep me out of trouble." He gave a half smile, but his pain was real. "I was a handful. Then we took Sam in. Sam had a shitty mom. Hell, he *has* a shitty mom. But that's another story. Sam needed us, and we took care of him. So Mom had another troublemaker to deal with, and she did. But Sam and I kept her from the moochers and the assholes out there. A few tried to push her around, but we wouldn't let them." He paused to drink again.

She rubbed his thigh, aware he was troubled. Feeling his pain pushed all anxiety about him away. "She had no one serious or steady, not in, gosh, how many years?"

"Twenty-nine," he muttered. "No, and I feel like a real shit, because now she has a decent guy, and I want him gone." He put his beer down and held his head in his hands.

"Foley."

"I can't tell Sam about this. He'll think I'm nuts. My mom is awesome. I love her more than anything. I want her to be happy, but I feel so fucking weird about the thought of her getting married or leaving. It's not like I live with her or anything. Like, we split *years* ago. It's just… I'm supposed to be the one who protects her. What if I leave it to this guy and he fucks her over? What if she gets really hurt because I wasn't there to stop it?"

She moved to straddle his lap and pulled his head to her chest for a hug. "Oh, Foley. You're a big dope."

He tensed and tried to pull away, but she held him tight. He gradually relaxed, then started to nuzzle her breasts.

"I can feel you doing that."

"You called me a dope," he said, muffled against her chest. "You owe me."

She tugged his head up so she could look into his eyes. "You are the sweetest, most devoted, perfect son I've ever met."

"Shut up, Cyn."

"No, don't look away. You should want to take care of your mom." God, how had she ever doubted he might be a good guy? "It's hard to let go, Foley. You know, she might get hurt. But that's what being an adult is about. Have you been hurt before?"

His expression closed, and he stared at her chin, not meeting her eyes. "Yeah. And it sucked."

"But you grew from that. You learned to be more careful. Or at least not to make the same mistakes again. Your mom raised you and Sam. Don't you think she can handle anything else life throws at her?"

He looked up at her. "That's a good point." He frowned. "Not very nice, but a good point. I know. It's stupid. Trust me. I've tried not to feel like this, but I can't help worrying about her. Plus, this guy is rich."

"Right. You said that. But that's good, because he doesn't want her for her money."

"But he could be a total rapey asshole, and he'll be too rich to take down. Then I'll just have to kill the fucker."

"Whoa. Slow down." She handed him his beer. "Drink and listen."

He sighed and obeyed.

"First off, no one is too rich to take down. Unless he's Bill Gates, and I'm not thinking your mom is dating him."

"No."

"Why would you even think about him being too rich to take down?"

"Lara—you met her, Johnny's girlfriend, fiancée, whatever the hell she is—nearly got raped by her ex-brother-in-law. The slime was a rich dude who barely got a slap on the wrist."

"Really?"

"Well, actually he's up on charges, but if he goes to jail, he'll be in some penthouse with see-through bars, most likely." Foley groaned. "It's dumb. Jacob is nice. I know that. He acts like my mom is awesome, and she told me she loves him. That he even told her he loves her."

"That's sweet."

"He's got a boat. His own private dock."

"And he loves her," she said slowly, trying to follow his train of thought. Which had clearly derailed.

"I just want to take care of her. That's my job. How can I hand her off to this dude I don't even know?"

"Foley, she's your mom. First off, you don't hand her off. Remember my rant about not being a baton in a relay race?" At his blank look, she drank some beer. "No one listens to me. Anyway, she's her own person. She doesn't need you to look after her. She needs you to support her. Keep an eye out, but let this guy step on his own crank if he's a schmuck. Your mom sounds pretty smart. She kept you two out of jail, didn't she?" she teased.

At his pregnant pause, she blinked. "Didn't she?"

"Mostly." He blew out a breath. "I was still in high school when Sam and I did something stupid. To impress a girl, if you can believe it. We didn't do anything wrong, exactly, but her dad wasn't thrilled his baby girl liked a dirt-poor kid like Sam."

She was shocked. "What happened?"

"I don't like remembering." He looked grim. "It was a long-ass time ago, and I learned my lesson. Never break into a girl's house to write *I love you too* on her mirror if you haven't checked to see if the place has cameras for security." He groaned. "Her dad was some rich tech guy. Rich people suck. Because of her dad and his ties to the police, Sam and I were charged as adults. A few other run-ins prior to that, for goofy stuff, added up to us doing prison time. Not county jail, the hard stuff."

"I'm so sorry." She truly was. She couldn't imagine what that had been like for a young man just out of high school.

"I know what you're thinking. I didn't get violated or anything." He was really red. "Never bent over to pick up the soap."

"Good to know." A huge sense of relief filled her.

"But Sam and I got the shit beaten out of us a bunch of times. Helped teach us some fine fighting skills though. How to hold out against some tough motherfu—ah, some tough guys. Also got us some experience working on cars." He paused. "Bottom line, I don't like rich dudes."

"But you like Jacob," she said, trying to make him feel better.

"Yeah, I kind of do. I guess." He hugged her. "Tell me I'm an idiot and my mom will be okay."

"You're an idiot and your mom will be okay."

He sighed. "Now tell me to relax and enjoy being with you."

She smiled and kissed the top of his head, wanting to offer comfort. "Relax and enjoy being with me."

"Now tell me I'm the most amazing man you've ever been with, and put your hand down my pants."

"*Foley.*"

He chuckled. "What? That's too much of a stretch?"

Unfortunately, it wasn't. She leaned back so she could see him. "Well, if it'll make you feel better." She slid her hand down his taut abdomen, unfastened the fly of his jeans, then eased her hand beneath his underwear.

Wonder of wonders, he was hard, huge, and hot for her. "Oh, Foley," she said in a deliberately breathless voice, "you're the most amazing man I've ever been with." She gripped him, shocked to find it difficult to make her fingers touch.

"Baby." He cupped her head and brought her mouth down to his.

While they kissed, she continued to fondle him, and the power she held—literally and figuratively—turned her world hazy.

He grew more enthusiastic, deepening the kiss.

She rubbed her thumb over him, felt his excitement, and whispered against his lips, "I love touching you."

He groaned. "Me too. But, Cyn, I want to make *you* feel good."

"This is doing the trick. Besides, you deserve it."

"Who are you kidding?" he rasped. "We both know I don't deserve you."

Before she could argue that, he tilted his head back to rest on the couch and put a hand over hers, stopping her. "Hold on. Let's slow this down, or I'll be done before we're started."

"Lightweight."

"You'll pay for that." He lifted his head and stared at her. "Now what coupon did you want to use first?"

She reluctantly let him go and fetched the booklet. "I believe the foot rub is where I'd like to start." She glanced at his erection, pleased to see him still hungry for her. "You sure you can handle me in that condition?"

"Don't you worry about me." He stood and dragged her with him down the hall into her bedroom. "Now get undressed and lay down."

"You're telling me that in order to get a foot rub I have to be naked?"

"Yeah. And there are no refunds. Drop the bra and panties, Nichols."

"Bossy." She undressed in front of him without a qualm, feeling sexy and powerful under his gaze. He palmed himself through his jeans while he watched her, and she thought it the most erotic thing. Foley wanted her. All of her.

It wasn't until she'd lain back on the bed, bared all the way, that her insecurities returned.

Foley, however, wouldn't let her dwell. He removed his jeans, keeping his boxer briefs on, and sat by her feet. He put her foot on his lap and started rubbing.

"Oh. You're good at that." She closed her eyes, not wanting to see him looking at her thick thighs and belly.

"You know, it's funny how you get shy on me. I get hard just looking at you, but you seem to think I don't like the way you look."

"That's not true." She sounded weak to her own ears.

"Yeah? Tell me something about yourself you like."

"I have nice hair."

"Come on. Something about your naked body. I'll tell you something about mine."

"Yeah?"

"I have a big cock. There. Now your turn." He dug into her arch, and she gave a low moan. He really was good at that.

"Okay. I have nice breasts."

"Spectacular tits. Big, round, with tight red nipples. Hmm." He leaned across her body and took a nipple into his mouth.

"*Foley*."

He sucked, licking and caressing her nipple into a hard peak. "Yeah, gorgeous." He leaned back and rubbed her foot again. "Tell me something else you like."

"Well, my hips are kind of wide, but I have a waist."

"Damn. I was hoping you'd get to your ass. But I can do a waist."

"What?"

He ran his hands over her hips, then her waist, stroking her until she almost begged him to stop the sensual torture. "How wet are you?" he murmured and maneuvered himself over her once more. He leaned down for a kiss.

She pulled him closer, her hands on his broad shoulders, and tried to draw him into her. But the stubborn man refused to budge.

When he eventually parted from her lips, he remained close, staring into her eyes. "Yeah. Gorgeous all over."

"Wh-what about you?"

"Me? I'm good with my hands." He moved to straddle her waist and put his hands on her breasts while he watched her. Her breasts fit into his palms, and the way he held her made her squirm.

She wasn't the only one affected. Foley had a large tent in his shorts, and she couldn't look away from it. "Take off your underwear."

"What will you give me if I do?"

"I'll tell you everything I like about you."

"How about you tell me everything you like about you?"

"That's stupid. I—" Cyn sucked in a breath when he scooted back on her thighs and ran his hands over her hips and in between her legs. Feeling the press of his palms over her sex distracted her, to say the least.

He grinned at her, then rose and removed his underwear. Foley Sanders, naked, was a treat to the senses.

She stared, wide-eyed. "I want to trace all your tattoos with my tongue."

"That nails it. I'm getting that dick tattoo for sure now."

She chuckled and reached up for him.

"First, tell me how great you are."

"Stop the feel-good crap. Come to me."

Foley shook his head. "You're wired to think you're too big or ugly or some bullshit I just don't get. You're a walking wet dream. I'm hard just thinking about you. And that's not because of your winning personality," he said drily.

"Shut up."

"It's that rockin' body. You have no idea how sexy you are. And I want you to believe it."

"What does it matter to you?" She didn't understand why they couldn't just have uncomplicated sex. But nothing with Foley had been simple. He aroused complex emotions in her without trying.

"What you think matters to me. Don't ask, because I can't explain it. I'm happy around you. But I want you to be happy too."

"I would be if you'd stop playing hard to get," she grumbled.

To which he laughed and joined her once again on the bed, this time lying beside her up on his elbow while he studied her from head to toe. "I sure would like to fuck you. Just waiting on you to do your part." He gripped his erection, holding himself like an offering. But he made no move to do anything more than hold that impressive shaft.

She swallowed a curse, determined to have him without begging. "I'm smart, financially independent, and I have a great family—well, only half-counting my mom. Oh, and my house is awesome."

"That's all stuff you *have*. Except for the smart part. Come on. You can do better than that." He pumped his cock once. "Unless you don't want this."

"Stop teasing." She scratched his chest with her nails, not hard, but enough to show she meant business. "If I tell you what you want to hear, will you fuck me?"

His eyes darkened. "I love that mouth. Yeah, I'll give you exactly what you need."

The growl in his voice nailed it. "Fine. I have a sturdy frame—I'm strong and can take some rough stuff in bed." He liked that, because his breathing grew harsher. "My breasts are big. My waist is small, and my hips make sense on my body. Oh, and my ass isn't half-bad."

"Touch yourself," Foley ordered, hoarse. "Let me see how sexy you are."

Watching him watch her while she trailed her hands over her body was its own kind of hellish foreplay. Odd, but having Foley pay such close attention to her made her flaws seem smaller, less important. Her soft, rounded tummy didn't seem so large when he watched her touch herself. And her thighs felt more muscular than thick when his gaze trailed over them.

"Between your legs," he rasped. "Spread your thighs and touch yourself there."

"Yes," she whispered as she ran her hands between her legs, grazing her folds while he watched.

Foley groaned. "God. I want you. Right fucking now."

She spread her legs wider and waited.

Foley didn't disappoint. He followed her hands and scooted down between her legs. Then he kissed her there, taking her clit into his mouth.

"*Foley*."

He made sweet love to her body. Not rushed, but moving with deliberation and a slowness that drove her insane.

His rough, callused hands were everywhere, plucking her nipples, stroking her belly, tracing her inner thighs. As he increased pressure on her taut nub, his tongue and teeth doing a number on her, his thick fingers found their way into her body. First one, then another digit sank deep inside her, and she thrust back against him, needing more.

Foley pulled his mouth away and rose over her. "I need you."

No pretense, no more teasing. He positioned himself at her entrance and shoved deep.

She cried out as he surged into her, and then he was fucking her hard. He kissed her while he took her, and she could do no more than hang on while he rode her into oblivion. She seized around him while he pounded into her, and she'd never been so satisfied with a lover as she was now.

Then he swore and pulled out, spending over her belly in great heaves.

Still riding a natural high, Cyn started to come down. She couldn't believe she hadn't insisted on birth control—*again*. What was it about Foley that made her mindless to everything but pleasure?

"Damn. Sorry, baby," he said between breaths. "I totally meant to put a condom on. Next time for sure." He kissed her, an entreaty of forgiveness and thanks she could feel deep inside.

She entwined her fingers behind his neck, holding him while she pardoned him with gentle kisses.

They broke apart, and he leaned his forehead against hers. "Fuck, you get to me."

"Yeah? Me too."

She felt his grin when he kissed her. "Good. God knows I don't want to be the only lovesick moron in this bed."

Lovesick made her start, but she realized he might not mean it as more than a token expression a guy might use after great sex.

"I am a moron for not insisting you use a condom."

He grabbed clothing off the floor to clean off her belly, then rolled to his back and pulled her on top of him. She leaned up so she could see him and just stared, still not sure what he was doing with her when he could have any woman he wanted.

"What's that look?"

"It's my breasts, isn't it? That's what has you coming back."

He grew serious. "Well, that and the hair. I'm a sucker for a natural redhead. It hasn't escaped my notice that your sexy landing strip is that same deep red curling around your breast." He trailed the lock over her chest.

Her lips twitched. "Yeah? Well I'm a sucker for big muscles and tattoos. Obviously that's got me hooked."

"And my big cock. Don't forget about that."

"Quit bragging. It's not that big."

He arched a brow, and she flushed.

"Okay, it's huge. Happy now?"

"Yeah. And I'll be happy again. I just need a little break. You wore me out."

More sex with Foley?

"This day just keeps getting better." She grinned. "For the record, I'm winning."

"Yeah? What game are we playing?"

"Having fun with friends?"

He chuckled. "Fun. That's one word for it."

Chapter 15

As they lay together, Cyn listened to Foley's heartbeat. Settled on top of him and astonished he seemed to like her there, she enjoyed the novelty of being in the position. "You're sure I'm not too heavy?"

"Ask me that again, and I'll switch positions and smother you. Now quit obsessing over yourself and tell me about your Christmas. I told you about mine."

"You really want to know?"

"I asked, didn't I?"

"Well, okay." She ran her fingers over his chest, tracing the colorful vines of tribal work that enthralled her. Such bright colors over such a lively man. "Christmas was actually fun. I enjoyed the family time. We played games, watched *Miracle on 34th Street*—my favorite holiday film, by the way—and then, oh yeah. Matt wormed out of Vinnie what happened." She pushed up to glare at him. "Why didn't you tell me about Jim Nelson and his dad?"

Foley flushed. "Hell. It was a guy thing. I didn't want to put Vinnie on the spot."

"You were worried I'd be upset. Admit it."

"Maybe I was."

She popped him in the chest.

"Cyn, come on, baby. Don't be mad."

"I'm not mad at what you did, just that you didn't tell me." She huffed. "I've been telling Matt he should have

Vinnie pound that little bully, but he's all antiviolence. I don't know why. He used to have no qualms about pulling my hair or punching me to get my attention."

"He *hit* you?"

She put pressure on his chest to keep him down. "Easy, big guy. Yes, he hit me—when we were kids. Rumor has it I might have been a bit of a brat."

Foley relaxed. "Hard to believe."

She tried not to laugh. "Not the point. You should have told me."

"Sorry. I just wanted to help Vinnie. It's not easy being a kid who's big for his age. Trust me. I know. I wouldn't have stepped in except the dad interfered."

"I'm glad you did. I'm only sorry you didn't punch him right in the face. Touching my nephew like that. He's lucky you didn't break his arm. Apparently Vinnie was more than impressed that you're a badass."

"Yeah?" He smiled, saw her warning look, and sobered. "I mean, I'll talk to him."

She sighed. "Don't bother. Nina is now your biggest fan, more than Vinnie even. Matt's coming around. He's trying to balance his stance against solving problems with violence with the fact that his way wasn't working."

"I learned early on that some people just don't respond to anything but a slap upside the head."

"You have a point." She would have liked to slap many an ex-boyfriend, as a matter of fact. And maybe a love tap to her mom, to get her off the diet bandwagon.

"So, that's your whole Christmas? How was your mom? Did you guys get along or what? She's your kryptonite, right?"

"Right." He sure did remember the things she told him. "For the most part the holiday was awesome. Then I ended up getting stuck doing dishes with her. Just Ella and me in the kitchen. She was actually nice…until the digs came out."

"Digs?"

"About how I need to be smaller to keep a man. That you're a good-looking guy, and to keep you interested I need to always look my best." And a dozen other belittling points she refused to get into.

Foley linked his hands behind his head and stared into her eyes. "She's got a point. I don't like my women without makeup, stilettos, or pasties on at all times." He snickered. "Please. If you can't be yourself with a guy, what's the point? I mean, the last few chicks I dated wanted tough guy Foley who fights a lot. Truth is, I only fight if I have to, mostly to keep Sam out of jail."

"Oh?"

"Punk gets into a ton of fights, and normally I'm the one left hauling his ass out of trouble. But me? I like to reason my way out of tough situations if possible. Problem is, I look meaner than I am. I figure if you don't like the real me, fuck you."

She traced the muscle car on his chest. "Fuck me?"

"I plan to again real soon," he teased. "But yeah, that's my general feeling. Life is short, you know? I don't have time for head games. You either take me as I am or get lost."

"I've tried that. I'm still single."

"No, you've got a boyfriend." He ran his fingers over her hair, sliding it between his fingers. "Me."

"Do I have you?" she asked, half-serious. "What

happens when some skinny woman who likes cars comes by? You'll drop me for her in a heartbeat, I bet."

He snorted. "I work with one of those, genius. Much as I love Del, the woman scares me. Besides, she thinks she knows more about cars than I do, which is just insane. I'm a god when it comes to mechanics."

"Confident much?"

"Damn straight. When it's about cars, I am. What about you, business lady? You're badass with numbers, right?"

"Yes."

"You're intelligent, independent. You kicked those losers to the curb."

"What losers?"

"Your exes. If they'd been man enough to handle you, I wouldn't be with you now. You don't strike me as the type of chick to tolerate bullshit. Why fuck around with second best when you can have a guy as great as I am? You wonder about what I'll do, well what about you?"

"Me?"

"What are you going to do when some Einstein with business know-how decides he wants to crunch numbers with you? You going to dump me for some nerdy genius? 'Cause I have to tell you, I'm not that book smart, and I doubt I'll ever be rich. Good-looking, solid in a throw-down, sexy, confident. I'm all that. But wiping my ass with hundred dollar bills? Not my style."

Yet that notion didn't seem to bother him.

"Frankly, people wiping with money seems problematic to me from a hygiene standpoint."

"You're a riot, Cyn." He snorted. "You get what I'm saying."

"I do." She never could have imagined a conversation with Foley like this. That he'd ever worry about *her* leaving *him*. "Does it bother you that I have financial goals?"

"Probably as much as it bothers you that I have no desire to be rich. I make enough to support myself and grab the occasional beer, and I'm good."

"Hmm. Moneywise we seem okay with each other's goals."

"And don't forget our chemistry in bed."

"That's a given." She smiled down at him and traced his artwork down his ribs. His abs tensed. "What about friends and family?" She moved off him to his side so she could further explore his amazing body. "You're loyal. But how far would you take it?"

"Take what?" He did some touching of his own, lingering over her collarbone and upper chest.

"If Sam wanted you to dump me, would you?"

"Why would he?" he asked absently and ran his finger over her breast to her nipple.

She inhaled and let out a shaky breath. "I don't know. Maybe he hates redheads."

"Nah. He wanted to do you when he first saw you."

"Don't tell me that." Now she couldn't look at Sam the same way again.

"Don't worry. I called dibs. He respects that."

"Great. Dibs. What am I, the last chicken leg?"

"I love chicken." He toyed with her other breast. "But not as much as I love your tits." He leaned down and took a nipple in his mouth.

Grazing his abdomen, Cyn found him aroused once more. She trailed her fingers through the coarse nest of hair surrounding his shaft, and he turned into her touch.

He released her breast and nuzzled his way up to her neck, then whispered in her ear, "You think too much. Go with what feels good, Cyn. I sure the hell am."

Then he kissed her, and she lost herself in his embrace.

Two condoms and several hours later, they lay in bed, still naked and a mess.

Cyn had never been happier. "You know, that picture you gave me makes me smile."

Foley stretched next to her. "That was the plan. You smile, you think of me. You come, you think of me."

"Really? All that from a smirk in a frame?"

He chuckled. "What can I say? I'm a simple guy."

"You're not that simple." Cyn sat up and fetched a robe. She donned it, then sat next to Foley on the bed. "I thought we'd have sex and goof around, but nothing too deep. You continue to surprise me."

"I surprise myself sometimes. But I try not to let that bother me." He yawned. "Hell, Cyn. I hate to fly, but I have work early in the morning."

"Me too." She hated that she wanted him to stay. Would that be pushing things between them though? "Monday comes so early." It was nearly midnight.

"Yeah." He left the bed to use the facilities. When he returned to the bedroom, he dressed while Cyn watched. "You want to get together this week?"

"When?" She loved that he'd asked her before she could ask him. Despite trying to tell herself to relax around the guy, she felt her heart thunder just thinking about him. His smile, his deep voice, the way he had of wanting her to feel good about herself.

"How about Tuesday night? We could hang out at my place."

"Your place?" She itched with curiosity. She knew he lived with Sam somewhere in North Beacon Hill. "Sounds good."

"There's a catch."

"Of course there is."

"You have to cook."

"No problem." She'd knock his socks off with her cooking. "What do you want me to make?"

"I'll pick up stuff for spaghetti."

"Spaghetti? *That's* what you want? That's too easy. I'll do something special to surprise you. What do you like?"

"You."

"I mean, to eat." At his growing grin, she blushed. "As in *food*."

"I like everything. Well, except for brussels sprouts. I'm partial to Italian, actually."

"Okay. I can work with that. Tuesday night at your place." Where he lived with Sam. "Should I cook enough for three?"

"Oh, you mean for Sam? Nah. He can get his own woman if he's hungry."

"He needs a woman for that? Why can't he just cook for himself?" She frowned, gearing up for a lively discussion on a woman's place in today's society.

Foley laughed. "Ease off the high horse, Red. I just meant he's as lame in the kitchen as I am. Except at least I know how to boil an egg."

"Oh." Deflated, she stood when he pulled her gently to her feet. "Okay."

"I wish I could stay, but I'll have enough on my plate, filling Del and Liam in on things tomorrow. The after-holiday crush is always brutal."

"I understand." She met his kiss, alarmed at how well they fit together and at how much she loved touching him. Should she admit what she felt? Would that be a good or bad thing? Then she threw caution to the wind. "I'll miss you."

He pulled back, and the tender look on his face melted her. "Aw, baby. Me too. I miss you all the time when we're not together." He kissed her again. "I'd better go, or I'll never leave."

Never leave. Would that that were true.

Oh my God, Cyn. Slow down. He's just a casual boyfriend who'll end up breaking your heart before you know it. Lighten up.

She walked him to the front door, determined to enjoy him while she had him. A glance at the counter showed a few beers left. "Want to take those with you?"

He glanced at the bottles. "Nah. You can drink it, or you can save it for me when I come back."

She liked the latter idea better. "See you soon."

He cupped her cheek. "Count on it. Now lock up behind me."

She rolled her eyes. "Don't think you can boss me around."

"Only in bed?" He pulled on his boots and grabbed his jacket. "What about foreplay before we get there? I mean, if I'm bending you over in the kitchen, I might want to order you to—"

"Go home, Sanders." She ignored the heat in her cheeks.

"Yes, ma'am." He gave her a quick kiss then left.

Cyn watched through the window until his truck lights disappeared. She missed him, and he'd barely left.

She was already in over her head with the man. Now she had no choice but to ride out this new relationship, because for some reason she refused to end it before she inevitably got hurt.

———

"So you finished the jobs on the desk?" Del asked for the second time Monday morning, nodding at several folders.

"Yes, Del," Foley said clearly. He told himself to cut her a break. She'd just come back from her first Christmas with McCauley and the kid. No doubt all that love and togetherness had fried her circuits.

He stood with her by the service desk, where Dale continued to input data the guys had collected into the computer. Normally they just plugged their work into the computer to save paper, keeping electronic files. But Foley didn't like fiddling with digital shit, and while Dale had been out, they'd recorded their work old-school. In notebooks.

"Damn." Sam banged something in the bay and said a few more choice words Del didn't counsel him on.

Must still be in the holiday spirit.

Sam was alone in the bay, working on a problematic Ford. Lou hadn't come in yet, and Johnny had the day off. To fill in for Johnny, Liam had decided to make an appearance. He sipped from a chipped coffee mug and watched Del's interrogation with an irritating grin.

"All the jobs?" she repeated, frowning, as she stared at the crap-ton of work orders he and the guys had completed.

Liam put his cup down. "Del, Foley told you three times that the work got done. You having some trouble hearing or what?"

Foley shot him a thankful look, and Liam slapped him on the back hard enough to crack a rib.

Del sighed. "Sorry. Just making sure I can take on the *other* work we've got piling up." She tugged at her braid. "Damn. I need to make sure we can commit to this. What the hell? I go away a few days, and everyone in Seattle is breaking down."

Foley shrugged. "Bitch or get it done. What would you rather do?"

Liam choked on his coffee while Del turned a blazing glare his way.

"What? I'm just saying what we're all thinking. Right, Dale?"

Dale grunted, the smart kid neither agreeing nor disagreeing. He didn't look up from the computer as his fingers flew over the keyboard.

"Apparently time spent with your new *girlfriend* has not smoothed your rough edges." Del raised a pierced brow.

"How can you know I'm dating Cyn? You just got back."

"I am all-knowing and all-seeing, Foley. Remember that." Her smug expression annoyed him all over again.

Liam snorted. "More like she grabbed some coffee and gossip from Nina this morning."

"Dad." Del shoved her father and Foley back toward the garage. "Stop sharing all my trade secrets and get to work."

"Who's in charge here?" Liam suddenly refused to budge. Like granite, the older guy could more than hold his own.

Foley liked watching him take a stand against his

daughter, since not many did, himself excluded. He'd never been one to back down from a fight, but he respected the hell out of the Websters, so he at least tried to be tactful when telling the pair they were full of shit.

Sam stopped working to watch, and Lou entered and took in the show as well.

"For heaven's sake, get to work, Dad. Please?" She batted her eyelashes at him.

Liam laughed at her and turned around to head toward the bay. "I can see that finger you're shooting me, Delilah. That's no way to talk to your father."

"I didn't *say* a thing." She tucked said finger away and stomped back to her office. "Dale! Get your skinny butt in here."

Foley waited until Dale rushed to join her and closed the door after him. To Liam, he said, "So she's still not swearing, eh? Too bad. We had a colorful breather while she was gone."

"I know." Liam sighed, "But what can you do? McCauley's civilizing her. My girl just ain't gonna be the same." He grinned, more than pleased Del had found herself a decent guy.

They all knew it.

"It's like she never left," Lou said as he walked into the break room and stored his things in his locker. "Aw, come on, guys. Nobody made coffee?"

"I can go grab you a cup if you want," Foley offered, always ready for an excuse to dart to Nichols and maybe see Cyn.

"I'll make a pot," Sam offered. "Just as soon as I get this freakin' truck to give up its spark plugs. I swear, I hate the 2005 Ford V-8s. Spark plugs stick like glue."

"Yeah, and it normally happens after the warranty is up. Bummer for the owner," Lou added. "That's why I drive a Toyota."

"Toyotas are for losers," Foley muttered.

"What's that?" Lou scowled.

Foley ignored it. "Hell, Sam, by the time you get those things out, it'll be spring. I'll make the coffee." That he could do.

"This time add grounds, would you? Foley, I swear, when you make the stuff, it's like drinking oily water," Liam complained.

"Hey, I'm happy to get some from Cyn."

"She giving it to you for free?" Sam asked, all innocence.

"Shut up, Sam. I pay for the coffee." After a pause, Foley added, "The kisses are on the house, though."

"Good to know." Lou stepped into his coveralls. "I might have to get some myself later."

"You wish."

Lou laughed at him.

"All right, bozos." Liam rubbed his hands together. "Let's get to work."

Foley cranked the radio, and everyone turned to. A few hours later, Liam stepped close and watched him leaning over the engine of an older GMC with attitude—Foley's favorite kind of car. No whiz-bang electrical circuitry, just good old plugs and gears and pistons. And a computer he recognized without needing a bazillion directions.

"So." Liam said nothing more.

"Yeah?" Hmm. Output voltage to the fuel pump relays was less than 11.2, yet the battery was supposedly new and had a full charge. Interesting. Time to check for loose connections and maybe some broken wires.

"You and Cyn Nichols, hmm? I hear you two are pretty hot and heavy."

Foley straightened. "Where'd you hear that?" Dinner at Johnny's had been great, but he hadn't been all over her. Unless Nina had said something. Had Cyn mentioned being really into him, maybe? Did she consider them hot and heavy? He sure the hell hoped so.

"So you *are* into her."

"Well, yeah. She's gorgeous."

"True." Liam smiled.

"Why the hell are you so interested in my love life?" Foley knew he sounded rude, but he worried about the guys screwing up his future with Cyn. So far everyone had been cool about it—not counting Sam's mouth. But the crew considered one another family. Hell, Foley himself had gone with Del to Johnny's to help him when he'd been drowning in his relationship with Lara. That made Foley fair game for interference, and he knew it.

"Just want to make sure my guys are happy and healthy is all." Liam tried to look innocent. It totally didn't work.

"Hey. I'm no Johnny Devlin. I'm not pissy and mooning over anybody."

"Yet," Lou added.

Foley ignored him. "Hell, I'm glad to be here. Webster's Garage rocks." He meant it. Foley loved the work he did, in addition to the guys—and gal—he worked with.

"A little testy, eh?" Lou tinkered with one of his

client's cars. "What's wrong, Foley? I'm sensing you want us to keep out of your private life."

"Like you kept out of Johnny's?" Liam had to add.

"Please. That boy was floundering big time. Del and I saved him from a lifetime of pain and suffering."

"How's that?" Sam asked.

"The pain and suffering he'd have gotten from the bunch of us telling him what an asshole he was. Only a tool—the dickhead kind—wouldn't see how great Lara is for him."

"Good call." Lou nodded.

"Yeah. I get that," Sam agreed.

The office door to the garage opened, and Del yelled, "Asshole and dickhead equal fifty cents." The ROP had returned.

"Shit."

"Seventy-five!" The door slammed shut.

Sam and Lou openly laughed at him.

"I'll put it in when I get change," he yelled back to be heard over the music. "How can she hear me? It's like she has wolf ears."

"To go with the wolf eyes," Lou said in a lower voice, still grinning.

"Quit changing the subject." Liam crossed his power-ful arms over his chest. "So you and Ms. Nichols are a couple now?"

"A couple of kids having a good time is all," Sam said for him. "Nothing serious. Just some good, clean, pornographic fun."

"Didn't need the help, Sam," Foley growled.

Sam saluted him before diving back toward his stuck sparkplugs.

"I'm good," Foley said. "Cyn and I are taking it slow, but yeah, we're a couple. She's mine, and she admits it. We're solid." Man, it felt good to say that. Foley felt warm inside and knew he was in the wrong place to get all giddy. He coughed to cover his joy. "So if we're done playing girlfriends and talking *feelings*, Liam, can I get back to work? I swear, Sophie is making you soft, old man."

"Not where it counts, boy." Liam winked.

The guys guffawed and got back to work. Foley took most of the afternoon to fix the Bronco and its corrosive battery connections. After a butt splice and a heat shrink, the truck proved roadworthy. A test-drive, and he'd returned, ready for more challenges.

He hadn't expected his biggest one would be on the ride home from work an hour later.

"So, you and Cyn. Things are good with your new *girlfriend*, huh?"

Foley watched the scenery pass by while Sam drove them in Sam's car, which he'd finally fixed. "Yeah. We're good." He paused. "What do you think of her? She was cool at Johnny and Lara's. I think Lara liked her."

"They seemed to hit it off." Sam shrugged. "She's okay, I guess."

"Do you like her?"

"You called dibs, remember?" Sam sneered. "Good thing you did, or she'd be crying out my name night after night." Sam turned back to the road, a grim smile on his face. "Or is she?"

"Ha-ha. Very funny." Foley had to laugh. "She's actually pretty religious."

"Yeah?"

"Mostly she's all, 'Oh God, oh God, yes, yes,' on our dates." He snickered and managed a laugh out of Sam. He figured Cyn wouldn't mind, considering he'd been just as *religious* under her talented touch.

Sam continued the drive in silence.

"So, ah, tomorrow night. I need the house."

"Huh?" Sam frowned.

"Cyn's coming over for a date. I want some alone time with her."

"Alone time?"

"You know. I can't score if she's worried about you hearing everything."

They'd been through this before. Typically, from what Foley had seen, early in a relationship, a woman needed privacy. She needed to feel out her space and his, to accustom herself to his friends and get comfortable enough to not mind the noises she made while he gave her orgasms.

Though he and Sam shared a big enough place that they weren't stepping over each other, they still shared the space. Sexing Cyn up while Sam sat in his room probably wouldn't go over too well. Not until she knew him better, at least.

"No sweat. I'll hang at Lou's or Johnny's." Sam turned onto their street. "So you cooking her up something big? Gonna impress her with more than your empty head and awful compliments? Maybe show her how neat your sock drawer is?"

"Yeah, right. We both know I can't cook. Since you finally cleaned the bathroom, I'm not too concerned with the house. Although…I might straighten up a little." Sam wasn't the cleanest guy. Foley inwardly groaned, recalling the state of his own room. "Shit. I have a ton of laundry to do. I have a feeling it's going to be a late night."

Sam shook his head. "Still in that have-to-impress phase. What's up, man? She should be hooked on the sex by now. You must not be doing it right."

"Please. She has no complaints."

"Whatever."

"But it wouldn't hurt to show her I'm a charming guy in and out of bed. One who's not a slob." He eyed Sam up and down, and Sam responded with a rude hand gesture as they pulled into the driveway. "I don't want her to think that the mess in our place is me. Clearly you're the hoarder here."

"I'm a collector, asshole. I *collect*. I don't *hoard*."

"Poor bastard, still living in denial." Foley shook his head and tried not to laugh at Sam's scowl. "Your bed sits in the middle of a maze of waist-high stuff. That's hoarding."

"That's organizing. And besides, I've seen that show about hoarders, and I'm nowhere near that. Those people have shit on their floors. Like, real turds. It's disgusting."

"The only reason you don't have that is I make you clean the bathroom."

They entered the house, and Sam stopped right in front of him, causing Foley to bang into him. "What the hell, Sam?"

"Since I got food, it's your turn to fix dinner. Oh, and if she's coming over tomorrow night to cook, make sure we get leftovers, okay?"

"If it'll keep you out of my hair, fine." Foley would

buy something for the guy. After all, Sam had agreed to stay away for the night. "I'll kick in a dessert too."

Sam brightened at that. "Maybe a cheesecake?"

"Sure. Why not?" He opened the refrigerator and sighed. "Hot dogs, again?"

"It's either that or frozen pizzas."

"Hot dogs it is."

Chapter 16

INSIDE FOLEY'S TOWN HOUSE, CYN GLANCED AROUND, impressed to find the living area clean. She'd noticed his section at the garage had been organized, while Sam's hadn't been. At all. So she'd wondered what to expect from their shared living space.

She hated to stereotype but had to face it—Foley was a guy's guy. The house had all the charm of a barely lived-in rental. Cream-colored walls, beige carpets, no artwork. She saw a few pictures in frames on the lone bookcase in the living room, along with some magazines and books on dogs.

A matching side and coffee table in halfway decent condition stood sentry near a large gray sectional. It faced an even larger television—what obviously passed for art in their home.

"It's clean." Foley seemed proud of that fact.

"So it is." She followed him through the living room into the kitchen, where he placed the bags she'd brought. The kitchen had Formica counters in the shape of a U, with a pass-through to the living room over the empty sink. A coffeepot, three apples, and a roll of paper towels were the only things on the counters. The cabinets and tiled floor had no doubt been selected for function and economy. They didn't offend with bright color and didn't overwhelm with high-end gloss either.

But the kitchen table had been set to look pretty. A

Christmassy tablecloth and plates, napkins and silver-
ware set for two charmed her. Candles sat on either side
of a Christmas cactus, and she smiled at the attempt to
liven the place with holiday cheer.

"I love the table."

Foley smiled. "Yeah? My mom gave us the plant and
the tablecloth. Said we looked pathetic with no decorations." Then he shoved his hands in his pockets. "But, ah,
that's it. I mean, I set the table and all. Just me. No help
from my mom. We're not joined at the hip or anything."

She swallowed the momma's-boy taunt, because he
looked adorable. Huge, handsome Foley embarrassed
because his mom had helped him decorate.

He nodded at her bags on the counter. "How much
do I owe you?"

"Nothing. I'm cooking for you."

"Yeah, but you picked up stuff for the cheesecake,
right? And I said I'd buy if you made us dinner."

"Don't worry about it. It's my treat. Besides, you
kicked Sam out for me. How sweet," she teased. "I owe
him too."

He flushed. "Nah. He had plans to hang out with the
guys. It's no biggie."

She doubted that. Foley obviously wanted privacy
for them, which she appreciated. She didn't know how
she'd feel knowing Sam was closeted somewhere in the
house. And it wouldn't seem right to eat a homemade
dinner without asking Sam to join them.

Cyn took items out of the bags. "Well, anyway, I
prepared some of this at home. Let me put it together."

"How about some music?"

"Sure."

"What do you like? I bet you like jazz or classical."

"I like all kinds, really."

Foley left while she started organizing the meal. She'd precooked the noodles and meat and blended the cheeses, so she only had to put the lasagna together, make the salad, and prep the cheesecake. Though Foley hadn't asked her to, she'd made plenty enough for him and Sam to share the next day.

A man as large as Foley who couldn't cook? A travesty.

Jazzy blues came through speakers with high-quality sound. Typical guy. He had no artwork to speak of, but he owned a big screen TV and high-end sound system.

Foley rejoined her in the kitchen. His eyes grew wide when he noticed the pan being filled with noodles, meat, sauce, and cheese. "Oh wow. Homemade lasagna."

"I would have gone more gourmet, but I didn't want to make something you wouldn't eat. Besides, I'm Italian. If I can't make a lasagna half as good as my grandmother's, I'm out of the family."

He grinned. "I get you. My dad was a mechanic, so it was kind of in the blood for me. Grease and car parts are what I do."

"Really?"

"Yep." He moved to the fridge and came back with wine and beer. "Which would you like? I have water and milk too."

"How about some wine?"

He opened it and poured her a glass of cold red. She didn't have the heart to tell him she preferred her red wine at a slight chill, just below room temperature. "This is good, thanks."

He took a drag on his beer and settled against the

counter to watch her. "You look good in the kitchen." He glanced down at her feet. "Barefoot would be good too."

"You add pregnant and I'm out of here."

He laughed. "Kidding. Though you'd look good pregnant too. What can I say? I'm a fan."

"A fan?" She blamed her heated cheeks on the warming oven.

"I'm all for the feminist movement."

"Ha. I'd be surprised if you can spell *feminist*." She finished prepping the lasagna.

"This isn't about spelling. It's about appreciating a businesswoman who can cook." Foley sighed. "I can't wait for dinner."

"You're so easy."

"Um, yeah. I thought that was obvious. Not like I'm hiding anything from you."

She snorted and put the lasagna into the oven. Then she started prepping the salad.

"Want me to do anything?" he asked.

"Nope."

So he watched while she worked, and they talked about his day back at work.

"…and I nailed the starter and figured out how to work out the power steering problem." He said more she didn't understand, but she wanted to. His enthusiasm for his work infected her as well. "Oh, and Del's still a huge pain. I owe her seventy-five cents."

"Seventy-five cents? That's all?"

"That's all she heard," he admitted.

She laughed. "I can imagine. You're a huge fan of the f-word, aren't you?"

"Well, yeah. I mean, you can use it any way you

want. But doing it, now that's what life is all about." He drank and stared at her breasts, his grin more of a leer. "Oh yeah."

"Foley, behave."

"Do I have to?"

She pushed the salad to the side. "Yes. Are you really just going to watch me do all the work? You're not going to offer to help at all?"

"Nope." He didn't sound the least bit repentant.

"But I bet you'll want to lick the beaters when I'm done with the cheesecake."

"Yes, please."

She showed him, step by step, how to put together a New York–style cheesecake. Once the lasagna finished, she'd pop it in the oven to bake.

"We'll eat it warm, even though it's usually best served cold. But it's cheesecake, right?"

"There's no way to eat it wrong." He nodded. "And can I just say I'm glad you're not going to be all weird about eating with me."

"Is this you being complimentary and insensitive at the same time again?"

He groaned. "Probably. Look, I'm just saying it's no fun to eat with a girl who says no to everything."

"You have this problem often?"

He nodded. "Look at me, Cyn. I eat a lot, and I always feel like a huge pig when I'm enjoying a meal and my date picks a salad and refuses dessert. She's never hungry. But I'm always wanting more."

"Hmm." They'd had this discussion before. She knew what he meant, yet she wondered if maybe she'd grown less sensitive about her size. Her mother continued to hound her, but it grew easier to ignore her when a man like Foley looked at her like he wanted to eat her up. How could a girl's self-esteem not be buoyed by that?

He put down his beer and stepped into her space. "You understand what I'm saying, right? We're over that mess from before. I do *not* think you're fat. A little hideous maybe, with all that ugly red hair, but I'm adjusting." That wicked grin made her want to kiss him senseless.

"Foley, you're an ass."

"One who's hooked on all of you, so gimme a break. How about a kiss?"

Like he'd read her mind. "Just one."

He took her hands and placed them behind his neck, then he leaned close and gave her the kiss she'd been wanting since he'd left her Sunday night. He tasted like beer and sex, and it was all she could do not to beg him to go straight to the bedroom for a little hanky-panky. Cyn lived with a healthy libido, but around Foley, she felt perpetually in heat.

Foley was special. She'd dated her share of men, but none of them had turned her on so easily. Foley had only to smile, and her panties grew damp. She thought about him all the time. And for more than his hot body. She wanted to hang around him, to watch him laugh, or hold hands while they walked in the snow. She wanted to know what he liked, what he hated, to watch him with Sam and his friends, or his mom.

I am seriously in trouble with this man.

He pulled back and stared into her eyes. "Hi."

"Hi," she whispered back, breathless. Ignoring the urge to bring him back for another kiss that could easily turn into a quickie over the kitchen table, she pushed him back, holding him at arm's length. She hadn't imagined that pole in his pants rubbing against her, and the sight of his arousal soothed that part of her that continued to wonder if she was enough for him.

"I guess you need to cook."

"And you need to go around the counter so I'm not tempted."

He grinned. "I tempt you, huh? Good to know."

"Yeah, yeah." She shooed him away. "If you want cheesecake, stop distracting me."

He didn't even bother to hide the fact that he adjusted himself.

"Jeez, Foley."

"Hey, you have it easy. No one knows if you're hot for a guy. I look at you and get a hard-on. It's uncomfortable." He walked out of the kitchen to lean on the counter over the sink. "There. Better now? I'm too far away to make love to you."

Make love, not fuck. Semantics, and yet... She flushed. The l-word and Foley kept cropping up in her thoughts, fitting together like the pieces to a puzzle, and it worried the heck out of her. Cyn took time to get to know a man. She didn't fall in love on a whim or even in an instant. Heck, it had taken her months to feel comfortable with Jon, and he'd turned out to be a mistake in the end. So why this fixation on Foley after only a few weeks?

She plugged in her mixer and started adding ingredients to a bowl. She hadn't known what Foley had to cook with, so she'd brought a lot of her own supplies. "Are your friends giving you a hassle because we're dating?"

"Nah. Well, maybe a little. How about you?"

"Matt is still a pain, but since you rescued Vinnie, he's a lot more in your corner."

"Your mom?"

She frowned. "I don't know. Over Christmas, she was weird. She acted like you were a bad thing for me, but in the same breath she pretty much said to do my best to hold on to you. If I can, that is." Cyn sighed. "I love her, but I don't always like her. That sounds horrible."

"It does."

"Oh?"

He hurried to say, "But I get it. My relationship with my mom is different than yours. Hell, it's different than most guys'. I love my mom *and* I like her. But I've always felt like I need to protect her, you know? Single mom, pain-in-the-ass kid, then add in Sam. She's always been there for me."

"She sounds terrific." What if she didn't like Cyn? That would be a deal breaker for Foley.

"She is. I love her like crazy. I'm worried about this new guy, but I'm trying to keep my nose out of it. Until he steps on his dick. Honestly, the minute this guy gets out of line, I'm going to rearrange his face."

She chuckled. "That's staying out of it?"

"For me, yeah." He sipped his beer and watched her. "She wants to meet you."

Cyn covered her unease by mixing the cream cheese, sour cream, and sugar mixture. She'd prebaked the crust at home in a spring pan, so she only had to pour the mixture then bake. "She does?"

"Sam talked about how you shot me down, and my

mom wanted to meet this woman with such poor taste."
He grinned at her. "Kidding. She knows we're dating,
and she wants to meet you." He paused. "I'd like your
take on dentist guy."

"Jacob," she said, staring at the cheesecake ingredients in the bowl.

"Him, yeah. So I was thinking we could go on like a
double date with them. She could meet you, and she'll
be on her best behavior trying to look good for Jacob.
You can meet him and tell me if the guy seems on the
up and up to you."

She poured the cheesecake mixture into the pie pan.
"You trust my judgment?"

"Sure. I mean, you think I'm awesome. You're obviously a good judge of character."

She unplugged the mixer and pulled out the beaters. "Here."

"Rockin'." He made short work of them while she
imagined his mouth on her body instead of the beaters.
She felt overheated, though she'd been careful to wear a
shapely dress that both showed off her curves and flared
at the knee, which should have given her enough air to
cool off.

But the way Foley was making love to those beaters…

"Yum." He glanced at her and froze. "Something
wrong? Oh hell, I'm mauling these like a hungry bear,
right? I look like an idiot."

"N-no." She cleared her throat. "You look just fine."
She took the beaters before he put his mouth on them
again—*dear God*—and placed them and the bowl in the
sink. "Now we wait for dinner to finish."

"That's it?"

"Yep. Lasagna has another twenty minutes then has to cool. Salad is done, and the dressing is ready to go. I'll put the dessert in once the oven is free." She decided to throw caution to the wind and let Foley take charge of the night. "We have time. So what will we do until dinner is ready?"

A loaded question if he'd ever heard one. Foley wanted nothing more than to fuck the hell out of her. That blue dress set off her hair and hugged her curves in all the right places. And she'd worn heels, the kind he wanted on either side of his head while he pounded into her. But Foley wanted her to know he respected her. That he liked her for more than that fine pussy and those breasts he could feast on for days.

So he remained behind the counter, his erection well hidden, and debated how best to be friendly without being *too* friendly. "How about a tour of the place?"

Was it his imagination, or did she look disappointed? No doubt his imagination, because she gave a wide smile. "I'd love it."

"This won't take long," he warned, forced his dick to stay down with thoughts of his mother, and after a moment gave Cyn the nickel tour. "You've seen the kitchen and the living room. Up the stairs is Sam's room. Mine is down the hall. Oh, and the bathroom is too if you need it."

"Just one?"

"Yeah. Stupid. My mom bitches they should have put two into all the units, but they didn't. So me and Sam got the place cheap. That and my mom is our landlord."

"Nice." She followed him up the stairs. "Will Sam mind me peeking in his room?"

"I want you to see what a catch I am. You see his room, you'll think I'm a prince. Sam—he's scary."

She said nothing after he opened the door.

He noted the mess had been marginally cleaned up, or as Sam liked to say, "more organized." Tons of car manuals, auto mags, clothing, tools, and weights had been haphazardly collected into piles and scattered around the room. But the room smelled like…mint? Odd, but better than the dirty-sock stench from the other day.

"It's like Stonehenge, only with stuff, not rocks," she whispered.

He laughed. "Like Sam-henge. I love the guy, but he hates to let anything go. See those magazines? They're from ten years ago. He says he's all about the classics."

"Is that *Mad Magazine*? Oh, and I see a few *Playboys* and *Penthouse Forums*, hmm?"

"He's a guy, Cyn. Let's give him a break. Plus I'm pretty sure he just reads those for the articles. I know I do."

She gave him a disgruntled look.

Under another stack, he saw what looked like an empty pet carrier. "What the hell?"

"Let's go. I feel like a voyeur looking in here." She tugged him by the hand. "How about your room?"

"I was thinking to hold that one for later, but if you insist. We've got five minutes. Should be plenty of time." He gave her a fake leer.

She popped him in the arm. "Dinner will be ready pretty soon. Your hormones will have to wait."

"They're always waiting. Hell." He followed her down

the stairs, unable to look away from the flounce of her dark red hair over her shoulders. Her hips had a gentle sway when she moved, and that ass just begged to be bitten. Or better yet, slapped hard while he rode her into orgasm.

Think of Mom. Sam. Jacob. Hmm. Liam and Sophie. Anything.

Fortunately, by the time they reached his room, he was only semihard. He pushed the door open, glad it no longer smelled like a sweatshop. He'd aired out the place and put a room deodorizer in the corner.

"Wow. It's nice in here."

He blew out a breath, relieved.

"Come on. You did this for me, right? You don't actually make your bed every morning."

He felt his cheeks heat. "Um, yeah. I do. Sam says it's a sickness."

"A neat freak. Good to know." She winked at him, and his heart beat faster.

"Go ahead. You know you want to look around."

"I do." She studied the dark blue blanket over the queen-size bed, which was small for his taste, but a larger bed wouldn't fit in the space. He had a dresser, nightstand, and a closet full of jeans, sweatshirts, and T-shirts. And lots of boots. Foley loved boots of all kinds, but mostly the leather, ass-kicking kind.

"Someone has a lot of shoes."

"Boots, Cyn. They're manly."

She laughed at him.

"Want to see something funny? Open that up," he dared and pointed to his nightstand.

She did, and her eyes grew wide. Condoms and a few toys sat, just waiting to be used.

"Got a few new things just for you, Red. What do you think?"

Her eyes turned glassy, her breath sped up, and her nipples beaded under her dress. Cyn's excitement turned him on like nothing else.

Before she could answer, the oven timer beeped.

She raced past him out of the room.

"Saved by the bell, huh?" He rejoined her in the kitchen, only to get a set of orders.

"No sex talk at the table."

"You take the fun out of everything."

"Are you hungry?"

"You bet." He couldn't wait. The food smelled amazing. Then he noted the garlic bread in foil on the counter. "Oh man. I think I'm in love."

He saw the nervous look in her eyes, realized what he'd said, and hurried to put her at ease. "I've never met a garlic bread I didn't fall in love with. Or a lasagna, for that matter." He saw her relax. "But garlic? You don't want us kissing later, is that it?"

"You know, I hadn't thought of that." She shrugged. "Oh well."

"Good try. If it comes to that, I have mouthwash and a few tubes of toothpaste. Hey, I like to be prepared. Two things I'm always stocked up on—toothpaste and toilet paper."

"Can't argue with that." She chuckled. "Foley, you make me laugh."

"Better than making you cry."

"Remember that when you decide we're done. It's much easier to stay friends when you end a relationship in a nice way."

His good mood left him. "Is that right?"

"Yes. Cheating on a woman to show her you're done, or ghosting, is not cool. At all."

"First of all, I've never cheated on a woman." Well, not since he'd left high school. But he didn't think that should count.

"Good to know." She put the bread in the oven, then set food on his plate. Hell, even the salad looked good, and he wasn't a man fond of too much green with a meal.

"So what's ghosting?"

"You know. When you suddenly cease and desist all contact with a person. Like a ghost, you simply no longer pick up the phone or visit."

"No shit? I'd call that a douche move."

"Exactly."

"Cyn, honey, here's the deal. When we're done, it'll be because *you're* tired of *me*. And that's a fact."

She blinked at him, blushed, then busied herself with the bread in the oven. "That's what you say now, but—"

"Hey, I'm your boyfriend. I'm all in." He figured he might as well give her a heads-up with a truth he was only coming to understand. "I ain't going nowhere. Especially not since I know you can cook."

"That's a double negative, implying you're going somewhere."

"What?"

She turned to make a face at him, and they traded barbs. Minutes later, she removed the bread, fiddled with the oven, and put in the cheesecake. "Okay, grammar king, how about some garlic bread?"

He held out his plate, then waited until she joined him

before sitting to eat. He was halfway through his first helping before he realized she hadn't said a damn thing. "What?" he asked with his mouth full.

"Do you like it?"

He forced himself to swallow and slow down. "Are you kidding? I haven't breathed since inhaling this. It's hard not to moan and groan over this food. But that would sound too much like sex, and you told me no sex talk, right?" He bit back a grin. "Your cheeks are really pink."

"Hush. Eat." She took a few bites, then relaxed. "It is good."

"*Soooo* good." He moaned a little, saw her grow even redder, then laughed. "I'm not sure I'll be able to save any for Sam. Seriously. I could eat that whole pan, and I'm trying to be polite and make sure you get some too."

Cyn shook her head. "I've seen your appetite in action. I made enough for you and Sam to have leftovers. That's if you're nice enough to give him some."

"I'll think about it. Holy shit, Cyn. You can cook."

She smiled. "I'm glad you like it."

"I love it."

I love you.

Foley shoveled another forkful in his mouth, wondering where to go from here. She'd made leftovers and cheesecake for Sam. That had to be a good sign. God knew it made Foley love her even more. Now he just had to see what his buddy and his mom thought of her, and he'd start looking for rings.

Rings.

Oh man. I'm so fucked.

Sam shared a bag of chips with Lou at Lou's place, which was currently filled with a bunch of women giggling, gabbing in Spanish, and giving him weird looks. He debated the idea of sleeping over. There had to be at least ten women—ranging in age from seven to sixty—in Lou's kitchen.

"Dude, what is up in there?" He nodded behind him.

"Sorry. My grandmother, my aunts, my sister, and a few cousins stopped over. *Uninvited*," he said in a louder voice.

The older woman said something that had big bad Lou sinking deeper in his couch. "You have no idea the hell I live in when I leave the garage," he whispered. "I'm surrounded by women all the time."

Sam stared at this Lou, one he'd never seen before. Lou always acted like a tough guy, so to see him trying to hide from his family was comical. "I know you have four sisters, but—"

"Yeah, and the mean one is here tonight. My mom has *five* sisters, and *Abuela*, my grandmother, lives nearby. You're talking all these women, who all have kids. And guess what? Only one of my cousins is a boy. It's like a plague of estrogen that never stops."

Sam grunted with amusement and saw one fine-looking woman giving him the eye. Doing Lou's relative would probably get him killed, though the woman looked more than worth it.

"No wonder you're so in touch with your feminine side," he taunted.

"Fuck you."

"Back at ya. Loser."

"I bet I could take you." Lou stared at him. "Yep. Pinned in less than three minutes."

Foley had warned Sam when they'd first started at Webster's to leave their fellow mechanics alone. No fights, and no mock fights, because Sam had a way of forgetting himself and causing major harm. Which made Foley's irritation with Sam's current bout of underground fighting so questionable. Sam needed to vent, and letting off steam by launching or taking a punch was fine with him.

Unfortunately, Foley didn't like it. A few minor run-ins with the law had been a little too close for comfort for Foley Sanders. But Sam couldn't blame him. Like Foley, he'd rather die than go back to prison.

Sam sighed. "Can't. Foley told me not to." At thoughts of his best friend—hell, his brother—he frowned.

"Speaking of Foley, what's up with him and Cyn? They looked real cozy at Johnny's."

Sam shrugged. "Hell if I know. I'm here now because he's got her at the house for a date. She's fucking cooking for him."

"Nice. Good work, Foley." Lou raised a cheese puff in toast.

Sam ignored it. "I don't get why I couldn't have stuck around. I think I scare her."

"Didn't seem that way to me at Johnny's." Lou shrugged. "My bet is Foley wanted some privacy. Pretty hard to love your new lady when your best friend is staring at you."

"I would have hid out in my room."

"And that's so much more comfortable, knowing your boyfriend's roommate is listening at the walls."

"Fuck you."

"Language!" One of the aunts glared at them both from the other room.

"Sorry," Sam apologized, and the hot girl giving him looks smiled.

Lou groaned. "It's my own house, *Tía*. And, Stella, quit flirting with Sam." Lou glared at him, and Sam held up his hands.

"Hey, I'm not dead. She's hot."

"Hamilton, I swear I'll—"

"I promise just to look, not touch."

Lou growled.

"Here. You eat."

Sam glanced up to see a tiny old lady wearing an apron, holding out a plate of what looked like tacos. Something tasty but small.

Lou frowned, asked her something in Spanish, and she responded with a smile. A pretty older woman Sam wouldn't want to mess with. Especially since everyone in the house seemed to defer to her.

"*Abuela*." Lou nodded at her. "My grandmother thinks that with all those tattoos you must be badass enough to eat one of her famous tacos *campechanos*. She uses homemade chorizo, and it's a little spicier than the crap they sell in the stores."

"A dare, Lou?" Sam stared at the food, wondering what Foley was eating. "Damn, they look good." He glanced up at Lou's grandma and accepted the plate with a nod. "*Gracias*."

"*De nada*." She smiled, showing a missing front tooth, which only made her that much cuter.

He took a few bites, washed the fiery food down with

the rest of his beer, and asked for more of everything. Lou's grandmother seemed pleased as punch to get him more food.

Once she stepped away, Sam leaned closer to Lou and said in a low voice, "Holy shit, Lou. You eat like this all the time?"

Lou groaned. "Figures you'd like the food. Now I'll never get you to leave."

"That's pretty much what happened to Foley back in the sixth grade. And here we are."

Lou groaned again, and Sam actually laughed.

But inside he wondered if this would be the start of something new. Of nights spent away from his home and those he considered family. They'd move on and leave him behind, finally understanding he'd never be more than he was. A man hiding a dirty little boy inside, one who'd never be clean.

Chapter 17

Dinner went off without a hitch. Foley ate to his heart's content, and Cyn was thrilled that she'd gotten to the man through his stomach after all.

They finished, and he demanded she let him clean up. After taking the cheesecake out of the oven and letting it sit, she turned off the oven, took her refilled wine into the living room, and messed with his music.

"I'm not asking for permission to touch your precious stereo," she called out as she fiddled with knobs. A test to see how far she could push her manly boyfriend.

"I can see that," he growled back. "If you don't like the presets, check out my phone. I have some channels you might like better."

He passed. No problem giving up control to his stereo. Interesting. She looked around. "Where's your phone?"

"Hell. I don't know."

That man and his phone. She found it a few minutes later in his jacket pocket—in the closet. She turned it on, sadly not surprised to see he had no password to protect his information, and selected a familiar music application. Then she chose a station she liked to listen to, a combination of old blues and jazz. One of her favorite Billie Holiday tunes piped through his Bluetooth speakers, and she closed her eyes, enchanted with the husky tones.

"May I?" Foley asked from right beside her. He took

her glass and placed it on the table. Then he took her in his arms and swayed to the music, dancing with her.

So slow, they moved together as one, leaning into each other, learning each other. She couldn't look away from his soft gray gaze, spellbound. "You're really good at this."

He smiled and asked softly, "At what?"

At making me feel special. "At romance."

"Is that what this is?"

She nodded and rested her head on his chest, totally falling for the big lug.

"Hmm. Guess I like it too. Romance. Who'd have thought?" He chuckled, and she felt his joy reverberate through her.

They danced together through several songs, until, as if by unspoken agreement, they decided to stop. She looked up into Foley's pale eyes, now hooded and hungry with the same need she felt inside.

"I'm going to kiss you." He cupped her cheeks. "Kiss me back, baby."

She closed her eyes as he neared, and his kiss took her breath away. It was the same enthralling connection she always shared with him, but tonight it felt like much more. She put her hands on his hips, holding him there, and he continued to caress her cheeks. They didn't press together, didn't mash in a violent frenzy of desire, one she felt all the same.

Instead, Foley seemed to hold back, kissing her as if afraid to let her go. He was so careful, so gentle, yet his kiss packed a punch that made her dizzy.

She clutched his hips, holding tight and wanting him more than she'd ever wanted anything. She pulled back and licked her lips. "Make love to me, Foley."

He didn't smile or make light of the moment. "Yes." He grabbed her hand and tugged her with him down to his bedroom.

Once inside, he closed the door. Before she could take off her clothes, he stopped her. "No. Let me."

He took his time feeling her first, running his hands over her body, touching her with care and a sensual lightness that made it difficult to hold still. What made it more erotic was that he stared at her face all the while, watching her take her pleasure. Then he knelt and hugged her, his head to her belly. Tears came to her eyes. Foley was treasuring her, making her feel precious.

She wanted to make this so good for him, but he wouldn't let her. Instead he pushed up her dress, exposing her thigh-high stockings and heels, as well as the sexy lace panties she'd worn just for him.

He looked up from her underwear, his face now showing strain. "Don't tell me. The bra matches?"

She smiled. "Would you like to see?"

"Take it off. Slowly." He moved to his feet and stepped back, ripping off his sweater and T-shirt in the process.

She removed her dress with care, taking it by the hem and lifting it over her head. She tossed it to the floor, hoping he liked the matching bra and panty set, as well as the pretty stockings and sexy black pumps.

"You are just…amazing." He stepped forward and cupped her silk-clad breasts. "So fucking gorgeous. So fucking mine."

He stepped closer and pressed his chest against hers.

She drew in a breath, her nipples hard, sparks of need flaring where they poked through her bra and brushed against his hot body.

Then he guided her until the backs of her knees hit the bed. "Sit."

She sat and watched him unbutton his jeans. So sensual. She was caught in his web. Ensnared by not only her lust, but his as well. He toed off his shoes, then removed the rest of his clothes. Standing naked and proud before her, he looked like an ancient warrior come to life.

"Here." He handed her something.

She took it. "A condom?"

"I didn't want to forget this time." He ran his fingers over her hair, and she was all too aware of how easy it would be to lean forward and taste him. "Put it on me, Cyn."

She was in her bra and panties, her hose and heels. He wore nothing at all. The mood felt heavy, sensual. She could still hear blues from the living room. The whole evening was surreal.

And she never wanted it to end.

"Come on, baby. Put it on me." He closed his hand around hers, which held the condom.

"Okay. But first…" She moved to the floor and knelt, staring up at him, watching his expression as she neared his arousal. His breath quickened, his belly contracted, and his jaw clenched. She opened her mouth, and he groaned.

Then she put her mouth over him, tasting his slick passion and wanting him to feel as needy as she did. As caught up in their moment.

She showed him more than desire, but how she truly felt, expressing her deepening feeling, sharing her trust. She took him deeper between her lips, still watching him while she caressed him. With hands and tongue and a gentle scrape of her teeth.

"*Jesus*. Cyn, baby." He moaned and put his hands on her head. "I can't… Oh fuck. Yeah."

She bobbed over him, no longer looking at him but closing her eyes and tasting him. She felt his tension, his thick, muscular thighs bunched in anticipation. Tasted the essence of his need and knew it wouldn't be long. Then he stopped her, trembling, his hand on her shoulder.

"Not yet, Cyn," he rasped. "Put it on me." He nudged her hand, still gripping the condom. "Please."

How he had the wherewithal to deny himself was beyond her. She'd been caught up in the moment, ready to swallow the whole of him, taking him deep within her. But she did as he asked, tearing open the packet and rolling his protection down the steely length of him.

Once covered, he dragged her to her feet and took off her bra and panties with methodical attention to detail. No stray touching, just a clean removal of her clothing, though he left her hose and heels on.

He eased her back on the bed. Everything about their time together was unhurried, savored. And she knew they'd turned some point in their relationship. Something she couldn't put her finger on, but the look in his eyes was just…more.

He climbed on top of her, the pressure of his body a comfort and an allure. She traced those inked muscles with her fingers, lightly clawing him with her nails.

"Yeah. That's it. Rake them over me," he said in a husky voice. Then he kissed her, and the need grew.

He touched her, so lightly she was sure she'd

imagined it. Foley explored her, caressing and petting her as if afraid to be too rough. The gentle press of his thumb over her sex almost had her up in flames.

She arched up, shifting and widening her legs. Needing him inside her.

But Foley continued his sensual torture, until she was mindless with desire.

He must have been as lost, because he moved with more insistence. He finally pushed inside her, not stopping until he'd buried himself as deep as he could go.

When he stilled, she opened eyes she hadn't been aware of closing.

Foley held her hands on either side of her head, their fingers entwined as tightly as their bodies. "Watch me."

He slid out of her until only the tip of him remained, and then he pushed back inside. With each push, he ground against her sensitive flesh, kissed her lips, rubbed her nipples against his hard chest—he drove her insane with need.

She clutched his hands and let him drive the pace until both of them reached for the completion they could only get with each other.

Foley chanted her name as he took her, and she responded in kind, needing all of him. The bed made its own music as it rocked against the wall, the low crooning of lovers and low bass coming from the hallway. He tasted like beer, like sex, and like Foley. Her man.

He pushed harder, and she couldn't hold back any longer.

"Foley, I'm coming."

"Take me, Cyn. Take me *now*." He slammed home once more, and she cried out and seized around him.

He didn't move except to jerk his hips, grinding into her as much as was humanly possible.

She hadn't realized she'd slipped her ankles behind his back, her heels interlocked, and she rubbed her thighs against his sides, sliding the silk of her hose over his hard muscle.

"God, Cyn." Foley kissed her between breaths. "What you do to me."

She returned the kiss, in wholehearted agreement. In love—and not sure what to do about it.

He deepened the kiss, and she lost herself in his affection and his touch, going along with the wave until it took her under, and she could think no more.

The next morning proved a serious turning point in their relationship. Foley watched Cyn blush under his study. She looked great even with bed head. Not that he could tell, but she insisted she had a flattened left side to her hair.

She'd spent the night. The *entire* night. They'd made love several times, and he'd lit candles during her stay. Talk about romance. The music, the dance, the kissing, and loving. And the candles.

He'd never, *ever*, made love to a woman, giving her everything he had inside him like that. Cyn had blown his mind. Not literally, but then, last night hadn't been the time for that. No dirty talk or fucking. They'd made love, laughed, talked, and made love again. She was so soft, yet a woman he didn't fear crushing with his strength. And so damn lovely in candlelight. The shadows played over her skin, drawing attention to the creamy gold of her breasts and the burning depths of her gaze.

Clad in her stockings and heels, she'd been the epitome of his own private pinup girl. His own wet dream come to life. But even better, she was real. A flesh-and-blood lover who made him feel—emotional, carnal, loving feelings that turned him warm all over, inside and out.

And she'd spent the night. He'd been able to hug her close, smelling and touching her all night long. God, she smelled good. Some blend of citrusy perfume and Cyn that went straight to his head.

His only regret was that he hadn't woken earlier for one last lovemaking session before seeing her off to work. She also refused to let him make her breakfast. Sometime during the night he'd put away the rest of the leftover food. She even turned down a slice of morning cheesecake.

"It's for you and Sam. Not for me." She relented to give him a last kiss, tasting minty fresh. She really had a thing against morning breath, he thought with a grin. Not that he could blame her. "I'll miss you."

"Damn. Me too, sweetheart." He saw her blush and sighed. "Come here. One more."

She walked into his arms, and he closed them around her, not wanting their time to end.

Reality was such a bitch.

"So about the New Year's Eve party on Thursday. Can you come? It'll be me and the guys at a friend's house. Joaquin throws a huge bash."

"Joaquin?"

"A motorhead with bucks who has a lot of friends.

It's pretty casual. Think grunge with money, so great drinks, probably designer drugs for those who use them, and a ton of jeans and anarchy T-shirts."

"Sounds interesting. You want to go?"

"It's a really fun time. I can introduce you to some more of my friends."

She didn't hesitate. "Okay. I'm in. Besides, you'll be saving me from my mother and possible matchmaking."

"I really need to talk to her about that."

"Later." She kissed him once more. "Now I need to get back and shower. I can't wear this dress to work. Nina will make fun of me."

"We wouldn't want that." He walked her to the door after pulling on a pair of drawstring pants, just in case Sam popped in.

She turned to leave and stopped at the door. "I don't have plans for dinner tonight. You'll probably be busy with Sam and the guys, but if you're not—"

"No. No plans. Your place?"

"Yeah. Just bring yourself. I'm thinking fish tonight."

"Awesome. I love fish." No matter what she made, he'd love it.

"Okay. Bye, Foley." She left, and his house seemed darker because of it.

He had a few hours before he had to be at work. He thought about catching some more sleep, but when he entered his bedroom, he couldn't see sleeping there without Cyn.

"Damn." As he'd feared, she was in his blood now. No way to get her out without removing his own heart.

He showered and dressed, made the bed, and cleaned up with no small sense of pride. He'd worked through quite a few condoms last night. Time to get more. And time to get a health check. He'd felt the magic of being skin to skin inside her. But coming inside her would be the ultimate connection.

To his shock, he started to grow hard again. He should have been too tired for another go-round after so much action last night. Foley forced himself to relax and had finished breakfast when Sam pulled up in his loud car.

Sam entered with caution, glancing around. "Ah, is it safe to come in?"

"She went home."

Sam tossed a bag on the floor and entered the kitchen, where he found Foley staring at an uneaten cheesecake. "She made it then?"

Foley sighed. "Yeah. If it's anything like the lasagna, it's going to be amazing."

"Lasagna?" Sam grabbed two plates and forks, since Foley already had a knife.

Foley cut him a large slice, but his own appetite had left with Cyn.

"You're not having any?" Sam asked.

"Nah. I'm still full from last night."

"I'll bet you are." Sam shot him a look, and Foley grinned.

"She made plenty so you'd have some too." Cyn. So thoughtful. So pretty and caring and fuck-it-all sexy, kind, intelligent—

"Holy shit. This is good." Sam devoured his slice and cut another. "You said she made extra lasagna too?"

"For breakfast?"

"Why not?"

Foley got out the pan and heated him up a few pieces.

For himself, he poured more coffee and tried to stop feeling lovesick. Because yeah, that's what he was. *Love. Sick.*

"Okay, I admit, the woman is a goddess. This is outstanding. Just…" Sam attacked his plate with gusto. "So we doing Ray's tonight? Lara's working, so it's Johnny and Lou and you and me."

"Oh, I can't. I'm eating at Cyn's."

Sam paused. "Her place this time?"

"I don't know if I'm staying over or anything. We're just doing dinner." Foley couldn't wait. He decided to bring her flowers. She'd like them. Maybe roses? Or was that too clichéd?

"Huh. Okay. But you're missing out on darts."

"I'll catch up next time. Whatever you do, if you play singles, make Johnny go first. He cares more about screwing with Lou than you."

"Thanks for the advice."

Foley shrugged. Time to get going and get to work. "I'll take my car today. I'll be heading to Cyn's after work."

"No problem."

Foley worked his ass off. Del hadn't been kidding. They'd been mobbed by breakdowns, frozen engines, and water pumps lately. He joked with the guys as he worked, taking their teasing about Cyn in stride.

That evening, as soon as he could, he arrived at her house, bearing a bouquet of flowers. His woman turned all soft and girly when she took them. He also earned one hell of a kiss for his thoughtfulness.

The meal was delicious, as he'd expected. And the conversation made them laugh. Stories about Sam and Matt growing up had them howling at their antics. He never would have guessed Cyn had annoyed her brother to tears so often. Hell. He felt for the guy. Hard thing to not be able to bring wrath down on a redheaded cherub like Cyn.

To his surprise, they ended the evening with some heavy kissing but nothing more. The break from sex felt…good. The closeness between them deepened.

The next day at work, New Year's Eve, he rode with Sam, and his friend seemed oddly quiet. They continued to work through the mounting breakdowns, with even Liam pitching in. Five mechanics, Del and Dale working overtime.

They'd found a rhythm, and the day flew by.

Foley searched for a socket and said to Lou, "Yeah, so I'm bringing Cyn to Joaquin's tonight. That a problem?" Joaquin was one of Lou's clients, though he'd turned into a friend to them all. As he'd told Cyn, Joaquin was a gearhead who loved cars as much as he loved women and booze. Foley's kind of guy. He had a habit of smoking a little too much weed, but since the guy didn't hit any of the harder stuff, Foley didn't much care.

"Not a problem," Lou answered. "How about you, Sam?"

Sam shrugged and moved back under the lift. "I'll figure it out."

"Better hurry," Lou advised. "Party's tonight. Gotta have a girl to kiss when the New Year rings in."

"I'm bringing Lara," Johnny announced.

"No shit? I thought you'd be bringing Del," Lou said with no small amount of sarcasm.

"Did someone say my name?" Del asked as she

charged through the outer door of the garage, barely holding back her dog.

"Seriously, Del. Who's walking who?" Lou asked with a grin. "Hey, Jekyll. How's it going?"

Jekyll barked and strained to reach Lou, until Sam walked out from under the car he'd been working on. The mongrel pup immediately shifted direction.

Sam wiped his hands on a towel hanging out of his back pocket and knelt. "Come here, boy."

The dog jerked the leash out of Del's hands and bounded for Sam.

"Shit," Del swore. "I mean, shoot."

"Hmm. Isn't that a quarter for the ROP?" Foley asked.

Del scowled at him. "Why is it my dog ditches me for Sam every time?"

"Dogs like me." Sam slanted a look at Foley. "Dogs are loyal."

Foley sighed. "This is about Cyn, right?"

"No, dumbass. It's about you ditching me with the wonder twins last night," Sam snarled. "They took me for twenty bucks apiece."

"Ouch." Foley felt for his buddy. "Why did you bet money?"

"He said something about feeling lucky." Lou shrugged. "I tried to feel bad about taking his money, but I just couldn't."

"Neither could I," Johnny, their darts master, said with pride. "Sam was seriously sucking last night."

"He was." Lou shook his head. "Maybe that's what Jekyll smells. The sad scent of defeat."

"Fu—" Sam paused at the glare Del shot him. "Screw you, Cortez." He sounded vicious, but his hands on the dog remained gentle. Like magic, Jekyll calmed under Sam's touch.

Lou snorted. "Heard that before."

"No doubt you'll hear it again," Del said, which made everyone laugh. Even Sam cracked a half grin.

"You coming to the party tonight, Del?" Lou asked.

Del had attended last year with her cousin and brother.

"Nah. This year I'm hanging with the McCauleys."

"How suburban of you." Johnny shook his head. "Will you watch the ball come down on TV? Talk about a wild night!"

Del just stared at him.

Johnny cringed. "Not the wolf eyes. Sorry for asking, boss. But hey, don't blame me because the McCauleys are domesticating you."

Foley chuckled, then coughed when she glared at him. "What? I like domesticated-family Del. Much nicer than angry-single Del."

Lou laughed at that

"Funny, guys."

"Do you know if Rena's coming?" Lou asked. "My buddy wants to know."

"She and my brother will be there. They're putting in an appearance at the family party first. Don't count on Dad being there, though. He'll be with Sophie. Liam's days with strippers are over. Finally." She gave Foley a look.

"What? I'm done with strippers too."

"Are you going to the party?"

"Yeah."

"With Cyn?"

"Um, yeah." What was she getting at?

"Look, moron. If you're planning on going to the party, you might want to think about all your 'old friends' that are going to be there too. Wouldn't hurt to warn Cyn she'll be rubbing elbows with your pole buddies."

"Damn—I mean, darn." Foley hadn't considered that. But what better way to introduce Cyn to his new life than by showing her the old one he was clearly leaving behind for her?

A great plan. What could possibly go wrong?

Chapter 18

THE PARTY WAS IN FULL SWING BY THE TIME CYN AND Foley arrived. They'd driven together, and she was glad. She never would have found this place on her own, miles outside the city. A veritable mansion with a garage that could accommodate more than a dozen cars, the place belonged in an architectural digest magazine. And that was to say nothing of the acres of green and meticulous landscaping surrounding the home, what she could see of it at least. She could only imagine the place during the daytime.

The driveway and road leading to the home were littered with high-end cars and a few buses.

Color her impressed. Joaquin sure knew how to throw a party.

They approached, following a few other couples. Electronic dance music thumped as she walked up the marbled stairway of the outer landing to the double-doored entrance of the grand home. Through the open doors, Cyn noted glitter and streamers dancing in the strobing lights that winked around a wall separating the inner foyer from the rest of the house, just beyond the guard checking people in. A heavily tattooed man with huge gauges in his ears and a Mohawk hairstyle high-fived Foley and shared a manly half hug.

Foley grinned and introduced him to Cyn.

Marlon looked her over and whistled. "Seriously,

Foley. I don't know how you do it. You, Cyn, are one fine lady." Marlon nodded to noise behind him. "Go on in. The gang's all here."

Foley slapped him on the back then put an arm around Cyn. She'd worn a pair of tight-fitting jeans and an off-the-shoulder short-sleeved blouse, because she'd figured any place that had dance music would get warm. Especially with the hundred-plus crowd Foley had mentioned.

The music grew louder as they walked through the impressive entryway into a living area that had been cleared of all furniture save a few tables and couches. She goggled at the rich detail. The house looked like a Colonial mansion, complete with archways and columns and marbled flooring. They'd driven nearly an hour toward Newcastle to get to the place, and she could see why. Joaquin had acres of land surrounding his mansion. Not something easily attainable in Seattle unless you'd grown up there and inherited the land or had megamillions to spend on real estate.

Outside, a massive pool patio looked congested. People danced under space heaters and around fire bowls scattered to increase the heat. The home wasn't so crowded that it was elbow to elbow, but as they moved into the *freaking ballroom*, where the DJ stood on a dais and several bars had been set up, the crowd seemed denser.

"Remember what I said about some of my exes being in the crowd. I wouldn't be surprised," Foley said loudly into her ear to be heard above the music.

Typical male. He'd told her to expect that they might run into an old girlfriend or two only when they'd already been on the way to the party. Had she known that beforehand, Cyn didn't know if she'd have agreed to attend. Silly to be intimidated by the thought of meeting one of Foley's old flames. But considering how attractive he was, she just knew his exes would be sexy and no doubt slender.

They ran into Lou, Johnny, and Lara, and she calmed down.

She smiled at Lara, pleased to see someone she knew and liked.

"Hey, Cyn." Lara gave her a hug. The woman looked amazing. She'd pulled back her long dark hair, which showed off her high cheekbones and full lips. Lara wore a short skirt and a tank top, and she looked like someone a rock star would choose to accompany him back to his room after a concert.

Cyn felt overdressed and clunky.

"Cyn. Lookin' good." Lou nodded and gave her an approving grin, one that Foley didn't seem to like. As usual, Lou looked fierce and lickable at the same time. He wore dark jeans and a black button-down shirt rolled up to midforearm. Wow, did he clean up nice.

"Back off, Lou. She's mine."

"Easy, jackoff. Just welcoming your girl to the party."

"Foley." She elbowed him, and he grunted. "Be nice."

"What? I'm not allowed to be jealous?"

She blushed and hoped the flashing lights hid it. "What's with the lights? It's like they're trying to get someone to have a seizure or something."

Johnny laughed. He looked sexy, strong. Masculine. Hell, all Foley's friends looked like buff models. Tattoos decorated both of Lou's thick arms and one of Johnny's.

Foley had worn what he called a dressy T-shirt—a solid black crew neck—with black jeans and one of his many pairs of black boots. All the black made his gray eyes look even brighter.

She had another moment of befuddlement. *What am I doing with all the pretty, muscular people?*

He gripped her shoulder tighter and hugged her close. Then he kissed her. A possessive gesture, and one that made her giddy. He was acting all macho in front of his friends.

She looked away from their smiles to see Sam approach with a gorgeous blond on his arm.

"Hey, man." He gripped Foley's arm with his free hand. "About time you got here. Look who I found?"

"Foley!" The blond jumped into Foley's arms, causing him to let go of Cyn.

"Hi, Cyn." Sam nodded at her, his expression distinctly less friendly than the one he'd given Foley. He greeted the others, giving Lara a half smile and a kiss on the cheek. Very different from the greeting he'd given Cyn.

"Ah, hey there, Stacy." Foley gently pulled out of her embrace. "Cyn, this is Stacy, an old friend of mine. Stacy, meet my girlfriend, Cyn."

Old friend—more like ex-lover. Expecting Stacy to be a cold bitch, because anyone with hair that golden, eyes that blue, and breasts that perky had to be nasty, Cyn waited.

"Oh, hi there." Stacy smiled at her and shook her hand, stepping away from Foley. "I'm sorry. I didn't mean to jump him." She blushed. "I just haven't seen him in a while. It's great to meet you. Want something to drink?"

Not wanting to appear unfriendly, Cyn pasted on a smile. "Ah, sure." She refused to look back at Foley while Stacy dragged her away.

At the bar, Stacy scored them two rum and Cokes without having to wait. "Sorry again for getting grabby with your man. Foley's such a great guy. We went out last year for a little bit."

Went out likely meant they'd screwed like bunnies.

"Oh?" Cyn took a fortifying drink.

"Yeah. It was just casual. I was starting out on a new modeling campaign, and he didn't want anything serious. But, honey, you are one lucky girl. He's a catch." Stacy showed her around, introduced her to a few *more* of Foley's exes—just awesome—then returned her to Foley and his friends.

"There you are. I lost sight of you past the DJ." Foley smiled at Stacy. "Thanks for grabbing her a drink. Great seeing you again, Stace."

"You too. I'm off to Paris in a few days or I'd say we could catch up." Stacy chuckled. "But I don't think Cyn would like that. I know I wouldn't if I were her."

"Right." Cyn latched on to Foley, not pleased with him at all.

Foley must have read the look on her face, because he looked suddenly nervous. "Ah, sure. Well, come on, Cyn. Let's dance."

He dragged her from Stacy and the others and steered them onto the dance floor, where bodies bumped and jammed to some rump-shaking music. "I'm sorry. I didn't know she'd pull you away. But hey, she and I were over a year ago. It was never anything more than casual at best."

"That's okay." Cyn smiled through her teeth and downed the rest of her drink in one long gulp. "Stacy introduced me to Brittany, Erika, Monica, and Tracy too."

He paled. "Hell. I had no idea they'd all be here."

"Seriously? How many women have you been *friendly with*, exactly? Or maybe not so past. How long ago did you sleep with all of them?"

He had the grace to look totally embarrassed. That made her feel a little better. "I had needs, okay? I've lived in the city for the past seven years, and most of my friends run in the same circles."

"Your *lovers*, you mean?" She was irked yet strangely amused. Foley seemed sincerely contrite and a little…scared.

He groaned again. "I'm *sorry*, okay? I knew I'd see one or two of them, but who the hell knew Joaquin had hired a bunch for his magazine?"

"And yet they're not *all* models, are they?" She had to laugh, that or cry. And she refused to feel like less because she wasn't in a magazine. "We have a few models, a yoga instructor, and a professional volley-ball player—oh wait, she happened to be in the *Sports Illustrated* swimsuit issue, right?"

Foley swore under his breath. "Cyn, this is not my fault."

She wanted to be angrier at him. "You're not getting off on seeing all your beautiful exes in one place, are you?" It would have helped if a few of them had been rude or nasty. But all the women Stacy had introduced her to had been pleasant and congratulatory to her about snagging Foley. Cyn felt, in a weird way, like she'd joined part of an exclusive club.

"I'm in hell. No, I'm not happy about any of this."
Foley hugged her tight. "I swear, I don't know what
they're all doing here. I'm not that much of a player.
It's been years since I've seen some of them. Please
don't go."

She pushed him back to get some space, startled.
"Go? Where? You drove us here." Wherever here was.
Model-land?

"Yeah. That's right. You can't go home without me.
Cyn, let's enjoy tonight. You and me. We can leave if you
want. Go anywhere. I just want to have fun with you."

She glanced over his shoulder to see his friends
laughing together, while Sam stared at them, his focus
intent. She turned back to Foley. "Are you having fun?"

"No. I'm worried you're going to ditch me."

She blinked. "Foley, I just spent half an hour with
the gorgeous ladies of the Foley ex-girlfriend club. If
anything, I should be worried you're going to ditch me."

"Are you kidding? Ask any guy here. Hell, Marlon
wanted to fuck your brains out. Lou still thinks you're
available, which you're not. It's all I can do not to
punch half a dozen assholes who won't stop staring at
your ass." He frowned. "Did you have to wear jeans
that tight?"

His jealousy, not that she'd meant to cause any of
it, soothed her wounded ego. She didn't see his exes
anymore. She only saw Foley.

She put her hands on his stubbled jaw and drew him
close for a kiss. Ignoring everyone around them, she
kissed him long and deep and hard, until he was lifting
her against him and grinding into her on the dance floor.

"Foley." She tugged his hair. "We can't have sex out

here." She blushed at some of the wolf whistles around them, as well as the cheering to see more. Which, to her consternation, started to stir the others around them to start removing clothing. She noticed poles in several corners of the room suddenly highlighted with spotlights, now populated with girls in thongs and nothing else.

Then one of the topless gyrators spotted Foley. She smiled and waved with enthusiasm.

"Oh my God. Strippers too?"

He swore under his breath and dragged her toward his friends. "I swear, the only one up there dancing that I dated was Celine, but that ended months ago."

She started laughing, a little hysterically. "You have got to be kidding me."

"I wish." He glared at Sam as they drew closer, who gave him a smug look back.

"Foley?"

"*That asshole*. Sam did this. What the fuck?"

He took a step in Sam's direction, and she grabbed his arm. She didn't like the look on his face, or his clenched fists.

He turned back to her, and his expression flattened. Foley looked...defeated. "Let's go."

"No. We can stay. I liked Stacy." And she refused to let herself feel intimidated. "It's flattering to know I'm in such beautiful company."

"Are you sure?"

She rubbed his shoulder, empathizing. What a crappy thing for his best friend to do to him. "It's okay. Really." But she didn't think things would go so smoothly for Sam when he and Foley next spoke.

They rejoined the others, and after Cyn pointed out

Foley's many exes, Lara laughed so hard she cried. "Foley's fan club," she managed to get out, which had the others laughing as well. Only Sam and Foley seemed immune to their shared mirth, the pair keeping some distance between them.

A song Cyn loved came on. Lou noticed, because he started dancing with her right there in their little group. Then Foley was behind her, grooving as well, and the bunch of them got down and dirty.

A hell of a way to kick in the New Year, for sure.

By the time Foley drove them both back home, the New Year had officially started. Even better, Cyn had kissed him to bring it in. He still had a chance with her.

Fucking Sam. A brief conversation with Joaquin had confirmed Foley's suspicion. Why the hell had his best friend tried to screw him over? Given the way Cyn doubted herself, Foley had been beyond terrified she'd dump him when she saw the others.

They had nothing on her, but try telling that to a tall, angry redhead. He still had no idea if she had been putting on an act by taking everything in stride, or if she really hated him for a bummer of a party.

Though with the exception of meeting his exes, the music, the booze, and the company had been stellar.

He pulled up in front of her house and turned off the ignition. He didn't want to wake her. She looked so comfortable sleeping. Instead, he found her keys and unlocked her door. Then he returned to his vehicle and carried her inside the house. She was no lightweight, for sure, but she fit in his arms perfectly.

Tired and no doubt still buzzing, she didn't stir when he kicked the door shut behind them. He put her down on her bed and hurried back outside to lock up. Then he joined her.

With any luck she wouldn't kick him out of her house—and her life—come the morning.

———∿∿∿———

He woke later that morning, his underwear down his thighs and a frisky woman all over him. She kissed and licked him to a happy orgasm before he could fully function in more than grunts and moans.

"Happy New Year." She winked, then ditched him for the bathroom.

Foley tried to control his breathing, but his heart wouldn't stop racing. He felt boneless, light-headed, and totally replete.

She'd gone down on him, no condom, all the way.

He struggled to a seated position on the bed and heard the shower running.

The perfect opportunity. He stripped down and joined her.

She raised a brow when he entered, looking like a sleek, stacked mermaid with the water racing down her body.

"You blew me."

"Yep." She soaped herself, watching him.

"So, uh, you're not mad at me?"

"Not exactly."

He groaned. His nightmare coming to life. "What can I do to make things right?"

"Two things."

"Anything."

"One, next time, don't tell me *on the way there* that we're going to a place where we'll probably run into one or two of your exes. Give me a chance to decide to go or not go. Okay?"

"My bad. Totally. I won't do it again. What else?" He could stand there all day staring at her. God, she was gorgeous.

"Why don't you return the favor?"

Before he could ask what she meant, she widened her stance, then spread her folds for him and waited.

He didn't need to be told twice and gave his girlfriend not one, but two mighty climaxes where she shrieked his name.

"Now that's how you ring in the New Year," he said with a chuckle. "Pass the shampoo."

———

He spent the day with her, returning home only to gather clothes and some personal items before leaving again. Fortunately, Sam hadn't returned. Foley wanted to smash his face in. What the fuck had Sam been thinking?

Foley understood Sam not taking to Cyn right away. But hell. If he'd give her a chance, they'd get along. She was kind, funny, and genuine. What was Sam playing at?

Foley and Cyn spent the day together enjoying board games, of all things, and joining Cyn's brother and his family for dinner.

Foley had a blast playing video games with the boys, until Nina threatened to twist Vinnie's arm if he didn't stop hogging Foley.

Then Nina had embarrassed the hell out of him by

hugging him tight and declaring him her hero for saving her son. Matt hadn't looked too pleased about the hug, and neither had Cyn.

Only after they returned from the dinner had Cyn let him in on the joke.

"Ha. You should have seen your face. You look so cute when you're mortified." She laughed at him as they got ready for bed.

"Cute?"

"Well, in a mean, brutal sort of way."

He flexed his biceps, satisfied when she sighed and stroked his muscle. "Brutal is right, baby. I'm a mean bastard, and don't you forget it."

"Oh, I won't. Because if I do, I'm sure Stacy or Monica or Erica or Tracy will remind me."

"Shit."

"Or Celine. Forgot about her."

He buried himself under the sheets.

She laughed at him. "Nope. Sorry, Sexy Sanders. You don't get to be in my bed unless you're naked."

"I'm just following your lead." He waited while she stripped out of her clothes. "Have I told you lately how much I like looking at you?"

"So you're objectifying me?"

"I'm sorry. I can't hear you. I can't look away from your tits."

She turned a delightful shade of pink. "You mean breasts."

"What?"

She leaned down to say it again, and he grabbed her closer and drew her breast to his mouth.

They didn't talk again until morning.

Cyn hadn't enjoyed a New Year's party in forever, but she had to say, Joaquin's hadn't been as bad as she'd thought it might be. Despite meeting Foley's past lovers, she came away from the experience feeling less intimidated. How funny to feel beautiful surrounded by such loveliness.

Yet even as she felt it, she chastised herself for allowing a man to make her feel one way or another about herself. She had to stop fixating on her looks. If she wanted other people to see past her body parts, maybe she should start with herself.

She and Foley spent the weekend enjoying each other's company and mentally preparing for dinner with his mother and the dentist guy—Jacob. Of Sam, Foley refused to say much other than that he wasn't talking to the jackass.

Not wanting to get in the middle of his relationship with his best friend, Cyn kept out of it. She had her own worries.

She hadn't expected to meet his mother so soon. And especially not after realizing Sam didn't like her. Foley had two close ties in his life. With his best friend and his mother. Because of Cyn, he currently wasn't talking to Sam. She could only imagine how long she'd last if Eileen Sanders didn't like her.

The car swerved to avoid a pothole, and she glanced out the side window at the muddied snow on the ground. The drive to Eileen Sanders's home filled her with trepidation, so she spoke to distract herself.

"I still think you should talk to Sam."

"I will, but not yet. I don't trust myself not to rip his head off," Foley growled as they closed the distance to his mother's house for dinner. Eileen had insisted on cooking them all a meal, not wanting to eat out, so they could have a family dinner.

More like bringing her foe in close, on her terms, so Cyn would be helpless and friendless on the battlefield.

"And not one more word about dining with the enemy," Foley said, no doubt recalling her earlier worries. "My mother will love you. Sam will too. He's just being an ass."

"So he's been like this before?"

"Once, a long time ago. But he was a lot nicer to Desiree. Unfortunately, she was a snot and a bitch. I tried, but I couldn't make it work with her. She wanted an executive, and I'm a mechanic to my bones. She also hated my friends."

Cyn knew some anxiety. "I like your friends. I just don't think your friends like me."

Foley squeezed her hand. "Honey, they love you. Sam will too. Just as soon as he gets his head out of his ass."

He'd worn nice jeans and a sweater, so she knew today was special. For the gathering, Cyn had dressed in her favorite black wraparound dress and her power heels. She looked good. Strong but feminine. She could only hope she'd impress Foley's mother.

Her brother and Nina liked Foley. Her nephews loved him. Cyn's mother… not someone Cyn wanted to spend time with right now. She'd fared the storm with Foley's exes well enough, but a little lecturing from Ella Nichols and Cyn worried she might fall into a crisis of self-doubt too easily. She could only hope her dad would like him when she got around to introducing them.

They pulled up to Eileen's home, a nice town house just a few streets over from Foley's. Cyn wiped her palms on her dress and saw Foley do the same on his pants.

She smiled. "Nervous?"

"My mom can be a tough one. But she's a softie on the inside. Tell you what. You play offense while I'm defense."

"Um, are we playing football or going to meet your mother and Jacob?"

"Yes."

"Funny." His nerves didn't make her feel any better.

They moved up the walkway and knocked. Foley fidgeted, and she squeezed his hand tight, giving him reassurance through contact. But when she tried to disengage, he balked.

"Foley, let go."

"To hell with that. We're a team."

"What?" She turned to him and was blindsided by his kiss. Foley went all he-man aggressive on her, turning her to absolute mush. She clung to him, barely aware of the couple standing in the doorway, gaping.

"Much better." Foley dragged Cyn under his arm and hugged her. "Mom, Jacob, this is Cyn. My girlfriend."

Tongue-tied, Cyn could only smile and nod. *Foley Sanders, I am so going to get you for this.* She pinched his side, felt him flinch, then stepped on his toe.

He swore, and she smiled through her teeth. She didn't call them her power heels for nothing.

Chapter 19

THE DINNER PASSED IN A BLUR OF POLITE MANNERS, pleasant conversation, and two couples dancing around each other with a skill that made ballroom dance look easy. Eileen had made a mouthwatering meal of steak, baked potatoes, and a Caesar salad. Simple fare, yet it went down easily. Too easily. Cyn had wanted to ask for seconds upon taking her first bite, so she ate slowly in between answering questions about herself and her businesses.

She finally placed her cutlery down, pleased she'd left a third of her meal on her plate. Enough to prove she'd liked everything without making a pig of herself. "What a delicious dinner, Eileen."

"Thank you."

"No kidding, honey. You're an amazing cook." Jacob shook his head. "I don't understand how Foley's so trim. I think I've already gained twenty pounds off your cooking."

Eileen blushed. "Oh stop."

Cyn thought Eileen and Jacob made a lovely couple. He complimented her, acted like she walked on water, and had offered to help at every opportunity.

"Good stuff, Mom." Foley had cleaned his plate. He glanced at Cyn's and raised a brow, which she ignored. "So let's get straight to it."

Cyn contained a groan. Eileen let hers be heard.

"Jacob, how serious are you about my mom?"

"Well, I—"

"Don't answer that." Eileen scowled. "Maybe I should ask you and your girlfriend the same thing."

"Yeah, maybe she should." Cyn glared at Foley. They'd agreed to be subtle and polite tonight. The only reason she'd agreed to come. "Your mother is a grown woman. And Jacob seems a few years past adolescence."

"A few," Jacob said with a grin.

Foley folded his arms over his chest. "Hey, I want to know."

"So do I." Eileen folded *her* arms over *her* chest, and mother and son locked glares.

Cyn sighed. "I'm not getting in the middle of this." She left the table to clear some plates.

A smart man, Jacob did the same. They stayed in the kitchen while voices rose in the dining room.

"Good idea." Jacob nodded at the dishes.

Cyn shrugged. "Better than getting caught between them." She filled the sink and started doing the dishes. Jacob grabbed a towel and dried.

"So what do you think?" he asked.

"About?"

"Me and Eileen."

"It's not my place to say."

"But you said enough already, didn't you? For the record, it's been forty years since I was sixteen."

She chuckled. "Sorry. I love Foley, but he, um, I—" Dear God. She'd confessed the *L*-word. Out loud. "I mean—"

"I know." Jacob patted her shoulder. "Don't worry. I feel the same way about Eileen. She's amazing, but sometimes she can be pretty stubborn."

"Ah, yeah. Foley too." She hoped her cheeks looked less red than they felt. "He sure loves his mom. I was hoping she'd like me, but the way he's acting, she'll probably never want to see me again."

"Nah. She was pretty excited to meet the woman who turned her son down flat."

Cyn groaned. "Who told her that?"

"Does it matter if it's true?" He chuckled and picked up another plate to dry. "I'm impressed. I have to say, he can be a little intimidating when you first meet him."

"True. Unfortunately I have a redhead's temper. He pissed me off."

They shared a laugh.

"Now Eileen and I"—Jacob paused—"the first moment I set eyes on her, I fell in love. Hard. Never felt like that about anyone in my life. Not even my ex-wife." He shook his head. "But something about Eileen pulled at me. I just knew she was special."

"Foley too." She let out a breath. "But I'm so different from his usual type." She didn't mean to confess that to Jacob, but talking to him felt oddly liberating. "I worry I won't measure up."

"Seems to me that man in there arguing with his mother should be measuring up to you." He nodded. "You're a beautiful, intelligent, independent woman. One who doesn't seem to need a man to make a living."

"Nope. Not a bit."

"Exactly. So it's not as if you're out to use Foley to get at his money." He gave a wry smile. "Just as I'm not out to rob Eileen blind."

She rolled her eyes. "Yeah, I heard. I can't believe Foley asked you that."

"It's a legitimate question. That boy loves his mother, and for that I can't fault him. Eileen might not seem like it, but she can be too nice sometimes."

She'd been pleasant to Cyn, but Cyn had seen the assessing look in Eileen's eyes. "Foley told me his mom has always looked out for him. And that he's watched over her too. So you have to know he'll be protective."

"I have no problem with that. It's Eileen that does."

"I'll bet." After a few moments, she heard nothing. "Does it seem a little quiet to you?"

He set down the towel. "I'm going to go check things out."

"Be careful."

He laughed and left through the swinging door.

A moment later, Eileen entered. "Oh no. You shouldn't be doing the dishes. You're a guest." She gently tugged Cyn from the sink and handed her a towel to dry off.

"So are you and Foley okay? I don't see any blood," Cyn teased, trying to make light of an awkward situation.

Eileen sighed. "I know his heart is in the right place, but that rock-hard head of his won't let him listen to reason. So I left him to Jacob while I interrogate you."

Cyn started.

Eileen narrowed her eyes, then gave a soft laugh. "I'm kidding. I have manners. So does Foley, when he chooses to remember to use them."

"Good luck with that."

Eileen smiled. "So, you told me about your family and your businesses. Now tell me about my son."

"Don't you know him best?"

"I do, but I'm curious as to how you'd describe him."

"Well, if you want me to be honest…"

"Please."

"Foley is sarcastic, swears a lot, and uses his size to his advantage."

"All true."

"He also hides a big heart behind that gruffness." He'd helped her nephew, constantly tried to make her feel good about herself, and was unquestionably loyal to family and friends. "He and Sam aren't talking now, and it's because of me. But Foley said he'd give it a day or so before making up. He loves Sam. He loves you. And he'd do anything for the people he loves."

"Yes, he would." Eileen gave a knowing nod. "My boy will pull out all the stops for those in his heart."

"Yes." Hadn't she just said that?

"So what is it you want from him?"

"Me? We're dating. Enjoying each other's company. Foley's fun."

"Uh-huh."

"What? You don't believe me?"

Eileen studied Cyn. "My son has dated quite a few girls in his time."

"Yeah, I know." *I met a bunch of them a few days ago.*

"But I've only ever met three. One in high school, one a few years ago, and now you."

"That's it?"

"Yes. So you're obviously more than one of his stripper friends at that club he sometimes works at."

"*What?*"

"Didn't mention that to you, did he?" Eileen's lips curled. "Far as I know, he's not working there anymore. Now he spends all his time at the garage or with you."

"A strip club?" Cyn wanted to smack him.

"And that bothers you because…?"

Cyn glared at Foley's mother. "You're telling me it wouldn't bother you if Jacob spent time ogling naked women?"

"Not as long as he brought his ogling home to me at the end of the night." Eileen shrugged. "I'm older and wiser. But, honey, it's not about looking. It's about feeling. My son brought you here so I could meet you."

"And because he wanted to know what I thought about Jacob," Cyn muttered.

Eileen cocked a brow, just the way Foley did. "Is that right? So you've been dating a little while, and he thinks so much of your opinion already?"

"I guess." Now Cyn felt foolish for having brought it up. "He loves you more than anything. He's just afraid of you being taken advantage of."

"Well, two can play at that game."

Cyn didn't trust the gleam in Eileen's eyes.

"Uh, Eileen?"

Eileen studied her from head to toe, then shook her head and smiled. "Damn if you don't remind me of a redheaded Marilyn."

"Excuse me?" Another of Foley's exes to contend with?

"Never mind. Look, I like you, Cyn. And I get the feeling you like my boy."

Cyn blushed, unable to help it. "I do. He can be a real asshat at times, but he's an amazing man."

Eileen burst out laughing. "I get the feeling you'll keep him on his toes. Don't let him push you around."

"That won't be a problem."

Eileen seemed pleased. "Didn't think so. You're too strong willed for that. But, Cyn? Go easy on him. He might seem like a steamroller, but he's got a soft heart. He's been through some shit in his life, but he's a good man. Not to say he won't make a ton of mistakes. I do know my boy."

"Yes, you do."

"I sense you know him too. You see more than the surface, don't you? My boy is much more than all that muscle and ink he insists on getting."

"Yeah." God, Cyn was feeling the urge to tear up. Nothing like hearing how much a woman loved her child. *This* was how she'd always hoped Ella might feel for her. Pride, love, concern. A true desire for her child to be happy, and not just because it reflected well on herself.

"Now that that's out of the way, what do you think of Jacob?"

Finally, a change of subject. "He's a lucky man, and he knows it." Cyn paused. "I think you two are perfect for each other. You're both smart, funny, and you look at each other like you can't imagine the world without the other in it."

Eileen's smile grew. "You're not just a pretty face, are you? Intelligent too. You're right. He's a wonderful man. I'm going to marry him."

"Congratulations."

"Shh." Eileen glanced warily at the door. "They're out there watching a basketball game, but Foley has ears like a bat. I'm going to tell him about us over pie."

"I hope it's a big pie. Soothe the savage beast first."

Eileen chuckled.

"He worries about you."

"I know." Eileen toyed with a plate Jacob had dried and left on the counter. "He needs to worry about his own life." She gave Cyn a sly glance. "I'm not getting any younger, you know. I'm more than ready to be a grandmother."

"Well don't look at me. Foley and I are just dating."

Eileen watched her, saying nothing.

"I mean, we just met, really. Heck, we didn't even like each other at first." That wasn't exactly true, but what should she tell his mother? That she hadn't liked him, but she'd lusted after his fine body?

Eileen continued to say nothing.

"What?" Right then, mother and son distinctly resembled each other, both masters of intimidation, this despite the fact that Cyn towered over Eileen's petite frame.

"Do you love my son?"

Cyn sputtered, trying to answer without confirming or denying a truth she'd only just come to understand. "I—well—I—I... That's pretty personal, isn't it? Besides, Foley and I just started going out."

"Is that a no, then?"

"You can't—I mean, that's just not—Foley and I are friends. We're dating. He's my boyfriend, and he calls me his girlfriend." So lame, she left it at that, feeling like a complete moron. A simple *no* would have sufficed.

Eileen nodded. "Right then. Tell your *boyfriend* and my fiancé that it's time for dessert." The woman winked at her.

Cyn tore out of the kitchen to find Foley and Jacob arguing about the Lakers' chances in the playoffs.

"Time for dessert," she said with more pep than she felt.

Jacob rubbed his hands together. "I can't wait." He left for the kitchen.

Foley held her back when she would have followed him. "Hey, you okay?"

"No. Your mother is a barracuda," Cyn snarled in a low voice, not pleased at the way Eileen had dug the truth out of her without trying too hard. How pathetic was Cyn to fall in love with this rough Adonis of a man after so little time? *It's like I'm begging to have my heart stomped on and torn to tiny pieces.*

Foley frowned. "Hell. I'm sorry, Cyn. I'll talk to her."

Before he could step away, she stopped him. "No. Wait." She took a few calming breaths. "She loves you, as much as you love her. And she has a big announcement to make."

Foley groaned.

"You'll like this one. Jacob is a good man, Foley. He really loves your mom. And from what you both have said, he's loaded. So he's not after her for her money. You met his daughter, and you liked her, right?"

"What does that have to do with it?"

"It tells you the character of the man. His daughter isn't spoiled or shallow, right?"

"No."

"So he's a decent dad. Follows that he's probably a decent guy. I mean, he fell for your mom, right?"

Foley stared down at her and wiped a strand of hair from her cheek. "Yeah, I guess." He let out a sigh. "I need to let go, don't I?"

Funny, it felt like talking to the father of a child, not the son of a parent. She fought a smile and answered in a tender voice, "Yeah, you do. If you love her, set her free," she sang.

He chuckled. "Okay, Red, let's eat pie."

"I'll be eating pie. I'm thinking you'll be eating crow."

"What's that?" He slapped her ass.

"*Foley*. Stop that."

"Fine. But you owe me when we get back to your place."

"For what?"

"For that kiss at the door before meeting my mother. What were you thinking, you hussy?"

She glared at him, but he was saved by Jacob's entrance.

"Come on, you two. Last one to the table gets the smallest piece of apple pie."

"With ice cream?" Foley asked.

"Is there any other way to eat pie?"

Foley nudged Cyn ahead of him, a hand on her hip, and squeezed. "Well, maybe he's not so bad after all."

Eileen gave her son a hug and watched him leave with his girlfriend.

"What did you think?" Jacob asked as he hugged her from behind, resting his chin on her shoulder, his hands on her stomach.

"I think my son is in way over his head with that one." She sighed. "But he did wish us well, didn't he?"

"That growling was well-wishing?" Jacob laughed. "Then I guess we have his approval after all."

She stroked his hand. "I know it's foolish. I'm his mother; he's not my father. But it's been the three of us for so long."

"Speaking of three, when are you going to talk to Sam?"

"I'm having him over for dinner tomorrow night. He's quiet but caring. Don't let him scare you off."

"If I can handle your son and his Amazon girlfriend, I can handle Sam."

She thought the description apt. An Amazon, but with a vulnerable heart. She'd seen the affection in the girl's eyes every time Cyn looked at Foley, along with a bit of puzzlement. "What did you think of her?"

"I liked her. She's smart, and she's not afraid of him."

"Yeah." Eileen had liked that about the girl. "Did you see the way she watched him at dinner? Like she's half in love with him but not sure what to do about it."

"Oh, I'd say more than half." Jacob told her about his conversation over dishes.

"Is that right?" She smiled, imagining the babies Foley and Cyn would have. Tall and beautiful and cared for—especially with a proud grandma on standby. "I think my boy has that girl flustered."

"I'd say you're right. Just as off-kilter as he is about her. Did you see him watching her during dinner? How many times he bragged about her businesses? Her smarts? Hell, everything about her?"

"Yes." It had done Eileen's heart good to hear her son infatuated with a woman she actually liked. Eileen had been able to tell that Cyn wasn't a stripper, barfly, or tattoo groupie, the kind Foley usually hung around with but didn't think his mother knew about. Please. She kept a watchful eye on her boy, even if he didn't know it. Good old Liam always kept her in the loop.

"I have a feeling my son is falling for that girl, and she has no idea."

"Not a one." Jacob hugged her. "Poor thing. It's tough when a Sanders has her claws in you and you don't know it."

"Is that right?" She turned her head and kissed him. "Well lucky for you, I've decided to take you up on that offer of marriage."

"Lucky for me indeed." He kissed her again.

"Oh, don't let me forget. After we talk to Sam tomorrow night, we're on for lunch on Wednesday with some friends of mine I'd like you to meet." Liam and Sophie—a woman after her own heart. A lady who'd finally found love after a lifetime of searching.

"Sounds good to me. Any friends of yours are friends of mine."

Such a sound, down-to-earth man. She glanced into his bright blue eyes. "I love you, Jacob."

"I love you, Eileen." He paused. "Even if you did raise a thug who wants to rip my head off."

Since she'd never made any bones about her son or Sam, she laughed. "Just think. In a few more months, he'll be *our* thug, dear. And don't forget about Sam."

Jacob groaned and hugged her tight. "Now you have to take me into the back and make me forget all about my angry future family."

"You poor man. What you'll go through to be by my side."

"Anything for you, Eileen. And I mean that."

Eileen had finally found the right man after so many empty years. She could only hope her son recognized his own happily ever after in the dark-eyed woman who was not sure of his feelings…or hers.

Chapter 20

FOLEY DID HIS BEST NOT TO HAVE THE CONFRONTATION with Sam he knew was brewing. He'd said little to Sam in the morning. They took separate vehicles after an obnoxious comment Sam had made about Foley no doubt going to his girlfriend's house after work.

Considering Sam hated mornings anyway, it was no problem to basically ignore his friend before heading to Webster's—in his own car.

Ignoring the dick had taken effort, but now, after a full day at the garage, he figured he and Sam were due.

Everyone but Lou had cleared out. Del and Liam had sequestered themselves in the office, doing paperwork the pair dreaded.

Lou looked from Foley's set expression to Sam's mulish features. "You guys okay?"

"Yeah." Foley nodded to the doorway. "I'll lock up. Sam and I need to talk."

Lou grabbed his things and clapped a hand on Sam's shoulder before leaving. "Go easy on him, Foley."

After Lou left, Sam scowled at the doorway through which Lou had departed. "What the fuck does that mean?"

"It means that Lou, like the rest of our friends, knows you almost sabotaged my relationship with Cyn over New Year's, you asshole." Foley spoke in a low voice, but his anger grew at the thought of what Sam might have accomplished with his stupid trick.

"Oh please. If she's that upset by a few exes, what good is she?"

"A few? You had *five* of them there."

"More like eight, but she never got around to meeting Tanya, Jill, and Micki." Sam shrugged, as if unconcerned. "Not my problem your old fuck buddies are hot. Joaquin told me to bring ladies. He had no complaints."

Foley put his hands on his hips so he wouldn't plant a fist in Sam's face. "What's going on with you? Why would you do that? You know I like her."

Sam ripped off his coveralls and threw them to the ground. "So what, you like her? She's just like all the rest, right? You'll fool around then dump her like the others."

Foley studied Sam. Sam looked annoyed as hell, but he sounded…worried. "Has Louise been bugging you?"

Sam's face darkened. "What the hell does she have to do with this?"

"Your mother has a way of making you unhinged." Foley offered no apology for the truth. They both knew it.

"No, asshole. Louise didn't call." Rage lit Sam's eyes. "Eileen did. Funny how you and your fucking girlfriend spent the night with Eileen and Jacob while I was home alone."

"You're jealous?" Foley knew Sam didn't like the attention he'd been giving Cyn, but he hadn't realized how deep the envy went.

"No, Foley. I'm not *jealous*."

He sure as hell sounded jealous.

"I don't get you." Sam paced, his huge fists swinging back and forth. "I understand the newness. I get you two fucking like crazy. And you know, good for you. But what's with spending so much time with her? You're never around anymore. And when you are, you're not really with us."

"Us?"

Sam shrugged. "Me and the guys. Ray's too good for you now?" He sneered. "Is your redhead too fine for us shit kickers you used to hang with? Funny I haven't seen her there yet. You embarrassed about your real family?"

"What the hell are you talking about?" Foley hadn't seen this coming, and a part of him felt badly that he'd misread the situation. This went beyond resentment to something deeper. "Sam, I love you guys. You know that."

"Oh, so it's just me then." Sam stopped pacing and walked into Foley's personal space.

Foley held his own, ready for a fist aimed his way. Sam seethed with hostility. "What is this really about, Sam?" he asked in a calm voice.

The hurt in Sam's eyes tore at him. "It's about you, dickhead. All of a sudden you're getting laid and you're dumping me—again. I'm nothing when you're in heat."

"Sam, I've been with plenty of women. I didn't dump you before, and I won't now." Foley shoved Sam back, feeling threatened. "Jesus, man. It's only been a few weeks. It's not like I've ignored you for years. Cyn and I are new. And you made it pretty clear you don't like her. Why would we hang with you?"

"That's my point. All this *we* bullshit. Since when do you and some chick need to hang with me? Everything lately is you and her. There's no just Foley anymore. Christ. It's like Johnny and Del and Liam. Everyone's all of a sudden fucking paired up, and none of them can breathe without their 'significant other's' permission."

"Sam, that's not how it is."

"Bullshit. You took her to meet Eileen and Jacob? Why wasn't *I* there?" Sam thumped his chest. "*I'm* the one who lived with you for the past ten years. Just you and me against the world, right, Foley? Well, what the fuck was last night? Eileen tells you and *Cyn* that she's getting *married*?"

Hell. His mother might have thought this through better.

"It's not like that, man. Mom and I love you. You know that. You're like a brother to me."

"*Like* a brother, not a brother." Sam trembled, his fists clenched. "Don't you see? This chick won't last. None of them do. It's just you and me, Foley. What do you need her for?"

The door to the garage behind them opened, but Foley ignored it. Sam looked awful. Pale, shaking, and his blue-gray eyes were pained. Behind him, he saw Liam and Del in the open office doorway, watching with caution. He gave a subtle shake of his head, and they closed the door.

Terrific. Now they knew Sam was upset. Foley had done his best through the years to protect his volatile friend, and he thought their time at Webster's had proven Sam had what it took to be considered a valued employee, with or without Foley present. But Sam hadn't become violent in the garage, hadn't destroyed things here the way he had at other places.

"Sam, let's take this argument home. This isn't the place for—"

"This is *exactly* the place," Sam roared, and Foley braced for a physical fight. "You're getting some fine pussy, and you forget everything else? What the fuck, man? She's not even up to your usual standards."

"What the hell does that mean?"

"She's not exactly slim and trim. Yeah, she's got a nice rack and she's pretty, but please. All that mouthy attitude," he huffed in disgust. "She must be really good in bed, because something's got to make up for that *big* personality that—"

Foley hit him before Sam could finish. His friend had gone off the deep end for sure, but Foley refused to listen to insults about the woman he loved. Cyn had spent so long dealing with size issues, that to hear Sam—someone Foley considered family—say the same, hurt deeply.

"She's more than what she looks like, you jackass. You of all people should get that."

"Why me? I'm not some fat-assed—"

Foley hit him again. Hard. No holding back this time.

Sam stumbled then hit him back. The fight got down and dirty in no time. They wrestled, swung, and landed punches that hurt like a bitch. The fight might have gone on except that Liam and J.T.—Del's brother—were suddenly between them.

"Whoa," J.T. said and ducked Sam's fist. "You bruise this pretty face, and I'll shove your head up your ass."

"Try it, shithead." Sam shoved J.T. back.

Foley struggled against Liam for a few seconds, then relaxed. He had no beef with his boss.

"You okay?" Liam asked.

"Yeah. But you might want to double-team Sam."

Sam started in on J.T., his rage building, blinding, and it took Liam, J.T., *and* Foley to pin him down, face-first, on the floor.

"Jesus. Is he on something?" J.T. asked. As large as his father but with considerably more muscle mass, J.T. was a force to reckon with. But Sam in a fury was no laughing matter.

"A heap full of jealousy, from what I heard," Del offered.

Hell.

Sam stopped struggling, especially when she gripped him by the hair and yanked his head off the ground. "Get the fuck out of the garage and cool off."

"You—"

J.T. knifed his knee harder into Sam's back. "Didn't you hear my sister, Hamilton? Fuck off."

"I said *cool off*," Del growled at J.T. To Sam, she said, "You don't come back until you and I have a talk." After a pause, she added, "You got that?"

Worried for his mental state, Foley gripped Sam's arm. Hard. "Don't blow this, Sam. Think, damn it. You're pissed at me, fine. But don't bring it to work. You like *them*, remember?" Meaning Liam and Del. "You keep flailing around, you might hurt Del. You want that?"

He stilled immediately. "No. Sorry, Del."

"You heard me. Go off. I'll call you later."

Sam swore then mumbled a "Yeah."

Liam, J.T., and Foley warily eased back.

Sam stood, refused to make eye contact with anyone, and tore out of the garage.

J.T. wiped off his jeans. "He forgot his jacket." When he saw everyone staring at him, he said, "What? He did."

Del made a face at him, then stomped back to the office.

Liam watched Foley, his gaze solemn. "He needs help."

Foley sighed. "I know. He's messed up, and it's partly my fault."

"I could talk to him," J.T. offered.

"Seriously?" Liam rolled his eyes. "Forgive him, Foley. I think he spends too much time sniffing that paint he tattoos with."

"Hey. Forget this. I was trying to help." J.T. followed Del into her office and slammed the door closed.

"Sorry, Liam. Sam didn't mean it." Foley ran a hand through his hair, feeling all the blows that had landed.

"You're going to have a shiner." Liam gestured to his eye. "Don't worry about Sam. We'll take care of him. He's family."

As aggravated as Foley was, he didn't understand how he'd missed the cues that his buddy had been building to such a storm. "It's my fault. I missed the signs."

"Nah. You're human. From what I hear, you're finally in a relationship with a nice girl. That takes a guy's energy." Liam gave him a grin.

"True."

"If she's anything like Sophie, you need to be gentle. My woman is used to the finer things in life. And that ain't me."

Foley groaned. "Yeah, me neither. I'm not what you'd call sophisticated."

"No shit." Liam chuckled. "But Cyn's got a good eye. Don't fuck it up."

"That seems to be your advice about everything."

"Works, doesn't it?" Liam stretched. "Damn. Haven't had a good brawl in months. And Sam is no slouch. Jesus, he's strong."

"I know." Foley hurt all over.

"So you going to talk to Cyn first or Sam?"

"Sam, why?"

Liam nodded to the back door. "Because she was in here for some of your argument. Left before it got crazy, though."

"Oh crap."

"Yep. If it were me, I'd probably deal with her then Sam."

Glumly, Foley knew he'd better talk to Cyn first. In person. "Shit." He left his coveralls behind, cleaned up the small mess they'd made— fortunately they'd only knocked a few of Sam's tools from his cluttered workbench—and left hugging his bruised ribs.

He found Cyn at her house. Sadly, he wasn't surprised by the cool welcome he received.

"You look like hell." She stood back to let him inside.

"Thanks." He entered and stood awkwardly, not sure where to start.

"So you guys are fighting, physically now." Cyn looked him over, sighed, then left him. She returned with a bag of frozen corn. "Best I can do. Put that over your eye."

"Thanks." He hissed when the bag made contact.

"And sit down before you fall down. Jeez." She led him to her dining table but didn't sit with him.

That didn't bode well. He sat, then removed his phone, which stabbed him in the butt, and put it on the table beside him. "How much did you hear?"

"Enough."

He blinked his good eye. "So, uh, this fight between me and Sam. It's not about you."

"Really? Because it sure sounded like it was." She crossed her arms. "I'm sorry you guys had to argue."

"Me too." He mentally reviewed what he'd said to Sam, and what Sam had said to him. "You know I don't just consider you a piece of ass, right?"

She nodded but continued to look aggrieved. *Shit.* What had Sam said to put her off like this?

"And I like you. A lot."

"Even though I'm not your usual type?"

He groaned and felt the ache deep in his gut. Not just emotionally draining, but physically as well. Sam sure packed a punch. "Damn it, Cyn. Not this again."

"Well, I can't help it," she snapped. "It's not like everyone isn't wondering what you see in me. Remember, I met your ex-girlfriends. They were all so pretty and skinny. I know I'm good in bed, but I'm not that good."

No, she was great. But he had a feeling she wouldn't take that as a compliment in the mood she was in.

Too tired to guess, he adjusted the cold corn over his eye and let out his frustration. "Fuck, Cyn. What do you want me to say?"

"I don't want you to say anything." She frowned. "But I think Sam was right."

"How's that?"

"We have been spending a lot of time together. Maybe we should cut back."

Panicked, because that sounded like easing out of the relationship in small bits instead of ripping off the bandage of rejection all at once, he snarled back at her.

"Oh, really? Seemed to me that you liked us hanging out. Calling each other boyfriend and girlfriend. We have one fight, and you want to end it?" Considering the fight had really been between Foley and Sam, and not her, he was duly annoyed.

"We've fought before."

True. "But not about anything that mattered. About fries or onion rings. What movie to watch. Not about us being together."

"Being together. What does that mean, exactly?"

"You tell me. You like fucking me, but other than that, I'm not sure what I am to you."

Her eyes grew wide. "Excuse me?"

"You heard me." Hard to glare with one eye, but he managed. "You seem to love being around me when it's about sex. Don't think I didn't see your nerves last night with my mom."

"Seriously? You were interrogating her in front of me. Even Jacob hid out with me in the kitchen."

"Nah. That's not it. You've been scared to be with me from the get go. A few tattoos and you're nervous of what your family will think when they see us together."

"That's not true." She drew her arms to her sides, almost leaning toward him in her anger. "I took you to my brother's for dinner, Foley. Remember that? That movie with my nephews ringing a bell?"

"I do remember. So you'd think you'd be a little happier about being with me. Instead, you keep harping on *my type*. What the fuck is my type? Because I don't think I know."

"Foley, just be honest. We have great sex together."

"You said it." She couldn't be mad at him for that. She'd admitted it.

"But what else do we have?"

"You can ask that after the time we've spent together?" Now more angry than tired or annoyed, he stood, needing this confrontation. "Let's be honest here."

"Oh, let's."

He knew it was wrong to be turned on by her fury, but he couldn't help it. She should add shallow and pussy-whipped to her complaints. "You're into me, and it scares you. So you harp on your size. Hell, anyone with a pair of eyes can see you're not small." Oh yeah. There went the steam out of her ears. "You're also fucking gorgeous, but you don't seem to see that. Your mother did a number on you, and I'm guessing your ex-boyfriends did too. But not me. So don't put your shit on me because you have issues."

"That's not the point."

"That's *exactly* the point. I like you, period. You're the one who doesn't like yourself. And you can use me, Sam, hell, my mother if you want, as excuses to back off. But if you're honest with yourself, this is you running scared. I'm into you. You don't think that freaks me the hell out? But I'm no pussy. I've been real with you from the first. Figure out if you can deal or not. Fuck, I'm tired."

He stalked to the door. "I'm keeping the corn," he snarled and left before he did something he'd regret. Like beg her to take him, bruises and all, and never let him leave.

Cyn didn't know whether to laugh, cry, or yell. Stupid Foley. He just had to say he was into her. What the hell did *that* mean? Hearing him defend her to Sam, and in the same breath tell his friend he wasn't into her looks, had hurt. Then the past had come back, the images of his exes imprinted on her brain. The fact that he had taken strippers to bed. Her mother's charming way of caring by telling Cyn, in no uncertain terms, that she didn't have what it took to hold onto a man.

She had a right to her anxiety. Seeing Foley injured — because of her — hadn't sat well either.

So instead of helping him, she'd plowed into him with her insecurities?

"Oh, sometimes I hate myself." She stalked around the house, consigning her exes to poor relationships and her mother to a universe of karma. She didn't wish ill on anyone, but it couldn't hurt to want people to get what they had coming, could it? Which meant she'd had this breakup coming.

Except Foley had acted like it wasn't exactly a breakup. More like a pause in their relationship.

The phone buzzed, and she didn't recognize the ringtone. Foley's phone.

She swore, picked up the phone and, recognizing the number, answered it.

"Hello?" came a familiar voice.

"Hi, Eileen."

Eileen paused. "Hello, Cyn. Can I talk to Foley?"

"*I* can't even talk to Foley," Cyn blurted, then groaned. "I'm sorry. This isn't a good time, and he's not here."

"What's wrong?"

Feeling horrible because she'd been mean to him when he'd needed comfort, and because as much as she tried, Cyn couldn't help feeling not good enough, she talked to Eileen. She'd give his mother the chance to tell her to run, to get far away from her son.

"What's wrong is that your son and Sam had a huge fight today, one that turned physical. And they fought because of me."

"Oh boy. Tell me what happened."

Cyn gave her version of events. "So I left before it got really bad. Then Foley showed up and tried to explain, but I made it worse." She paused and dabbed at her tearing eyes. "I just don't know why he's with me, Eileen. He can do so much better."

"Really? That's not what it seemed like to me at dinner the other night. Both of you couldn't keep your eyes off each other."

"It's new. Probably all about sex anyway." Great. Now she'd mentioned having sex with Foley—with Foley's *mother*.

I'm in hell. I know I am.

"Well, physical compatibility is important, I'll grant you." Eileen sounded amused. "But I know my son, and he would never bring a girl home to meet his mother if that's all it was. Foley cares for you, Cyn."

Cyn wiped a dratted tear. Crap. "You mean '*cared* for.' Past tense."

"Did he say it was over?"

"No. He told me to get it together. But what if this is all just us being new to each other? I feel a lot for him." She couldn't admit—aloud—love. Not yet. "I also know you can be with someone for years and it doesn't work out."

"That's true. But maybe you're right about this."

"Huh?"

"Give yourself some time apart. See how you feel after being away from each other. Makes sense to me."

"It does?" Was Eileen telling her to drop Foley in a nice way, maybe?

"Yes, it does. You're right. A relationship takes time, and you two have been in each other's pockets lately. So take a break. It's not over if you're on a break, is it? And it gives you time to think."

"That's true." Relief at not being done with Foley shouldn't have been so strong.

"While you're on break, how about you and I have some girl time?"

"Uh, what?"

"No pressure. This isn't about Foley. To be honest, I could use a levelheaded female to talk to. Believe it or not, you're not the only one with doubts. I'm fifty-three years old, and I've only been married once, and that was over thirty years ago. I'm nervous about Jacob, but I can't tell Foley or Sam. They won't understand."

Didn't the woman have friends of her own? "I see."

"I know this seems strange. I have friends, but they know Jacob, and I don't want them to know I'm unsure. If it ever got back to him, he'd be hurt."

Cyn understood. "You want a neutral party to talk to."

"Yes." Eileen sighed. "I'd appreciate it if we kept this between us. If Foley knew I was talking to you, he'd see it as interference in his love life. But really, it's interference in mine."

Cyn liked Eileen. "I have some meetings tomorrow. How about Wednesday? We could do lunch."

"Yes, let's. How about some place downtown? Where my son will never find me?"

"It's a date." Cyn disconnected, then stared at Foley's phone. She quickly called Eileen back.

"Yes?"

"I'd better give you my number. This is Foley's phone."

Eileen laughed. "Right. Go ahead. And don't worry. Unlike my son, I keep my phone close at all times."

Not a coward, or so she kept telling herself, Cyn dropped by Webster's the following day. She went straight to Del in her office.

"Hey, Cyn. Problem with the car?" Del sat behind an organized desk, sorting through a large stack of papers.

"Um, not exactly. Do you think I could talk to Foley for a minute, in private?" Her cheeks felt hot. "I hate to be unprofessional, because I know you have a business to run, but I really—"

Del had already opened her office door and yelled, "Foley. Get your ass—ah, butt—in here." She turned to Cyn. "Got a quarter? I'm tapped."

Cyn blinked, fished through her purse for her wallet, and handed Del a quarter.

Del smiled. "Thanks." She put the quarter into a nearly full glass jar.

Foley arrived at the doorway, wiping his hands. "What? I'm in the middle of a..." He tapered off when he caught sight of Cyn. "Oh, hey."

"I'll be back." Del dragged Foley in, then left and shut the door behind her.

Foley looked bruised and haggard, and she wanted to give him a big kiss and a hug. But the more she'd thought about things last night, the more she realized Eileen—and Cyn herself—had the right of it. "Here's your phone."

She handed it to him, careful not to touch him in the process.

"Ah, thanks." He pocketed it, staring at her with intensity. "You look nice."

She'd worn business clothes for her meetings downtown and a Skype session later. "Thanks. Look." She wanted to get right to business. "I've been doing some thinking. And I think we're both right."

"We are?" He looked a little lost, her giant bear of a man. All fierce and rough, and vulnerable.

"I have issues. I don't deny it. But we're also moving really fast. I'm not saying we should break up, but maybe a break would help."

He swallowed. "So you want some time apart."

"Yes." Easier to say than she'd thought.

"So do you plan on seeing other guys or what?"

"What? No. I just meant we should take a break from each other. Why? Do *you* want to date other people?" She hadn't considered that. She panicked, then realized if he wanted that, he wasn't the man for her after all.

"Hell no." He glared at her. "You're all fucked up, you know that?"

"Watch your mouth, Sanders." She glared back.

She swore his mouth threatened to curl into a smile, but he remained tight-lipped.

"Fine. We're now officially on a break. But we're still just with each other. So no sex for you."

"God, Foley. This is about more than sex."

"Good to know you realize that. Call me when you're ready to un-break." He took two steps, then turned around and grabbed her.

"What—"

He gave her an angry, soul-stealing kiss before stomping out of the office.

Cyn stared after him and rubbed her lips. Then she left before she forced him to finish what he'd started.

Chapter 21

"I'M SO GLAD YOU AGREED TO MEET ME FOR LUNCH. I'VE had a wonderful time," Eileen said again.

Cyn smiled at her. She'd enjoyed herself as well. Eileen was such a refreshing change from her own mother, someone maternal, caring, and reasonable.

"Well, for what it's worth, talking about your problems makes mine seem smaller," Cyn admitted.

"What problems would those be? Not Foley."

They'd discussed him at first, but not for long. Eileen really had wanted to talk about Jacob, which had put Cyn's mind at ease. Foley wasn't using his mother to get to her, and Eileen didn't seem to have a hidden agenda.

"No. My mother." Cyn toyed with her salad, hoping she didn't come across as unloving. "I have a tough relationship with my mom. She's a good mother, great with my brother and his wife, her grandkids. She loves my dad, and I know she loves me. But she's always on me about my weight and the way I run my life." Cyn looked up at Eileen, hoping she wouldn't see censure.

"That's a tough one. Mothers and daughters, fathers and sons. Sometimes we rub each other the wrong way."

Cyn nodded. "My aunt Sharon was a lot like me, I guess. She wasn't petite, like my mom. And she wanted a man, to get married. Honestly, marriage is all my mom seems to care about with me. That if I get a man, all my problems are solved." Cyn snorted. "Trust me. I've dated my share, and I can tell you that I'm much better off being financially sound on my own. You know."

"I do." Eileen nodded. "I spent the past thirty years struggling to make ends meet, then to get my business on a profitable track. It took a lot of work, and I didn't have time for a relationship, what with keeping Foley and Sam on the straightaway and managing my business. But why does your mother assume you need a man to be happy? Because your aunt did?"

"I don't know. That's what she says. My aunt committed suicide when I was a kid. Out of depression, I think. But my mother attributed her depression to her size, not to a chemical imbalance."

"I'm so sorry." Eileen grabbed Cyn's hand across the table and squeezed. "That's got to be tough."

"Yeah, but it happened over twenty years ago. I know it bothered my mother. Heck, it's not an easy thing to think about, let alone deal with. But my mom uses it as an excuse to belittle me." Saying it out loud resurrected her bitterness.

"She never makes fun of me around my family. Only when we're alone together. She makes digs, and whenever I'm with her, I feel like a loser." Cyn was startled to realize she was on the verge of tears. "It's stupid, but just once I'd like to feel like my mom is proud of me, no matter what I look like. You love Foley. He's got so much ink and looks so mean sometimes. He swears like a truck driver, and he's been in trouble with the law. But you don't tear him down. You love and accept him, and he loves you like crazy."

"I love who he is, not who I want him to be." Eileen sighed. "Being a mother is difficult. You fear for your child. You want the best for him." She paused. "I don't mean to sound judgmental, but honestly, what your mother does to you doesn't sound right. Have you told her she hurts you?"

"I have. She doesn't listen. She says she only wants me to be happy. Heck, I've told my dad and brother about her, but they don't believe me. It's like she has two faces. The perfect mom, and the passive-aggressive, nasty mom." Cyn dropped her fork, her appetite gone. "Then I feel terrible, like I do now, for questioning that she loves me. She's done a lot for me over the years. Sacrificed everything for her family."

"And never let you forget it, hmm?"

Startled, she glanced into Eileen's eyes. "Yes."

"You never asked her to give up what she's given up for you. You love and accept her decision to stay at home and raise her family, don't you?"

"I do. I know being a stay-at-home mom is a job all by itself."

"Yes. So why should she get to poke at you, in private or otherwise? Because she's your mother? Because you owe her something?"

Cyn nodded. "That's it exactly. I've always felt like I owed her something."

"Have you ever talked to anyone about your feelings?"

"No. I thought about it. Trust me, I did. But when I moved away, I could put Mom on the back burner. She didn't bother me as much. Now I'm back home, to stay, and anytime she can get me alone, I'm a fat, ugly teenager going nowhere unless a boy likes me. It's crazy."

"It is." Eileen looked her in the eye. "Let me tell you something. If I had a daughter as amazing as you are, I'd be smiling all the time. Real love is accepting someone's good and bad habits. And, honey, there's no law that says you have to like your family." Eileen snorted. "Hell, I haven't spoken to my brother since I married the 'wrong man' thirty years ago." She smiled. "I loved Foley's dad something fierce. He was a rough-and-tumble mechanic, a lot like my son. And I've never been loved so well. Until Jacob." She let out a wobbly breath. "Oh damn. Now I'm going to cry." She blinked to dry her eyes. "Let's be real, Cyn."

"Let's." God, Cyn liked this woman.

"Your mother has issues. So do you. You can either deal with them yourself, get counseling to deal with them, or be miserable for the rest of your life. And this has nothing to do with Foley. Your relationship with him is apart from how you feel about yourself. Get a grip, girl. If everyone else can see how great you are, don't you think maybe the ones who can't are the assholes?"

"Oh wow. Can I quote you on that?"

"Feel free." Eileen nodded. "Now stop with the salads and let's get some real food. How about dessert? Something with a lot of unnecessary calories and carbs?"

Cyn felt her heart open again, loving this woman and her unquestioned acceptance. "Sounds perfect."

───※───

Foley couldn't take it anymore. He hadn't seen Sam all week, not since their fight Monday evening. The asshole had been home when Foley wasn't, because Foley had noticed things moved around in Sam's room. The pet carrier had disappeared too.

Sam didn't answer his voice mails, his texts, or show

up to work. He hadn't talked to the guys or Eileen either, and Foley had grown beyond worried into thinking about contacting Louise Hamilton, which he'd sworn years ago never, ever to do again.

He finished stowing his crap and prepared to leave work for the day, not looking forward to another lonely night without Cyn or his best friend.

"Yo, Foley. Can you come in here?" Liam called from the office.

"Ooh. Someone's in trouble," Johnny teased.

Lou chuckled. "No shit. What did you do now, big man? Fight some other guy for his air ratchet?"

Foley flipped him the bird.

"Pathetic. That's all you got?" Lou frowned. "How about a darts rematch?"

"Since he can't beat me, he's going for third best," Johnny explained.

"You two are hilarious." Foley thought about it. "Yeah, sure." Been a while since he'd been to Ray's.

He entered the office. Liam was the only one present. "Sit down."

Foley couldn't stop staring. "Who died?"

"Shut up." Liam flushed and tugged at his dress shirt and tie. The big guy was wearing a suit, minus the jacket slung over the back of the chair. "Sophie and me are going to the theater tonight." He groaned and sat. "She threatened to burn my favorite T-shirt if I wore it with jeans."

Foley laughed, feeling better than he had all day. "She's good for you. But I can't see her burning any-thing. She's so nice."

"Not all the time." Liam tugged at his tie again,

looking pitiful, and Foley chuckled some more. "Like I said before, shut up. Del talked to Sam yesterday."

Foley straightened in his chair. "Is he okay?"

"He's better. Boy is seriously fucked-up lately. Like his head's on wrong." Liam stared at Foley. "He needs you, son."

"I know." Foley felt terrible. Looking back on it, he had spent more time with Cyn than he probably should have. He—

"Just stop. I can see the guilt on your face, and it doesn't belong there." Liam shook his head. "This is Sam's mess. The guy has to realize you're both gonna grow up some-day. What? You both going to marry women and live in the same house forever? Or maybe you never get married and bring all your dates home to your bachelor buddy. Whatever. Point is, are you always going to be the same, living the same lives, stuck in the same rut?"

"I'm not in a rut."

"Please. You going out with Cyn has put a bounce in your step, boy."

"I hate when you call me boy," Foley growled.

"I know." Liam chuckled. "But it's true. Girl is good for you. She'll put you through your paces. But if you stick, you'll find she's worth it." Liam paused. "I like her. She's perfect for you."

"How so?" Finally, someone who agreed with him.

"She doesn't take your shit. And you can't charm her out of a bad mood, apparently."

"So you admit I'm charming."

"Nah. But the women around here—even Del—think you are."

Foley grinned. "So you're saying I could take Del

away from McCauley?" As if he'd conjured the man, Mike McCauley poked his head in the door after a perfunctory knock.

"Come on, Liam. We're going to be late." McCauley wore dress pants and a dinner jacket, but unlike Liam, he seemed more comfortable in his clothes. "Hey, Foley. How's it going?"

Foley glanced from McCauley to Liam and grinned. "I'll give you twenty bucks if you take pictures tonight. Del's all dressed up too, yeah?"

Mike chuckled. "I like my head where it is, thank you. But if Liam happened to snap a group pic, I'm sure I could post it somewhere online. Anonymously, of course."

"Awesome." Foley couldn't wait to tell Sam—"So, ah, Liam. Can you tell me where Sam is?"

"He's at your place, I gather. I think he wants to talk to you."

"Great. See you Monday." He left before he could rethink it. Time to talk to Sam and put things right. And to consider what Liam had said. At some point he and Sam would have to realize their futures might split them apart. Not forever, but finding love and starting a family would change them.

Foley wanted, with everything in him, to start that family with Cyn. But even if she didn't agree—and it would kill him if she didn't—he and Sam had to acknowledge change was inevitable.

He drove home carefully, wanting to go faster but dealing with an unexpected snowfall that made the roads treacherous. After parking, he entered the house to find Sam waiting for him.

Foley looked him up and down. "You look like hell."

"Thanks. Back at ya."

Foley tucked his hands in his pockets, and Sam did the same. "So."

"So." Sam blew out a breath.

"I'm sorry," they said at the same time.

Sam gave a ghost of a smile. "You first."

"Asshole." Foley's relief at that smile made the world a brighter place. Granted, he and Sam would have to deal with change, but he couldn't see his future without Sam somewhere in it. "I'm sorry I was leaving you out of things because I was with Cyn. It's just—"

"You love her. I know." Sam made a face. "Still not sure how I feel about that, but I had no cause to belt you. Sorry I beat on you."

"Sorry I beat you back, jackass." Foley frowned, annoyed to see Sam smirking at him.

"I beat you up. Admit it."

"Look, you—"

"Kidding. Sorry, man. This is weird." Sam took a deep breath before letting it out. "I fucked up. I was all jealous of you and Cyn, and I took it out on you. It was my fault. I'm sorry."

Foley just blinked at him. "Come again?"

Sam scowled and stared down at his feet. "I said I'm sorry. I acted like a horse's ass."

"Yeah, you did." Foley remembered what he'd said. "And Cyn heard you too. We're on a break."

Sam glanced up in shock. "You are?"

"Don't look all hopeful."

Sam had the grace to blush. "I'm not. I'm really not."

"Looks like it to me."

"Damn it. I'm sorry, okay?" Sam threaded his fingers in his hair and walked away, then came back to face Foley. He had the saddest eyes Foley had ever seen.

"Shit, Sam. What's wrong, man?"

Sam shocked him by grabbing him in a bear hug and holding on for dear life.

Not sure what had happened, Foley hugged him back, giving his buddy all the reassurance he wanted.

Sam finally pulled back and surreptitiously wiped his eyes. Foley pretended not to notice.

"Fuck. I'm such a pussy." Sam swore again.

Foley normally would have teased him, but not today.

"I got scared, okay? Eileen's getting married to that dental dick, then you get Cyn, and she's all your type and hot and—"

"Everyone has this fixation on my type," Foley growled. "What the hell?"

"Can I finish?" Sam glared at him, and Foley shut up fast. "It's just, I'm losing Eileen. Then I'm losing you too. And, man, you're all I got. I'm so pathetic."

"You're an asshole," Foley said bluntly.

"That's what Del said." Sam sighed.

"Sam, I love you. Mom loves you. Just because she's getting married doesn't mean she'll stop."

"But she'll have Jacob."

"So? It's not like we live with her or even see her all that much now. You think she'll stop with the breakfast invites just because she's marrying Jacob? He's not a total douche, by the way."

"I know. I had dinner with them last night," Sam mumbled.

"I'm sorry I took Cyn to meet him with Mom and not

you. I'll be honest. I wanted Mom's opinion of Cyn, and it was a good excuse to get them all together. Plus Cyn told me what she thought about Jacob. She's not biased against him like you and me."

"Oh."

"Yeah. She liked the guy. And Mom seemed to like her." Which made it odd Eileen hadn't been on his ass to see how things were going with Cyn. Did she know they'd broken off for a bit? Or didn't she care now that she had Jacob? "Fuck. Now you have me doing it. Mom loves us, Sam. No matter what. Hell, she waited thirty years to marry a guy because she wanted us to be all settled and shit before she did."

"Not us. You."

Sam looked so lost. It tore at Foley. "You are so clueless. *Us.* Mom is going to marry him. Great. She still loves us. I might or might not be going with Cyn. That doesn't change the fact that you're my best friend and always will be. You're so fucking stupid. How could I get along with anyone but you? Don't you remember?"

Sam knew exactly to what he was referring. Their dark days in prison, protecting each other from the abuses so many younger, innocent men suffered in those places. Beatings, rapes, knifings. They'd protected each other from the worst of it, and they'd come out stronger because of it.

"I know. I didn't think you thought about it anymore though." Sam looked surprised.

"How could I forget us fending off Leroy and his gang? Or you getting knifed and me scared as shit you wouldn't make it?"

"It was a scratch."

"That bled a lot." Foley glared. "Shit, Sam. We protected each other. Brothers, remember?"

"Of course I do. But we were only in that hellhole because of me."

"Because you left her a note in her house. Okay, dumb thing to do, yeah. But we were eighteen and stupid. Her fuckhead father was the reason we went to prison."

Sam sighed. "Yeah." He brightened. "You know what? I heard the guy was indicted last week on embezzlement charges. Made the papers."

Foley smiled. "Guess karma really is a bitch."

Sam laughed then sobered. "So are you and Cyn really over? Because of me?"

"Nah. We're on a break. Because of her." Foley rubbed his eyes. "Woman is such a pain in my ass. And I love her. Ain't that some shit?" Sam blinked, but before he could get weird again, Foley cut him off. "So, yeah. Cyn's taking a break from me, and I love her."

"You told her, and she dumped you?"

"I'm not stupid. I didn't tell her." Foley huffed. "She said we needed to take some time because she has a mountain of issues she needs to deal with. I'm just hoping she comes to her senses, or she's missing out on some prime stud potential." He gestured to himself.

Sam grunted. "Yeah, all that ass. Imagine that."

Foley knocked him in the arm. "You done sulking yet? Coming back to work?"

He blushed. "I wasn't sulking. Del ordered me back. Said the shop was a wreck without me." He puffed up a bit.

Del was awesome. No doubt. "She was lying, obviously."

"Please. She told me Lou was starting to act like he was the number one man around the place."

"That's me." Foley gave a mock frown.

"Nah. You're number two, behind me."

"You're wrong, but we both know Johnny's a solid four."

"True." Sam smiled, and Foley knew things would be all right, come what may between him and Cyn.

"So now that you're no longer acting like a girl, all emotional and shit"—he ignored Sam's middle finger—"how about darts at Ray's? Lou challenged me."

"Oh, it's on." Sam smiled.

They left in Foley's SUV, which was better able to handle the snow than Sam's car. "So, Sam, I have to ask you something."

"Yeah? What?"

"What's with the pet carrier?"

"You know, we're back to getting along. Let's save that answer for tomorrow, okay?"

Foley groaned. "Hell. I'm not going to like this, am I?"

"Sure you will. We're best friends and all, remember? But you know I'm sensitive. You have to be nice to me."

"Ass."

Sam laughed, and it was the best sound Foley had heard all week.

Cyn couldn't believe the weather continued to be so bad. Last Friday a storm had hit, and it continued to snow like crazy a week later. She also couldn't believe Foley hadn't called her *once* during their "breakup." She'd talked to Eileen a few more times though, and they'd met for coffee twice.

Nina sat next to Cyn as they waited for Ella to finish cooking supper. Her mother had gathered the Nichols brood for a Friday fun night. What she didn't know yet was that Cyn had another gathering in mind.

With Alex and Vinnie spending time with Nina's parents in Portland for the weekend, Cyn wouldn't get a better opportunity to finally deal with her mother and family all at once.

Cyn had taken Eileen's advice. Since she'd been unable to handle her mother on her own for the past thirty-four years, she'd found a therapist to consult. The woman had happened to come into the coffee shop by chance while getting her car fixed. Apparently she had some connection to the McCauleys, who had a connection to the Websters. Spotting fate at hand, Cyn had decided to do something about her lacking self-worth.

Two sessions later, she found herself ready to talk to her family about her issues, to get them out into the open. No more feeling shame about anything. She intended to, nicely, let her mother have it between the eyes. It hadn't surprised her that everything Eileen had said, Dr. Rosenthal, her therapist, had seconded.

Was Cyn cured of all self-doubt? Hell no. But seeing the problems through Dr. Rosenthal's eyes had definitely put things into perspective. Cyn was no slouch, and she knew how best to put that advice to good use.

Confrontation—my middle name.

She waited until everyone had enjoyed their meal, making sure to take a normal portion and not skimp the way she usually did to make her mother happy.

Ella had frowned, but she said nothing.

"Let me help clear those," Cyn said while her mother

also cleared the table. Nina stood to help, but Cyn shoved her back down.

Matt stared. "A little forceful, eh, Sis?"

"Just sit tight. I'll be right back." She took the plates to the kitchen, then tugged her mother from the dishwater. "Mom, we need to talk."

"Fine, dear. We'll discuss whatever you want after dishes. Thanks for helping, by the way." Her mother frowned. "But did you realize how much you ate, tonight? Is everything okay?"

Cyn bit her tongue. "Everything is just fine. I need you to come with me. This won't take long, then you can get back to the dishes. I promise."

"Well, all right." At that moment, her mother looked small, frail, and Cyn had second doubts about the firestorm she intended to unleash. "Are you gaining weight, sweetie?"

Nope. Time to deal. Right the hell now.

Chapter 22

CYN DREW HER MOTHER BACK TO THE TABLE AND SAT her next to her father. Then she stood to face everyone.

"What's this?" Vincent asked. He leaned back in his chair, patting his belly. "Great meal, Ella."

"Thanks." She grabbed his hand and held on.

"I'm glad we're all together tonight," Cyn began, "and that the boys aren't here."

Nina perked up. She probably thought she had an inkling of what tonight might be about—Foley. Nina knew Cyn had been doing some soul-searching about "the protective stud," as she liked to call him.

"Oh?" Ella leaned close. "What's wrong, honey?"

"Cyn?" Vincent asked, frowning.

"I've decided to be honest with you all. So I'll come right out and say it." Her heart raced, and her palms felt sweaty.

"Is this about that boyfriend of yours?" her mother asked.

"Is it?" Nina smiled.

"Hush." Matt elbowed her. "Go ahead, Cyn."

"What boyfriend?" her father asked.

"No," Cyn said over the commentary. "This is about Ella Nichols and thirty years of verbal abuse."

Everyone quieted. Her mother gaped.

"I have spent my entire life being told I'm fat, I'm no good, that I can't hope to have a wonderful life unless

I'm married. To be married, apparently, I need to lose weight and that attitude that comes with it. Because men want a sweet, biddable, slender woman in this day and age."

"Damn straight," Matt teased.

Nina glared at him. "Not now, Matt."

He sobered, and Cyn continued. "I've spent years trying to explain how Mom acts toward me, but no one ever believed me. You all said I was too sensitive, that I must not have understood her. Well guess what? I moved away for ten years because I couldn't take it anymore."

Her father stared. "You said you had opportunities away from here, that you couldn't do them from Seattle."

"I lied. I've tried for twenty years to get Mom to see me as more than a fat albatross around her neck. Do you know how many times she's compared me to Aunt Sharon?"

"Ella?" Vincent grasped at the hand Ella tugged away. "Is that right?"

"Of course not," she snapped. "Your daughter is too sensitive."

"To you. But you'll notice I never had any problem being with Matt or Dad. Dad, did you ever wonder why I took such pains not to be around Mom by myself?" Cyn's eyes grew wet. "She says horrible things. Then she ends every lecture with wanting me to be 'happy.' You know, Mom, I'd be happy if you'd just accept me for me."

"Cyn, that can't be right," Matt tried.

"Just keep out of it. You're the perfect son. You have a wonderful wife and two amazing boys. I love them, and I love you. This is about Mom and the way she treats *me*." Cyn locked eyes with her mother. "From now on, the minute you say something negative, I'm leaving. No more digs about my weight. No more snide comments about my social life and how I'll never fit in wearing a size twenty-four. For your information, Mom, I've never worn that size in my life. But the fact you're petty enough to tease about it says volumes about you, not me."

"I never said that." Her mother's face was on fire.

Cyn turned to her father. "Dad, I'm tired of you always taking her side. That goes for you too, Matt. Nina's the only one who ever listened to or believed me. And I'm thankful for that."

Nina nodded, studiously avoiding Ella's glare.

"I am not fat. I do not need a man to be worthy. And I sure the heck don't need Mom to ask her friends to bring salads and low-fat food to her parties because I don't need the added calories."

"Ella, you didn't do that, did you?" Her father looked disappointed.

"I just wanted to help her." Ella pointed at Cyn. "She's gained more weight. She'll never keep a man if she's so big. Jon left her. So did all the others. I just want her to have someone to care for her, to love her as much as we do."

"Seriously, Mom?" Matt looked surprised. "Is that what you really think?"

"Ella?" her father asked.

"I love my children, and I won't defend wanting a better life for them."

"Better than what? What your suicidal sister had?" Everyone stared at Cyn. "Yeah, I went there. But only because I'm constantly compared to Aunt Sharon and her miserable life. Mom seems to think I'll commit suicide if I'm not stick-thin. Then I'll make the family look bad. Right, Mom?"

"That's a horrible thing to say." Her mother rushed from the room in tears.

"You've gone too far." Her father stood.

Before he could go after her mother, she stopped him. "Hold on, Dad. Why don't you think about why I stayed away for so long, when I could have easily done my work from here? I didn't have to move away ten years ago. I did it to get away from Mom. I think she has a real problem. It's not normal for a mother to be so fixated on negatives with her child. She never did it in front of any of you, either. Just to me, behind your backs. That's not healthy. And that's from a therapist's perspective."

"You saw a therapist?" Nina asked.

"Yeah, I did. Because I'm tired of thinking I'm not good enough for anyone ten seconds after being around Mom."

"Damn." Matt looked blindsided.

"Um, so you guys know, Cyn's being honest," Nina said, drawing everyone's gaze. "I've overheard Ella saying some wacky things when she thought she and Cyn were alone." She turned to Matt. "Remember? I told you a few times, but you made me think I was overstating things. It's easy to believe, because Ella's so nice to everyone else. But, Matt, she really did say those things to Cyn in private. Calling her a fattie and a loser and a sad addition to the family. But she says those things in such a nice tone, and she cages her insults around how pretty Cyn is, how much she loves her. It's just bizarre."

Cyn's father paled. "I can't believe it."

Cyn sighed. "Then don't, Dad. I couldn't make you believe it then, and I doubt I can now. But I'm taking control of my life. I'm not going to visit Mom anymore. Not until she gets some help. I'll even go to counseling with her. But being with her, alone, isn't good for me." She left the table. "I'll see myself out."

Before she got to the front closet to retrieve her coat, Nina and Matt were there.

Nina took her in a big hug. "I'm so sorry, Cyn. I should have been vocal about this before."

"No. It was up to me to put a stop to it."

Matt looked baffled. "I don't get it. It's so…weird. How could she be so mean and none of us knew?"

"Or didn't want to know," Nina said quietly. "Even you told me your mom was harder on Cyn than you growing up."

"Harder, but… She really said those things to you all these years?"

"Yes, Matt. She did. It wasn't just once every now and then. It was all the time until I left."

He looked upset. "I'm sorry, Cyn. I never realized."

"I should have gotten counselling for this a long time ago. My therapist thinks Mom has unresolved issues with Aunt Sharon and her own mother. It makes sense. If Grandma Isabelle was abusive to Mom and Sharon, then maybe Mom is doing it to me and not realizing it. But I'm done."

She shrugged into her coat and put on her boots. "I'm not scheduled to come in tomorrow. But I think I'll take Sunday off too, if that's all right."

"Don't worry about it. We'll have it covered. That's if

we're even open." They looked out the front window at the snow. Matt gave Cyn another hug. "Text us that you got back home okay. I don't like the look of the weather."

"Yeah, better get going before you're snowed in here," Nina whispered, and all three shared a low laugh.

Feeling much better than she had in a long time, Cyn hustled through the snow to her car. She had an urge to call Foley and tell him what had happened. Would he want to hear from her? Considering she hadn't made up her mind about him yet, should she call him?

The answer was taken from her when her phone buzzed. She glanced down to see a text from Foley.

> Mom hosptal. Virg Mason. Acidnt. Thawt u shld no.

Foley couldn't stop pacing. He'd gotten the call from Jacob two hours ago but had only just been able to reach the hospital. His mother had been in the ER for a while, and no one would fucking tell him anything!

"What happened?" he asked Jacob.

Jacob sat with Sam, his head in his hands, bandages on his wrist and forehead. He looked terrible, and he'd been crying. "The car came out of nowhere. It hit a patch of ice, I think, before hitting us then ramming into a telephone pole. The driver was dead before the ambulance came for your mother. That damn car hit us in the wrong spot. God. It should have been me." He looked up, and Foley saw the twisted pain on the poor guy's face.

"Should you be out here?" Sam asked, his voice a low grumble.

"I'm fine. I need to know if Eileen is all right."

Foley swallowed hard. "How was she when they took her in?"

More tears appeared in Jacob's eyes. "Not good. She wouldn't wake up, and there was blood." He blew his nose in a hankie. "She broke her leg. Her shin, I think. Bone went right through the skin."

"Jesus." Sam looked pale.

"But she'll be okay." Foley kept thinking that. Anything else just wasn't acceptable.

"She'll be okay." Sam patted Jacob on the shoulder, being careful.

Foley wanted to plant his fist into something. Someone. "What the hell were you guys doing on the road?"

"It was my fault. Your mother insisted on going to a friend's party. I should have put my foot down and said no. But she wanted to go, and I wanted t-to—" Jacob wiped more tears and took a soothing breath. "Make her happy."

Foley pinched the bridge of his nose, knowing Jacob wasn't at fault. "An accident, that's all it was." He didn't know how to feel. Someone should have been by to talk to them by now, right? So where was a doctor? A nurse?

The waiting room had filled, the road conditions fucking everything up. But Foley didn't care about anyone else. He wanted to know about his mother. Then a horrified thought struck him. What if Cyn had been caught out in this weather?

Nah. Smart girl like that would stay indoors, where it was safe. Best not to borrow trouble.

He saw a nurse hustle by and was on his feet. "Hey. I need to know about my mother. Hey, you." He grew louder, knew he sounded belligerent and didn't care, not even when he heard someone call for security. If anything happened to his mother, he didn't know what he'd do.

Cyn was out of breath by the time she finally found Sam and Jacob in a large hospital waiting area. "Where's Foley? How's Eileen?" she asked, panting.

Sam saw her and nodded. "Eileen's still in surgery. We think. No one will tell us a goddamn thing," he said, raising his voice.

A nurse at the front desk scowled at him.

Cyn hurried to the woman. "I'm so sorry. I'll keep him quiet."

"You'd better."

Cyn didn't like the woman's attitude. "I know it's an imposition, but is there any way to know if Eileen Sanders is doing okay?"

"You'll know when I know," the nurse said stiffly. "Now if you don't mind—"

"But I do. Mind, that is." Cyn put on her sales face, the one that had pushed her past mediocre to financial success. "You see, those two men over there and another big one that's no doubt caused all sorts of trouble, love that woman to death. She's sacrificed everything for them. Single mom, multiple jobs over the years, taking on loans, doing anything and everything for her boys."

The nurse started to soften.

"Then after thirty years of being alone and worked to death, she gets a chance at love, only to have it taken away in a horrible accident. So I'm sorry they're being a pain, and that they yelled. And yes, you get this type of trauma and worse all the time. But surely if it was you in that seat, hoping your mother or father, husband or wife, son or daughter lived, you'd be that anxious to know something, wouldn't you?"

The nurse stared at Cyn a moment then sighed. "Hold on." She made a phone call and hung up. "Ms. Sanders just went into surgery. That's all I know."

"Thank you."

The nurse nodded, and Cyn rejoined Sam and Jacob to give them the news. Where the heck was Foley? "What happened?"

Jacob described the accident. "It's a hell of a mess. Let me find Foley for you."

"I'll come with you," she offered.

"No, sit here with Sam. I'll get him." He groaned when he rose, but otherwise seemed steady on his feet.

Sam sat and tapped his foot. She sat beside him on the three-person bench and shrugged out of her jacket.

She felt awful for him. "I'm so sorry, Sam."

"Shitty day." He frowned at her. "I thought you guys were on a break."

"I got Foley's text." She sat next to him and took his hand in hers, startling him. "I'm so sorry. I know Eileen loves you all so much. She'd feel terrible knowing you were scared for her."

Sam stared at her, then lowered his gaze, his blue-gray eyes narrowed on her hand holding his. Like a wolf in pain, wondering whether to gnaw his hand out of the trap. "How do you know what she'd want?"

"She and I have grown close. She's a wonderful woman. You and Foley are lucky to have her."

His gaze whipped to her face. "Are you crying?"

"Yes, dumbass," she snapped. "I'm crying. Happy?"

He shocked her with a flash of a smile that appeared and disappeared in a heartbeat. "I'm not happy you're sad. This situation sucks."

"It does." She clung to the strength in his large hand. "She's told me all kinds of stories about you guys, you know."

"Yeah?" He didn't let go of her.

"Yeah. The one where you two glued your teacher to his seat was a funny one."

He gave a surprising chuckle. "Good times." He paused. "She paddled my ass for it too. Same thing she did to Foley. And I was twelve at the time."

"Then she told me about you two fighting over what she thought was a girl in high school. Said you broke three lamps and almost lost a tooth. Only to find out the girl was actually a car. Man, was she mad about those lamps."

"She's a stickler for keeping the house neat." His voice broke. "A tight-ass for sure." He bit his lip and blinked at her.

To her shock, tears filled his eyes. "Oh, Sam. She'll be okay."

"She'd better," he growled, making no effort to wipe his cheeks dry. "She still owes me for inviting you and Foley to that stupid dinner without me."

"She really does," Cyn agreed and drew Sam to her in an awkward hug.

After a tense moment, he lifted her onto his lap and buried his head against her shoulder. She couldn't feel him crying, but her shirt turned wet.

Poor Sam. She cradled his head and stroked his hair. "It'll be all right. She's strong. She'll make it."

"She's all I have," he whispered.

"Nah. You have Foley and the guys at the garage. And me, if you'll have me."

He lifted his head, staring as if he could see into her soul. "Is that right?"

"And not in a sexual way, you perv." She smiled through tears. "Any friend of Foley's is a friend of mine. Well, except for Celine. I'm not fond of dancers."

Sam cracked a smile then hugged her.

When he pulled back, he set her next to him on the bench. "I'm sorry, Cyn."

"For crying? Please. It's nice to see you're human under all that toughness."

"I'm sorry for being an asshole."

"Which time?"

He frowned, and she was forced to admit that even teared up, Sam Hamilton had a rare male beauty, full of pain and pleasure and a raw wildness that Foley had never possessed. That wildness was a little too much for her to handle, but not too much to be friends with.

"Kidding." She continued to hold his hand, pleasantly surprised he let her.

"I could see from the start you were different than the other girls Foley'd been with. You're special."

"Nah. I'm just—"

"*Special.*" He squeezed her hand. "You're too good for him. Hell, too good for all of us, but you fit right in. I only said that shit about you in the garage that day because I was jealous and scared," he said in a raw voice. "You could take him away from me, and I don't have that many good friends."

"Sam, don't you know Foley would never desert you? Not for me or anyone. He's loyal, and you're his best friend. He's told me so on more than one occasion. And that's great. I wish I had a friend like you. Nina's probably it, but she got stuck with me because of my brother."

His breath hitched, but he pretended not to notice, so she did too. "Yeah, well, you're smarter than I am. I got scared, so I hit you where it hurt. I saw you come in, so I made that crack about you. Damn, Cyn. You'd have to be a complete idiot to think you're ugly or fat. Yeah, you're tall. You have breasts and hips and a kickin' ass."

She clapped a hand over his mouth when a few men in the waiting room looked over at them.

He wriggled his mouth free and continued in a lower voice, "He called dibs first, or trust me, we'd have been hitting it."

"Pretty sure of yourself, aren't you?"

He shrugged. "All I know is my boy fell hard for you. Real hard. And I get the feeling I'm the reason you're not together. It's not his fault. You're special. I'm the nobody. You matter, Cyn. Without you, he's not right." Sam paused and brought her hand up for a kiss. "He needs you."

Cyn could only stare at him in shock. Then he nodded to the stairwell. "Go find him. He's losing his mind. Security dragged him away, and he needs comfort. Even if you're not getting back with him, could you help him out?"

"Oh, Sam. Of course I will." She stood. "Keep an eye

on my jacket for me, okay? And if Foley knows what's good for him, he'll take me back."

"Hell, woman. He never got rid of you in the first place. You ditched him, remember?"

She blushed, knowing he was right. "You're a pain, you know that?"

"Yeah, but I'm family." His sweet smile lit up his face. "Now go help my boy before he kills someone."

"Mr. Sanders? Oh, Miss?" The crabby nurse called out to Cyn. "We have information on Eileen Sanders."

Cyn and Sam stared at each other, then rose as one and approached the nurse behind the desk.

Foley couldn't think. They'd put him in some stupid room that locked from the outside. They'd threatened to call the cops, but fortunately Jacob had arrived in time and explained the situation, pleading for understanding.

Foley couldn't do more than hold his head in his hands as he sat, praying and swearing and demanding to whatever power-that-be that his mother make it through the night. The door opened and closed, and he felt the presence of someone close.

"Not now, Jacob."

"Been so long you can't tell me from Jacob, hmm?"

He gave himself whiplash jerking his head up to see Cyn watching him.

He stood in silence, not sure what to say.

Her eyes dark with compassion, she gave him the hug he'd been needing for so very long. They remained still for a while. The only thing he felt was her hand stroking the back of his hair.

Her steady heartbeat and the faint scent of her perfume filled his senses, until he could almost accept she was really here. He lifted his head. "Cyn?"

"I got your text. Came as soon as I could."

He frowned. "Text?"

"Your mom is in surgery. Sam's up there waiting. Jacob went back to be with him." She smiled, and her beauty made his heart ache. "Sam and I made up."

"G-good." He cleared his throat. "Thanks for coming."

"I'm so sorry, Foley." She kissed his cheek, and he felt her warmth all the way to his toes. "Your mom will be okay. She's pretty stubborn. Must be where you get it from."

He gave her a watery smile. "Yeah. That's me. Stubborn."

"Can we sit?" She motioned to the chairs in the small, otherwise empty room, and they sat. "Nice cell, by the way."

"Ugh. Not funny."

"I was kidding." She seemed nervous. "I talked to your mom, since we went on our break, actually."

He started. "You have?"

"She's a pretty smart woman. Jacob is lucky to have her."

"Yeah."

"You're not upset with him for this, are you? He told me what happened."

"Shit. No. It's not his fault. Stupid accident." He told himself he'd stop crying. But fuck. His mom was up there, halfway to dead for all he knew. "Cyn, what if she doesn't make it?"

Her eyes filled. "Sweetie, she'll make it. I'm telling

you. If only to kick your ass to make sure you're nice to Jacob. You know her better than I do. What do you think?"

"She has to make it. She's tough." He only wished she hadn't always had to be. "I'm glad you're here."

"So am I." She clasped his hands in hers, holding them on her lap. "I missed you, Foley."

"You don't have to be nice to me just because my mom is bleeding out."

"That's horrible." Her frown turned into a reluctant grin. "I mean, really horrible. You're pretty dramatic, aren't you?" When he didn't smile back, she sobered. "She is *not* bleeding out. The nurse told us they have her on the surgery table. She broke her tibia, and it's an open fracture, but she should be okay. She woke up for a few minutes before they put her back under for the surgery too, so that's another good thing. The nurse said something about an epidural line, so anesthesia wouldn't be a problem. Eileen's going to be okay," she repeated.

"Yeah?" He felt weak with relief.

"Yeah." She kissed his hands, then set them back on her lap. "Can I take your mind off this with an even better story?"

"God. Please do."

"I told you I've talked to your mom this past week. More than once."

"What?" Shocker number two of the day. Or was that three? He'd lost count.

"She's an awesome woman. I mean, I wish she was my mom." She sighed. "She made me see some harsh truths I've known but never dealt with. So tonight, I dealt with them."

She told him about her mother and the dinner, about her seeing a therapist, and he sat, stunned. "Are you kidding me?" He laughed, his first since arriving at the hospital. "So you're not going to see your mom anymore?"

"Not until she gets help for being such a wackjob," Cyn said, sounding like him.

"Wackjob. Huh. Makes sense. I mean, who the hell undermines their kid for years? So that therapist helped you."

She flushed. "Yeah. I always considered that kind of stuff for crazy people. I mean, normal people don't see a shrink, right?"

"Uh-huh."

"I know. Now *I* sound like a wackjob."

"You said it."

They sat in silence, and he took comfort in her presence. That she'd come when he needed her meant the world to him.

"Foley?"

"Yes?"

"I love you."

He blinked. No way he'd heard what he thought. "Huh?"

"I do. It doesn't make any sense. I'm not saying this because your mom is being operated on. And not because I'm scared of losing you or want to get you back or anything. I just thought you should know."

"Are you on fucking crack?"

She frowned. "What?"

"You just thought *I should know*?" He gave an angry laugh, confused, elated, and annoyed all at once. "First off, I was supposed to say it to you first. 'Cause yeah, it takes balls, and that's more my department than yours. I've loved you for a while now. Ever since that dance at my place. Maybe it was your lasagna. Hell. I don't know. But *I* love *you*."

She just stared at him. "O-kay."

"And that's not that easy to say. I think I've said those words to maybe a handful of people in my life. Like my mom and Sam. And Sam not in a gay way. I love the guy like a brother."

She coughed. "Right."

"Right." He stared into her velvety brown eyes, losing his train of thought.

"So you're angry I said it first."

"Yes. Yes, I'm angry." He tried to get his anger back, because tears threatened once more. "Because no way in hell should you doubt how amazing you are. And you should have known that because I loved you first. I mean, I don't just share Foley-love with every woman who wants it. And they all do, you know."

She quirked a brow. "You have a name for it? Foley-love?"

"What's wrong with that?"

"Nothing."

"So maybe I was with a few women *over the years*. Hot chicks. So what? I picked you, didn't I? Hottest one out there, bar none. I mean, everyone at New Year's knew it. The guys all want you. Sam knows to be hands-off. Johnny's pissed he's stuck with Lara."

"Oh, he is, is he?" She was openly laughing at him now.

"And Lou... I don't trust that bastard. We need to watch out for him."

"Sure thing, Foley-love." She smiled.

"That's it. We're officially off break."

"Okay."

"And… Okay? That's it?"

"Yep. You were right. I'm an idiot. I missed you, and I love you. Oh, and I'm going to work on my issues."

She'd taken the wind out of his sails. "That's so unfair."

"What?"

"I had a speech prepared and everything." His euphoria faded under worry for his mother. "God. I can't be this happy. Not now."

"You deserve it. Knowing Eileen, she'd demand you have it. Now let's go back upstairs, act like nonviolent, worried people, and wait until we hear she's okay." They stood together, and he knew he was holding her hands too tight. But he couldn't help it.

"What if she's not okay, Cyn? What then?" He didn't know what he'd do. Eileen Sanders had been his rock forever.

"Then we'll be together. You, Sam, and I will find a way to go on." She kissed him, so tenderly, and brought tears to his eyes again.

"Quit making me cry."

"I will if you will." She wiped her eyes, and her mascara ran.

"You look like a raccoon."

"You sweet-talker." She knocked on the glass, and the security guard grudgingly walked them back upstairs.

An interminable length of time later, the surgeon came out.

Chapter 23

FOLEY DIDN'T THINK HE'D EVER BEEN SO PLEASED TO hear his mother bitch. She was itchy. She hated that stupid wheely-thing—the knee walker—that allowed her to walk with her cast. Where had Jacob gone, and was he back yet? All that on top of a pre-wedding party for the boss. It was like he was in pre-matrimonial hell, except his mom was back and Cyn sat by his side.

"You know," Cyn whispered, seated next to Foley, "I had no idea your mother was such a terrible sick person." Eileen and Jacob sat next to Cyn.

"If Jacob can handle this, the guy is seriously gearing up for sainthood," Sam whispered from Foley's other side.

A month after the accident, the three of them sat across a large banquet table from Lou, Johnny, and Lara. Liam sat at another table with Sophie and a bunch of his annoying relatives, the Donnigans. Mike McCauley's aunt, uncle, and four cousins—two obnoxious ex-Marines, a lanky teen, and a pretty little blond.

To Foley's amusement, the Donnigans seemed to be just as annoying as the McCauleys. Even J.T. seemed to be keeping his distance from the table, despite Liam trying to urge him over. Foley understood the big dudes being irritating, but the daughter might have drawn him for a closer look if he'd been in the market for a sweet blond.

But his honey had no worries in that department. As it was, he had to refrain from knocking Lou's teeth in and rearranging one of the Donnigans' faces. He studied the blond giant and noticed the dude's siblings rolling their eyes at him.

Hell. Even the prick's family found him annoying.

"Why are you staring so hard at the hunky Donnigans?" Cyn asked.

"Excuse me?" He glared at her, only to hear Sam chuckle. "You find that funny?"

"You're jealous of *that*?" He waved at their table, making no effort to keep his voice down.

So of course the prick looked their way. He gave the ladies at Foley's table a smile, ignoring the guys. Foley didn't care for the way blondie seemed to linger on Cyn. From Johnny's frown, his friend didn't like the way he'd looked at Lara either. Blondie smirked at Sam then deliberately turned his back on them.

Foley thought he heard the words *tough guy wannabe* and *asshole* and had to grip Sam to keep him from leaving his seat.

Cyn took charge. "Sam Hamilton, if you start a fight at this pre-wedding party, Del will have your head. Not to mention dealing with Liam, who's glaring at you. Landon seems nice enough. Why don't we give him the benefit of the doubt?" Eileen said something, drawing her attention.

"Landon? What the hell kind of name is that?" Lou asked.

"Amen," Johnny agreed.

Sam muttered, "The dipshit's lucky I don't shove my boot up his ass."

Foley laughed with the guys. Even Lara cracked a smile. Fortunately, his mother and Cyn didn't seem to have heard him.

"Not nice, Sam," Lara said, trying to wipe away her grin. "Landon is a great guy."

Johnny rounded on her. "How the hell do you know *him*?"

"For God's sake, Johnny. Liam introduced both of us to him when we arrived." She snorted. "I swear. Del was right not to invite you idiots to the wedding."

"Oh, we're invited. Johnny too, I think." Foley shrugged. "Maybe not smart, but Johnny's her call."

"Hey." Johnny frowned. "Pick on someone your own size. Like Mount Rainier," Johnny added, not quite under his breath.

Cyn chuckled.

Foley sighed. "Not sure what this party is for though. I thought you were supposed to have a big celebration *after* the wedding." Hadn't Del just mentioned having to postpone the big day due to some problem with the venue anyway?

"It's not a reception." Cyn and Eileen shared a sigh, and Cyn explained, "It's just a party. The upcoming wedding is an excuse to get everyone together for some fun. Did you not read the invitation?"

"Not much longer until Del will be Delilah McCauley." Eileen dabbed her eyes. "I'm so happy for her. She's wonderful."

"She is," Lara agreed.

Cyn nodded as well.

"A few more months of the ROP. Now *that's* something to celebrate." So saying, Sam left the table, encouraged the DJ to play some funky tunes, then crossed to the Donnigans' table to ask the blond woman to dance. Apparently her brothers' glares and large, clenched fists meant nothing.

"Now that's trouble waiting to happen." Cyn finished her wine and poured another as Sam and his partner hit the dance floor.

Foley could almost hear Liam's sigh from here. He laughed when he saw Liam grab the golden-haired Landon to stop him from following his sister. "Come on, Cyn. Let's go join the festivities." As if that had set the others free, almost the entire table departed for the dance floor. "Hey, Mom. Here comes Jacob."

Her smile made Foley warm inside. The perfect ending to a hellacious week.

He'd owed Del's ROP two dollars in quarters, and that had been her taking it easy on him. Cyn still dithered about where they'd live together, her place or somewhere new, because *"No way in hell am I living in your beige, bland town house. No offense to Eileen."* And Sam was secretive as hell staying God knew where all the time—away from home.

But at least Eileen and Jacob had set a date. And Cyn was all his. All the time.

"Have I told you today I love you?" he asked as they grooved to some European track.

"Nope. Say it again."

"I love you."

Del's soon-to-be stepson, Colin, and some little red-headed kid bumped him as they raced by, laughing and jamming, while Mike and his brothers grabbed their women to dance. The party was well underway.

Foley kept coming back to that little red-haired boy.

"See something you like?" Cyn asked.

"Besides you?" He kissed her and brought her in for some closer dancing.

"Hey, Foley." Del smacked him in the head.

"Damn it. What?" he snarled.

"Keep it clean. There are kids here. And let's not offend the delicate McCauleys." She snickered.

"Not funny." Mike glared at her.

Foley grinned and put a little distance between himself and Cyn. "Better, Sister Serious?"

She scowled. "Watch it or I'll hit you with my ruler."

Mike sighed. "Seriously. She's no fun anymore."

"Mike." Del sounded hurt.

"Delilah. What did I tell you about our ruler?"

"It's only for bed?"

"Exactly."

Foley made a face. "Ew. Go away, you two. Be happy somewhere else."

McCauley gave an evil laugh and whisked his fiancée away.

Cyn seemed caught as well by the kids playing in the corner. "You think our kids will have red hair or black?"

He tripped. "Damn, woman. Don't say things like that."

She laughed. "I didn't mean we'd make them now." She pulled him in for a kiss and teased the nape of his neck. "But maybe when we get home?"

He just stared. His physical had come back clean, as he'd known it would. Cyn planned to go on birth control, but she'd been so busy lately she hadn't had time for an exam yet. And man, he hated condoms. But kids? "You mean it?"

It felt right.

"I think so." Cyn smiled. "I have to take advantage, big boy. It's not every woman who's entitled to some Foley-love, now is it?"

He gave a whoop and carted her over his shoulder toward the exit, laughing all the way.

*Keep reading for an excerpt from the first book in
Marie Harte's new series, The Donnigans*

A SURE THING

WORST DAY OF THE FRIGGIN' YEAR. SEATTLE HAD ITS doozies, but this one by far smacked of depression. In addition, it had been overcast and miserable all day, with rain continuing into the early evening. A glance around the surprisingly crowded gym full of men *and* women made Landon Donnigan wish for a return to the scorching heat of Afghanistan. Better that than the danger of desperate singles looking to hook up on Valentine's Day.

God save me.

Though life in the Marine Corps had been fraught with risk—and not the bullshit emotional kind of risks—he'd enjoyed his time both overseas and in the States. During his service, he'd thought a civilian life behind a desk would be worse than anything he might imagine. Now he took his current job in stride, pleased to be useful once more.

But Valentine's Day surrounded by flirting singles, in *a gym* no less? Sacrilege. He did his best not to make eye contact with anyone, especially the small group of women who kept looking his way. With any luck, they hadn't noticed him, their attention on his supposedly charming younger brother standing next to him. He placed the hand weights he'd been using back on the rack, figuring he'd cut himself a break on his workout, just this once.

His brother glanced over his shoulder at several of the staring women. "Is it just me? Or do you feel almost hunted right now?" Gavin waved, and they waved back. "I mean, I *have* to be here. I'm a trainer. But shouldn't all these women be out with their significant others celebrating with flowers and chocolates? I thought lonely women on V-Day stayed at home, sobbing into their Earl Grey and fighting their twenty-plus cats for bonbons. Kind of like you on any night of the week—alone and lonely."

"You're an ass."

Gavin chuckled. "Yeah, I am. I'm kidding…about the women." He ignored the finger Landon shot him. "Seriously though, most of the women I know are either out with friends or pissed off at men in general and sitting at home."

"Like Hope, you mean?" Landon drawled. Their little sister had supposedly broken up with her latest dickhead boyfriend yesterday. God willing, the next guy she dated wouldn't be so toxic.

"Yeah. Like Hope." Gavin nodded. "No worries, Bro. Hope's situation will work out." Gavin took after their father in looks and temperament. Dark-haired, *too* laid-back, and for some reason, was well-liked by the ladies, who continued to watch him.

Landon followed his brother's gaze to the attractive group. "They seem interested. Why not go ask 'em out?"

"No way in hell." Gavin frowned. "We don't fraternize with clients. Mac's orders."

"Really? Because you've got a mess of opportunity right over there."

"That group is way too loaded for my blood. And by loaded, I mean richer than shit. They're looking for a boy toy to play with. And rumor has it they break their toys." Gavin glanced around him, then murmured, "Mac didn't actually say I couldn't date gym members. But when I tell them that, they leave me alone. I mean, they don't want to get me fired from my job."

With any luck, Gavin would hold on to this one for a while. The last two jobs hadn't gone well. Landon wasn't the only one adjusting to civilian life after the Corps. He subtly leaned closer to Gavin. Good. No scent of alcohol on little brother's breath tonight.

"Smart excuse," he said, trying to cover the sniff check.

"Smart. That's me." Gavin didn't do smug as well as he thought he did. Not like their youngest brother, who'd come out of the womb smirking at life in general. "But why are *you* here? I'd have thought you and Claudia would be getting romantic. Hell, man, it's Saturday. You can't use work as an excuse."

Landon shrugged and retrieved his towel and water bottle from the floor. "I thought I told you we broke up. We were never more than friends anyway." *Intimate* friends. He'd been smart enough to end their casual relationship two months ago when Claudia had been hinting about changing their status to something much more serious. He'd been getting bored, and her constant neediness grated on his last nerve. As if Landon had time for more trouble when he had so much work to do fixing his dysfunctional family.

"Yeah? That's not what I heard." A pause. "From Claudia."

Crap. "She's been to the gym lately?" She'd quit when they'd broken up. Landon had only seen her once since then. Just last week. They'd exchanged a pleasant greeting, nothing more.

"Yep. Heard her talking to Marsha about you yesterday, as if you two were still an item. Then she told me to say hi from her." Gavin smiled wide. "So hi."

"Shut up."

Gavin snickered.

Landon glanced around, praying the woman hadn't arrived tonight. He hated hurting anyone, and he'd been surprised she'd taken their "friend" breakup so hard. Which only reinforced the notion he'd been right to sever the relationship in the first place. Dating should be fun, not a minefield. He'd had enough of *those* to last a lifetime.

He scowled, feeling hemmed in. Jameson's Gym was supposed to be his refuge in this chaotic, civilian world. Landon appreciated the hell out of the owner giving his brother a job. Mac Jameson seemed to be a stand-up guy. He'd been a master sergeant in the Marine Corps before doing permanent damage to his knee, ending his time early. They shared that connection—common core values, an appreciation for discipline and order, and medical bullshit ending a guy's dream.

"Mac here?" he asked.

Gavin shook his head. "Seriously? You've seen his wife, right? She's hot as hell. No doubt they're hanging at home for some 'alone time.'" Gavin sighed. "I miss uncomplicated sex."

At his words, a pretty blond in tights stopped behind him and gave a toothy grin. "Hey, Gavin. How's it going?"

His younger brother cringed, then turned around and gave her an insincere smile back. "Oh, ah, hi, Michelle. How are you?"

"Great. I just finished my workout." She eyed Gavin the way a lion would a helpless gazelle. The comparison made it hard not to laugh, especially with the hunted look on Gavin's face. "Shouldn't you be out with your girlfriend tonight?" Michelle asked, her voice breathy. "Hope, right?"

"Hope's my sister."

"Oh, so you *are* single then. Megan and I were talking."

"I'm single, yeah, but I don't mingle with—"

Michelle grabbed him by the arm, her sharp nails a bright pink. "How lucky for me you're here. I could really use a spotter."

"I thought you said you were done with your workout."

"I mean I'm *almost* done."

Gavin couldn't rightly refuse to help Michelle train. Landon ignored the beseeching look his brother shot him and subtly stepped away.

"Ah, sure." Gavin blew out a breath. "Are all of you training together?" he asked, staring at the three women watching them.

"Yep. We need someone to show us the proper way to use some of the equipment." The same equipment she'd been using for as long as Landon had been coming to the gym. She tugged Gavin with her. "Then after, maybe you and I can do a casual dinner." She blinked at Landon. "How about you, Landon?"

Gavin hemmed, "Well, I don't know. My brother and I were supposed to—"

"Go ahead, Gav." Landon almost felt sorry for him. Then he remembered what Gavin had said and smiled. "Sorry, Michelle. I have plans. I'll be at home drinking Earl Grey and playing with my cats."

Gavin scowled at him. Michelle shrugged, her claws still hooked into Gavin. "Oh well. Gavin, I know there's a no-dating policy, but it's not a date if it's just dinner. Or dessert," she purred.

Knowing his brother could take care of himself, at least when it came to women, Landon headed for the men's sauna before Michelle's rabid pack of singles decided not to take no for an answer. Not that he considered himself God's gift to women, but he'd been doing his best to avoid several of her friends since he'd been coming to the place. He'd never hurt for bed partners, blessed with his parents' good looks and a body built from constant exercise.

He didn't spend his free time at the gym to hook up. He wanted a workout.

As he sat in the sauna, he struck up a conversation with some other poor fool with nothing better to do on Valentine's Day. At least Landon wasn't the only guy not all that keen on hearts and flowers.

"Yeah, well, don't feel bad for not getting all the

hype about V-Day, man. Frankly, I'd rather soak in here than deal with trying to figure out what women want."

"Or what men want," his companion griped.

"Amen." Landon chuckled, not surprised that any relationship could give a guy a headache. "Time for me to go. Later." The guy nodded, and Landon left to grab his stuff and head home.

The house he—and now Gavin—rented sat in the heart of Queen Anne. He lived close to his aunt and uncle and a bevy of annoying cousins, but a neighborhood over from his parents, who had a big home in Fremont. Since moving back to Seattle, he'd already been to an engagement party and had invites to three weddings.

At least his cousins were getting married and growing up. To hear Linda Donnigan tell it, her own children could take lessons from their McCauley cousins. The Donnigans were seriously screwed up.

Frankly, Landon agreed.

He entered the house after locking up his car and grimaced at the mess Gavin had *once again* left in the kitchen. After doing the dishes and straightening up the living room, Landon took his things into his bedroom and put his laundry away before taking a quick shower.

Yeah, his mother had it right. She was a type-A workaholic, balanced by his mellow father who thought the world would be all right with a little more love. Landon snorted. If love came in the form of some hand-to-hand combat or a grenade, then yeah, he agreed. It never failed to amaze him that his father had served as a Navy Corpsman, taking care of Marines in combat, with that peace-love attitude. But while Van Donnigan didn't worry about much, Linda and Landon stressed for the lot of them.

Landon finished his shower and dressed in comfortable sweats, dwelling on the mess his family had become. Gavin had a bad case of PTSD he was trying to drown in booze. Hope kept bringing home clones of Jack the Ripper, and Theo had his head buried up his ass, in denial that high school was over and he had to grow the hell up.

With a groan, Landon settled on the couch and pulled up a kung fu movie on television. After the week he'd had, he deserved the break. Though he'd been relieved to find transitioning to civilian life a lot easier than he'd anticipated, his job had taken some getting used to. No longer able to take long runs during lunch or bark orders at his subordinates, he'd gotten back into the swing of business management, landing a sweet job thanks to an employment recruiter and some old friends. Being an officer had its perks, even on the outside.

He could manage the employees of D&R Logistics with his hands tied behind his back. His biggest challenge had been learning the company's mission and getting on board with their management structure. That and convincing his buddy Daniel to stop treating him like a friend and act like a boss.

With a sigh, he ran his fingers through his cropped blond hair, aware it had never been so long, not in over thirteen years. But a high and tight haircut in Seattle, during the winter, was sheer idiocy.

He grabbed himself a beer and settled in for some amazing martial arts. Between one blink and the next, the show had ended, the room seemed much darker, and the front door opened. Gavin stumbled in. A glance at the clock on the mantel showed a glowing two in the a.m.

"Yo, Bro," Gavin slurred and chuckled. "What a night."

Landon sighed. "I thought you were done drinking."

"I was. But it's Valentine's Day! A night for lovers." He walked out of his shoes, dumped his bag on the floor, and tripped into the couch, sprawling next to Landon. "Michelle's a real snob, but she sucks better than a Hoover."

"TMI, Gavin." Landon shook his head, concern for his brother growing. "You didn't drive, did you?"

"Nah. Took a cab."

Thank God for small favors. "Come on. Let's get you to bed."

"Sure." Gavin grinned and closed his eyes. "Not gonna dream tonight. I'm plastered."

Landon dragged him to the nearby bathroom and nagged at him to piss. Then he half carried the idiot to his bedroom and covered him up in bed. Hopefully Gavin would get a decent night's rest. Then tomorrow, Landon would arrange for the family to plan that intervention little brother needed, before it was too late.

He returned to the living room to lock the door, turned everything off, then went to bed. The world around him might be spiraling out of control, but he controlled his own environment.

He snorted. Valentine's Day with hearts and flowers? More like a drunken brother, a half-finished kung fu movie, and a beer. Yeah, that sounded about right.

COMING NOVEMBER 2017

Acknowledgments

This book wouldn't have been possible without the help from the amazing folks at Sourcebooks. Thank you.

About the Author

Caffeine addict, boy referee, and romance aficionado, *New York Times* and *USA Today* bestselling author Marie Harte is a confessed bibliophile and devotee of action movies. Whether hiking in Central Oregon, biking around town, or hanging at the local tea shop, she's constantly plotting to give everyone a happily ever after. Visit marieharte.com and fall in love.

The McCauley Brothers

the hot new series by Marie Harte

Meet the rough-and-tumble McCauleys, a tight-knit band of brothers who work hard, drink beer, and relentlessly tease each other.

The Troublemaker Next Door

Flynn never thought he'd fall for the girl next door. But when he's called to fix Maddie's sink, he's a goner. Too bad the fiercely independent interior designer wants nothing to do with him. Even worse, he's forced to rely on advice from his nosy brothers—and his five-year-old nephew!

How to Handle a Heartbreaker

It's lust at first sight for Brody when he sees Abby Dunn. But Abby's still trying to get over her last relationship, and he isn't getting the hint. It doesn't help that she keeps casting Brody as the hero in her steamy romance novels. Will Abby write her own happily ever after or stay safe in her shell?

Ruining Mr. Perfect

Vanessa Ann Campbell is a CPA by day, perfectionist by night. But she can't stop thinking about the youngest McCauley brother, even though they tend to rub each other the wrong way. Cameron's dying to get Vanessa to let loose—but if he succeeds, can he handle it?

What to Do with a Bad Boy

Mike had his soul mate for a precious time before she died giving birth to their son six years ago. He's sick of everyone playing matchmaker...until he meets Delilah Webster, the tattooed mechanic who sets his motor running. But the closer they get, the more the pain of the past throws a wrench into their future...

For more Marie Harte, visit:

www.sourcebooks.com

May the Best Man Win

Best Men

by Mira Lyn Kelly

USA Today bestselling author

―――∾∾∾―――

Four friends. Each a best man at a wedding. One chance to get it right.

Jase Foster can't believe his bad luck. He's been paired with the she-devil herself for his best friend's wedding: Emily Klein of the miles-long legs and killer smile. She may be sin in a bridesmaid dress, but there's no way he's falling for her *again*.

They can barely stand each other, but given how many of their friends are getting married, they'll just have to play nice—at least when they're in company. Once they're alone, more than just gloves come off as Jase and Emily discover their chemistry is combustible, and there may be something to this enemies-to-lovers thing after all…

―――∾∾∾―――

Praise for Mira Lyn Kelly:

"Mira Lynn Kelly is a master storyteller." —*Romance Reviews*

"Mira Lyn Kelly's writing always sparkles."
—Lauren Layne, *USA Today* bestselling author

"Sexy and with a truly fresh voice."
—Tina Leonard, *New York Times* bestselling author

For more Mira Lyn Kelly, visit:

www.sourcebooks.com

Trouble Walks In

The McGuire Brothers

by Sara Humphreys

New York Times and *USA Today* bestselling author

He could be the man to rescue her

Big-city K-9 cop Ronan McGuire loves women, loves his dog, loves his job—but when old flame Maddy Morgan moves into his jurisdiction, he can't think about anyone else. Ronan knows she's way out of his league, but he's determined to help Maddy live life to the fullest.

In more ways than one

With tragedy in her past, Maddy has immersed herself in work and swiftly made a name for herself in the hot New York City real estate market. She's looking for safety, not love, but Ronan McGuire is as persistent as he is sexy, and his crooked smile is hard to resist. But all other concerns are wiped away when Maddy goes missing and Ronan and his bloodhound K-9 partner are tasked with finding her and bringing her home.

Praise for *Brave the Heat*:

"Boasts suspense that burns as hot as the love scenes."
—*Publishers Weekly*

For more Sara Humphreys, visit:

www.sourcebooks.com

Beautiful Crazy

Rock-n-Ink

by Kasey Lane

—∼∿∼—

She's a rocker with attitude and ink...
He's a sexy suit who gets what he wants

Kevan Landry is trying to keep her life on track and her brother in rehab. If her fledgling marketing firm can sign the hot new band, Manix Curse, it will make a world of difference. Mason Dillon heads the most successful music PR firm in Portland. He's desperate to breathe new life into the company by signing Manix Curse.

The last thing either one needs is a one-night stand with a smoldering stranger...

The stakes are high when a battle for the band—in the bedroom and the boardroom—becomes a battle of the heart. But if these two can set aside their differences, they may find they're the right mix of sexy savvy to conquer both their worlds.

—∼∿∼—

For more Kasey Lane, visit:

www.sourcebooks.com